HEXATRON TALES

RESPECT

Printed in Australia
First Printing: November 2022
Shawline Publishing Group Pty Ltd
www.shawlinepublishing.com.au

Paperback ISBN 978-1-9227-5158-4
eBook ISBN 978-1-9227-5161-4

A catalogue record for this work is available from the National Library of Australia

HEXATRON TALES

RESPECT

CRAIG CARDENAS

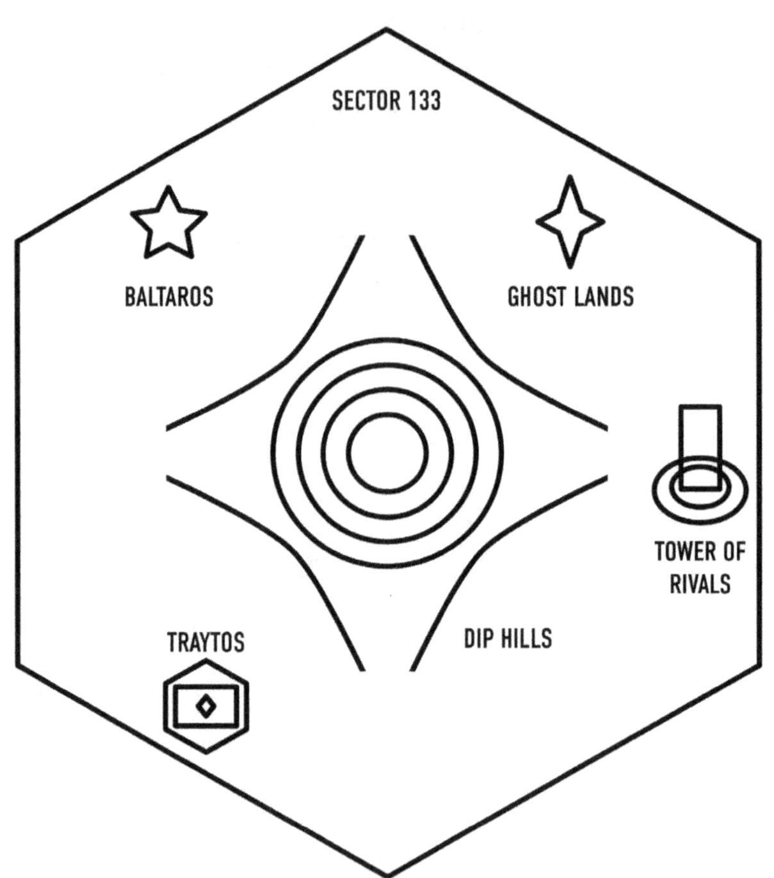

SECTOR 133
BALTAROS
GHOST LANDS
TOWER OF
RIVALS
TRAYTOS
DIP HILLS

PROLOGUE

The realm of Rippel is a place of chaos and advancement. Like a stone dropped into water, it creates ripples and depending on where these waves or ripples meet, it shall change its outcome. The places in Rippel consist of many factions. There are two main factions that define it. The faction of Tranquillity, whose people require immense amounts of arcane or divine concentration to search for true advancement or perhaps ascension and the faction of Chaos, whose people find experimentation is far more effective in advancement and transformation. There have been many wars fought and lost in the struggle over which faction will succeed the other. During a time, perhaps an eon ago, there was a great war more catastrophic than any battle fought, which changed the face of Rippel for the next generation. By great tranquillity, the Void was opened and by the erratic nature of chaos, the Pulse had warped time and space itself. No one of any race or existing faction has any knowledge of how the Void or the Pulse were thrust onto the land of Rippel, but they remain for the brave and foolish to explore.

– Father Eirths of Sector 228, 437AT (After Thrust).

CHAPTER 1
A PAUPER'S LIFE

My life is a struggle every day. As a halfling and as someone who has been born through war and anguish. The land where I was born was one with life and full of joy. A life short lived when the war began. We small folk had no way to defend ourselves. We hid. We ran. But the war was just too big for us. Too violent, too cruel, and indiscriminate. We were not part of the war. We did not take sides, as we as a race, thought neutrality a safe answer. But the fighting was so intense, both sides drifted from one part of the continent to another. This is why magic and technology should stay apart. I only know of the stories of how our race was blasted from our homes during the battles of equilibrium.

I was no older than a young boy when the battles were fought. The surviving elders have always told the stories of how they were saved by the knights. Saved from the war. Saved from the suffering and most of all, saved from the pain. Lives can always continue, but life must change. After being rescued, we were discriminated against, as the rumours of halflings being thieves spread like wildfire. We were treated as normal refugees, but after a few weeks, maybe months, all halflings were treated like thieves. I only remember the slums. I lived in the slums and even then we were treated like rats. Traytos was a place of technology and we were mostly farmers and breeders. Stealing was not in our nature, but looking like mischievous children all our lives, we gave off an impression of being thieves. I was always good, but sometimes, larger races such humans and half-orcs would force us to steal just to stay alive.

The beatings happened very regularly, unless you were fast or discreet. I learned quickly that to survive in this city; we halflings needed to rely on the bigger races. But our old allies, the elves and dwarves, had their own problems. So I decided when I grew up I would be a knight to save my fellow halflings. A knight of my dreams.

CHAPTER 2
THE IDEAL KNIGHT

A person with virtue. Someone with bravery. The courage to inspire. Victory for all that believe in justice. Valour in combat and finesse in conflict. A tall, dashing man that strikes fear in his enemies and encourages those all around him to treat others better.

A man in shining armour, a warrior that can do anything, to be able to aid the sick and help the people. I want to be like a soldier that can gain the admiration of the people without the scorn of their race. To have great passion for life and to have a path of good and righteousness. To serve and to protect, to save and to provide. To have the nobles esteem, I want to be their reliable fighter, to have their influence, to partake in their wealth.

I want a place filled with companions and comrades of the same views. The same path, a life filled with adventure and to live life to the fullest. To see the cheers of the people with each triumph. To defeat the evil and allow good to prosper. I want a life like that. I want it to be filled with joys and cheers. Happiness and laughter. To live a life that can endure and conquer the struggle of sadness and suffering. To fell the wrong doings of the wicked. To defeat those who use evil as a means of power.

I want to be a man, a warrior, a soldier, a shining force of truth and justice. A force that protects the weak and helps the innocent. An authority to uphold good tidings and laws to protect those that need it most. Someone to rely on. A good person. A person like me.

CHAPTER 3
THE TALE OF SECTOR 133

Now all tales start with valiant heroes and malicious villains fighting for either justice or perhaps chaos, but in this story it at least has both of those elements in mind with one exception. The hero of this tale was born to be one, bred from noble stock and just as arrogant as any large knight with only his honour to lose and a beautiful maiden's graces to uphold. The story is of a kingdom of magic and chaos full of jealousy and greed, so much so, they had decided to kidnap the beautiful princess of gears and technology to gain, not only the control of the sector but also for, the utmost dominance of the ways of supremacy for advancement.

That's just what the king of Traytos had told its people, to rally them to his side, but the real story goes back before anyone in any of the clan wars would remember or even before the metal arachnids were manufactured. It was a time of two sides trying to out best the other through chaos or the magical and divine arts, or through wild, unpredictable experimentations and inventions. Sectors all over Rippel were indeed at war; physically, politically and pragmatically, but violence was always the result to prove who was right or who was weak.

All beings in Rippel have learned from history and the mistakes that have formed our rock of a world, but unfortunately, two sectors in the country have been duelling for supremacy ever since they were separated from a single sector. The reason for such a split was made for the children of royalty, the twins born from such a family. The king at the time thought it best to have his most prominent son to rule the kingdom, but boys will be boys and a rivalry soon formed.

A simple chore became a contest of who was the best. Chores became contests, training became duels, duels became battles and battles turned to conflict. And every sane person knows what happens to over exaggerated conflict… it turns to all-out war. The fighting needed to be stopped as it started to become yet another Thrust, so the great ruler at the time decided to cut the sector in half.

Now you might think the king should have simply said, 'Son, my son born four clicks – four seconds – before the other, here have this part of the map… and my little boy born four clicks after, here have that part of this map.' It would have been a gallant speech. No, he actually (or at least that's what I have studied) used his most powerful spell to blast the centre of the fighting and split the north and south sections of the land apart. The spell was rumoured to be the size of grey moon and supposedly the shape of a glaive. Anyway, with the fighting, it was at least halted by the ruler's declaration that his sons would be at peace once they both ruled their own kingdom.

Sure it worked. His sons were at peace for as long as the great king lived, but a single generation of boredom after the sons' descendants and they were again at each other's throats. Sixty-three descendants later, I continue this history lesson. Now then, this story begins when the princess of Traytos is captured by one of the wily assassins of Bataros. That is when the greatest hero of Traytos valiantly risks life and limb to traverse enemy territory, defeating their residents and monsters alike to rescue our fair maiden.

CHAPTER 4
PROCLAMATION

Yes 'twas I, Lord Wilbur L. Fameborn, that raised his small man at arms and defeated all the obstacles in my wake, to rescue my fair lady. I traversed great lands and defeated terrible monsters and out witted clever traps of the most vicious of men, the Batarians. The fiends had amassed forty-three thousand desperate raiders and monsters to battle our great warriors of only a few hundred or so.

Lord Fameborn interrupts the bard retelling his heroics and stands in his most majestic pose to impress and stun the gathering crowds, as well as provide his own emphasis and elaboration of his struggles and triumphs. He is a human of thirty odd watches – around 30 years – and has a height of a small goliath of almost two metres. His outfit is of a casual linen many of his stature wear, with enough frills to look like a wizened sage, but not enough to look like a miser of nobility. His tale is one told and retold many a time and the more he recalls his foe, the greater they become and the smaller his force he admits with each new version.

The king bestows upon me his blessing, when I alone volunteer to sacrifice myself to rescue his one and only beloved daughter. Our great king begged and begged, warning me the true dangers of my campaign but I just told him this, 'If I must be the one to die so that your liege can continue, then I will gladly unsheathe my sword and end my life here and now. Justice will always triumph and honour is all the reward I wish to receive.'

As he recites his most famous monologue, the hero reveals his blade; a shining sword made by the great dwarves of technology. He raises the blade in front of him and re-enacts a more theatrical version of the scene, then raising the sword in a single hand, he declares all his rights to justice and honour by serving his great majesty, the king of Traytos. The crowd reacts as if enchanted by some magical force and roar and cheer for the hero and great knight of Traytos. Though magic is forbidden in these parts of this country, the thought is dismissed by the bard. Perhaps some kind of alchemical potion to create charming illusions, but maybe not.

CHAPTER 5
THE HERO?

Hey… hey… hey… said a rather quiet voice among the roaring crowds. *I don't remember any of that part of the story,* said a squeaky, exasperated voice from down below.

The bard, being quite learned in perceiving even the slightest of moans a satisfied woman would make after a rueful session of copulation or the sneaky taste of forbidden fruit, slowly moves towards the corner of an empty side street. The bard looks around for the strange sound of objection and motions towards a set of rusted iron bars. A sewer grate. Looking down, the bard sees nothing, nothing but darkness and the smell of faecal matter.

I was the one who saved the king's daughter, I was the one who traversed danger and saved young knights from a pointless war and I was the one who sacrificed my whole being in rescuing her without reward. And what do I get for my service… a sentence to the gallows. A sigh of regret and disappointment follows.

CHAPTER 6
SPECULATION

As cheers gather around the great Lord Fameborn, children of all ages re-enact the valiant motions of Fameborn's tale. A young boy with a bent stick fights his friends cheering and gallivanting about being, or at least wanting to be, the great hero himself.

So I heard that there will be a festival in honour of the return of our princess. The greatest honour must go to lord knight Fameborn for his courageous deeds. I heard the hero had slain a great boar of ferocious proportions. No, no, no, it was a wild and terrifying behemoth with two heads and horns all over its monstrous body. You're all wrong in that sense 'cause I heard it was a giant with two heads and a club in each hand, the size of an alchemists' tower.

More and more exaggerations were told throughout the sector about what lord knight had indeed defeated, but a dancing minstrel retells the story of Lord Wilbur L. Fameborn, though some may call it a poem rather than a story.

I, the knight Fameborn, am hero of this land.

Born from great knights of old and chaos of man.

I, the warrior of justice and valour.

Traverse the lands of Bataros the betrayers.

To rescue the maiden of this land, the great land of chaos, Traytos.

I, the saviour of truth and beauty.

Fight the wicked and the terrible enemy.

I, the courage of warriors and knights

Climb the tower and break through with might.

To rescue the maiden of this land, the great land of chaos, Traytos.

I, the clever and wisdom of great sages.

Endure their foulest and illusion of mazes.

I, the freedom and righteous of my order.

Defeats the wicked and rescues the king's daughter.

I, the great Lord Wilbur L. Fameborn.

With the final strands of the minstrel's poem, comes the great merriment of the crowds and the many who believe in epic ballads, come to throw their appreciation – or payment - of a great story. This is mostly in coins of copper and silver, but sometimes it is of fanfare or the flirtatious women, their bodies – to the bowing performers. The men and women of the crowds still enjoying the celebrations rather than working at their stations, start singing, continuing their uncouth merriment.

CHAPTER 7
THE KING'S SCHEME

Father, father look down there. I think I can see my hero among the crowds of peasants. My great hero and honourable knight, why do you linger in the mess of the masses when instead you could be in my bed regaling me of how you rescued me from the evils of our enemy? Says the Princess of Traytos as she leans against the balcony of the palace.

The king ignores his lubricious daughter and sits on his throne, mulling over and over the real story behind the hero's account. His thoughts are of the recent past, on the occurrence of the planned kidnapping of his own daughter by his distant niece, the princess of Bataros. The thought passed him like some nefarious scheme, but of course, he knew of its significance. The place of the meeting and the time and accomplices that joined them flashed through his mind as his foolish and stubborn daughter continued to regal the distant hero.

A place of seclusion, a place of secret, a place of history and tradition. The king and his agent stroll toward a common destination. Steam bellows with each passing step as the surrounding pipes release a mist of liquid. The path ahead is narrow and walled to support a massive structure up above. The conversation the two have is one of private importance.

'Now then, you do realise why I have brought you here instead of my uncultured daughter, RIGHT!' said the king, with a demanding tone.

The agent replies with a nod and with the utmost reverence, formal but precise.

'This meeting is more important than your whole being and it must be regarded with the utmost discretion, as we will be meeting with someone of similar stature to myself. Now, until we conclude this meeting, you are not to speak to me or the other party unless spoken to or provoked,' said the king, continuing to warn his servant of the dire consequences of failure.

The agent again does not say a word but responds with another nod to confirm the message is understood. The pair stop at a lightly lit chamber with low burning torches at each corner and a round stone table in the central most part. Two other figures gradually approach the same but opposite side of the table. The king motions his agent to move to one of the corners. The figures on the other side of the table place both hands on to the table and greet each other with a coded message. 'Srerecros fo tsetaerg emoclew,' says the king. While the others respond with 'Tsigolonhcet tnaillirb emoclew' and then both men share a strange chuckle and welcome each other with a spirited hand shake. The meeting has begun.

While both the king and my father share the ancient tongue, I observe the other in the corner of the room. This person does not look like my cousin and for the most part, this person looks very much like a man, considering his build and stance. As silent as he is, he seems to have no interest in the meeting whatsoever. I, on the other hand, am quite curious as to why uncle has decided to set this meeting up with a stranger rather than his own daughter. I remember the history of our sector and its traditions. I know my father, the sovereign of Bataros and his brother, the king of Traytos are blood siblings, so why is this stranger, unrelated to the crown of either sectors, here? As I ponder the possibilities, I hear an unfamiliar voice in my mind. It says, '…because she is a fool…' the voice lingers for a few seconds but then vanishes. As I look over to find where the voice might have come from, the stranger in the corner gestures subtly, hinting that it was him or perhaps her since they are heavily cloaked to hide their gender and physical features. The voice sounds feminine but with an odd inflection to the tone and nature of the statement. As though it was formed through arcane means rather than a mechanical device.

'Daughter, you know of your uncle and my brother, king of Traytos,' proclaims her father. Before the girl could even reply to such a question, he continues '…we have proposed an arrangement to keep the peace in our lands and his.' Again, just before she can interrupt his line of conversation he continues with '…we are going to participate in kidnapping your cousin and having his liege choose a puppet to control as his daughter's rescuer…'

The king comes back to his senses as he realises that his idiot of a child has tried to - but failed - accost him with an obscenely large mechanical broad-axe. He commands his guards to gently stop her, as he slowly steps down from his throne. He then engages in some light conversation. She wants to inform him – though it was the same old princess babble that all young naïve maidens prattle on and on about – then he kindly apologises and sends her away, so as he can mull over the events that have transpired.

CHAPTER 8
IN JAIL

A small dark vestige of a child in a very large room, unfit for its size. Sitting down on the filthy dirt floor of this semi dark room, the figure stays silent, not even making a slight breathing noise. The child notices light piercing the darkness as the new cycle arrives, but still makes no motion to react. As more and more light enters the room from a barred opening, the vestige of the child becomes clearer.

A boy perhaps, or a young man, but with such small stature and rough features, it must be a man. He finally reacts to the shadows of the world and he breathes a sigh of annoyance. He shuffles and struggles to move as his hands are bonded to his hips, not his back or perhaps to the wall. The chains and restraints are positioned in such a way as to restrict him from escape as well as stop him from moving at all. The man is restricted this way, not for his crime but for his race. He is a halfling after all and they have a reputation for being notorious thieves and vagrants. Even though his legs are not bound, they still have bells attached to them. These bells will react to any kind of movement and the ringing in the silent cell will echo to alert the guards.

The noise from the world outside the room becomes more and more prominent, with cheers and shouts and comments of 'the hero has returned' or 'the saviour is here'. As the loud noise outside slowly fades away, the man exhales yet another sigh and says in a very subtle voice,

'…but I'm the one who saved her…' As the sounds and cheers slowly move away and silence once again remains in the room, a single voice, an inquiring tone asks, 'and who might you be? Mr Saviour!' Strangely enough, there is no mockery in his voice or an unsavoury remark.

With such a query being proposed in such a quiet atmosphere, the remark seems like a booming demand. The others near this cell loudly react to this inquisition as though this were their one and only visit or friend. The man sitting in silence only looks up at his cell room window and reacts with yet another sigh, as though he is still exhausted from a prior experience. Though there are indeed more rooms in the place, with even more people of sorts in them, the sounds become muffled as all their shouts and demands for freedom are drowned out by the sound of water and fire. Shouts and screams of freedom and innocence and cries for reverence or just the curses of being wronged.

After the sounds of the other occupants cease, the silent sighing man, having waited for this moment, finally answers very sincerely, 'I am … I am Torbiro … I am a knight or should I say ex-knight of Traytos.'

CHAPTER 9
TORBIRO THE HALFLING

'Look here, ya little speck,' said the bard.

'Why don't you tell me what actually happened, huh!' the bard gestured some faint interest. The man in question is indeed small, as he is not a member of the human descent. He is of a halfling descent or more to the common description, a sneak-thief. A lowly creature that has absolutely no real value in any sort of society ~ structure of social upbringing ~ and is just a creature born to leech and steal and laze about throughout their life. Though it is known halflings are borne into a farming culture, many see their action in the city sprawl as evil and criminal.

'I can see you just fine, bard,' said Torbiro, seeing the lengthy shadow extending away from the sewer grate.

'Let me tell you the real story if you would reframe from putting more salt in my wound, with your sarcastic comments,' said Torbiro with genuine words. Torbiro is indeed a halfling. But his story starts on a day just like any other. Although many will not take his words with a grain of salt due to many opposing factors. He is what many people have described as a good person.

'Well, what do you have to say for yourself?' said the bard, demanding more from the squeaky little voice and irritated at being stopped from participating in the joyous festivities. Torbiro started to clear his voice and began with, 'it all started with…' but unfortunately the shadow of the bard from the sewer grate had vanished. 'Well that was rude,' said Torbiro, feeling left out. 'I guess everyone must believe in the king's propaganda, rather than the truth.'

'Hey, little boy,' said a short figure crouching from the sewer grate. 'Heard you say something about a story.' He showed interested curiosity.

'Well, I can tell you, but it might be a long one,' Torbiro explained politely.

'Well, I can wait, 'cos I'm lost and there is too big a crowd,' said the figure.

'Well, as I was saying, it all started one morning just like any morning in Traytos. I was in my master's attic working for him as his apprentice clockwork repairman. I fixed old clocks and broken clockwork toys and other bits and pieces when a cloaked man burst into his shop.'

CHAPTER 10
TO BE A KNIGHT

Clicking, clacking and sounds of springs and a rusty old gear scraping against another. The room is filled with clocks, big and small. Rotating devices, with springs and gears and filament with precision slots and ball bearings, moving in intricate and dynamic motions. The sounds of springs reacting to the pull or weight of the device as it hits a cylindrical object. More and more ticking sounds and rolling sounds as though the room is alive with motion.

As though every second and 'click' had filled such a room with the absence of quiet. A clock or more precisely, half a clock ticks, ticks and ticks some more until the hammer of this particular device is about to reach its zenith. The hammer is released and it strikes a bell. But the sound is muffled. It is a soft 'ting' compared to the chaos of noise in the room. The hammer again strikes the bell, but this time it is off its mark and strikes, not the bell but a makeshift bed.

'Tor… Torro… Torbiro,' says a very disgruntled man. 'Torbiro, wh're 're ye? Ya lazy excuse of an appr'ntice.' A surly sounding man, trying to look for Torbiro.

A makeshift bed with makeshift feet constructed of strong but old clock hands, support the bed in a very unusual position. A boy laying in a foetal position, curled up in a ball like some sort of cat. The tattered rags cover him as a form of blanket to ward off the cold, though not really. The bed is mostly made of softer and more flexible clockwork pieces. Leather straps, flexible tin filament, copper springs and lighter than cloth mithril rings. He rolls left and then rolls right in the same fashion of a ball, moving to the tilting of a moving platform. Torbiro too, is like a ball moving with the sway of his bed as it is also not a stationary object.

He rolls left just as the hammer of the clock strikes his bed, missing him by a hair's breadth. Well, missing his body by a hair's breadth, but trapping his cotton shirt between the hammer and his bed. He rolls to his right and he strikes the iron hammer, which wakes him abruptly from his sleep. He, like many of us, tries to return to the euphoria of sleep but then quickly realises he was, in fact, in mortal danger.

'AAAAAAAAAAAAAAAAAAHHHHHHHHHHHHHHH' screams Torbiro in obvious distress. He tugs his ragged leather smock in a chaotic panic when he hears his master's morning call. 'Ma… Master, Master Dorian… help me!' yells Torbiro in a stressful panic, as he fails to remove his trapped shirt.

'Boy git ou' ta bed dis instan'' or no buttered sweet rolls for you,' said master Dorian as he yells at Torbiro. Dorian pulls open the latch of his attic, to rustle up his much needed apprentice to handle the day-to-day duties. He enters the room and pulls on a rope-like pulley. This action seems to have halted the percussion of noise from the bits and bobs in the room. The parts and pieces of the room reset and move in a reverse motion. With that, large amounts of warm steam and thick condensation of gas fill the attic.

Torbiro, having been saved by his master yet again, gathers himself and rushes over to thank and praise his master. Unfortunately, instead of getting the 'I came rushing to save you' speech, Torbiro is pounded to the ground by his dwarven master, getting the 'Stop wasting time and get back to work' lecture.

After regaining his senses, Torbiro heads down to the shop where he has to work to earn his keep, paying for living quarters and cycle meals. Days in many areas of Traytos are referred to as cycles. For those few non-technologists that use the word 'days', they are treated with scorn, prejudice and racial ignorance. The duties of a clockwork engineer's apprentice is a brutal job. Though the job itself is easy and extremely boring, the master engineer's neglect is the result of many deaths of young enthusiastic apprentices.

Master Dorian is just one of many dwarves that has a terrible habit of strong drink as priority one, rather than cleaning up the scraps of a masterpiece. He is a master of his craft and is one of the more noteworthy steam crafters. But I have always dreamed of being a knight of this realm. To fight for justice and valour and to right wrongs of the world. Too bad for me, I won't be able to become one because of a law of this sector. 'Halflings are forbidden to be knights.'

'Torro, stop yer day dreamin' an' get yer 'hic' arse back to work,' says Dorian in a drunken stupor, 'ye 'hic' waach' da shop I gotta pic kup sum lubricant, I'll bi baak 'hic' lat'r.' He is red faced drunk as he stumbles out the door. Torbiro glances down to where he last restocked the shop's supply of lubricant and finds cases and cases of them. He sighs with thoughts of relief and feelings of sadness that his master has yet again dumped all the remaining work on him.

Many clicks and turns pass while fixing and re-gearing clocks, locks, music boxes and other intricate devices. A man, a human man, bursts into the shop. He wears a ratty old cloak; it is brown and covered in muddy patches at the bottom edges of the garment. He wears leather armour under his cloak, but it looks like the sort anyone could buy if they wished to go adventuring. He holds no kind of weapon, but it appears he is a swordsman from his form, stance and stature. He looks desperate and distressed as his eyes dart left and right as though searching for something. 'How can I be of assistance to you?' asks Torbiro, using his best welcoming voice.

The man responds with, 'Keep it safe…', then drops a sack on the shop counter and rushes back outside.

'Sir, you forgot your sack,' yells Torbiro as he grabs the sack and chases after him. As he exits the shop, he notices the man has collapsed a good two or so metres away from the shop. Torbiro quickly approaches him to return the sack. As he gets closer to the collapsed man, Torbiro notices blood stains on the ground. Small drops of blood but then as he reaches the man, he realises he is dead. Merchants of that sector are of no help, as they place no trust in the likes of halflings.

Being as honest as a young man trying to be a knight can be, he drags the man's corpse to the back of the shop's scrap yard. He searches the man's belongings and finds a bloodstained crest. The crest of a sprocket and a key. He also finds a strange weapon concealed underneath his clothing. It is a dagger Torbiro has never seen before and it is the cause of his demise.

Torbiro pockets the strange item as well as the crest, so he can inform the guards of what happened.

I knew that leaving a corpse in my master's yard would get me fired, so I moved him to an empty crate and dragged it to a common alleyway. This took me hours and by the time I finished, I was sore all over.

It was late, but I knew I should, at the very least, tell one of the local militia about the incident. I went to the guard post at the edge of the sector and explained what had happened. The guards on duty just laughed and shooed me away. I tried to tell them again, but this time they threatened me with their muskets. I ran for fear of my life and as I turned a corner, I crashed into someone.

'Hey, what was that for?' asked the girl. I got up, apologised and started to run again, but she stopped me. 'Oh, it's just you Torro, what's wrong?' At the mention of my nickname, I looked up to see that it was Myra. I tell her the situation that a man was killed in front of the shop and she too laughed. I waited for her to stop and told her I was not joking and she should come see for herself.

I took her to the place where I left the body in a crate, somewhere only halflings could enter, under a pile of garbage to hide it from salvagers' and scavengers' prying hands. When we got there, I showed her the body to show her the truth. She had disbelief written all over her face until she saw the body. Myra, at that instant, was felled by shock and fainted. I brought her back to the shop where I found my master speaking to some important-looking officials.

'Torbiro, wh're hav' ye been? When I got back, the shop was closed and I had to break down the door to get back in?' shouted Dorian. He complained to his apprentice that if the shop was closed, business would suffer and therefore his payment would be less. Torbiro explained the situation and Dorian laughed at the poor excuse. The officials, on the other hand, questioned the little halfling about the man. What the man wanted and the whereabouts of his body. He told them the truth and then showed them the hiding place.

Once I had answered all of their questions and showed them the corpse, they shoved me aside like some piece of ill discarded scrap from the dismantler's workshop. I left, knowing I did the right thing and went back to where I had left Myra.

She was sitting on my bed next to the rather large but broken clock hammer that nearly killed me this morning and said, 'Have they left?' I was confused by her question so I double checked and when I thought about her question again, I came back in the room flustered as though I was made fun of.

'Who?' asked Torbiro.

'The suspicious officials of the king, who else?' said Myra with a quick reply. She told me they were looking for something of importance when I had left to show them the location of the body. We talked it over and I told her there was nothing else to be found from the body aside from the murder weapon and crest. She stopped me, stood up and walked with an arrogant strut before revealing the sack I had forgotten about.

'And what about this?' asked Myra with smugness in her tone. I could not even reply to that face of hers and stayed silent. She dropped all of its contents and found a broken old music box and a letter. Myra grabbed the box and tried to forcefully open it. I instead looked at the letter.

'Yes!' I yelled in surprise. 'This is my chance to be a knight.' Myra was startled by my sudden outburst and dropped the music box. It struck the floor and broke into several pieces. A round metal piece hit my foot and I looked down. I saw scraps of metal being scattered by the force and I yelled at her.

'What are you doing?'

'Look, it wasn't my fault. You're the one that broke it with your proclamation of knighthood!!' said Myra, flustered.

'I, um… you still dropped it. Now help me find all the pieces,' I said, gathering the scattered pieces of the music box.

'Fine.'

After all the pieces were collected, I found a similar crest to the one I found on the dead man. The box seemed to be a disguise to keep the item a secret. I wondered why, but those questions could be answered later. The next day, I took the letter to the castle to inquire about becoming a knight. They refused and got the shackles ready, but when I showed them the letter and the crest, they were dumbfounded. They still arrested me and escorted me to the palace. The king was called to address the matter personally. He had a shocked face when checking the document in question and the notable crest. He yelled at the guards that apprehended me and told them to release me.

Once the shackles were off, the king announced, with the most foul of looks, that I would become a knight. Though it was only a provisional position, I did not care. I was honoured by this opportunity and I promptly walked to my new station. The training was tough and the other warriors hated me, but I persevered. Basic training took almost three watches – three years – but I managed to tough it out and prevail.

The king later announced there would be a trial for all young knights to test their mettle. My commander told me I was to be stationed in town to capture criminals in the marketplace, like some lowly guard. I took this mission very seriously so as not to disappoint my liege and fellow knights, but they all laughed at my attempt to be gallant. I ignored their insults and headed off to complete my mission. Unfortunately, my first mission was to capture a rather well-known thief by the name of Memyra.

CHAPTER 11
MY FIRST FAILURE

A cloaked child living in the kingdom of Traytos runs and jumps and dashes quickly. This child hears merchants and workers curse at the annoyance of the creature that crashes and hits obstacles as it gets further and further away. This child hears shouts and cries of travellers and day-to-day people as she runs to a very common corner.

This corner is the typical corner of a building or alleyway, or perhaps a small hideaway from the common folk. Removing the hood of her cloak, the child is no more than 10 years old. She catches her breath, for these moments are of great importance. Just a few more seconds and she will run again and this time she must get away for good.

After a moment's rest, perhaps it was just too long of a moment as she hears shouts of, 'Where is that thief…where did that thief go?' A young man is looking around menacingly. This man was a typical watchman or guard depending on where you're from, but they all have one thing in common: they hunt down and catch law-breakers. She then notices a crowd saying, '…over there…over there, she went that way?' Slowly this girl hiding in the shadows of a corner, takes a slight peek and finds the people shouting are also pointing in her direction, to the location of her path. She looks around in a startling panic for an escape, but from what she can see, in that alley are two paths - into the alleyway or out in the streets.

Her choice at that moment is to run into the depths of the alleyway and get trapped at the end or at the nearest opening and climb up the sides of the building walls and try to get away from the rooftops, only to be caught once she arrives at the top. Has she already forgotten her plan of escape as the adrenaline pulses through her tiny body? She decides to take a fool's route and run, hoping for the best. This change in her plan will get her ambushed by other guards further down this path. She is not thinking until struck by a protruding steam pipe knocking her down. 'What in the name of the pulse was that?' says the girl with the silent whisper in an already silent alleyway. She looks to where her path was abruptly stopped and sees an unusual-looking pipe. Its shape is very different from normal steam pipes as they usually have an L-shape and spit steam regularly. This pipe, on the other hand, has something about it that is familiar to her and she quickly examines it with a slight touch.

She finds this pipe so familiar, as though it was part of her escape plan in the first place. This is the strange contraption she bought from one of the dwarves selling pulleys and winches by the lower marketplace.

With a simple pull of the device, it can provide the wielder with an accelerated lift, allowing one to mysteriously vanish from their pursuers. She quickly tries to remember how this contraption is supposed to work, but around the corner she hears the guards coming closer and closer, as their steps clunk on the wet cobblestones.

She is forced to hurry, trying to find the lever to work the machine and the rope where she is to hang on, but alas, she is in a panicked state and therefore caught. 'So this is where ye've been hidin',' says the guard as he gasps for breath. 'Now drop all dat ye've stolen and come peaceful like, ye know the penalty for stealing.' He is not one for the workout of chasing speedy thieves. The girl continues to work the device and finds the rope and pulley are taut enough to hold her escape.

'Well good sir, I believe you have me red-handed and trapped, but I must say fare-thee-well.' As she makes this sly remark, she pulls the lever and is shot to the sky so quickly the guard is left astonished. This is not his day. He looked around frantically but finds no trace of the thief. Was it magic, perhaps?

As the girl reaches the roof of the adjoined building, the rigging which holds on to the pipe-like container holding her loot, has also travelled up with the young thief. She hears the guard cursing down below and the footsteps of the other watchmen as they arrive much too late to have witnessed the scene. The thief breathes easy and checks for all the loot she has acquired during her morning run. A small bag hidden away inside the container is filled with only a few things. A loaf of bread, a length of copper wire, a broken dagger and a small jewel with a white lustre. She has the bread but only a few pieces before she hears a commanding voice up on the rooftops with her.

'Hmmm, it seems I've caught yet another apprentice thief…' says a man in heavy bright armour.

'Um, who are you? You haven't caught me yet!!' replies the thief, in a panic as she tries to hide her loot.

'Oh, but I have. You have no place left to run or hide. That makes you caught… didn't your master ever teach you the basics of thievery?' he says.

'I have no master of which you speak, only a …' she replies, trying to think of the right word to say that does not reveal her master's name or an association with her, 'only a companion of sorts. You might even say a guide to this large city to which I should tour.' She ends her sentence, not to add suspicion.

'Well then, let Myra know I said hello when she frees you from your jail cell in the dungeon,' says the warrior as he explains that criminals will pay.

'But Torro, why not say it now, while I'm here… for old times' sake?' says a cloaked figure just behind an exhaust vent.

'That's Torbiro, Sir Torbiro to you, Myra.' He grins, proudly stating who he is. 'Thief child, I advise you not to follow the corrupted occupation of halflings and start over.' Torbiro says with the deepest voice he could muster, putting on an act of confidence.

The warrior in the bright heavy armour appears more like a child in an iron suit than a warrior of the watch. He speaks with a high-strung tone, as if hiding the fact that he too is a halfling. The voice coming from the vents, the opposite side of where she has hidden, sounds like her master Memyra.

A few minutes of looking at the self-proclaimed knight and it is very obvious he is in fact a halfling. He might wear the armour of a knight of Traytos, with the insignia of the gear and the shape of the screw, but there is something else about it that is magnificent. The other knights or soldiers are not as sheen as this one. His chest plate is shiny, with brilliance only the clerics of the void could ever possess or obtain and the condition of the steel is unlike anything made by a smith but or an artisan. His gauntlets and greaves are so well maintained this knight must have taken days of care to possess such radiance in the reflecting light. And of course his boots… what I saw were just feet. Feet with fur, or maybe it was hair.

She looked down to her own grubby little toes and saw a similar sight. This knight was truly a halfling like herself, but different. Moments later, the knight named Torbiro approached the young halfling girl and said once again, 'Like I said before, I have you caught, so stand up.' Her master, an acquaintance of this knight, dashed forward and for some reason or another both of the thieves were up and away from the knight and her master said, 'Hey, Torro see you in the usual place to settle this… bring as many of your knightly goons with you if you can.'

The words of her master were calm and collected, as if they were meant to taunt or tease this knight. A name could be heard from such a tiny creature as a halfling. 'Myyyyyyyrrrrrraaaaaaaaa…' This town or city or sector of Rippel is known as Traytos. It is where I live as a knight and a man of honour and justice. This sector is filled with all sorts of characters and peoples. Shops and guilds of many kinds exist here in Traytos. We are a sector of advancement and science, but some do not oppose the ways of the arcane and mystics, for where business exists, there are those that practice the forbidden or lawless acts.

CHAPTER 12
MYRA THE THIEF

A figure staying silent in the shadows paces forward and backward as if waiting for someone, impatiently. This figure appears to be clad in rather light attire geared up for quick escapes. She prepares her instant escape device and waits some more. In the distance, she hears a familiar voice berating some foolish thief. She peers out from her hiding place and sees Torro, her childhood friend who had left for knighthood and had forgotten to resign from his job. He had been gone for three watches after they found an important letter detailing information on Bataros' plans to attack Traytos.

She hadn't seen him in such a long time that she wished to greet him in the usual joking manner. Myra also notices he now wears the crest of the kingdom as well as the crest of the sprocket and key. He seems not to notice her at all, as though he had forgotten what she taught him about 'being aware of your surroundings'. She felt superior because she has kept her racial pride in her abilities to be a halfling.

'Where in the pulse is she?' mumbles Myra silently, disgruntled at being kept waiting at the appointed location.

At that moment, her apprentice appears but is confronted by Torro. Being caught by the likes of Torro is funny in itself and she can't help but watch her apprentice being lectured to by a poor excuse of a warrior. She waits for the signal before helping, but it seems the young thief has forgotten everything she has been taught, so Myra equips the instant escape device, much like a steam-powered jet pack and jettisons into the air upon activating it. The acceleration of the device is so powerful Myra has to run and grab her apprentice as quickly as possible before turning the device on.

CHAPTER 13
THE SKIES OF TRAYTOS

Soaring into the sky, one could see what the city of Traytos was made of. To the south were the guilds, mainly artisans and crafters that specialised in making engines and pipes and tubing for powering and sustaining energy for the city. To the north were places for the rich to languish in rare finery and delicacies and fashion that the common folk could only imagine in their wildest fantasies. To the west was where the forgotten and wretched people lived. This place was filled with the slums and old ruins of a great accident in the past. Taverns and brothels and old remnants of homes were scattered in this place. To the east was where we thieves never trod. This place was known to all as the military training sectors. It was also the place where the jails and execution blocks were located. Warriors and Sellswords were the only ones welcome here as outsiders, with the exception of magic folk. Adventurers used to be in that list but due to the increase of prejudice among the races, they have turned to the life of trade.

The centre of the sector was where the castle of Traytos lay and also where the marketplace was located. Thieves, thugs and pickpockets thrived here. The risk and reward were one and the same. One's survival.

CHAPTER 14
VALUE OF FAILURE

After shouting my frustration at the shrinking distant figure, I note our favourite place, a tavern known as Cold Beer. The sign to the place has been broken ever since I was much younger, making mischief. I heard this place used to be called Gold Beer for its honey-like brews and precious tastes that were referred to as 'Golden' liquor. Or at least that is what adventurers used to call it.

Torbiro arrives at the old, abandoned tavern and walks right in, though not through the mouldy old wooden doorway but instead through one of the windows just low enough to step over. He notices all the nostalgic places where they used to sit and play and pretend to be great rogues of old. 'Myra, I'm here,' Torbiro announces his arrival. But after yelling it out, he feels foolish, as if he has forgotten this is a dangerous place where one might lose their life over a misplaced insult.

'I know,' says Myra using her joking and sarcastic tones, 'I'm the one who invited you, after all.' She places her dagger to his throat. Torbiro reaches for the fake dagger only realising it is real as he feels the sharpness of pain in his hand as he grabs it so abruptly. He cries out in pain and deflects the dagger away from his neck.

'Torro, what are you doing?' asks Myra, mocking the fact she purposefully used a real weapon rather than one of the toys they used to play with.

'Great, now I'm bleeding... are you trying to kill me?' Torbiro is in disbelief. She laughs and hops down from the pile of refuse she was perched on.

'So how many goons did you bring?' Myra asks with sarcasm.

'None,' says Torbiro. He explains that after they escaped, the only one to follow their pursuit was him. She laughs some more and starts a coughing fit from his story.

'Look, I told them I knew where you would be and I had a plan to catch you but... they wouldn't listen,' Torbiro whines like a complaining child.

'So,' more laughing and chuckling, 'you...' heavy exhausted breathing, 'came alone?' Myra was laughing and losing breath from the hilarious tale.

'Stop laughing already, Myra. It's not that funny,' said Torbiro with a scowl from being made fun of.

Myra didn't reply until her laughing fit was mostly over. She then snapped her fingers and her gang of thieves popped out from everywhere. She pointed to the young girl who had been cornered on the rooftops and demanded she bandage up my hand where it had been cut by the fine dagger. The girl was named Natie and was good at bandaging the small wound. 'Come Torro, we have much to talk 'bout,' said Myra, collecting her winnings from a bet she had made.

'Look Myra, I just came to arrest you for the crimes that you have committed in this kingdom,' said Torbiro declaring his purpose for being in the rundown building.

'So?' said Myra in reply, not taking his presence seriously. Torbiro explained it was his first mission and if she came quietly without a fuss, then he could convince his commander to give her a light sentence. Of course, she wasn't going to come quietly, as they both knew the punishment for theft was brutal. She proclaimed that Torbiro should join her as a spy for their gang. But he too stubbornly refused, saying there was no honour among thieves.

The next thing I knew, I was tied up with rope, gagged with a filthy sock and blindfolded by some kind of thick leather. I was freed by an elf in one of the sniper units. She spoke sweetly, like many of her kind. I heard mention of her name. Cyan. I was found tied up on one of the main flag poles of the castle, with a message from Myra saying, 'Try again, turdbags.' The 'a's were written the wrong way, indicating Myra's mark.

CHAPTER 15
OFFICER'S LIFE

The new morning was never really new. In Commander Peren's mind, the city of Traytos was a scheduled disaster waiting to be cleaned up and restored. The first signs of morning for this particular knight was the sound of the explosions north, north-east of his sleeping quarters. Followed by the screams of 'fire' if it was the second cycle of the revol, or 'elements' if it was the fifth cycle of the revols and 'oddities' every other day. He knew the protocol to deal with each and every occasion, so long as there were no elves or others of the magical race involved besides himself, of course. Quickly and gracefully, he donned his protective gear and then his uniform on top. He then headed out to direct his men on whatever the problem was that needed to be solved.

CHAPTER 16
CONSPIRACY

Several turns after dealing with the oddities from the morning gnomish explosion, one of Peren's men approaches him with some urgent news. It is a summons from the king. Peren gives his men one final order and heads off to the castle, but not the front door. There are many ways to his destination and the quickest is by using the lay lines. Lay lines are dwarven marvels of transportation, which allow a person to be sent to his or her destination via the steam tubes. They were later named lay lines after a gnome had a terrible accident while travelling and experimenting at the same time.

Upon arriving, Peren and other knights of similar rank were assembled and then seated. To Peren, this was very strange. Council meetings were usually scheduled on the second revol on the sixth cycle of the toggle. But today's date was 1985AT, third cycle of the first revol of the ninth toggle. Thinking and sighing to himself, 'I miss the elven calendar '.

The proceedings went on for turns – hours – but the subject that truly rattled my nerves was not the reports of monsters from different sectors or the advancing forces of the void cultists of Bataros, but of the probationary knights' enlistments. One in particular had been mentioned that shocked me the most. Torbiro, the halfling. Most of the knights were human or of half breed descent. But a halfling? The king hates their kind and now he was giving this short stack a chance.

Something else must be going on. I kept these thoughts to myself, but some of the other commanders roared in outrage. This was not to my surprise. I kept my composure while the others argued the choice of recruiting one of these cunning creatures.

Once the gaggle of arguments subsided, the king himself singled me out to hear my silent opinion. Our king, Aroduct the golem master, told me to speak my mind. I said nothing. I made a rather confused look on my face as I gave a long, hard stare at my current ruler. I then answered, 'His majesty's choice is the right one.' I said this in the most monotone manner I could muster, not hinting at the fact that I too, thought this was a farce or a mockery to the knights that serve and protect. As I started to bow and return to my seat, he answered, 'I agree, this day will be the beginning, for halflings to serve this kingdom.' I expected him to add 'protect' but it was not mentioned. Just as I sat, the king stopped me and ordered me to hear his new orders concerning Torbiro.

King's orders:

I hereby declare that the halfling by the name of Torbiro becomes a knight of Traytos. I pledge that you, Commander Peren, will be his acting commander in the upcoming missions and help him aid the kingdom of this beloved Traytos. All responsibilities of knighthood will be provided to this new recruit upon completing his graduation mission.

He must protect my daughter, Dawn of Traytos. His assignment will commence in three cycles from now.

What say you, commander?

I was shocked at this formal declaration. I was so speechless that all I could do was bow and recite the credo of the knights of Traytos. This meeting was adjourned and all knights and soldiers were dismissed. This was a ridiculous farce. I must be on the king's blacklist. But he cannot possibly think of breaking the elves from his alliance, or could he?

CHAPTER 17
KINGDOM'S HATRED

After the meeting with his army representatives, the king needed to inform the lesser sect of his kingdom's officials, the nobles and the council members. The annoying lot that handle the petty change they like to call the 'economy'. The knights were the easiest to handle. They have more bark to their bite, but if they bite, they know their fangs will be removed. The nobles are even louder in their bark but would never dare to bite. They are spineless. But useful.

Arriving to this unscheduled meeting, Aroduct had the members of Traytos' nobles and other guildsmen and kingdom officials be announced and then seated. Much to the leaders' and officials' sudden concern was who entered next. A halfling of all things. In the castle, but not in chains, nor for execution. Even though a respected knight and commander was escorting 'the thing' all the council members were outraged. They ordered guards and other men and women at arms to arrest it.

As the soldiers followed their orders, King Aroduct, with an authoritative 'SILENCE' demanded the attention of them all. The council men and soldiers halted to a stop. Interrupted from continuing to arrest the halfling, the hall was put to order.

First, there was a speech from his majesty about the wrongful persecution of halflings. This prejudice must stop and new laws must be changed to accommodate all races, great and small. Second, he announced this halfling was to be a knight of the realm. All soldiers laughed, but the council members only revealed their grim distaste for such a thing. The king simply sighed and that was enough to silence the crowd. Those among the council that knew the king personally, knew of his silent wrath. The soldier had only heard stories of such events and those who were new to their posts continued the verbal riot in the proceedings. These soldiers suddenly vanished with a cry of pain, as a stone hand appeared out of the walls of the great hall and grasped the fools in a swift and crushing motion. Blood splashed from the dead. Many soldiers gulped in horror but said no more. Men with weak constitutions released their breakfast to the floor ~ away from the king, of course ~ women simply covered their mouths in shock. While the others were just stone-faced as they knew the consequences of his majesty's wrath from prior experience.

Third, the king asked his trusted council to judge the knight. Not by his race, but by his worth. His loyalty. His strength. His measure and mettle.

CHAPTER 18
BLIND SUSPICION

My head was bowed for most of the proceeding, as I was told by Commander Peren just before we entered the great hall, to be courteous and formal. There was a lot of noise about my arrest, but that was to be expected. I had faith the commander would defend his own, but then again, he might not. There were screams and then sounds of some people throwing up, but after all that, just silence. There were a few whispers here and there, but nothing that I could hear myself.

My name was called several times and I waited for a command, but nothing. Then the king himself ordered Commander Peren to leave the room. With a slight click of the heavy doors closing and the poorly oiled hinges quietly creaking, I was alone in that hall.

'Stand, Knight!' was all Torbiro heard next and there he was judged.

After Peren exited the great hall and left the bean sprout to his inauguration, he started to passively listen in on other knights and see if there would be some sort of coup. Most of the generals and soldiers of respectable rank only spoke of their disagreement and that they would keep a close eye on the ex-sneak thief.

Once Peren had left the castle, he noticed another young knight being escorted by another commander he had never met before. He thought it strange, but perhaps they had only returned from their mission. Peren greeted the knight with a salute and he, in turn, gave a very old but formal gesture. Peren wasn't able to get much of a conversation with the knight but managed to gain his name. Jimmy. With more formal gesturing, they headed to the great hall. Peren thought to himself that he had a strange sense of arcanus, but it couldn't be. Arcanus was the energies of magic and it was outlawed in this sector. With all the protective barriers in place, there would have been an alarm as they entered the walls of the kingdom.

I watched their backs until they disappeared from view and headed back to my post.

CHAPTER 19
THE ANNUAL MEETING

Morning had arrived once again and the air was still and cold. It was just like any other day where light slowly seeps into a room. A rather spacious one with heavy velvet curtains to block out the light. But the light of the morning and of this cycle was at first subtle, soft and dim, thanks to the heavy curtains. It gradually beamed brighter, like magic had intensified it. The light chased closer and closer to the bed of the room as the morning light settled.

A light groan of irritation. The tossing and turning of a man still chasing midnight dreams. The light breaks free of the curtains as a soft breeze pushes it away. The cool air leaving morning dew on the open window. The man continues to elude the light and ducks under the covers of his pristine silk sheets and warm, expensive elven cotton bedding. A subtle sound, the softest and slightest knock. The man ignores the sound and again tries to return to the bliss of his dreams. The sounds at the door repeat in ascending amplitude. Louder and louder does the knock rapped on the door.

'…Sir, Sir please wake,' says a servant. King Aroduct stirs in his bed. He says softly in his mind, 'What in the pulse is it now?' He gets up from his bed and hears the morning sounds of his palace. His rather loud daughter is ordering her servants about to get her the latest clothing. The word 'Fashion' being screamed by said daughter as though saying the word louder and louder will make the servants work fast. The lords and ministers are harking calls for an audience. As if they think their matters are important. The sounds of early morning executions out in the parade grounds. The knights doing their morning drills and of course, the sounds of hazing the grunts, better known as testing the new recruits.

Aroduct, king of Traytos finishes getting decent to showcase his dedication to morning routine and not just lazing about in bed trying to avoid the responsibility of his own kingdom. He opens the door to reveal the stern and regal looking king that he is, but as he does, to answer one of his servants, he encounters his agent and spy. 'Oh, it's just you.' He feels rather foolish in front of this person as he already knows the truth of his majesty. That he is, in fact, the slovenly, lazy king that wishes for an even easier life.

'Do not be too disappointed with seeing me, your highness.' The spy replies in a formal, but teasing, manner.

'I have news from your brother. He agrees with your proposal and would like to discuss it in more detail if you will allow it?'

'Tell him, to the caverns. He should remember what that means.' The king is obviously irritated to give such an order. He waves the spy away and tells him to get his breakfast ready. His majesty only hears the door lock click to acknowledge that his agent has left. He breathes a sigh of relief. 'Finally he's gone.'

CHAPTER 20
THE SCHEME

After having his morning meal with his daughter and other invited guests, the king prepares for his morning council with the ministers that handle minor problems in his kingdom. Matters of the people, matters of crimes and matters of the outer region's welfare. Once these issues have been dealt with, the king needs to provide private lessons to his layabout daughter in the smaller matters of the state. The girl is a dunce and never fully aware in these lessons. To get the frivolous girl back on track, King Aroduct needs to call the experts to provide tutelage to his brainless daughter. He always wonders why not just let the tutors do this job and why he, the almighty king, has to waste his time with such frivolous tasks, but it is tradition and a last request from someone in the king's past. He wishes every morning he could have changed such a law, but his late father had stated the penalty for such a change. A beheading.

Holding his neck and sighing with disgust, he continues to his next meeting. The great hall, where most of the most important warriors and generals and councilmen are here to discuss the threat of the northern kingdom of Bataros. This threat detailed the approach of magic and of the chaos it would bring to Traytos. Generals and high-ranking knights informed that large armies were approaching from the northwest and northeast, moving around the Valley of the Pierce as if trying to move into pincer position. The councilmen spoke of strange happenings in the abandoned tower to the northwest, where the farmers and peasants mentioned eerie sounds and flashes of ghostly colours.

The king, sitting at the end of the meeting table, wonders in silence. 'Brother, I think you have moved too early.' He continues to acknowledge the 'supposed' threats to his kingdom and agrees with the generals there needs to be a plan or manoeuvre to repel those armies. He thinks long and hard on the situation when suddenly the main door to the great hall is opened with such force. the bang of the door resounds in the halls of the castle, as the warrior bursts into the meeting.

Guards, warriors and soldiers immediately draw their weapons and point to the disruption. 'Everyone at ease. It's just Fameborn,' said the king with a scowl at the pompous nobleman. At the order of the king, the soldiers withdraw their weapons and return to their discussions. The councilmen have come out of hiding from behind whatever furniture they could find to cower behind. There were men that hid behind the king and he makes notes of these cowards to execute later if they disobey him.

'Sorry for my late arrival, your majesty but I had a few important matters to deal with. I also had to retrieve my son from training the probationary knights before he seriously hurt any of them.' Lance Fameborn bows, using his most apologetic voice. The king acknowledges him and accepts the man's apology, but thinks, 'Perfect, just what I need. Another arrogant blowhard.'

With all parties mostly present, the king quietens the room. He gives out orders to his general on how to deal with the threat of Traytos. The plan involves guerrilla warfare, where traps are to be set to destroy half of the approaching armies and rout them once they are distraught. This way, the armies of Bataros can have reserves to thwart other threats that might occur.

The generals, being just as devious as the king, agree with the plan, but the Fameborns suggests they should be the ones that lead the charge against the first wave while they are setting up obstacles to annihilate scouts and the vanguard of Traytos in an honourable battle. The king first opposes the idea, as he knows the reason for the oncoming threat but then reconsiders, stating they must march as soon as the 'traps' are set.

Upon agreement of the king's plan, Lance suggests his son Wilbur take the honour of rear guard. Since he had been training the newly formed knights of this sector, he will have the trust of his own troops. King of Traytos thinks to himself, 'Hmmmm, the young Fameborn will be the one to marry my stupid daughter, sooner or later. Then it should be he that rescues her from that tower. I wonder how smart he is...' At that moment, the young Fameborn makes such a foolish decree, it almost makes the king fall out of his throne from laughter.

'I, Wilbur L. Fameborn, will serve his majesty at the risk of my own life and limb. I decree that if there is a task to be done, it must be done with honour and might rather than magic. With the blade of my ancestors I shall protect this land...' said the young Fameborn. The king only heard this part of this arrogant fool's decree, as he needed to concentrate and hold off his true reaction until he was alone. The need to burst out laughing and relieve himself of the stress of the day was starting to catch up with him. He signalled to one of his servants to bring the midday meal. This was enough to startle the men and leaders of the room, since it was quite early in the cycle.

As the food started to arrive, the Fameborn representatives bid their farewell. So they may prepare their troops for the plan and train more recruits to add to their forces. The king sighed with relief and noticed there was a strange light coming from outside. The window that viewed the lovely courtyard garden seemed to blink with a strange tint of orange light. It reflected off the window and bounced all around the room, from a large bronze statue to the copper chandler to the crystal bowls filled with a light brown serving of consommé, to his majesty's silver cutlery. The light flashed some sort of code only for the eyes of the receiver.

The king stood up from the table and excused himself. He did not say why he needed to leave, but not a single person, warrior or statesmen wondered or questioned him. He walked to a wall just outside the great hall. It was there he touched a sequence of bricks. A moment later, soft sounds of gears and mechanical parts clicking and clacking could be heard, until the hidden door opened. He entered and it closed behind him.

CHAPTER 21
UNKNOWN ASSISTANT

Walking down the secret passageway, the king thought of the message. 'Your highness, your brother waits in the cavern. Shall I bring the girl? If not, take a sip of your soup and excuse yourself.' What in the world has brought you here so early? It has only been a few turns since I sent him to give you the message. It must mean they are in a dire situation. The king sighs with worry in his mind as he remembered how pathetic his brother was at controlling servants, when they were children. 'Brother, you must be stronger,' the king thought.

After passing a few private rooms underground, he finally meets up with his agent. 'You know why I have brought you instead of my uncultured daughter, RIGHT?' says the king in a condescending tone. 'Don't speak, I don't like hearing the sound of your disgusting voice,' interrupts the king just before the agent can respond to the king's question. The agent simply nods in the formal manner of his tribal race. Under the agent's cloak, he is actually an Orc. A breed of savage barbarians or nomads that wreak havoc as they traverse the land. They are known for the destruction of small villages. Selling, pillaging and the occasional rape and mass sacrifice.

This Orcish agent is actually part cyborg and part wizard. Magic in all of Rippel has a dangerous effect on technology. Normally, magic is simply disrupted by the powers of mechanical energy and technology. It has an overloading effect towards magic as it might absorb such uncontrollable or chaotic amounts of power without having the ability to contain it. As a result, most technology will either stop working or explode. But this agent has been given a piece of lost technology from before The Thrust.

As the two continue to walk at a more brisk pace, they arrive at another doorway, but unlike the others, this one is far more decorated with murals of the past and depictions of the time before and after The Thrust. The king taps a few stones in a certain sequence, as if this door is some lock to a vault. Once he has finished, the king says a few ancient non decipherable words. 'Gnik rouy rof nepo.' The archway glows red, then green, then silver, then a faint violet. The door vanishes and there is a room with a stone table at the centre. A man and a girl stand on the other side of the room.

The king and the man greet each other with the same words used to open the door. They speak quite fast, so it is very hard to understand what they are discussing. I stand in one of the corners of the room and wait for my liege to finish his meeting. The girl looks at me as though questioning why I am even there. I use my telepathy to communicate with her and an illusionary power to disguise myself as well as to deceive her. 'Who are you?' she asks mentally while my telepathic connection is still projected.

'I am just a lowly servant of his majesty. And may I get your name, young one?' I say, answering her question.

We exchange formal curtsies as well as some information. I find out she is the princess of the Bataros, Lady Kitreth. I tell her one of my many names, Zephyr Spike and she concludes that I am not what I seem.

CHAPTER 22
LADY KITRETH

Father and I had been informed by one of our spies there would be an important meeting with my uncle. I am the next heir to the throne of Bataros. My father is the mighty sorcerer, king of Bataros, King Kerem the Terasol. I am just his daughter. I am just as capable of a mage as most of my age. I just lack experience and a rival. Once father was ready, we approached a secret passageway under our garden in the palace. The room under the garden is only known to those of the royal family, so father and I were the first ones in a long time to use it. The room was full of cobwebs and thick layers of dust. Father cleared the place with just a simple gesture and the chamber was clean. I was about to clean it myself with a small bolt of fire, but I was just too slow. We arrived at a room that had depictions of all ancient Rippel where magic and technology were in heavy conflict, like some stubborn boys arguing over who is the best. There were depictions of 'The Thrust' before and after.

Father motioned for me to stand on a magical glyph. I did as instructed and with some ancient words 'Nrevac eht ot levart' we were teleported to a chamber with a stone table in the centre of the room. There, father and a man in a regal outfit greeted each other in the ancient tongue. That is when I concluded that he was my uncle, the ruler of the Technologist south of our kingdom. Rumours back home tell of strange machines that give off energy to light the entire city or other machines used to ride in instead of using horses or other mounted animals. I look around the room to see if cousin Dawn was here, but all I saw was a heavily cloaked figure at the opposite corner to me.

I tried to listen in on what father and uncle were discussing, but they spoke far too quickly in our ancient tongue for me to make anything out. I did manage to understand the main gist of the conversation. It was about obtaining peace in both of our restless subjects by staging a kidnapping. Of who, I just did not know. But I presumed someone important, like a statesman or a noble.

The figure in the corner was covered so well it was hard to notice him at all in that dim light. It could be a man or perhaps a woman, but they stood still as I tried to identify why they were here instead of Dawn. They spoke to me in my mind and I asked, 'Who are you? And why is the princess of Traytos not here?' Rather than revealing anything of subsequence, they answered back, but only in my mind, without even a gesture that a wizard or mage might make when casting a spell. The voice that answered was a woman's, but it was distorted as though this creature wanted to reveal very little information about herself or himself. The only significant information I got from them was a name - Zephyr Spike.

I waited for father and uncle to finish their discussion as all I wanted to do was head back home and perfect more spells to my repertoire as a Fire-mage. Father then started to radiate in magical energy and slammed his bare palms on the stone table and shouted something to uncle who only laughed with absolute glee. I looked at father's face and it was as red as one of my fire spells. All I heard was, 'Nrob erew uoy yad eht sa diputs sa tsuj era uoy' and father had the cutest scowl on his face. I had to keep from reacting in a sisterly way to avoid his strict punishment.

His face remained this way for a few minutes, but then it started to retain its normal complexion. He turned to me and father and uncle stopped speaking in the ancient tongue as he introduced me to my uncle Aroduct, the golem master. I formally introduced myself as Kitreth the Flame. Father then said he wished for me, his proud successor, to handle the execution of the plan. I agreed so long as I was rewarded by the end of such an escapade. 'Well, aren't you a greedy little minx?' said uncle as he patted the shaggy part of my hair. I wanted so much to blast him then and there for such insolence, but I knew why he did so, without any care for danger and that was the still creature in the shadows of the corner. I stated my firm desire to obtain my reward of either ancient spells or a rare artefact and that is when father put his hand on my shoulder as if to say, 'yes, I promise.' Father and I bid uncle farewell and we returned to our palace to prepare the plan.

CHAPTER 23
THE CULLING

Rehtorb sgniteerg. Said Aroduct with a light greeting.

Ees on emit gnol rehtrob olleh. Said Kerem in reply.

Gniteem siht fo tniop eht ot teg tsuj dna seirtnasaelp eht piks ew llahs llew? Said Aroduct, trying to hasten their time together.

Etsah hcus rof deen on. Said Kerem, trying to have a proper reunion. It had been a while since they last saw each other.

Ora, thgir elihw elttil a rof tahc dluoc ew? Kerem continued the conversation.

Seiduts reh htiw rethguad ruoy si woh mek. Aroduct asked, pushing his brother's request, and complimenting the young sorceress.

Nwad toidi ym ekilnu ssalc reh fo pot eht ta eb tsum ehs. Aroduct complained about his own foolish offspring.

Rehtaf etal ruo fo swal eht wonk uoy nehw noitidart siht fo tuo Nwad peek ot dediced uoy taht desirprus yllautca ma I. Said Kerem, worried his brother had broken the laws of this sector. As karma would bite those that disobey.

Rehtom reh ekil gnihton si ehs. Sselesu yletelpmoc si enim fo tarb taht. Erac I lla rof retsef dna tor tsuj nac rehtaf llew. Said Aroduct, breaking his oath nonchalantly.

Rewop ni rehtaf ekil tsuj emoceb ot detrats sah dna noiger eht ni loohcs egam eht lla morf detaudarg ydaerla sah Htertik llew. Kerem was proud of his daughter's achievements.

Thgir dnim ni ton tub? Asked Aroduct, noting her lack of experience.

Yltcaxe taht yb naem uoy od tahw? Said Kerem, insulted by the comment. She had worked hard, but Kerem had thought it to be a cheap jab as he misunderstood.

Yressabmud tnatalb ruoy esruoc fo llew. Said Aroduct, insulting his little brother. Forgetting how proud his first comment was.

Smodgnik ruo ni smelborp eht fo tsom evomer ot nalp emos klat ot gniog erew uoy thguoht I. Ora won siht pots! Kerem was frustrated that his brother was right. There was no more need for pleasantries and he wanted to get back to the topic at hand.

Ysae si taht llew! Said Aroduct, with such confidence that it sounded sarcastic.

Si tahw? Said Kerem, confused at his statement.

Nrob erew uoy yad eht erew uoy sa diputs sa tsuj era uoy. Said Aroduct, stating the obvious. But continuing with his idea.

Raw a trats ot gniog era ew! Aroduct revealed his cunning plan. He paused, waiting for Kerem to react, but ultimately continued.

Rehto hcae llik meht evah dna elbbur gninialpmoc eht tiurcer. Aroduct really was cruel.

Ti trats ot gniog ew era ohw tub? Asked Kerem, as he was never good at anticipating his enemy, even as a great mage.

Uoy ot tuo ti lleps em tel! Aroduct was feeling irritated at his brother's lack of mental insight.

Esle. Enoemos. No. Emalb. Eht. Tup. Dna. Rethguad. Ym. Pandik. Said Aroduct very slowly, so Kerem would understand.

Sruoy fo nalp suorcidul siht ni yug dab eht eb I ton lliw tub? Kerem worried such a scheme could backfire. Aroduct sighed with irritation. How did his brother even run a kingdom with such a soft constitution?

Esucxe na pu ekam tsuj ti yub ton od yeht fi. Nopaew WEN fo dnik emos htiw rotces ruoy reuqnoc ot snalp evah I taht elpeop dna nem ruoy llet tsuj, On! Said Aroduct, starting to get frustrated, thinking that he would have to govern both kingdoms himself. Such a pain.

'Aro, you truly are father's true heir. You should have just united the two kingdoms when you had the chance years ago. I wonder why you chose not to. Was it because of Ratchet? Or maybe because you knew something else?' These thoughts ran through Kerem's mind as Aro teased young Kitreth on her purpose in the plan.

I look to my lovely Kitreth and notice she is about to angrily cast a rather powerful flame spell at Aro. I place my hand on her shoulder just in time and calm her down. We say our farewells and return to our home. Aro, your plan better work.

CHAPTER 24
BELOVED RACHET

Taking a stroll in his garden was one of the only things that reminded him of his late wife. Ratchet was the most beautiful of all the trashy mechanics of her region. She was different. She loved her craft. To make, to build, to fix and to invent. She loved it all. She was like the gears of a clock. Rough and smooth, precise and almost chaotic. But when you took a step back and viewed her like a tree in a forest, she was one of a kind. The day of her time was a tragedy. More for the king than anyone else. Not even his silly little daughter could remember her face. 'But I. I still do,' thought the king.

'My Lord,' said a quiet little voice, interrupting the king's thoughts.

Turning around, his majesty released all thought of his darling Ratchet and answered his servant's call. 'What is it now?' asked Aroduct with irritation in his voice.

'The meeting leaders await your decision,' said the servant, trying not to stutter as he spoke. The king acknowledged this and walked past the trembling man and without a word, headed in the direction of the great hall to conclude and commence his wily plans.

Upon entering, many of his councilmen started talking up a storm on the plan of the trap and ambush, as well as the logistics, whether they be economical or domestic. The king ignored such concerns. Instead, the king wore a grim face as though something absolutely terrible had just happened. Some of the men seemed not to notice such an expression, but one woman, a scholar perhaps, had noticed. But protocol of the great hall had her preoccupied. As the king reached his throne, he simply sat there in silence while statesmen and warriors bickered back and forth on the priority of the plan. The king ordered them to silence. 'Here me now!' shouted the king. The members of the council, as well as most of the warriors of this sector, were stunned by such a commanding voice.

Now he had their attention, the king told them of some more grave news. (Though this news was still fabricated at the time of his announcement) The king told his men that his 'lovely' daughter Dawn had been kidnapped by a band of rogues. These were no ordinary rogues of Traytos, but were actually mages of the malicious Bataros. The last known heading of the band was north east toward the Tower of Gadgets. A place where the previous kings would tinker away before their demise.

The response of the councilmen was expected. They showed worry and concern for Dawn while the generals and warriors responded in anger. They had eyes of devils wanting revenge straight away. Many men were in absolute panic and others were already performing the needed actions to gather a search and rescue team, as well as obtaining more information on who to blame. Councilmen ran about the room ordering soldiers of lower rank to quickly find their precious Dawn. The generals and warriors, especially those of noble lineage, were quick to the charge. A blind rage had consumed them over such a useless child.

I hope that clumsy fool doesn't mess up his part of the plan. First, he must get a scapegoat. Second, he must kidnap Dawn and injure her without it being fatal. Third, he must join the scapegoat, to observe his actions while reporting to that ignoramus Fameborn. And lastly, he needs to make sure the scapegoat is caught so we can put the blame on them.

These thoughts recycled through Aroduct, as more and more panic ensued in his great hall. Warriors declared promises and something about honour. While servants rushed out to gossip about the news which spread so fast that only twenty-six minutes and thirteen seconds later, the young Fameborn burst into the chamber declaring his promise of rescue and some other nonsense the king had no real interest in. The great king of Traytos silently grinned behind his fake grim expression as more and more pledged their allegiance to their chaotic and malicious king.

CHAPTER 25
FIRST IMPRESSIONS

Having lost his only chance to prove to his peers he was indeed a worthy knight, Torbiro showed much shame and regret as an elf girl helped untie him from the 'care package' of his childhood friend Myra. Captains of the guard punished their subordinates for crudely mocking a fellow ally, even though he was a halfling. 'Thank you,' said Torbiro to the elf girl. He stood up to report his failings to his commander.

'Sir Knight, I believe you need to be escorted to the infirmary,' said the elf girl and awkwardly continued without knowing the protocol in which to address someone of higher rank, 'to… to get you checked for any injuries great or small!' The soldiers hearing this, burst out laughing at such a jab of Torbiro's stature. Captains and lower-ranking guards laughed at the mistake of words used. The elf girl apologised and introduced herself as Cyan Robyn. She told Torbiro she was very new to her post here in the bustling city of Traytos.

He accepted her apology and told her he was not at all injured, at least not physically. Torbiro, with as much pride and control as he could muster, walked up those tall steps and ignored all the negative and slanderous comments thrown at him as he headed to report to his commander. Having pride and justice is the way of the knight. Such thoughts began to mull over and over in Torbiro's mind as he got closer and closer to his commander's quarters. Thinking about pride, he decided to stop and prepare his apology speech. 'Sir, I have no excuse for this failure...' or 'My captain, the thief was just as wily as you had said and I should have been more prepared...' or 'If it will please, I shall make haste in capturing that fiend...' Torbiro paced back and forth trying to come up with such an apology in a way he would be regarded as a knight that tried and failed in his first mission.

Three more steps and he would be right at the door. More and more thoughts of apology came to him, but they did not sound very proud. Then he heard his commander through the large oak door. '...failure means death in the battlefield and I want you to realise that!!! Now you are dismissed.' He was lecturing some subordinates. At the sound of his commander, Torbiro reflexively hid underneath a bench to the left of the door.

Using his innate racial skills, Torbiro was able to evade the knights and soldiers being lectured. 'Next time, let me do all the talking...' said one of the soldiers. 'But I couldn't help it, his glare is said to break even the hardest of veterans, let alone... let alone his...' said one knight, hesitating to finish the rest of his sentence. Torbiro, having heard part of the lecture, steeled himself for his own. Taking deep breaths, he allowed himself to calm down. This enabled him to finally crawl out from under the bench and make an attempt to report his mission. As he started to get up from the floor, he heard, 'So, it seems hiding under a bench comes first, hmmm?' in a very blunt and ominous tone.

Inside the commander's chamber was a worn table. Its colour was a light ebony and it had a lot of dents and deep carvings that weren't part of its original design. There were also a few simple chairs so visitors could sit or relax in. These chairs also had the same forceful cuts as the table and they were strangely deep, as if the indenture was more forced into the wood rather than intricate elvish sculptures. He also has the standard bookshelf I'd seen in many other officer's rooms. But this too had such deep gouges in random places of the wood. After a closer inspection, I finally realised what these odd carvings were. Looking toward the large scimitar leaning on the right side of the table, I put two and two together. With whatever monstrous strength my commander has, he had either used his upholstery as target practice or for some kind of savage elven mediation ritual.

After coming to the conclusion about my commander's strength, I wait at attention until Commander Peren gives me the order or some kind of signal to do otherwise. Standing patiently was the most difficult thing when Commander Peren was in the room. It's like waiting for almost an eternity, but it had only been something like 12 seconds. Every so often, he taps his elegant fingers on his worn oak table. I count every time he does it. 1,2,3 tap, 1,2,3 tap. But then he pauses and that pause is so long, I think I might have broken a sweat from the heavy tension in the room. Then again, 1,2,3, tap, 1,2,3, tap.

I knew there would be a lecture and I just couldn't handle the silence anymore, so I spoke. 'I am sorry commander…please just tell me my punishment… I can't handle this silence anymore.'

I blurted this out, breaking the short silence of five minutes and startling Commander Peren out of his usual routine. The look on the commander's face was 'You're getting it now, boy?' with one eye slightly squinting and the other outrageously open. His eyebrows were angry and surprised and amused all at the same time. I immediately bowed in a sincere manner, rather than what knights would do. I thought I was going to be sent to the gallows, but instead I just heard laughter.

CHAPTER 26
COMMANDER PEREN

After scolding some lazy new recruits, I notice Mister Short stack quickly slip away to the right side of my door. I waited to see if he was coming in because he heard the news. But it seemed he was coming in to report something else. I waited for maybe 10 clicks - 10 minutes - and then I decided to see if the little beansprout was waiting to be informed to enter. He was always a stickler for formalities. 'You may enter.' I said. But there was no response and when I looked through the door to the hallway, he was not there, standing in his jovial attempt at the knight's stance. Instead, I saw him cower under a bench, as he whispered to himself some kind of encouraging mantra.

I simply couldn't hold my laughter at the sight. But I knew I must keep my form. I slowly approached him and kindly let out my hand to assist him up from under the bench, but he had quickly crawled out and started to brush the dust off his armour. I waited again for his acknowledgement that I was there, but with the thought of him under the bench, it twisted my words into some kind of snide remark to scare him rather than tease him.

Once the door was closed, I had to calm myself before I could tell the mouse in tin-can armour his new assignment. It took much longer to get the image out of my mind. The small soldier under the bench chanting an encouraging chant of 'by the pulse, by the pulse, by the pulse' to give himself the courage to enter my office, was absolutely the funniest thing I had ever seen. Laughter skewed my face from the elegant and graceful demeanour of the elves into some sort of gnomish abomination. Like an asymmetrical golem.

It would take more than 10 minutes to gain control of my emotions, but it was luck and impatience that let me release these feelings when the half-pint exploded into such a loud demand. I laughed my loudest in more than a century as this action pushed me past my limit of concentration. The echoes of my laughter finally subsided. I turned and told that tiny soldier his news.

CHAPTER 27
PRINCESS DAWN

'That was definitely disturbing,' thought Torbiro as he exited Commander Peren's office, 'my new mission is to guard some female aristocrat by the name of Dawn?' Torbiro tells himself, 'That name seems familiar, I wonder who it is.' While he goes to his new assigned post, he continues to march through the barracks to get the proper papers at the registry.

After the proper papers and forms are properly notarised, he headed to the appointed place where he would start his mission. The castle of Traytos. Thinking he had been promoted, even though he failed in his first mission to capture the notorious Myra, he remembered the words of his commander.

'Listen here short stack, too tiny to even matter. The council has chosen you and another probationer recruit to handle this task. You may be honoured to the task or the people you need to deal with and handle, but just act accordingly. The guidelines will be provided as soon as you report to the east wing of the castle. Yes, I know this is out of protocol but I was not the one to handle this rather delicate task or the decisive mind on who chooses…' 'concocts' he coughs under his breath, '…these personnel. Now then pinch-pockets, we need to confirm you do not go back to your old habits and steal any or all of their possessions. Do I make this clear? Now go to your post and this time do not screw up.'

During this speech, Commander Peren seemed to loom farther and taller away. I felt smaller and smaller every time he started a new sentence.

With this memory fresh in my mind, I thought of the missions new knights were stationed in. Guard duty, patrol duty and in-city captures or bounty hunts. If this task involved a team, then it must be patrol duty.

These were Torbiro's thoughts as he continued his journey to the castle. He stopped just a few steps away at the extremely large steps that were inaccessible to his kind and those of the shorter races.

The steps were massive. They were all about 10cm taller than normal. I was struck by the awe and stupidity of such a construct. 'Didn't the dwarves build this thing?' the thought of it struck me with an unbelieving question of why?

Torbiro looked around for another way of making it to the east tower of the castle and noticed no real openings or paths that would allow him to travel up these 'royal' steps and just climb the thing. The size of the step was the size of Torbiro's leg. How in the chaos do humans even climb this monstrosity? That lingering thought vanished as he heard strange sounds coming from his left. A large legged golem was being operated to scale the 'Anti Halfling stairs'. Several humans and dwarves were riding the device.

Now, how do I get on one of those things? Looking around, I saw that once a person makes it to the fifth step, there was a tower one could use to ride, rather than mount the golem. I saw a distant golem approaching and I panicked. I worried it may be the last golem of the day to take people up to the castle grounds.

'Hey, Hey... wait for me,' cried Torbiro as he frantically tried to climb the very steep step wearing the knight's mail he so proudly maintained. His first attempt was fraught with failure, dropping him flat on his back. Straight up climbing was just improbable, as the weight of the armour had encumbered his dexterous movement. Thinking was more his style anyhow, so he ignored the incoming golem taking passengers to the top and calmed himself. He thought of one, two, or three possibilities. But such thinking was fraught with risk. Using a rope to climb would display his race's typical ways. It could most likely be cut from the top by any of the guards. Doing a run up to the first step would be pointless as the second step will most likely have less space for a second charge. Plus, the guards up top would be able to just shoot incoming enemies or intruders from their vantage point. Third and final thought was to discard his armour and just carry it on his back as he climbed, but that would be against regulations and it would also mean he had given up on his oath. The oath of knights and their armour. His creed as a knight.

While pondering for a few hours and missing several travellers pass him by (as well as several of the golem transporters) a shadow blocked his way. Torbiro shooed the figure away with his hands, indicating they were covering his light. The figure simply waited. Then finally, Torbiro looked up to unleash all his frustrations on this creature, when he saw it was a dwarf. He seemed to be waiting politely, which was rather strange as most dwarves are known to be quite gruff (or at least the ones Torbiro has met so far). Torbiro asked what he wanted so he could finally get back to his thinking. And the dwarf plainly answered, 'Sir Knight, do ya need a lift?' Torbiro was a little taken aback and said 'Yes…' in the politest voice he could muster, but turned into the meekest squeak of a voice. Almost sounding like a girl, or even a human child.

Looking again, Torbiro saw there was indeed a transporter craft he could ride. It wasn't like the impressive golems that carried other soldiers early or the typical golems in the shipyard, with its man like form. Usually having two legs of thick iron or clay-earth, a rather solid structure for the body and two arms to carry a variety of materials. Passenger or transporter golems usually had four legs or wheels and seats for its passengers. The controllers were usually situated on a much higher seat, with many levers and a control box to move the vehicle. But this… was just a flat metal cage. I did not understand how it was going to get myself up those steps, let alone move.

'Lad, whatcha waitin furr? Ar ya comin or naught?' said the dwarf impatiently, yelling at the little warrior.

I quickly forgot my pondering and ran towards the steel-like platform and asked, 'Is this really a transporter?' But before I realised it, I was already at the top of the stairs. I was shocked and amazed at first but quickly realised my situation. I unsheathed my sword and demanded that magic was illegal. The dwarf looked at me, perplexed. He explained it was a new type of technology. The technology was flight. With a much slower demonstration, he showed me the craft. It levitated. Right off the ground. I blanked out with awe.

CHAPTER 28
DARK THOUGHTS

After the discussion with my lord, I started to survey the movements of the princess. I had servants report to me. Maids, serving girls, tailors, and some of her wastrel friends. Some of the cooks, waiting staff, bards and ministers trying to gain favour from the king. Beggars, traders, bakers and soothsayers, she passed by on her daily wasting spree. All reported back to me. I have many spies working for my faction and used them willingly. Not brutally like most of the ministers or corrupt knights or soldiers. It won't take so much as an hour to find the scapegoat. I needed no reward for his majesty as I was quite free in this cage of a sector.

Walking towards the ridiculously large steps, I wondered why the king even built such constructs to 'prevent' the lower tier from reaching the upper class. Why not just use a wall or a trench? The filth of the lower tier should just be exterminated, with fire or a destructoid or a chaos golem those crazed goblins are so proud of. I could kill every single one of them in an instant, but I do not have the authority to do so. I also do not understand why we even need the lower tiers, since production lines can be controlled by two or three technologists (they don't even have to be THAT skilled). His majesty must have a grand scheme for them.

Waiting for the damned transporter to arrive, I notice a dwarf and a halfling at the bottom of the steps arguing about something and within a blink of an eye, both of the figures vanished. Thinking it was some kind of gnomish warper, I looked around only to find the halfling had removed his weapon and threatened the dwarf for using magic. It couldn't be magic as it was for one, illegal and there had been alarms to detect such mystical arts. No alarms had triggered, so it must be gnomish. But I had never known a dwarf to touch, let alone use such devices, saying their dwarvish devices were superior in every way, as well as not having explosive tendencies.

The transporter had arrived and started to board some of the passengers. I was asked if I was going to board as well, but I declined. I told them I would get the next one. I slowly approached the two, once the transporter had left, but also stayed some distance away. The halfling was wearing what appeared to be armour. A knight's uniform, at that. Then he suddenly squeaked and collapsed. What perfect timing. The fool that would take the blame was right in my grasp. I had not even started the search yet and here he was.

CHAPTER 29
NEW PARTNER

The craft of the dwarf was amazing. I had not ever thought of such a device existing. He had called it a LIFTOR. Levitating Ionised Flat Top Orbitizor Reflector. It was a marvel of chaos. Just thinking of all the possible uses, just overwhelmed me. It seemed the mass of ideas rendered me unconscious. I opened my eyes to the sight of a small circular room. It had an active fireplace and the smells of fresh meat being cooked on an open fire. The delicious wafts of spices and sizzling juices of meat melded within the room.

What woke me is not the sound of the cooking, but of my growling and groaning stomach as it reacted to the unknown food being prepared. I noticed my armour had been removed and I was just wearing simple garbs. I quickly checked the surrounding area to find my knight's uniform and armour neatly placed on a small coffee table. It was strange, but I was relieved it wasn't on a regular table. I climbed out of bed and slowly and quietly approached the smell of the food. I reached the door and heard, 'Well I hope he likes this' before quickly heading over to my armour to get dressed. The door opened before I got to my armour and a gnome popped into the room carrying a tray of food and a large jug. From the smell, it must have been some kind of sweet beer gnomes consumed religiously after an experiment or 'successful' explosion.

'Well, it seems you are awake,' said the gnome. I nod in response.

'Then you must be starving, here have some,' the gnome continued as he sets up another small table. I started to ask if the food was safe to eat, but before I could, I was already in some kind of gnomish contraption. I don't even remember it grappling me to a seating position, but I was there, sitting in this mechanical chair as attached to a mechanical table. With the food, plates, cutlery already in place. Well, in front of my reach. I wondered what sort of meal it was as I looked at the dishes on the table. He pressed a series of buttons in front of him and was eating in no time. I looked at his side of the table and realised he did not use cutlery. After observing for about three clicks, this gnome just stared at me with an odd-looking anger. His chair extended an arm that wiped his mouth of the food scraps and he said, 'Don cha worry, it's good…' while pointing with his eyes to the food, then to me, then back to the food again. I did not want to take on a gnome's wrath and also not to be impolite, I started to dig in. The meat was not actually meat but some kind of sweet potato dish and the soup was very, very sweet. I pushed it away, saying it was far too sweet for me and the gnome laughed, saying it was a dessert. But a soup? The bread though, was the only normal thing I had and when I said it was delicious, the gnome said he bought it from the market three cycles ago. After more laughter and just before this gnome needed to be revitalised with air from laughing too much, he had somehow introduced himself as 'Jimmy'.

CHAPTER 30
GUARD DUTY

The day after Jimmatricgeoletrictransdynamicformersamazingsum-
monrektor ~ or 'Jimmy' for short ~ was revitalised with some air, we
were introduced to our princess and this was the person the both of us
needed to protect. I was very forward about my opinion regarding the
protection of someone so important in the care of two probationary
knights, rather than fully qualified knights. I was then masked and
gagged for three cycles of punishment. But we did manage to get the
reason for this and it was because 'Her majesty likes small, cute animals and things!' The princess' quarters were filled with many gnome
attendants and very pretty, gorgeous young girls. Most were human,
but the rest were gnomes. Jimmy and I were the only guards to protect
her and were also the only males within a close vicinity ~ of 10 metres
while in the castle and 40 metres during her expeditions to the town
market ~ during our scheduled shifts. I was the only halfling within
the castle. This I found was quite annoying. As every so often, one of
the maids would demand me to empty my pockets. How rude of them
not to trust me.

Princess Dawn of Traytos had a very strange schedule for a royal. I
expected her daily plan to be filled with much more elegant activities.
Dancing, studying or even training in etiquette. But most of her days
were filled with complaining about food being uncooked (though they
were prepared with careful skill and cooked with precious admiration

as there was an artistic image of the princess with food), the creases of her gown to be too sharp and that she had been cut by such fine silk (I had never been cut by silk, even the roughest type of silk made from titan silk larva) or her complaining about the length of time it took for the royal carriage (five clicks is not an eternity and when the carriage arrives in two clicks there should be some thanks to be said or to be more gracious). Jimmy and I were used as her personal errand boys. To get her next meal or to get messages from his majesty and to send the responding message back. I had never experienced the rush and exhaustion of darting back and forth, up and down the castle. But every time I stopped for breath, one of the maids would eye me with disdain for being a halfling.

CHAPTER 31
DARK OMEN

Running errands and guarding the princess was very much an honour, but the image of the princess degraded with every errand and random outburst about not getting what she asked for (even if Jimmy or I brought her the exact item). Her emotions were described by the king with every procession or Traytos festival as being bountiful. I always thought she was the greatest princess of the ages, or from the fantasy tales from the orphanage. But the king was right. Her emotions were absolutely bountiful in the most negative manner possible. Her complaints were those only one in her position could make or understand.

'Little thief, get my lunch,' said the princess in the most whiney voice. 'Like, right now!!' she continued. I tried not to begrudgingly respond to her stupid nickname of my race. I collected her hardly touched food cart and quickly raced towards the kitchen to retrieve her meal. Traversing through the castle, I noticed Jimmy was speaking to someone. I knew he had other errands to do as well and must be talking to the princess' lecturer. I dropped off the cart and collected the next to deliver it to the princess' royal dining quarters. On the way back, I misheard something odd.

'So the plan is going according to plan?' said the cloaked man.

'It is. No need to check up on me every time you see me!' said Jimmy.

'So the mark doesn't know what's about to happen! Right?' said the man.

From the corner of the corridor, the person speaking to Jimmy was cloaked in a red leather cloak. He wore a mask with a star where his right eye socket would be and circle patterns on the left side of the mask. From the view around the corner, it appeared to me he also carried a weapon. Most likely a sword. A lord's blade. A rapier. The rest of his attire was that of a mercenary, rough and rugged leather pants and worn and scarred boots.

The conversation piqued my interest as it started to get darker and darker. The contents of the conversation revolved around someone being a mark and having to deal with Princess Dawn. I needed to quickly finish my duty to the princess, even if she was a bitch. I hurried to push the cart to the dining room.

As I entered the room, I heard the princess yelling at how slow I was, with her hysterical screaming. I left the food cart at her side while she yelled and screamed orders at me. Panicked and winded, I took the neatly arranged plates and bowls of food to the princess to calm her down. I then tried to inform her of the dire news that involved her in the near future.

'Is that a threat?' said the princess with a mouthful of bread and meats.

'No, not at all!!' Torbiro said. Telling Princess Dawn it was a conspiracy towards the royal family. She ignored him in the most childish fashion ever. After revealing all this information, Torbiro was sent away for being a 'naughty little thief' and disturbing her gracious eating time.

Torbiro knew such news would be important and rushed towards the great hall where the king of Traytos dealt with the problems of the country. But before Torbiro dashed off, he noticed Jimmy heading back towards Princess Dawn's sleeping quarters in a rather suspicious manner.

CHAPTER 32
PRINCESS KIDNAPPED

Torbiro had trailed him back to Dawn's room and watched what Jimmy was up to. Inside the chamber was the same man Jimmy had been talking to earlier. But the princess was just being her usual self and ordering them around. I felt a relief there wasn't a conspiracy to harm the princess. So I headed into the room. My first step had a lot of confidence, but once I had taken the second step, I felt a strange unease in the air. The third and fourth step were just moving too slowly for the danger I sensed. On the fifth step, I yelled, 'Everyone watch out!!! Som…' but before I could finish the warning, there was an explosion.

It came from under us. It erupted so suddenly I was slammed to the wall near the princess. Jimmy had fallen down through the fissure the explosion had torn on the stone floor. I didn't get to see what happened to the man serving the princess. The last thing I saw before I lost consciousness was Dawn's fine hands reaching out to me.

I awoke hours later in the castle infirmary. My arms had been lightly bandaged. I had a few scrapes and bruises, but I was well enough to go searching for the princess. I tried to leave to get back to work, but I was told I was still in danger from some of my wounds. Another officer was told to guard me until my supreme commander came to discharge me. I told them I had urgent business to attend to. Such as rescuing the princess or finding out what exactly happened to my partner, Jimmy.

The soldier told me Jimmy was also in this infirmary. He pointed out where he was resting and I went to see if he was still alive. The guard allowed me to leave my bed, but not his sight. As I got to the bed where Jimmy was resting, I saw he was very comfortable. His injuries were even less grave than mine. But how can that be, when he had fallen down the hole of the princess' room? The room below was at least 100 metres of a drop. I wanted to talk to him, but the guard escorted me back to my bed. I was only able to inspect Jimmy for 1-2 clicks.

'Can I please leave this place? I need to check on the princess! Is she alright?' Torbiro said with concern, even though he did not like the bratty princess.

'Look 'alfling, you are 'urt and I 'ave orders to keep you 'ere! So stay put!' said the guard while aggressively threatening Torbiro with the butt of his clockwork spear. After poking the halfling a few times, the spear started to rattle and the spear point rocketed off.

'Blasted t'ing, keeps breaking on me...' the guard said as he headed to where the broken spear point lay. After retrieving the disconnected piece, he forced it back to the top of his clockwork spear. Only this time, one of the spring coils shot out. 'I'm sick of t'is infernal contraption, just give me an old fashion spear, damn it.' the guard said in frustration.

'Um, maybe I can help you there, mister guard?' Torbiro offered his services.

'And w'at can a 'alfling do besides steal it 'ey?' asked the guard, suspiciously.

'Well, I can be a knight and I'm pretty handy with fixing things! I'll have you know that I used to be the apprentice of the Famous Dorian, the ...' said Torbiro before the guard interrupted him.

'Well, stop your boasting and fix it already?'

The guard forced several pieces of the clockwork spear on to Torbiro to repair, but the halfling told him he needed at least a screw-twister and a screw-gripper to do the deed. So the guard asked one of the other attendants for some tools as he needed to remain to keep a close eye on the sneak thief. A few moments later, with the proper tools, Torbiro finished doing the proper maintenance on the weapon and returned it to the guard.

With some grunting and little appreciation, the guard thanked Torbiro for fixing the spear. 'Well, sneak t'ief, t'at's a fine job. Looks like you got more talent than just sneaking and stealing, ay?' said the guard while inspecting his weapon.

'I have a name, you know! And it's not sneak thief! I'm Tor…' Torbiro was interrupted by a loud crash from the infirmary entrance.

'Short-stack and Sir Gnome, attention!!' said Commander Peren with a grim expression. Looking around, Peren noted Torbiro was fine while Jimmy was still quite injured. He then relieved the guard from keeping watch of Torbiro and to return to his prior duties.

'I have your new orders from the king himself! Short-stack, tell Sir Gnome his detail will be to accompany you. Is that understood?' As he had more pressing matters to attend to, Peren told Torbiro his next mission was to stay within the kingdom of Traytos and capture the notorious sneak thief Memyra.

'But commander? Shouldn't we be investigating the tower?' said Torbiro with genuine concern.

'NO!! You have your orders and I have mine. Now rest up and meet me in my office,' replied Peren.

Torbiro, still feeling duty bound to guarding the princess, decided to make a detour towards the tower before heading to Commander Peren's office. As he left the infirmary, he wished Jimmy well and placed some sweet breads that gnomes truly enjoy, on his bedside table.

Quietly sneaking towards the ruined tower, Torbiro arrived to see many dwarven builders cleaning up the rubble and making sketches on the possible repairs and other calculations to effectively and efficiently do the job with the proper materials. Torbiro was able to sneak past them without being noticed, as dwarves are naturally noisy as they sleep, which, in Torbiro's experience, is the time when they are the quietest. He could hear the sounds of writing tools, scratching here and there as well as the shouts of poor dwarven designs.

Inside the ruined room, there is a hole the size of the door. From the looks of the burn marks at the edge of the hole, this was either caused by halfling trick fire or dwarvish mining boomers. Trick fire was never strong enough to make such a hole and dwarven boomers tended to destroy all things. 'What exactly made this hole that used fire?' Torbiro thought, as he continued to hide and examine the ruined floor.

'What are ye doing there, boy?' said the dwarf clearing debris, finding the poorly hidden Torbiro among the scraps of wood, previously chairs. Torbiro, very startled, had instinctively hopped to the front, forgetting there was a large hole in the floor. The dwarf was not fast enough to catch Torbiro, so he started to fall. 'Lad, are you all 'ight?' said the dwarf as he looked down to see Torbiro hanging by the loop of his sling. Torbiro, only now feeling the pain of his action, tried to stifle a scream but the pain was just too much and he let out a squeak.

Once the dwarves pulled Torbiro out of the hole and warned him that this area was one, dangerous and two, restricted to non-authorised personnel, was sent back to the infirmary to be healed. Before being sent away, Torbiro was able to pocket a piece of the burnt floor board that had come loose. Heading to towards the infirmary, Torbiro heard a very familiar voice speaking to the king. Wanting to know more, he decided to listen through the door. Listening, he found out Princess Dawn had been spotted leaving the walls of the city, in a simple wooden cage, by some hooded figures. Suspects may be magic users.

Before rushing off to rescue Princess Dawn, Torbiro needed to report to Commander Peren's office or he would risk the wrath of an elven commander technologist. They had tracking shots. Torbiro arrived late to the arranged meeting to report.

'Short stack, you're late!!' said Commander Peren angrily. Peren then strikes his dwarven-constructed, elven oak table. The sound of hard leather striking worn wood, resounded in the room as Torbiro enters.

'S-So… Sorr… Sorry Sir, but I have news of…' said Torbiro as he stuttered in fear. But is then interrupted by Commander Peren's second strike.

I don't care what new information you have found, you have orders to follow.

But it's about Princess Dawn?

The trackers will find her and bring her back. Now, here are your new orders.

But sir...

No, buts probationary knight! You know the law. Now then, your new orders are your old orders. Go and hunt down Memyra, the master thief of the Gearspark Thieves Guild and arrest her. You will be proved...

Sir, the princess needs our help and from the direction they are going they're ...

Probationary. Knight. Torbiro. Your orders or your honour?

While saying these words, Commander Peren unsheathed his elven rapier and raised it towards my throat. I stubbornly and angrily stare at the elven-made blade. I took a step back, realising the meaning of his words. I accepted the orders, begrudgingly. Commander Peren also introduced my team that will engage with the mission. An elf called Robyn; she seemed to be related to the commander. A half-orc called Tulip Spinner; she looked like a full bred orc but her accent was very elwarnian. Elwarnian was the language half-breeds used. It was a combination of elvish and dwarven. It was rather odd, but very useful as inventors and engineers. The last name Commander Peren revealed was Jimmy, but he was still injured so, our orders were to plan and rest. As well as learning all of our strengths and weaknesses.

Robyn was our scout and scope shooter. I had expected her to be using an elegant longbow made from elvish maple with intricate elvish inscriptions, but she wielded an elemental blunderbuss. A miniature portal cannon that used clockwork gears for rapid shots and different alchemical infused capsules. The only problem with an elf – a semi-magical creature – using a dwarven designed and gnome-made weapon was, the void and pulse complexion. That magic disrupted technology and technology deconstructed magic. It usually ends with an explosion, Torbiro thought as he sneakily took a step away.

Tulip, on the other hand, used typically large weapons. But her weapons were more intricate with gears and clockwork that provided an extra pop and range of a melee weapon. She brandished a light lance with spring action shot to increase the range of any strike. I thought it was light by the way Tulip swung it around, but the device was as heavy as dwarven golems. She also had two blades; they appeared to be dual swords but with gears at mid-blade. They also had a pair of initials, W. S. Must be the maker of the fantastic weaponry.

I told them what I could do, but Tulip just laughed a very primal orcish chuckle. Robyn simply tried to consult me as she understood the indifference of others, especially towards her. I tried to hide my scowl, but Tulip had seen through my attempt.

'Come now li'l cap'n,' said Tulip with the utmost sassiness and sarcasm. I knew then Robyn was trying to mend our ties, but she too was unsuccessful. Instead of arguing with Tulip, I just sighed a big sigh and told them where we needed to go next.

To capture Myra was going to be extremely hard, as she was the most agile of thieves. I made a plan of ambush but Tulip wanted to just storm the Gearspark Thieves Guild – or GTG for short – and Robyn just wanted to test her new weapon – from long range, I assumed – on the thieves. We had no clear leader even though I had been appointed by Commander Peren.

So the plan of Ambush became an Ambush and Storm in and Snipe plan. No, it was not plan ASS. I called it plan SAS because storming in was 'technically' first. We made this plan with Jimmy of course, and he never gave any input. Must be in his training to just follow rather than argue like Tulip.

The medical team had stated that normal recovery would take at least three toggles, but we didn't have that much time. I wanted to catch Myra, then help with the rescue effort of Princess Dawn. Yes, I was naïve. I never considered the time at all. It was simple in my eyes.

Catch Myra. Rescue Princess. The hows and whens didn't matter. Or the fact that traversing outside of Traytos was more than a journey.

Anyway, we had our plan. So we headed off. To GTG. And to Myra. My childhood friend.

CHAPTER 33
GEARSPARK THIEVES GUILD

We arrived at the mission point, but there was something wrong. I felt it in the air. I warned the others, only Tulip seemed to ignore me. We were just 20 clicks – 20 minutes - away from the point where we would all take our positions, but there was still that feeling of something wrong. I just couldn't pin it down. I told my team my concerns but Tulip, being too head strong, just told me to 'tin it' rather than can it. So we all continued our plan and then all hell broke loose. In just 15 clicks -15 minutes - of our mission, we had already been captured. We fell for a trap. I knew storming the place was a bad idea, but what got us caught was actually Robyn with a misfire and malfunction from her blunderbuss. I was about to order a fight to the death when Myra and her band ambushed us. I was 'literately canned' in a very small trash bin. Tulip, ironically, was bedded in a flower garden and Robyn was netted. Jimmy, on the other hand, was nowhere to be found, until we were all brought before Myra herself. Jimmy was jammed. Not sure how or where these thieves had gotten so much apricot jam, but he was brought in on a silver platter. Literally.

'Well, well, well. If it isn't Torro,' said Myra in her very sarcastic, smug tone used when she beat me in some game. I couldn't reply as all of us were gagged. Mine was a simple cotton sock with dwarven syrup to keep it stuck. Robyn and Jimmy had a thick piece of wood. Perhaps it was elven or maybe gnomish. As magical timber tends to glow with a touch from the void races. Tulip, on the other hand, had been stuffed in a small cage with her arm as a gag. I knew of the cage as it used to be my safety place. I called it my safety place as it protected me from all the outside cruelty, such as beatings, torture and experiments. My cage was like a second home. To all other races, they would look at the cage and say 'how cruel' or 'what a poor soul' or 'caught like a rat'. The cage itself was made of reinforced dwarvish steel. It was used for catching horned-rammers. A violent beast out in the caverns of Mithral Valley. These beasts were the main source of mithral, a type of metal, until recently. The beasts were not big but had a nasty habit of sticking together to make themselves bigger. The cage was designed to catch and separate them once captured. So this cage was strong. The impact of those monstrous creatures was enough to break down iron and unrefined mithral.

That being said, we were trapped. Getting out was not going to be easy. I definitely needed the key for Tulip. I don't care what the orcs say, but there is no way she would be able to burst out of that cage with brute power alone. I watched and waited for Myra to talk. I was always good at that. I must have waited a good couple of clicks since the last time Myra had spoken. 'Memyra, what do you want?' I said, just wanting to break the sudden silence. But due to the sock in my mouth, it just came out as muffled sounds. Myra started with a snicker and then continuous laughter.

She walked beside me and whispered, 'You can't run from me.' I could see Robyn and Jimmy doing the same. Trying to speak, even though they were gagged. Myra then waved her hands and snapped her fingers. Her goons were at the ready. Ready to kill us or worse. I tried to struggle, but I was tied down to something heavier than myself. Since we were in dim light, I must have been tied to an old slag engine or something. Myra asked me again about 'what we were doing?' but I refused to talk about the plan to capture her and send her off. I knew her tactics. They were very familiar, nostalgic even, but that meant we would be tortured and interrogated next. But because we had Tulip on our side, they needed to subdue her first. Myra again whispered in my ear, 'Come on Torro, join me so we can have fun.' Her tone was sarcastic and sadistic, just like those days when I would get beaten and bullied or when I'd boasted about some game I was unbeatable at, only to be beaten by her.

Myra stood in front of me. She was so close, I could smell the sweet scent of lavender in her hair. The fragrance was soft and gentle. It reminded me of the fields and gardens outside of Traytos. In my dazzled state, distracted by the memories of youth, I failed to realise what Myra was about to do. She had commanded her men to take us to jail cells to later question us. Her hand then went to my cheek.

The honey or syrup had already hardened around my mouth like thick amberite. Her hand was in position to the left of my mouth. Then it happened. I was pulled right out of my daydream and what I felt next was the tearing of soft skin from my face all the way across from cheek to cheek. The nerves of my lip and mouth were pulsing with pain. I tried to resist, but I just couldn't. I yelped in pain, while lightly patting my lips and rubbing my cheeks. Once the throbbing lessened, I could hear laughter, which started soft, but as my senses gradually came back, the laughter got louder and louder. It was almost a piercing mockery. I tried to get a word in, but my lips were still sore and my words were still a mumbling mess. I could see Myra holding her sides with absolute amusement. She had tears in her eyes and was having a hard time breathing from the sight of me patting my lips. They were swollen, but I still didn't know what was so funny.

CHAPTER 34
TORBIRO'S KNIGHTS

A goblin dashed through the ruins of a dilapidated factory, passing agents and operatives similar to him. They all wore the same leather armour with a symbol depicting a gear and spark. He dashed all the way to the back, passed the training hall where new recruits were being trained and punished alike, passed rooms with operatives planning some nefarious action against the city and dashed through to a room with a female halfling. She was beautiful in appearance, but was more ruthless and deadly than any ogre with a large bludgeon. She wore a leather jacket with cuts and nicks from multiple skirmishes. She also wore a set of cracked goggles around her neck and a pair of slim kylor pants. These were no ordinary kylor either. Rumour had it that it was enchanted with magic to protect the wearer from damage. She wore herself with a level of threating importance. She was our leader, Myra the Kramnor.

'Hey Punkgirl, we have a report of knights in our area,' said a goblin agent. His face had been burnt on the left side. This was a result of him resisting or being stubborn when he was marked as a slave.

I nodded slowly to acknowledge Firecrow. We had ranks in my gang. Torro was the one who came up with it back in the day. He wanted even the low ranks and new recruits to have something to have. He was nice like that, but naïve. I half listened to Firecrow as the knights of Traytos were always around the bend. Just because we wanted what everyone else wanted, wasn't a crime. Well, it was a crime to steal, but prices weren't fair in the first place. Bloody merchants and those rich money bag nobles. This report got very interesting fast as Firecrow explained that a very short knight was with them.

'Torro must be with them.' I said under my breath. This was going to be fun. Messing around with Torro was always amusing. He had a dreamer's mind and would always fantasise about being a hero of some sort. I knew my place in this world. I needed to be a survivor and the only way was to become a thief. Sure it was unlawful, but it was the only way for a race discriminated against for being thieves at first encounter. Torro and I were always treated like scum. We were bullied, threatened, punished and terrorised. Just for being halflings. I wanted revenge as early as I could remember, but I also had Torro. His dreams and faith were fun and amusing. We started this guild, though it was just to rally all the people in this god-forsaken place and create a haven. Torro's place was to start a 'knighthood' but I knew this band would only have unruly thoughts in their mind. At first we were only four, but as we met more and more of the downtrodden and the misjudged, we grew in numbers quickly. Torro eventually found out what we had become. What 'his knighthood' had become and left us for a cheap living.

We had reports coming in every day about knights hunting me down. But they were minor reports. They had never found our trail. We were more than careful; we were devious and cunning. We used everything we could get our hands on. Whether it was technology or magic. But we also learnt they could not be combined. It was dangerous. We'd use cloaks of invisibility confiscated from wizards or unfortunate adventurers. We used dwarven dynamos and flying crafts to travel this city of Traytos.

But I also had a few reports of unusual disturbances, such as the princess being captured and a war band being mobilised to the north, to halt the advancement of war wizards from Bataros. It was strange; Bataros was never this ambitious. They were even less interested in an event that would have aided they're magical enhancements when a meteor had collided and fused with one of our celestial gears. The warriors and knights of Traytos were more interested and we managed to procure some samples of the meteorite that crashed in a place once known as Tanrole village. It was my old home, before the war that split this sector in two. But now it was called the Devils Invert Partisan Hills 'officially' but there was another name most common folk referred to it as. Dip Hills.

I was most interested in why the princess was being captured. It was something that was very odd, very out of place. Any fool or sane person knew that messing with King Aro was more than just suicide, it was voidicide. This was a punishment of death by agonising torture, but with each stroke, the person or creature would lose pieces of their memory. How do I know? Well, having spies in almost every corner of this city can get you the best information. I also knew Torro was coming to try and capture me again. This was going to be a fun encounter for today. I also wondered why Torro wasn't going to rescue the princess, as the reports concerning the princess in any way had Torro's name mentioned. Sometimes as a candidate while other times as the accused. It was strange and very bizarre at the same time. I needed to talk to Torro to get the whole story.

I had prepared my spies and magic agents in the north and east entrance, near the old dwarven-styled saloon. I made sure to watch him from above, as he still knew some of our old tactics. We finished our preparations a bit late, but it seemed Torro had brought an Orcish knight, along with a technologist elf gunslinger and a gnome. What was he up to? But no matter, we were in position and could strike at any moment's notice. Torro gave some signals, but the Orc just charged ahead. I signalled my agents to proceed as planned. In 10 clicks it was checkmate. Torro knew nothing about magic and his tactics were spot on. We made each one of them think they would be defeated by the most ironic means. A precise Suggestion spell. If the elf hadn't misfired, he would have had more of a fight or a chance to play out his plan. I brought each one of them to the interrogation room. Before I brought in Torro, I had each of them talk. The elf girl was the quickest to break. She shared the plans that we were to be captured and hanged for thievery of the highest charge. We laughed at her weak demeanour and recorded everything she said, after which we gagged her. I had thought elves were more fearsome than this, but I guess rumours are just rumours. The gnome was oddly friendly but refused to speak, so we gagged him with silence bark. The orc was very violent and needed to be restrained quickly. I had my magical agents paralyse her then put her to sleep, so we could avoid more casualties. We stuffed her in Torro's old 'safety' cage and made sure she was bound by iron chains. Torro was much more stubborn than the rest. I knew he was going to be annoying to deal with, so I shoved a honey-soaked sock in his mouth and pasted some sticky syrup like liquid on a slip of discarded parchment big enough to cover the entirety of his mouth. I taunted him and used all sorts of embarrassing comments for him to talk. But he was just as stubborn as a dwarf. So I revealed the state of his comrades. But I knew this tactic was not enough to push information out of him. My comrades were starting to get blood thirsty, so I had to quicken my fun teasing Torro. I blindfolded him to trick him to talk.

I gave the signal and had my men leave with the exception of a sorcerer, just in case the orc broke through the cage. I then had the caster create an illusion of a jail cell and of Torro's team being tortured. Once I knew Torro was in position to live the illusion, I removed his blindfold and bindings, but not his gag. I stood directly next to him so I could have a bit more fun. Like I thought, Torro was more convinced his friends were being punished and tortured in front of him, and he became more talkative. He was a good-natured person, after all.

Once he had inadvertently revealed his plan, I spoke to him in a booming voice. He looked around to locate the voice. I was no further than two arm's lengths away. Maybe half a metre or so, with a pipe used for diverting steam in certain machines, I spoke through it to make my voice sound further away than it really was. I snuck next to him just to reveal myself and scare him a bit by pulling off the sticky paper covering his mouth. But his reaction was so unexpected that all my men and his crew laughed uncontrollably. Even the Orc he brought had laughed so hard at Torro's plight that she fell unconscious.

CHAPTER 35
CAPTURED BY THIEVES

Once the laughter had stopped, Myra and her thieves invited us to a different room for refreshments. Apparently, we would be treated more like guests than prisoners. I wasn't sure why. I hadn't talked about our plan and I assumed none of my friends had blabbed either. Myra was a mystery. Only three of us were invited, as Tulip was unconscious by some unknown means. Our hands were restrained enough so we could not battle with them. But the restraints were loose enough to allow us to eat and drink. Only our hands were shackled. The shackles were simple iron. I could probably slip out of them, but what of Jimmy and Robyn? I wanted to finish this job quickly and pursue the kidnappers that had taken the princess. It was my chance and possibly all of our chances to redeem ourselves. To either prove our worth and perhaps our existence.

'Well met, knights of Traytos,' said Myra as she exclaimed her leadership of her band of criminals. With flair and grace in her gesture. Too much flair, of course.

'Well met to you too,' said Robyn, of all people. I had thought she was the same kind of warrior as Commander Peren. But I suppose she was just a girl in comparison. Commander Peren had an air of leader about him. Robyn was more of a relaxed market girl, having a chat with an old friend at a clothing stall or accessory shop.

'Robyn, what are you saying? Memyra is our enemy. We have our job to do!' Torbiro tried to get back on track of the situation. He knew this was some sort of ploy. A Rogue's Ploy or scheme.

'But Torbiro, I was just replying to our nice host. Even if she is who we are after,' said Robyn, as she unconsciously revealed our main objective. What a fool.

'Nooooo, why did you just have to reveal all that? Now we're done for!!' Torbiro was in a panic and irritated at the revelation of their plans. Now Myra had the upper hand. They were screwed.

'But I.... I was just being polite. My elders always told me to be polite to the one I'm speaking to,' said Robyn, proving her manners with her polite tone and a graceful bow. She was the complete opposite of the stories I had heard about elves of her kind. She was more bubbly and carefree than I had anticipated. I told her to hold her tongue and Robyn started to whine and cry like some disobedient child.

'Torro, you don'ta hav ta be mean to the young elf. What are you anyway? A bully of girls? Some soldier of justice you've become,' said Myra in a display of fake empathy. I knew what she was playing at. Using people was her forte. Next, she would unshackle Robyn and consult her with some sweet beverage.

'I am a valiant knight. Thank you very much. I am more of a soldier of justice than a bullier of girls. I just thought she was a soldier too,' said Torbiro in his defence, but the two girls were already off to the side. One freed from her shackles and the other comforting her. I was right. Myra had released Robyn. Now was Robyn's chance to capture Myra. Just knock her out and this mission was done. But instead both were having a light conversation about me. Why me, of all things? I looked at Jimmy and he was at the central table gorging on the sweet treats Myra and her gang had called 'refreshments'. This is when I had to make my move.

'I could walk out of here and get a key to free ourselves. Get Tulip and defeat all the thieves and finish the mission. Afterwards, I could race after the princess and rescue her. Commander will be proud of me and the king will give me commendations as a knight. A true knight of the realm of Traytos. Just like the knight of my dreams,' I said, a bit louder than anticipated. I was planning in my mind and when that happened, I tended to narrate what I was planning.

93

CHAPTER 36
THIEF ACQUIRED

I had sent Torro's crew to the banquet hall for some refreshments, to show him my usual gratitude at his amusing show. He was clumsy and naïve after all, but he had quite the skill at being a jester or an unintentional comedian. There I welcomed them. I was faking my introduction with some flair and grace. A bit too much flair though, but I liked the theatrical nature and drama of sarcasm. I could see Torro saw through it. I mean, why wouldn't he? We did this a lot when we were younglings to impress elders or people to join our guild.

The elf named Robyn was very much amused and captured by my actions. The gnome was not very interested in my showmanship but was far more interested in the sweets gnomes truly could not resist. We spoke a bit and Robyn really could not keep from revealing the truth. She must still be young by elf standards. She was joyful and very bubbly like the girls I con at the marketplace. Torro even made her cry. He is just as naïve as ever. So to show my 'empathy' I consulted her by telling her a story of Torro. I managed to calm her and get a bit more information about the current guard situation in the castle and the city's defences.

After I calmed Robyn, I heard the most astonishing thing come out of Torro. His plan. Torro had a bad habit. It was a tactician's worst nightmare. It was more of a panicked tick of his, where he would mumble his plan. Most of the time it was just his normal quiet voice, but while he was wearing that particular helmet, it was amplified. I knew he was crafting a plan the moment he started to pace back and forth. His voice was pitched a bit higher than normal. It sounded like a young human girl squealing for some sweets from her mother. But add a bit of manly tone to it and there you have Torro in a tin can. I had to hold myself from laughing, but then everyone in the room seemed to notice him too. More astounded than assumed, we all watched and listened to this ridiculous halfling knight.

Torro was in shock after finally realising he had been talking aloud rather than just lightly mumbling. His eyes first darted left and right, then all over the place. Dropping his head downward, he first whispered something. It was quiet, but I could hear a forced laughter. The laughter was getting louder and louder at every tick.

'Ha ha ha,' said Torro repeatedly, trying to make a false laugh just before he would deny what he was planning from the narration a few seconds before.

'It's just a joke. Ha ha ha…' said Torro, trying to play off his mistake as a lie. But Myra and the others, with the exception of Robyn, knew the blatant lie. A poor excuse at best.

Myra approached me slowly and wrapped her slender and dexterous arm around me. Slowly, she brought her face down to mine and showed me her very devious grin. She was dark, scary and I knew I could not get away with what she would propose next. That smile was devious indeed, something that looked like that of a Cheshire cat, a magical creature able to transcend reality. It was rumoured this creature could phase in and out of a realm. From realm to realm.

Torro, you want to rescue the princess, right? Why not?

Well, my current orders are to…

Come on Torro, orders can be broken and no one will find out, hmmm.

But I must follow my orders from the commander…

Who cares about what Peren will say? Come on Torro, let's save the Princess together, it'll be like old times, you and me.

Myra, I can't disobey! I'll lose my knighthood. I'll lose my dream. Please understand.

Torro, what if I tell you I have a plan, hmm?

No, not one of your plans, Myra. I could get executed for disobeying direct orders. I can't, please don't make me.

Look Torro, my plan is simple. Since you need to capture me, I'll travel in the direction of where my scouts have reported the princess was last being carried to and you just so happen to be chasing after me.

Myra, please. No.

Come on Torro, you can even bring your knights as allies to combat the dangers of the wilds. It makes sense to bring Robyn and Jimmy along. It's a great excuse!

But what about Tulip? What about her?

So Tulip was her name, aye? Well, you can bring her along too. Of course we won't be travelling together 'officially'. So what do you say?

But what about my report? How would I explain this to my commander? I can't just leave the city of Traytos without consent. That would be breaking procedure and over stepping my authority as a new knight.

Well, how about this? I have one of my men convince Tulip to report back to your commander about your current situation of your mission to 'capture' me.

How are you going to convince an Orc?

I have my ways, Torro. I have my ways.

But will she be all right?

She will have no real memory of the report before and after the report is given. That way, your alibi is secured. You are doing your mission and you have reported back with a trusted ally that has gained your admiration as an upcoming leader. For future missions.

Wait… You have wizards in your rank? Magic is illegal in Traytos.

What else is new?

But magic is dangerous and unpredictable. It cannot be controlled. Plus, you could have us all blown up and make a new THRUST. Are you insane?

I've been using magic or rather utilising magic for two watches now and no THRUST has ever happened. Maybe an explosion, but nothing as crazy or mythical as the THRUST. Besides the THRUST is probably just a story to scare little. Naïve. Fools like you.

Hey that's going too far. I'm no fool, I'm just being cautious, is all.

So are you in? Or are you a fool?

I am no fool Myra, but I'm still unsure. Maybe if I discuss it with my crew. Then I'll decide.

No time for that Torro!

Why? And what do you mean?

Well, I am well informed about the information in and out of the city. And with what Robyn has told me, my reports are disturbingly accurate.

What do you mean? What reports?

Our agents from Bataros speak of war with Traytos. And with the low number of guards around Traytos, it must mean most of the warriors and engineers have already gone to oppose them.

With Myra's last statement, I was more worried about the war than rescuing the princess. I looked to Myra, then to Robyn to ask her if what Myra had told me was the truth. Unfortunately, both Jimmy and Robyn had not understood any words of the conversation, as Myra had been speaking in our halfling tongue. A language I rarely used, but I tended to not notice the difference when I switched from Traytarian, the common tongue used in Traytos and of the neighbouring towns near this sector. I asked Robyn politely, about the reports of guards being reduced for an operation to defend against Bataros war-wizards. She explained her older brothers work to gear up the soldiers sent for war. She explained what she had heard and it seemed to match with what Myra was talking about. I also asked if she had told this to Myra. She was very reluctant, but Robyn confirmed she had.

War again. Why was there going to be war again in my lifetime? It seemed like there was always conflict in this sector, or maybe it was following me. I looked at Myra and she just shrugged. She must not have cared much for the lives to be spilt on the battlefield again. I was worried at first and then a thought came to mind. What if this war had something to do with the disappearance of the princess? This was bad, worse if it could cause another Thrust which would destroy all the inhabitants that dwelt in this sector. I guessed Myra might be right to lead me on, but this was serious. I had never heard of war besides the war that destroyed my home 16 years ago. I must have been a few revols old when it happened. I looked at Myra and agreed to follow her out to rescue the Princess, but it did leave a bad taste in my mouth.

Torro was easy to manipulate once you broke through his stubborn shell. But if you broke him out of anger or sadness, he would try to fight you off. He was a weird one, after all. But lucky for me I had a nature for embellishment. The lie about the war was my luck. That was thanks to Robyn. But that didn't really surprise me in the least. There was always a war with Bataros or maybe with a neighbouring sector if there was a pricing dispute here or a breaking territory lines there. King Aroduct loved his war. He waged war like it was a game of sorts. Or maybe a Revoly hobby. I could see in Torro's face any mention of war was enough to sway him to my plan, to find out more about the state of things with Bataros and Traytos. Now then, I'll have to make use of more magic to get a move on.

First the orc, next would be to mobilise my guild to Bataros for safety and get a few of my technologists hidden away in Traytos during this mission. I collected my supplies, weapons and gadgets and some restorative elixirs and magic potions. I was ready, but I knew I needed help in this mission, so I informed my best lightningpigs, as well as my apprentice, Natie. Why are my best operatives called 'lightningpigs'? Well, that would be thanks to Torro. Like I've said before, he was the one who started this guild. The names are yes, ridiculous, but are also very confusing when others are trying to decode some of our encrypted messages. It is funny and genius. We were going to war, after all, to reach the designated location the princess was being held in.

I relayed my plan to Torro, but only to Torro, as I had some suspicion something was off. I just wasn't sure. It could have been Jimmy or one of my men. I had a sinking suspicion of a spy or mole among us. Torro agreed, but was a little adamant about keeping his men in the dark. I told him only leaders should know, just in case. He frowned at my last proposal, but in the end he too agreed. My plan was simple. It was the shortest and quickest path besides teleporting to the location. As Torro had made his stand on magic. Especially around technological items like Robyn's blunderbuss exploding when magic was cast. His ignorance was justified. I was like him once, fearful and suspicious of magic around technology, but with experience and information, I changed. His view and prejudice on the subject will change in time. Torro was smart, he'll understand one day.

The plan was to escape the city walls, then head toward Dip Hills and in just a few days' travel, we would arrive in the sanctity of the tower. A rumoured place of riches and death.

CHAPTER 37
THE WAR BEGINS

Traytos was located near the edge of the southwest most part of the sector. A single sector was determined by a hexagonal range of mountains or valleys. The location of Bataros, in comparison to the size of the sector, was that on the same location. But the kingdom of Traytos was precisely 350km away from Bataros. The single mountain range that separated Traytos with the neighbouring sector was forty-five times that distance. So the size of the planet itself was quite large in comparison to that, as there were approximately 169 sectors in total. The sector number in which Traytos and Bataros were located was number 133. It was positioned to the south of the equator of the planet. What did this mean? Well, it meant the seasons were far more chaotic than normal. Seasons and temperature changed from winter to summer, then back to winter, then to autumn, then to summer, then to autumn, then back to summer and finally to spring.

The seasons were erratic due to the effects of the Thrust event in the past that had shifted the orbital access. It would oscillate. Like some electrical wavelength constantly harassed by a magnet. This made war quite easy to mobilise. The cold season was best for any technologist army to mobilise, as the alchemy of their fuel would have the most stable reactions. As for magical armies, they would prefer climates on the warmer side as the celestial energies were what they used to propel their attacks, defences and support.

So war was quick and easy to formulate. If a sector fought another sector, it was most likely a similar type of warfare. Technology vs technology. Magic vs magic. But sector 133 was different. Both kings of Bataros and Traytos had used war as an excuse to cull the herd, so to speak. The King of Traytos had always used war or deadly battle as a test for the loyal or the death of the useless. The King of Bataros had never been a very diplomatic man and the excuse for war was always at the ready just to remove troublesome subjects or unfaithful citizenry. This war that Aroduct the Golem master had set up was just another culling of the overgrown hedge known as his citizens. As for his less conniving twin brother, it was to subdue the frequency of complaints from his newly appointed magic professors. Resources were always low as the nobles and monarchy kept all ready supplies to themselves. Demand was always high, but only the truly selected were given the chance, even if it were a waste. But once any person, besides the monarchy, demanded more, they were culled in an exercise called war.

The war mages of Bataros were just minor citizens trying their best to survive the demands of the city. They only marched to Traytos to receive the promised supplies not available in the markets of Bataros. The wants and desires of these men and women were one of desperate survival. They did not wish for a war and they were all innocent. They had been used by their own desperation. They would even pay for the exchange, but unbeknownst to them, the knights and soldiers of Traytos were marching to meet them in martial combat.

These warriors of Traytos had grown fat, boring and useless in the eyes of the Golem master. Their refusal in other campaigns had made them targets for Aroduct's culling. Some of these warriors were being discriminated against due to their race. For in the past, they were the enemy. They could be trolls or ogres that had been reformed by the government itself to make it easier to control them. Aroduct had many he wished to cull, but a mass culling would mark him as a dangerous foe to other sectors. It would incite perhaps another Thrust if he was not a calculating tyrant. His real army could wipe out all the creatures on this planet and many more, but that prospect would become a stalemate with the next higher power come to oppose him. He would control the masses by leading them to destruction.

So every year he made it clear to those that knew he would start another war. To clean the mistake created by broken parts of his kingdom. His brother was not too bright, but still wanted to live in the same sector. So in truth Traytos was just one kingdom and Bataros was just a kingdom with a puppet king strung up by the hands of the calculating Golem master.

CHAPTER 38
THE FRONTLINES

At the foot of Dip Hills, Torbiro's team had arrived late into the battle of magic and technology. The mages of Bataros were in magical barriers to protect them from the fierce and ferocious clockwork cannons and anti-magic piercers. The soldiers of Traytos advanced with every blast of a cannon. There was an order to charge only a few clicks later. There was another order for retreat as beams and waves of energy were sent toward this side of the battlefield.

We are at war. A concept I had only thought to be one-sided and victory would provide wealth and honour, but this was terrible. Many were already dead and it was a horrible sight indeed.

Although we had arrived at the foothills of Dip, Myra suggested we stay low and keep out of sight. I had wanted to aid the soldiers, but the horrors of this battle made my entire being stiff. I was scared. I was scared of death, the path and the fighting. I was not ready for this. I looked at my comrades to see how their reactions were to this sight. Beside Myra's cloaked allies, I could see the same fear and stiffness had affected both Robyn and Jimmy. More so for Robyn, as she could see her kind fighting on both sides of this conflict. Why were there any elves in this army at all? I had thought the major troop of Traytos were human gunners, human knights and the holy paladins. The clockwork cannons were a dwarven marvel and yet there were no dwarves here to man them or fix them. Instead, there were goblins and mecha-ogres to move and fire the weapons. I needed a closer look, but Myra had a firm grasp on my shoulder.

'Torro, stop what you're thinking,' said Myra, as she held my shoulder to stop me from going to the battlefield. Her hand was trembling. She must have been afraid. I clasped her hand to calm her and looked her way. My first thought was that she must have been crying from the view of death and destruction of life. But her stern face only revealed irritation. The sort seen by a parent irritated at their child for disobeying their warnings again and again. The kind of irritation a master would show their apprentice when they were using the wrong techniques, after learning the right ones only moments ago. It was not anger Myra showed me, but a warning distress. As if I was about to forget about the mission at hand and go off and die for glory or false honour. Her eyes were sad and full of worry, but not a single tear was coming out. Her stubborn look was saying, 'Go ahead and fight, because if you don't die out there, I will kill you myself.' The smile on my face quickly disappeared and now I had the same fear from the view of the battlefield to the devastated look in Myra's eyes, piercing my own. I nodded slowly at first, then put the same smile on my face to hide the fear of death.

'Ok, I won't fight but I can still help, right?' said Torbiro to the very cross Memyra. His face showed concern on a more mutual level. The type of kindness for the people. To meddle in the business of war was deadly at best but there was always hope. The smile on Torbiro's face was filled with the fear of dying and a courage to help those in need. Torbiro revealed a very cheeky grin, then turned back to the battle at hand. He knew fighting was not an option as it would only be the death of him. He needed to think of a way to help but not fight. The path to the princess was shortest if he went through the battlefield, but the risk was high. Going around was also an option but with Torbiro in heavy armour, it was not a practical idea, as by the time he arrived at the tower, he would need a significant amount of rest to recover.

Lost in thought, Torbiro started to mumble and ramble about what to do. All present could hear him and Memyra was the only one who laughed. From a scoff to light laughter. Robyn and Memyra's agents looked at the ridiculous pair of halflings and could only shrug and nod. A few sighed with regret. Though all had been preoccupied with the halfling reactions, Jimmy had snuck away, using the immediate distraction to lose his companions for some nefarious scheme.

While the others were busy with the battle upfront, Jimmy had used his innate ability to create a silent image to fool and trick his allies, as well as his enemies, making out he had been next to the oblivious elf the whole time. From the noise of battle and the unusual commotion of the halflings, casting his spell was an easy feat. Once done, he retraced his steps to a more private location. When alone, he scanned the area for any onlookers, even if they were minor, as you could never be too sure if someone else was watching or listening to you. Peering side to side from the opening of a small cave just a few metres away from the group, Jimmy made sure it was safe to make such a secret report. With a scowl on his face, Jimmy pulled out a viewing crystal. It was in the shape of a simple-looking scroll, but once extended, the holder could communicate with someone who had the same type of scroll.

As the scroll opened, there was no image at first, but soon a man appeared in the viewing crystal. Jimmy spoke very softly, but it was loud enough for this man to acknowledge him. He reported his location and where the halflings were. He reported on the number of the group and that he would report again once in the tower. No words were heard from the other and once the report was done, Jimmy simply made a strange gesture and quickly closed the scroll. The strange gesture was a salute. It was very simple, motioning his right fist, palm toward his face and fist clenched. His left hand was crossed over to form a cross with his left fist palm towards the viewing screen. Once his secret message was sent, Jimmy quickly headed back to the others, making sure he was not seen.

Torbiro finally came to from his thoughts and completed a safe and sound plan. Memyra had also calmed herself as she too remembered where she was, by the sound and vibration of a nearby explosion. Magic or technologically making an explosion was always dangerous. Flying debris had also reached their location and they needed to move. Torbiro's group was relatively small, but the battle continued to wage. Torbiro's plan was to take to the ripple-made trenches in the Dip Hills, then find a cave or passageway through to the tower, but they may come across fighting on the way, so they needed to be stealthy. Quick and quiet was the plan. To do this, Torbiro needed to remove the encumbering armour he so proudly wore. But to discard it would also remove the only protection he wore. He would be exposed. Exposed to the elements, to the battles ahead and to the war. To Torbiro's knowledge, Memyra was involved with magic and magical items. But he had no knowledge of special items to store and disguise. Items such as a Bag of Holding, which could store almost unlimited items, or a Cloak of Illusion, which could protect its wearer with illusions strong enough to deceive its opponents.

'Torro, how are you going to go on with your plan?' asked Myra with concern but also mockery.

'What do you mean, Myra? I'm ready,' said Torbiro with determination but a bit of confusion.

'Your plan is to save the princess, right?' said Myra with derision.

'Well, of course. Why else would I have gone this far?' said Torbiro with stubborn pride.

'Well, how are you going to do that, huh? Like a knight or what?' said Myra.

'Well, I have my plan, and… and…' said Torbiro with more confusion and fluster than confidence.

'Come on Torro, you can't do anything in rags.' Myra interrupted Torbiro.

'Come here and let me take care of your armour and other gear. What do ya say?'

Another explosion interrupted their argument and pushed the group further from the edge of Dip Hills. With the explosion came cries from soldiers and other warriors. They were not cries of victory, but cries of pain. With the dangers, the bickering stopped for the moment and had the team move to a much safer location. Although the battles raged on, there was far more danger as it continued. The shape of the terrain changed with each blast and the casualties rose. The shape of the hills was pretty odd already.

Like any hills with soft slopes, there are valleys that connect them. But the main differences are the multiple hills and valleys in this single location, creating a ring. They have the shape similar to a heating coil used for cookery. At the bottom of the hills, a low slope starts all the way around to the other side, like a round pastry with a hole in the centre. The strange thing is the Dip Hills have four separate valleys within the region. But the valleys themselves are not connected. The hills are more like mounts but the Dip Hills is on a single mountain top. A single peak that rises at the central point of the hills.

With the battle raging on, more and more of the hill coils were being turned into craters by the steam cannons or bubbled and pulsating soil from the magical blasts and incantations. They needed to move, but safely. Torbiro shouted, 'to the caves' as one of the cave entrances near them is blasted with bright solar light. The group moved quickly and in chaos as the battle of magic and technology continued. They wormed their way through the battlefield but they weren't able to evade the troops of Traytos as they too, pushed and pulled with each command and attack. The terrain was already a factor for movement, but the sheer number of Traytos warriors and soldiers outnumbered those of the mages. The movement of the group was chaotic, sometimes back-tracking due to dead ends or meeting either forces, as they tried to reach their destination. Their elven companion Robyn has given them insight on where to retreat to. Torbiro pushed the team, but Robyn guided it to safety. There was much communication between the two and though they moved quickly and clumsily, they managed to work out a way to a safe destination. As the group moved from danger to brief safety, Torbiro managed to put on simple pants that Memyra handed him, then a shirt, a leather jacket, and lastly, a pair of goggles. Though Torbiro was wearing his halfling sized plate armour, his allies had helped him out of it with each pass of the Dip valley from hill to hill, across to safety with elvish insight, perception and coordination. With each piece of armour came a simple item of clothing from Memyra's mysterious satchel. Memyra still reacted with amusement but had not the time to express her enjoyment due to the constant and continual effects of the battle. The group reached safety in an abandoned medical outpost to heal the troops of the terrible war.

This particular area had many injured soldiers. Goblinoids, orc tribes, trolls with brain enhancers and human soldiers. There were very few physicians to aid each creature and it seemed the critically injured were left to die or suffer the pain of surviving whatever battle they had been in. Those with only minor injuries were quickly patched up with first aid and ordered to go back out to battle. It was horrible. The men and women here were treated like expendable troops. They were treated worse than criminals. No breaks. No meals. No rest. Who in the pulse was managing this war? Just throwing lives like mouldy bread in the waste bin. These were people and they desired better. Torbiro felt the anger and frustration from the suffering and dying. He was about to scream at the staff who were healing the lightly injured and charge their leader to organise better operations, as he had learnt from the knights' teachings and training.

Memyra could see and sense the emotions welling up in Torbiro. She ordered her agents to stop and restrain him if he made a move, with a simple but complex set of hand gestures. Torbiro was not the only one in shock. Robyn also showed emotions of sadness and sorrow for the soldiers and quickly moved to the ones nearest her. She was too agile and nimble to be stopped by Memyra's agents, but she could do nothing to aid those that needed medical care. Memyra could see it was not the physician's fault either, as they too were shorthanded and leaderless. They had no organisation and could only help those that were quick to aid. To think even the fabled trolls would be this injured, their regenerative abilities were simply far too weak to heal them in this battle, was unbelievable. In Memyra's memory and knowledge of hospitals and healing facilities, there would be more healers than patients. But here in this large outpost, there were only three physicians for every fifty soldiers. They too had no time to rest or eat. This was a mess. Who in all of Traytos was commanding this war?

As Robyn reached her first soldier, she had asked the simplest question. 'What can I do to help?' But from under the covers, the soldier could only groan in pain. Robyn could think only of compassion and slowly removed the covers to see what best she could do to help. But the sight of this human's injuries was so ghastly that tears started to fall down her face. She noted the brutal lacerations on the left side, from the left shoulder all the way across to the right foot and ankle. Like some kind of blade had cut the left arm right off, as well as the left leg right up from the thigh. It was a horribly ghastly sight. The cut was not made by a blade, which would have had external signs of blood, but that of burns from the intense friction of energy. Magic was indeed deadly in the hands of powerful creatures. The external appearance of the man was enough for him to die, but so painful to survive the experience that it set Robyn's insides turning.

If the injuries of the covered were all like this, then she knew they were in serious danger. Torbiro could only think of ways to aid these men and women, these soldiers, but as the rage and fury of inability started to fill Torbiro's mind, it also sparked deep anger which showed on his face. Memyra had seen this before in previous comrades and acted quickly to hold her friend back and bring him to the present. With pain showing in both Robyn and Torbiro's eyes, they acknowledged the situation here could only be stopped by rescuing the princess. Torbiro calmed his emotions and dried his tears. But first, he needed information. Who was leading the army? To find out, he needed to speak to the soldiers, or at least the soldiers heading back to the fight. But he was ill equipped to continue on. He did not have armour, nor did he have any authority symbols to converse with the soldiers. He looked at Robyn, but she was still an emotional wreck. He looked for Jimmy but he was nowhere to be found. Odd. Finally, he looked at Myra for advice. At first she ignored his 'suggestion' and said they should continue towards the tower, but seeing how stubborn Torro was, Myra decided to aid him with more magical means.

With Memyra's items and extra clothes, Torbiro, not trusting magically enhanced items, was at first stubborn like a dwarf, but being an ever changing and challenging halfling, he agreed to the use of Myra's items. A cloak of disguise, a few mithril daggers of returning and clockwork speed shoes. The cloak was magical and would allow the wearer to create illusions about the wearer. It worked like a mental mirror. Think of what you look like and become just that. The cloak was not all powerful and had many flaws, too. As it could only make illusions of the wearer's approximate size, so if you were the size of an arctic giant, you could make illusions of that size but no smaller. And since Torbiro was a 106 cm tall halfling, he could only create illusions of his size, give or take a few centimetres. The daggers were simple weapons that could be returned to the wielded with a simple command. To Torbiro's misfortune, those command words were already assigned by Myra, when she purchased them in some desert bazaar. The command words were, 'Now kiss me' which were odd in Torbiro's mind and very embarrassing to say. As for the shoes, they were the standard wear of Accello-engineers back in Traytos. They ran on friction power, or at least that's what Myra had explained. Torbiro, on the other hand knew more about the items in detail as his master Dorian, had constantly boasted about being the true inventor of them. It could have been fiction, as the dwarf was always plastered when he told such grandiose tales.

The strange thing was Myra. She had all sorts of items in that infinity bag of hers. She had provided items for not only the unprepared Torbiro, but also his companion, Robyn. As to where Jimmy was, she too did not know. Myra had seen how the elf handled her rifle in the alleyway and had given her something a bit more stable. She provided a Triphil, a life jacket and belt of location. The Triphil was a triple barrelled rifle, hence the name. This weapon was similar to the rifle Robyn had used in the mission to capture Myra, but Myra had explained it to be more 'stable'. Whatever that meant. But Robyn was still full of emotions. Some were sorrow for the gruesome injuries of the suffering soldiers and others were joy of addiction towards receiving a new marvel or the latest toy a child would receive on their birthday. The life-jacket was a magically enchanted leather that could heal the wearer of injuries and other ailments. What those ailments were, no one knew, not even Memyra as she had 'procured' them from somewhere. The belt of location was meant to aid the wearer if they got lost. Torbiro had his doubts about this item as well, but it could be useful for the journey which lay ahead. The belt was not for Torbiro's benefit, but for Memyra's. This item allowed her to locate its wearer at all times.

CHAPTER 39
FAMEBORN'S COMMAND

A few hours ago, when the call for re-enforcements was made by the main force to encounter and repel those dastardly spell slinging shits, I, the great Fameborn, have readied all I need for this command and conquest. Wearing the Fameborn armour and wielding the Fameborn blade, I march to the balcony to hail my men. To rally them to the cause and to inspire them with the same conviction as I. The responding shouts rally others to do so. The sound of roaring warriors and paladins echoed slowly throughout the grounds. Then outward from the Fameborn estate to the town. The sounds were quite melodic but much more similar to the sound of clockwork. Synchronous like gears of a machine but as it resounded and reflected off each other, the sound created a soft harmony. Only those very far away could hear this and only those with 'that' creative soul could identify it as rustic barbershop.

As the army marched forward, their commander launched out orders left, right and centre. His orders were all about attacking formations so he could quickly defeat the enemy encroaching on the borders of the motherland. He had no care for the men following the orders. He had no care for the survivors returning with their lives and grave injuries. His orders were simple but cruel. Attack. Attack. Attack. Attack the right flank. Attack the left flank. Attack the centre flank. These were the orders of Commander Wilbur L. Fameborn. He was relentless, but foolish. He saw only victory, a swift victory by his hands. He had no idea what the men and women of this war had to overcome, what pain they had to experience. He was in command and he believed he was never wrong. Any soldier who revolted was executed on the spot. The remains of those that revolted were used as incentive to rally the troops, then the bodies would be used as meat to those cannibals, those monsters. The trolls, ogres and goblins of Traytos were monsters and Fameborn treated them with seriously harsh prejudice. No man was above the commander. He had been given this position by the true king of Traytos. He too had orders and these orders were strict, without compassion, without mercy and without chaos.

So with these orders being followed, Fameborn made his preparations to lead his troops to the quick victory of his mind. Unbeknownst to Fameborn, Torbiro was a knight like him, but one with friends to aid him and council him with his decisions.

CHAPTER 40
HEALING TOUCH

With the items and gear provided by Myra, Torbiro headed straight for the main medical tent to better address the chaotic nature of the healers and doctors. All of his companions followed him there, with the exception of Jimmy. The team had discussed their plan with Jimmy present, but once they started to head out, he had vanished. Without the luxury of time, Myra had ordered one of her men to search for Jimmy and rendezvous with them at seventeen turns – or 17 hours – near the tower. As the team had made a search attempt but were unsuccessful in locating Jimmy. Torbiro had a plan to aid the injured by confronting the medical team and providing them with better instructions.

As the four of them approached and entered the main medical tent, Torbiro and Robyn took the lead, while Myra followed and her agent stayed by her side. There stood a tent lacking patients. No soldiers, bandaged or otherwise. Only the fluttering of tarp leading inside. Where the major doctors were to wait until ordered. The tent's location was very odd as it was far to the back of the healing area, a good 2km away. As though the commander in charge of this battle had thought healing was not necessary. It was common knowledge to both Robyn and Torbiro the med-team should be with each assault team for quick relief and not be too far from the fight itself. Not completely separated from the whole encounter. It was also general practice for a member of the offensive team to have a medical member or two on hand. So fighting and co-ordinated attacks could be performed by the teams engaged by whatever opponent they were facing.

Upon entering the tent, the Torbiro and Robyn saw twenty-five doctors waiting for orders.

They were all ready and were very surprised only two of us had entered. They at first thought we were the enemy, but I quickly explained my attire and mission and that they needed to go to the main healing area for major assistance. As their assistants were under-staffed and needed all the help they could get. The head doctor did not believe Torbiro at first, but as Robyn spoke, one of the other practitioners spoke up. This particular doctor was perhaps a relative of Robyn's as they were both elves, but one could not assume this simply from a racial trait. This doctor was very familiar with Robyn, quickly speaking in their native tongue and embracing each other. Torbiro was glad at least one of the doctors would listen, but he was quickly forgotten once the other doctors had seen the two elves together. The elf Robyn was speaking to was male perhaps but Torbiro could not tell. He had only known two elves in his life, Robyn and Commander Peren. But this elf looked almost identical to Robyn, his hair, the shape of his eyes and his slender frame. Besides the fact Robyn had a darker tan of skin, Torbiro believed they must have been twins. He tried his best to get the attention of the other doctors for aid as the war raged on and all of those soldiers were dying without the much needed care they deserved.

Although Torbiro had pleaded his case with them, there was much prejudice from them and this led to distrust and more aggression than he could have anticipated. Some of the doctors just ignored him yet again, while others threatened to harm him if he did not leave. Torbiro knew if he did not get the doctors' help, this war would escalate and more people would die than needed. He stopped by jumping off one of the beds, more like an instant cot used in workshops where inventors or fabricators would rest. It was a marvellous invention, the instant cot. It was marvellous because the initial size of the device wasn't bigger than a normal sized book. The length was about 15cm by a height of 25cm and a thickness of 2 to 10cm, depending on the actual size of the intended cot. But these cots needed a lot of cold steam or air to keep their shape. Torbiro moved towards Robyn to convince her friend to help them, but thinking that he was hidden due to his size, one of the doctors had noticed him and, without warning or caution, threw a small surgical knife at Torbiro. Though it was meant to be a warning only, it was going to strike true and only Robyn could see the path of the knife's flight path. To his luck, Robyn moved to block the knife, rather than catch it. Elves were known to have quick and agile reflexes, but not all of them could catch small knives. With a shout of pain from his ally and friend, Torbiro leaped back on one of the instant cots and berated the knife-thrower.

'What are you doing?' Torbiro shouted, glaring at the assailant. His eyes were grim and shameful.

'I was… just… trying to warn… You!!' said the doctor with an accusing finger pointed at Torbiro. But before he could continue, he was interrupted by gunshots and thermal blasts just outside the tent.

'What's going on?' Memyra said as she entered. She could not be seen by anyone aside from Torbiro and Robyn's friend.

'Robyn got hurt from a knife, thrown by that doctor.' Torbiro said, pointing at the assailant.

'I'm ok, by the way…. Ow,' Robyn tried to get up.

'Cyan, you shouldn't push yourself,' said the elvish doctor. He helped Robyn up.

'This is nothing, Silver,' said Robyn as she held her arm tight. Her face was just as tight as her grip, to keep herself from crying.

'Robyn are you ok?' Torbiro's voice had concern in his tone. But to his surprise, he heard two voices in reply.

'I'm just fine,' replied both Cyan and Silver in coordinated synchronicity. It was very odd. Though they had both answered at the same time, it was as though only one of them had spoken.

At which point, Cyan and Silver looked at each other and smiled. then laughed until Cyan, not Silver, remembered one of them was still injured. Myra's agent then appeared at the other side of the tent, behind the retreating doctors and loudly cocked his weapon. The doctors did not know what to do, but offer to surrender. That they were not at fault and to punish the one that was. Myra whistled twice in succession, to message her agent about his next actions as he started to corral them. I looked at Silver and asked how long it would take for Cyan to be healed. I was going to say 'Robyn' instead of Cyan, but that might have been confusing. Doctor Silver informed me the knife did not go in too deep and within a few minutes, it would be out and he could start mending her. I could clearly see the few tears that had escaped Cyan's eyes, showing she was more embarrassed than scared. With a few complaints from Cyan, the healing was done in just a few minutes, just as Silver said. But while that was happening, Myra and I spoke to the others about the urgency of my request.

Myra decided to order these stubborn doctors to their jobs instead of using compassion to get them to listen to us. Once they knew Myra meant business – by shooting one of them, no less – the main medical team headed to the healing sector, all twenty-five of them. In a matter of a few ticks, the doctors went to work. Healing the heavily injured to the ones left to die. In the rush to aid the soldiers, Silver was the only one who spoke to me. While bandaging one of the critically injured trolls, he asked me to protect his sister. With a simple nod, I agreed and started to head to the next location to aid the war. I needed to head to the commander's tent next, to coordinate plans and update them on the situation in the healing sector. As I left, Dr Silver must have said something in elvish, as I didn't understand it. But I remembered the word. Valpra.

CHAPTER 41
TORBIRO'S COMMAND

With the first part of his plan a success, Torbiro needed to go to the source of confusion. The commander's tent. He knew Myra protested this as a waste of time, but if saving the life of the princess was his mission, then saving the lives of soldiers could aid him with this task as well. Currently, there were no defensive positions made anywhere on the battlefield as they ran from the incoming fire and energy blasts of the sorcerers. There were no cover or small camps for communication. For a battle this size, there should at least be small bases around the Dip Hills so soldiers could rest and find refuge from the fighting. Something needed to be done and said. But the first problem was locating the right tent.

I had spoken to the soldiers coming and going from the healing sector and none of them could tell me where they were getting their orders. The only thing they knew was once they had moved to the battlefield, it was all about fighting for survival. There were no orders to attack certain areas and no place for them to rest.

Myra and I searched for the commander's tent, but we could not locate it. Myra even used strange stones that glowed, but they could not help locate the tent. It had to be somewhere. I thought of the most logical places this tent could be. The top of the Dip Hills or on one of the Dip Hills to the east or west vantage points where you could get cover from incoming fire but still get a good view of the enemy's positions. It wasn't at the back of the hills either, as that's where the healing sector was located. It puzzled us both. As the group climbed the second hill to the top, Robyn spotted a tent in the weirdest position. Near the front lines. In fact, it might as well have been in the frontlines.

Torbiro could not see what Robyn had spotted in the distance, but with the help of one of Myra's spyglasses, he could clearly see the commander's tent was on the other side of the hills. It was in the complete opposite location of the healing sector. Why in chaos was it there? It was located in enemy territory. But from the view atop the hills, the sorcerers were nowhere to be found. Had we already won? Or had the enemy forces just been driven into the hills? If it was the latter, it would explain the rapid dangers in the outer sectors of the hills. If not, the fight was becoming worse with every turn. This battle was becoming more like guerrilla warfare. The commander needed to be told of the situation. Our forces were wounded, scattered and confused. The fight continued and nothing was being done to rally the troops. Torbiro needed to right this wrong. Something needed to be done and quickly, as the magicians were either closing in or laying traps.

Traversing down the hills was no easy task. The battle scars and scorched earth did not make the journey any easier. The team moved quickly down toward the commander's tent. As quickly and safely as possible, that is. With the skilful agility of elvish acrobatics, the dirt and earth appeared to not move with every step, but as Robyn ran and jumped, the earth and soil would shift and sink. This delayed movement of ground would be due to the combination of the energies. The magical residues and technological toxic wastes. The culminations of such energies had corrupted the very land they ran on. Without the magical assistance of Memyra's items, the team would have been enveloped by the chaos of corruption. After a few turns of the clock, Torbiro arrived at the foot of the Dip Hills on the north side where the commander's tent was sighted.

On their arrival, Torbiro and the crew were met with harsh looks and confusion. The men guarding the front of the tent were clean of wounds, unlike the soldiers at the healing sector. They awaited the arrival of a certain man. There were about one hundred strong troops awaiting orders from command. Torbiro had many questions for the commander of this war. Such as defensive tactics, effective use of healing facilities and what were the offensive plans of this war? He was small, but his thoughts were much bigger than himself. Torbiro could no longer stand the waste of lives being used in this battle. Rather than confronting the entire force with questions, Memyra decided to use stealth and go directly to the tent. Torbiro did not like this tactic, but knew any other method would be time wasted, when his mission was to rescue the princess. Sneaking in to the tent was easy, but once they entered, the three of them were stunned. No one was inside. No one was here at all. There were, however, plenty of battle plans and tactical maps of the surrounding area. Standing on the only chair in the room, Torbiro and Memyra investigated the battle maps and plans. Robyn, being tall enough to see the plans laid out on the table, looked the maps over. The plans were pretty simplistic but the three were still quite puzzled at their stupidity.

The table was filled with many charts and battle maps. One map in particular had pin marks and small figurines marking locations on Dip Hills and the plans of the continued offensive. From the markings, the commander in question was a knight named 'Fameborn' and he was leading the assault against the sorcerers of Bataros. Fameborn's plan was a fool's errand. Torbiro and Memyra thought he must have been some fool or a glory hog. The attack Fameborn led might have been successful if he was using the rest of the army more effectively. Like placing traps to capture the enemy or ambush points to deal a fatal blow when their numbers dwindled. But a reckless and relentless assault would only split the enemy into smaller groups, which would make them harder to deal with. The enemy was wizards and sorcerers and one might be easier to deal with if they were out in the open, but the Dip Hills was another story. The magicians could use the lay of the land to their advantage. Myra had mentioned illusion magic and nature-based spells could be used to hide and confuse soldiers not used to such tactics. With all the information from the maps, such as the network of tunnels and the use of different natural terrains in the hills, this war could be dealt with in a single tactical manoeuvre.

Both Torbiro and Memyra looked at each other, with a similar idea of how to deal with the problem at hand. As they turned, their faces were only a few centimetres apart. So close that each could see the steam from the other's breath. They both smiled and they both had a thought about how to proceed, but only one of them showed affection for the other. There was a light blush on Memyra's face, showing her soft rosy cheeks as she faced Torbiro, her friend from childhood. Torbiro, completely oblivious to her feelings, showed a toothy grin. With a short exhale of breath from each of them, the moment passed and having realised her reaction towards Torbiro, Memyra covered her face with her cowl. In the same instance, Torbiro started to collect the maps on the table to use and make proper plans.

CHAPTER 42
COORDINATION AND COLLABORATION

Emerging from the tent after a short discussion between the three of them, they encountered the soldiers and knight outside the tent. At first, the knights refused to listen to Torbiro's orders due to his stature and race, but quickly retracted their troubled opinions. Mainly due to Memyra's threats and the real threat that Lord Fameborn may have bitten off more than he could chew. Torbiro's plan was twofold: one; they needed to find where the enemy was hiding in the Dip Hills and two; they also needed to form camps to provide better networks of communication for the entire army. This campaign needed to stop wasting lives. From the reports in the commander's tent, the enemy's numbers were only about one to two thousand mages.

Our forces numbered three times that number and yet they were yet to be defeated. Since leaving Traytos with Memyra, ten cycles had already passed. Which meant this battle or war had been going on for at least twenty one or twenty two cycles. About half of the initial force had died from both sides and all the soldiers were still in disarray. This battle needed to end. But before it could end, we needed more information. About the enemy and about the hills. As well as Commander Fameborn's whereabouts. So I split the soldier stationed at the commander's tent into five regiments. All of them had very specific roles. Each regiment had been split according to their role. Scouts, trackers, defenders, chargers and trailers. Scouts were meant to act with the utmost speed. Trackers had a good sense of nature and direction. Defenders were for reinforcements. Chargers were also for reinforcements but used for offense. While Trailers were the main supply lines to provide support and communication for the army.

Despite these soldiers not being well equipped for anything aside from offensive or defensive tactics, they could still be instructed for different roles. What Torbiro needed now was more men. More soldiers. But he knew most of them were either at the healing sector or wandering around the Dip Hills fighting a battle without any plans or orders from Fameborn. Commander Fameborn, that is. Torbiro ordered three of the fastest knights to guard Robyn while she scouted the hills. He also sent ten of the soldiers to go to the healing sector to provide new orders for them, to make small camps at crucial points in the hills. Torbiro's plan was simple: rout the enemy by closing their exits. To better use the terrain as natural blockages while slowly advancing to deal with the enemy. After seeing siege engines around the hills, Torbiro wanted some of the soldiers to team up with veteran knights to man and defend them as they were moved to more tactical positions around the hills and valleys of Dip.

With the orders made, Torbiro and Memyra led teams of soldiers to find the enemy as well as Fameborn's location. Torbiro took his troop west and Memyra agreed to take her warriors east and then south to meet up and gather more soldiers to form a web to rout the wizards. Many of the soldiers refused to follow the halflings, but with positive reports from the healing sector, they begrudgingly agreed until Commander Fameborn was found. Memyra was more annoyed she had to lead the soldiers, as she only wanted to help Torro with his princess rescue. So she planned to leave them and trail her childhood friend. The soldiers knew their orders and Memyra couldn't care less about this war or this operation. Torbiro, on the other hand, followed his plan, leaving men in the natural choke points of Dip Valley. Most of these choke points would lead out of the Dip Hills. The terrain was rough and mostly battle scarred by cannon blasts, but they could be traversed. The soldiers moved much slower than Torbiro, but they were able to manage a similar pace. The siege engines they found were mostly clockwork cannons. These were heavy but were quite mobile.

Although the clockwork cannons could be moved easily, they had trouble moving up hill. This was due to their design. The cannons were set in a rotating gear which moved clockwise. Once the cannon was in the lowest position, they would be loaded by one of the turning spring sprockets. As the cannon rotated, it would fire once it reached its zenith on the gear. While it was firing, it had anchors to hold it in place, but while it was being moved from different locations, the large gear would be used to move the engine. Due to its design, the weight of the cannon actually assisted the soldiers moving it. So long as it was not going uphill. As the main gear would dig into the ground and hinder rather than help the soldiers operating the siege engine.

The soldiers from both the healing sector and the command post made their stand, according to Torbiro's plan. The soldiers started to encounter the enemy wizards. Many of the wizards were very quick to surrender so long as they could leave alive. Others started to argue about the promise of the king of Traytos, but soon found themselves dying for petty materials. The wizards were not what Torbiro had expected. They were more like merchants or students fulfilling orders. What kind of war was this? As more and more of the Dip Hills were connected by small encampments, Torbiro slowly conquered the hills without unnecessary deaths, but many captured enemy troops. The map Torbiro held first looked like dots on the scroll, but as he filled those dots, they started to connect. The image on the scroll almost looked like an intricate cogwheel. Torbiro was very perplexed. His perception of wars was one from the great tales in taverns or from the tactical lessons he received from his short knight's training. But this battle had no honour or glory involved. It was just one side's greed and the other's relentless defence.

With every step up the hill, Torbiro and Memyra found themselves in the middle of a very complex situation. It was weird that after Robyn was sent to scout almost one revol - or eight cycles, to be precise – to find the location of Commander Fameborn and to report back, she had not returned or given any other report. Torbiro wondered what had happened to her, but had been too busy expanding his perimeter of the Dip Hills. Time was ticking and Torbiro had to finish with the Dip complication. But as Torbiro's team had reached near the top of the hills and the valley accompanying it, they found both Robyn and Lord Fameborn. They were fighting.

CHAPTER 43
BLOODLUST OF A KNIGHT

'My lord, we have found some rogue elves. What are your orders?' asked a soldier.

'Where? And how many of the savages are there?' demanded Fameborn, while sharpening his large twin blade. He had beads of sweat all over his muscular body as he cleaned and polished his armour by lamp light.

'Second mound. Toward the east. Seven males, four females and five children,' said the soldier in monotone.

'MEN!! Gather your things and we march in three clicks,' said Fameborn as he ordered his soldiers.

The soldiers under Commander Fameborn were mainly comprised of human soldiers who had been worked to the bone. They were exhausted and hungry. They had only a few turns for rest, but they were drilled to continue. His troop was a grand number at first, but due to Fameborn's lack of morals and ethics for his soldiers' lives, that had reduced. He had pushed them to the brink of death. He had used them like tools or automatons. But soldiers and warriors needed rest. The only warriors that had any rest were the venerable veterans. His father's knights. They were well rested and well fed. With each charge, that grand number dwindled to a few dedicated soldiers and some simply insane killers.

'Sir, is it possible to rest just for a few clicks? Many of...' A tired soldier approached Fameborn.

'Soldier, you have your orders. Rest is for the dead or the dying,' a knight countered.

'But sir, we've all lost a lot and a bit of rest will do us wonders. Please, sir…' the soldier pleaded for his comrades. They had bags under their eyes and they all had growling stomachs and trembling bodies due to lack of human care, even for soldiers at war.

'Come men, even our honourable veterans have more energy than you lot. Think of the glory. Now march!' said Fameborn, ordering his troops. Lord Fameborn used his rank for privileges that other soldiers simply could not argue against. He was like the veterans. Well-fed and well rested. He could not understand why many of the soldiers were tired. He could not see the problem with his command. He foolishly ordered all his soldiers to keep watch. But he had forced all his soldiers to keep watch and not in efficient shifts. So, of course, those soldiers were exhausted.

As a reply, the soldiers, whether tired or teetering on death, answered, 'Yes Sir.' But due to the forced march, many of these soldiers could only collapse from exhaustion. One by one, Fameborn's troop was reduced. By the time Fameborn found his prey, he only had the venerable ones and a handful of proud warriors. He was reduced to twenty warriors. Twelve old knights and eight warriors pushed by the insanity of honour and glory. They reached the top of the mound and Fameborn signalled his men to charge at the first sign of the savage elves. The eight warriors were sent to the perimeter to block the escape routes and the venerable knights ordered to ready a swift charge. Fameborn was at the lead, a grin of excitement on his face as he waited for the enemy to appear.

The site at which Fameborn had arrived was a ridge among some trees and beyond was an opening to some connecting caves. Here, there were to be a number of elves and magic users for the commander to defeat. Though one could say it was more of a slaughter than a defeat, as the current occupants of the cave were a family caught in the war. They were in the wrong place at the wrong time. They were a simple family of elves, just seeking Traytos to migrate. As their home was ravaged by powerful beasts. They did use magic. But their magic was not powerful enough to do any harm. They knew only simple spells and cantrips. Though they were not a threat, they had still been hunted for being magical in nature. They hoped for salvation, but they had no idea that death was nearing them. Waiting just outside to slaughter them. Cruel, cruel slaughter. These elves were tired and exhausted from their previous trek, but their children were full of energy. They played and would, on occasion leave the cave to play and explore nature. Most of the time when they left the cave, one of their parents would remind them of the dangers outside. But this time, they would be the ones to warn their own.

One of Fameborn's tired soldiers finds herself near the entrance of the cave as she searches for a good spot to take a well-needed break. She was ordered to make sure the enemy could not escape. The enemy to her was surrounded and she really needed to eat something or just get some shuteye. Even if it was just a few clicks. She found a strong tree and leaned on it with all her weight. She put her pack down and managed to find some bad tasting rations out of her pack. When something kicks her leg as she knelt. At first, she did not notice it. She was exhausted to near death. The only feelings she had were the numbness and the empty growl of her stomach. But then it happens again. Something had kicked her. Her ration was in her mouth and she had shifted to stand. Fallen on the ground was a small elf. A child. To her shock, she spat the stick of dried meat out of her mouth to shout 'Elf!'

Fameborn had not ordered one of his men to scout. They had waited in their positions for more than a turn. Too foolish to acknowledge his error, he blamed his men for not mentioning any clear sign of the elves, when one of the smaller children had been noticed. His face red with anger, he ordered a loud charge. Fameborn led the charge. The old knights followed very slowly behind and the soldiers did not take notice other than the one who found the elf child. Fameborn had his blade held high to strike down the first target he met. The knights had shields at the ready as they charged at their slow pace. Once Fameborn got to the cave, he was met by an elf girl. With all his might, he brought down his sword and to his surprise, their weapons clashed.

CHAPTER 44
COMPASSION VS ANGER

Robyn had scoured the hills for the commander, but all she could find were scattered soldiers who had been pushed to the brink of exhaustion and the fear stricken magi seeking safe haven. Each encounter with the soldiers she had were to ease their pain and allow them to rest. She had cared for them with compassion and kindness to ease their burden. With enough first aid and the reassurance that reinforcements would come soon, she had provided them comforting rest.

As for the magi, Robyn had considered defeating and detaining them, but these folk were of her kin. Many of the mages were simple merchants heading to Traytos for the opportunity of trade and resources, but the others were mainly poor apprentices who needed ingredients for initiation rituals to progress to the next stage. At first Robyn and her scouts engaged with the magi in martial combat, but the spell slingers were no match for the swiftness of an elf. Blades were useless in ranged combat, but any unprepared caster would have a severe disadvantage in a melee. With a simple trap here and an ambush there, the magi she had encountered first fought, but then calmly considered a formal surrender. Robyn was aghast at first, knowing the situation was a serious one. They were at war. She gathered the spellcasters in a nearby cave where she found more of the Bataros fugitives. Her team wanted to kill and slaughter the magi, but there was protocol to follow. The Batarians would be taken in as prisoners of war, but as soon as Robyn saw the casualties, she instead negotiated with them.

After a calm discussion about the wants and needs of the prisoners, she thought about the oddly common situation with the soldiers she had found along the way. The needs were all basic, from shelter to food. It was nothing like the drills and lectures from her days of the academy. She had even prepared for a heated argument, but that didn't happen either. She was perplexed at the commonality with the soldiers. They too, only wanted the fighting to stop. Now, why did the fighting start in the first place? Only Commander Fameborn could answer these questions. Robyn promised these magi she would protect them from the dangers of the wild until her scouts returned with new orders. The cave Robyn had found was very spacious. Only moments had passed when her scouts returned with injured soldiers they had encountered on their search for the missing commander. The cave was large enough to accommodate both soldiers and prisoners alike. The first thing Robyn needed to do was assign areas for either side to take up residence, but after more and more soldiers arrived, the Batarians started to help the injured. Some used magic, others used medicinal herbs and salves. The cave was like a small community assisting and helping each other in times of crisis. There were a few children who at first were so full of fright they would only peer from behind their mothers. But after the healers and casters started to aid the soldiers, they too wanted to help. The people of Bataros were not what Robyn had expected. They were very similar to tribal communities, like orc tribes of the east. Robyn even saw two half-elf children helping one of the soldiers get some water. It was precious. Robyn had forgotten her task to find the commander, in the peace and helping nature of the Bataros magi and Traytos soldiers working in harmony.

Robyn's reverie was put to a stop when she heard a cry from outside the cave. The cry sounded like a child. With her rifle in hand and two handy leprechauns — leprechauns were curved swords, elven craftsmanship but tricked out with gnomion ingenuity - by her hip she prepared for the worst. By the entrance of the cave, Robyn saw another soldier, eyes bloodshot, stomach growling and trembling legs. Another exhausted example of Fameborn's troop. Robyn was relieved to see no danger afoot, but then her elven ears heard a command call for a charge. With rifle in hand, she sprinted out toward the entrance of the cave. There she saw an elf child on the ground, prone and injured with small cuts, most likely from thorned vines and plants, but the image of a crazed, bloodthirsty soldier charging at a helpless child made Robyn act.

Thoughts swirled and befuddled Robyn as the assailant moved closer and closer to the child. It was as though time had slowed. Thoughts of defence, thoughts of attack and thoughts of motion bombarded Robyn. What should I do? Perhaps I should fire a warning shot to stop her! Perhaps I should go inside to warn her parents! Perhaps I should shoot him in the leg to halt his charge! Perhaps I should… NO I must act.

No time for indecisive thoughts. Robyn rushed to put herself between the child and the assailant. Quickly, she raised her rifle and clashed with the warrior. A large sound echoed as both weapons met. Robyn held her rifle in both hands to protect the child, but the attack was so heavy and fierce she started to yield. It was slow, but the assailant was indeed much stronger than Robyn. This was not good. Robyn was in a dire position, but the child needed to be protected. Robyn was an elven warrior and a knight of Traytos. She needed to follow her oath. Protect the weak and uphold balance.

Being pushed back was one thing, but a pointy-eared elf was no match for the power and strength of a knight of Traytos. Fameborn only saw an enemy in front of his eyes. His first strike was blocked and parried. But with the momentum of his attack, he had the advantage. Again, Fameborn struck as hard as he could, this time from the right flank of the elf. She blocked and rolled from the force of the attack. He had cut her. Perhaps she would die in his honour, but she was quick. She managed to take a crouching position, coming off the roll.

She appeared like a small demon, pointed ears and as pale as a ghost. Fameborn eyed his prey and charged again. This time, he would strike wide to cleave both in half. What was that saying? Finish two birds with one strike?

Robyn was in trouble, but she knew if the child was safe, she could at least stall the assailant and wait for reinforcements to come to her aid. The first strike was easy to parry, simply change the angle of the attack and push. Cousin Peren… I mean Commander Peren was right, hand to hand training would come in handy.

I felt my blood quicken and the world around me slowed even more. Here I looked at the child and my surroundings. I saw seven, perhaps eight, more soldiers following the charge of this blood-crazed warrior. I turned to look at the child and a possible escape route back to the cave. It was easy. Pick up the child and run back to the entrance of the cave, then roll back with my blades to protect the entrance. A smile started to form on Robyn's face when the assailant had returned for another heavy strike. It was unexpected to come from her left. Robyn had seen the man's form and thought he would be coming in from her right. The child was already in her arms when the sharp, serrated edge struck her. There was no time to block, so Robyn turned to take the full brunt of the attack. Doing this would protect the child from death.

Robyn was flung about five metres, but to her luck she managed to roll to avoid causing harm to the child she hoped to protect. Incidentally, the armour she was wearing had also protected her. It was magical in nature and had healing properties. Unbeknownst to both Robyn and the child, the jacket she wore had healed the fear and small cuts from the child. With all the adrenalin and the rush of her elven blood in Robyn's system, the damage was severe but had healed very quickly. A third strike was coming in quick but the warrior had taken foolish steps and gone wide. The warrior spun with his sword like a crazed gnomish gyro-top. Robyn ducked to avoid the clumsy attack and rolled towards the entrance of the cave. Recovering from the roll, Robyn stood and released the boy in her arms and warned others of the danger of the assault.

Are you okay?

Yeh, that 'twas fun... can we do it again?

Okay good, now go inside and warn... wait what? Do what again?

The crazy rollie pollie rollie pollie...

Not right now! You must warn the others and call for help. I cannot hold them for long.

Aaaawwww but...

Not buts, you're in danger and I need help!!! Please call my friends to help, please go.

Lady, watch out...

As the boy starts to object, he points his muddy little fingers behind Robyn. His warning comes slowly, but Robyn manages to push him away from the incoming attack. He stumbles forward and falls down in the passage of the cave. Robyn screams in pain from the vicious attack. It is dishonourable to attack an enemy from behind. Robyn fell to her knees but used the momentum to turn it to a roll and bounce off the nearby wall to catch her footing. Her rifle out of reach, she pulled out her leprechauns, one in each hand. Robyn knew she would die if help didn't arrive soon. She also knew small leprechauns could not match the might of human eterium swords. Eterium swords are the culmination of dwarven craftsmanship and human cruelty. The sword is more of a cutting saw than a weapon for honourable duels. The blade is two metres long, twenty centimetres wide and about two to three centimetres thick. Unlike traditional greatswords, this monstrosity has an extra edge that rotates the main blade, which is intended to critically wound any opponent. But the main weakness of this design is the massive weight and bulkiness of the weapon.

The attack went into Robyn's back quite deep. Even with the aid of the armour's magic, healing such a wound would take much more time. From the pain on her back, Robyn tried to ignore it and continue the fight. Leprechauns were the best weapons to catch and parry attacks, but blocking and parrying was forcing Robyn back towards the defenceless. The attacks got heavier and heavier with each strike. Was she getting weaker, perhaps? She was full of energy and with each attack, her arms moved slower and slower, getting small nicks and near misses from the assault.

What Robyn didn't know was the armour she wore had a price for the healing properties. It was life. Even Memyra did not know of this price, as small cuts were nothing to be noticed. But the energy, the life energy of the wielder, was sacrificed or more to the point drained from the body. This energy is known to all practitioners of the tranquil arts as 'the void'. The void is where life is said to have originated and by returning your life to the void, you are able to use magic. The armour was healing her physical wounds but draining her years into the void. To a traditional elf that has embraced magic in all forms, it was nothing more than a droplet of water in the vast ocean. But to an elf that had trained and embraced technology, it was creating a conflicting effect similar to 'The Thrust'. The Thrust effect is a massive explosion that forms when both magic and technology are combined.

With each attack, Robyn was feeling the conflicting fatigue of a small Thrust effect within her. It was making her vision blur, her reflexes slow. It was making her whole body stiffen like a rigid plank or dwarven stone. She was in trouble, another attack could fell her. Robyn's thoughts went to moments of joy when she neared death. 'My Valpra, please save me' were the last thoughts in Robyn's mind. But to the fortune, someone had come to save her.

CHAPTER 45
THE VALPRA

'By the pulse,' thought Torbiro, as he cursed and assessed the situation with Fameborn and Robyn. Sure, Fameborn was his commander and Robyn was wearing rogue-like clothes. No, it was all wrong. Why were they both fighting? They were on the same side. Both knights, both warriors in this war and both from Traytos. With a very loud, disgruntled grunt, Torbiro yelled, 'What are you idiots doing?' To Torbiro's misfortune – or one could also say 'fortune', depends on how you look at it – no one had heard him yell over the clash of steel and cries of battle. Not even Memyra, who was right beside him. Torbiro was filled with anxiety, frustration and confusion at the situation unfolding before him. He needed to stop this, but how?

I needed to stop the commander, but I also needed to save Robyn from the commander. How am I to aid one and not betray the other?

As more and more questions bombarded Torbiro's mind and as his eyes darted back and forth to the situation, something unexpected happened. Before he knew it, Torbiro was upside down, lying on his back, facing the clouds. His right cheek throbbed as if someone had just punched him. But the questions had stopped and an idea struck him. A possible solution. A method to stop the madness. It was crude, but plausible. His idea was not simple at all, but it would stop the chaos. In the few moments from formulating his plan and listing the priorities in order, Memyra had picked him up and started to brush off much of the dust on 'her' cloak. She had known Torbiro all her life and she knew he needed to be forcibly 'jogged' out of his reverie or his confusion. Otherwise, her friend would just get lost in his thoughts and there was no time.

Within a few moments, Torbiro had asked Memyra for help. Before Torbiro had explained the details of his plan, Memyra had agreed to it. She knew him well and knew this plan was going to be one of his harebrained schemes. Therefore, it was going to be fun. She had to stop Torbiro talking about the intricate details of measured distances and the reasons why he was going with this plan. She had asked for a simple explanation, but every time Torbiro would answer, he would explain his loyalty to his homeland and the pride a knight should maintain. But such policies did not apply or concern Memyra and to quicken Torbiro's explanation, she forcibly grabbed her friend from under his chin and squeezed his cheeks with her thumb and forefinger and dragged him to the scene of his friend fighting a crazed human knight.

Understanding the need for haste, Torbiro explained his plan to Memyra with three words. Distract, attack and push. The plan was simple but made complex due to Torbiro's over analysing the situation and formulating all the variables. Torbiro had made another brilliant idea, to distract his opponent and drive them away, saving his friend and confusing his enemy. Though it would have been a lot easier just to kill the foolish knight and his comrades in Memyra's mind, she could not help but feel the excitement for one of Torbiro's plans.

CHAPTER 46
HYPER SONIC HALFLINGS

'Myra is in position and with my signal, we will save Robyn and Commander Fameborn from their misunderstandings,' Torbiro had thought as he braced himself on the shoulders of his friend. The both of them were on an adjoining slope opposite the cave Robyn was near. She was carrying a small child like a bundle of hay and was being assaulted by Commander Fameborn. There were a lot of fallen logs and bushes in this little outcrop which would pose as a problem. But Myra argued it was fine.

Her confidence might be the end of my plan, as well as the life of Robyn. Commander's forces were also there, but most of them were extremely tired. Some soldiers were inebriated by sheer will to push on and others were recovering from an intoxication of potent liquor. They were, in a word, sluggish and insane. My plan was to use a distraction and drive them away. I gave the signal to Myra and we were off.

With my imagination, I transformed into a flock of native birds and with the help of Myra's cloak, the image was set. Upon my signal, Myra used her rocket boots and dashed extremely fast. It was hard to concentrate, but I managed. From a small bush to a large tree stump to a fallen log, both of us dashed to towards our targets. First, it would be to deal with the soldiers. Confusing them would be easy. They were in such a paranoid state that a flyby scare should be enough. I commanded Myra to turn left and right, here and there, to make our movement erratic, like a berserk swarm of gnomes on pay day. But Myra was ignoring my orders and was going in at random.

Aaaaaaaaaaaaaaaaaaaaaaaahhhhhhhhhhhhhhhhh.

Torro, you have to sound like a falcona…

I told you to turn left… T-tree…

Wow… that was close and your illusion is kind of gnomish.

Gnomish!!! How dare you, Myra? They're black falconas…

What? Blast forward… ok, then full power.

Myra slow down! Flower powder?

Yasss! <insert sinister grin here> Maximum charge…

No Nooo Noooooo. Myra listen to me. I said. SLOW. DOWN.

Super Drive? That'll be fun.

Super drive what?

Think bird Torro. Your cloak!

Aaaaaaaaaaaaaaaaaaaaaaaahhhhhhhhhhhhhhhhh.

With the two halflings whizzing around the soldiers at hypersonic speeds, chaos was created. At first Torbiro's plans were working the soldiers to boredom. Some saw the flock of falconas as a sign of peace, like a relaxed stroll with a lover or a loved one. But once Memyra had taken control and gone beyond the speed of sight, the birds vanished, but not altogether. They simply transformed into a multitude of afterimages. The new problem was the rate at which Torbiro was now zipping and zooming past the soldiers. The acceleration was too much for him to have enough concentration to hold the illusion as one thing. After the first thousand passes at Mach speed, his falconas turned from one animal to the next. Sometimes the illusion would be muck rats or gnome-hybrids. These images were still in a swarm and with Torbiro screaming at the sight of every near-missed tree. The sound produced by the terrified halfling was of an even high pitched shrill. It was like a gnomish ballad. Too many words and not an understanding for pitch control. It was horrible. The soldiers, incapacitated by soothing birds, woke up with a fright. This was worse than battles they had experienced before. As for the soldiers and knights held up by their tenacious wills, they were at odds with attacking both each other and the afterimages of Torbiro's illusions.

The noise was so ear shattering that a few of the knights had indeed distracted them, but due to the intensity, many of the knights were inflicted with deafness to the point of defeat. In a matter of a few clicks, all those under Fameborn's command had been subdued. Torbiro and Memyra had won, but the rocket boots had malfunctioned and the brakes had broken under extreme pressures. Memyra could see the soldiers had been defeated but there was the next target. Commander Fameborn himself.

Moving at 100% speed of the rocket boots' capacity was not only dangerous but completely reckless. Memyra though, was having the time of her life. The rush, the pressure, the excitement and the danger made her grin. A smile of reckless excitement. She knew the next part of the plan, but moving at this speed would not have the same effect as outside in the wide-open wilderness. In a cave tunnel, it would have grave effects on the occupants, either in the tunnel or farther in the cave. She needed to stop and reset her boots. But the brakes did not respond. She thought they were just delayed and activated them again and again. But the brakes were not responding. This was bad.

Speeding at a deadly velocity, riding on top of Memyra in a magical harness was not only dangerous, but it was completely insane. Why had Myra gone faster? I'm going to die! Why wasn't Myra stopping? I'm going to die! I knew I should have detailed the plan more to Myra. This wouldn't have happened if she just stuck to the plan. These words ran through Torbiro's mind as they completed the first part of his plan. But why were we not stopping? We could just stop and reset the plan. Torbiro tried to talk through the pressure and wind, but it was extremely difficult. Like trying to swim in syrup but having your arms and legs chained to orcish iron. It was impossible, but he could still signal Myra by tapping her back. There was less wind pressure there.

Next time we do this, I have to remember to wear a ping-talker. Ping-talkers were communication devices that orcs and dwarves used when working in a loud environment, such as welding metals or drilling in a mine. But there was a flaw with ping-talkers, they could only be used by two people. It would have been nice to talk to Myra about the plan, but what can I do?

After ten or so laps on the Dip Hills, Myra had made her revised version of Torbiro's plan to rescue Robyn. The problem was the speed. How could she catch Robyn without killing her? We were going too fast and it seemed that grabbing things would ignite them. This was a problem for sure, but she needed to do something quick. No pun intended. But after a while, Myra had noticed Torbiro was indeed alive and was trying to talk to her. The tapping on her back was not random, but a form of remorse mode – or Morse code for the rest of you – that Torbiro had used when he was younger and weaker.

He had tapped on my back a message of his 'updated' plan. His plan was to save Robyn by creating a whirling wind around her and catch her, like a glider or a bird in flight. Another crazy plan.

CHAPTER 47
VANISHING ELVES

As I stood above the accursed fiend, I prepared an ending strike. My thoughts were of justice and may this abomination, this spellcaster, this elf be condemned by the holy blade of my Traytos. I could see the fear and anger in her eyes, but justice needed to be served. I gave the elf a chance of redemption, a chance to change her wicked path and follow in the righteous true path, but she threw her look of contempt. Her last chance wasted. My hand of mercy, of charity and of grace, disregarded. With regret and frustration on my face, I swung my holy blade. I cut her as she rolled to the side. With nowhere to go, she threw her spawn and cast it to the inner cave, where I could hear my frightened men. The thoughts of torture from those magicians, those harlots, those false prophets angered me.

A tear fell down my cheek from the thought of the horrible atrocities the wicked elves were doing to my men. It gave me a fury. A fury so overwhelming, it turned to an energy to prevail. To defeat the wicked. To destroy the source and to drown the painful thoughts out. I raised my blade and struck again. The attack was so full of fury, I must have eradicated the elf in a single slash. The assault was indeed quick, so quick it was a blinding flash. My foe had been defeated but more were farther in the cave. I needed to save my men.

With all the adrenaline and momentum of my prior victory, I pushed on. I saw the small spawn up ahead and with another attack, it was destroyed, leaving only its ashes on my blade. I continued towards the entrance to the cavern and there I saw it. My men, blocking my path as though they were protecting the enemy. No, that couldn't be. They must have been put under control. It must be the doings of the spell slingers. Those unethical demons, using my own men against me. I needed to set them free. I shouted a warning and pressed my assault. In but a few cuts, slashes and thrusts, my foes were gone. Some of my men were still in shock, but I needed to free them all.

Once the dust cleared, the only people left were the freed soldiers, as well as some of my own knights. They had joined the fray and had helped vanquish the evil elves. We had won. Victory for Traytos. Defeat for Batarians. It was time to celebrate. The men did need the rest and though the battle must continue elsewhere, these men needed this. A banquet for the victory and a report for the commander and a tale for the people.

CHAPTER 48
HYPERSONIC GNOME?

In no time at all, Torbiro and Memyra had rescued all the elves out of the small cave. But due to the method, they could not put them in one place. They had to pick them up quickly and drop them off safely. But doing so was very erratic. In fact, it was random. They had no control over where they could place those elves. Travelling at hypersonic speed was not an easy task. Nor was it safe for the passengers. Even with Torbiro shouting at Memyra, where and when to circle so he could 'gently' release an elf. But picking those elves up was the easy task, it was similar to dropping them off. Picking them up, the two halflings had time to approach more carefully. Robyn was first and she was dropped off in the eastern pass, which was on the other side of the Dip Hills. The little elven boy was next and dropped off in what Torbiro had thought was the northern edge. But Memyra had no interest in coordinating and just wanted to finish the task at hand. One by one, they saved the elves as well as 'stolen' some travelling gear.

Once the task was done – the elves unaware of how and who had rescued them – Torbiro and Memyra needed to stop. But the brakes were ironically broken. The intense speed had damaged them beyond use or repair. So while Memyra was enjoying the rush of the wind, naturally Torbiro was in a terrified panic. Although Memyra and Torbiro were in different states of mind, their thoughts were as one. How were they going to stop?

In Memyra's mind. By the pulse, this idea was great, but now that we actually need to stop. This was a terrible idea. Oh, well. What's done is done. I can only think of two ways to get out of this situation, but I know Torro. He won't approve. One: I could slip out of the boots and hope we land on a flat savannah of soft and moist grass, but landing on it would probably kill Torro and seriously injury me. Two: I could use a spell to freeze the boots and slow us down, but I don't like cold feet and Torro would probably get launched off his perch and die on impact. Hmm. What should I do? I know what I should do next time, though. We need a Talk-a-box. So I can at least talk to him. Shouting is just not a realistic way to have a chat. I wonder what he's thinking. Huh… what's that up ahead? Is that a gnome?

In Torbiro's mind. By the pulse, this was a terrible idea. I shouldn't have come up with the rocket distraction idea and now we need to stop. How was this a great idea, anyway? I think I need a new pair of pants. I must have wet myself several times. Coming close to death at every turn can kill a man. But having to grab and catch elves was insane. How did I manage all of that with Myra without a single word? Ahhhh, Tree. Branch. Duck, Torbiro, duck. What in chaos was Myra doing? Ahhh. I can only think of two ways to get out of this situation safely, but none of them could work without putting Memyra in danger. One: I could push down the back of the basket I was sitting in and slam Memyra to the ground so the boots would be pointed towards the sky, but it could kill my friend and I don't want that. Two: I could jump out of the basket and roll to safety, but then Memyra would still be going at top speed. I couldn't leave her alone. That's not how a knight should act. Think Torro, think. There has to be a way. Huh!? What's that? Why is Memyra going towards it? Now that can't be, can it? Is that a gnome?

Both halflings were perplexed at the sight ahead of them. It was a gnome. It was a gnome riding a box. It was a gnome riding a box with valves, tubes and several exhaust vents. Kind of like an engine or maybe a rocket. But the rocket was more like a missile that humans used to launch to declare war. The rocket was no bigger than a small market cart, used to carry produce from a warehouse to a market stall. It had a small cockpit, big enough for the gnome, but it did not have a hatch or maybe it was missing. The gnome was also in strange attire. It wore tattered wizard's robes, flopping about from the wind at hypersonic speed. Its attire was not functional at all. Its hat covered its head and wrapped around it like a scarf. Its robes were so loose they wrapped around the creature like they were strangling it.

As shocking as the sight of a creature heading towards them, no less a gnome, at close to the same speed, the two intrepid adventurers needed to solve the issue of stopping before it caused them irreparable damage to themselves and the surrounding environment. Memyra was the first to stop looking at the endangered gnome and its insidious device. She returned to her senses and thoughts to solve their current conundrum. Torbiro, being more concerned than curious, wanted to make sure this creature was alright and made an attempt at communication. He shouted and shouted to get a response from the gnome, but the hypersonic wind was just too strong for the concerned halfling. As for the gnome, it had noticed our hero but had no control over the machine it rode on. Which meant very little, as the situation was quite dire for both parties.

In no more than a few ticks, the already dire situation had a turn for the worst. The gnome was heading towards our heroes in a perpendicular direction and was now on a direct collision course. Memyra had weaved and turned to avoid the creature but it seemed to move closer and closer to them as though it was trying to eliminate them. On the other hand, Torbiro had managed to communicate with him by using his magic cloak. At first Torbiro had used verbal methods but it not only exhausted his throat but also damaged his tongue and mouth due to the pressure of the air. Using the cloak was a dangerous idea, as there was technology nearby and he was worried about what chaos it might cause. Unfortunately for Torbiro, his idea had caused both his salvation and his peril. His salvation was being able to communicate with the creature and his peril was the machine the gnome rode on had malfunctioned, but Torbiro didn't know that. The movement of the rocket continued to swerve left and right in such chaos, there were many opportunities for a near miss here and there. But then, out of the eyes of creation, an explosion.

CHAPTER 49
FAMEBORN'S MARCH

After the battles with the dishonourable spell slingers, my men and I received new orders to rescue the beautiful princess of my land. The shining star in the twilight, Dawn of Traytos. She had been captured by the nefarious fiends of Bataros and our scouts had reported a newly found sighting of my bride to be. I mobilised the troops and called for reinforcements to siege the infernal tower of magic. The path ahead was reported to hold deadly traps and terrain that would hinder the mighty siege machines from taking the tower. I say, for Dawn we must push on.

CHAPTER 50
NEW ORDERS

Commander Fameborn had just finished his victory celebration when a report came by a drill messenger called sphrill. A drill messenger was a type of digging machine with a single purpose. To deliver a message, via a direct path, underground. The machine was quite efficient and it would not be interrupted by means of magic or outside forces. Now you might say that travelling underground would have its problems, but the device was a sharp and dangerous weapon once it had a message to deliver. Nothing would stop its journey. The device was spherical and had burrowing blades all around it. How did it work? Well, that is another can of gnomes to explain its operation. As the inventors of this device were earth gnomes. Earth gnomes were a very dangerous breed of the chaotic gnome sub-race. as they had an affinity with both machines and magic. Many believe they were the cause of the historical 'Thrust' that has divided the planet into the great sectors.

The sphrill would come from the ground and burst out without warning. This device was not commonly used unless it was an emergency, as it would cause much havoc in its journey and arrival. Lucky for Fameborn, he was the beacon for the device and had a platform prepared for its arrival. Unfortunately for the commander's men, who were not notified of such messages, they were the bearers of its assault. With his soldier's cries of dismay as the sphrill approached the commander's camp, Fameborn received it at the cost of a few soldiers. Though Fameborn could care less for the 'minor' injuries of his men, he still needed them to fight, he needed them to do the leg work and he needed them to take out the small fry while he gloriously took care of the greater prize. He would tell the tale of defeating all the foes in his way, to come out triumphantly on top. But he would never mention those that actually fought in the frontlines while he pushed his troops forward.

The way forward for Fameborn at least was straight. Even if it meant ploughing through traps. Even it meant losing large numbers of troops, he had no concern for the weak and incompetent. He only wanted soldiers that would follow his example and follow orders. Most soldiers were highly trained and had little expectations on the outcome of their life, but more on the outcome of the mission as a whole. If the mission succeeded, then they succeeded. But after the battle with the mages in the Dip Hills, only his loyal knights had the same conviction as the commander. The soldiers had seen the war with Bataros as a way to propel their careers to the next level. Unfortunately, expectations and reality were far from each other. A soldier's life was more like discarded trash in the streets and slums rather than a pawn on a chess board. Which meant that morale was very low for the soldiers. They all saw the outcome if they continued, but they also knew the result if they fled from battle. It was a lose-lose situation.

The message the commander had received was a report detailing the location of the princess and the dangers of the surrounding tower. Once he had looked at its contents, usually a commander or general or a leader of an army would inform some of the details of what to do next. The message even warned him about a certain outcast that was trying to thwart his efforts, but what Fameborn did next would threaten the plans of the king. He disregarded these warnings and ordered his men to charge at the tower of evil. Destroy all enemies of Traytos and rescue the princess.

CHAPTER 51
INFORMATION FROM THE KING

Report 23 – 4th Cycle of the 2nd Toggle

To Commander Fameborn,

I congratulate you on your victory against the vile enemies of Traytos. But I must inform you we have received news of the whereabouts of my dear daughter Dawn. Please, I request that you send a strong but small unit of knights to save her. I would be honoured if you would lead these men and come out with my Dawn in your arms.

I wish to learn that my soldiers have served you well in the conquest, but I must heed that I will need my soldiers to return to guard and protect Traytos. I have also learned there are many shadows making their way to thwart your efforts in saving my Dawn. Please be swift. Signed King of Traytos, Aroduct Golem master.

PS: If you find a wandering pair of halflings, I want you to execute them. They are traitors to Traytos and betrayers of Bataros. BEWARE of them, they are dangerous and if you bring their pathetic corpses back, I will reward you beyond your wildest imagination.

CHAPTER 52
DARK RALLY

The letter was quickly discarded and the commander leaped out of his protective tower to land with a powerful stance. A crash and the crumbling of the ground upon such an impact made a lot of dirt and dust to spread to the surrounding area. Fameborn was a man for the theatrics and wanted to make his mark. He certainly made his mark on the soldiers he landed on. He unwittingly killed two heavily injured soldiers by the sphrill, as it came through the camp. As the commander emerged out of the dust and dirt, he made his command known. Shouting orders to his men, shouting orders to his knights and shouting orders to his able-bodied soldiers to ready themselves for the next conquest. The conquest to the tower.

Many of the soldiers were still disoriented by the chaos and havoc of the sphrill. Some soldiers were aiding those that were injured by the deadly machine and when their commander started to order them around, they felt much dismay and negative emotions. Many of them only signed up for the war against the mages of Bataros. Many soldiers still had duties to take care of in Traytos and some even had assignments much more urgent than rescuing a damsel in distress. The able knights were all for the next venture, as thoughts of glory and honour swooned their minds. Fameborn too, was one of them. He had disregarded the important points of the report and pushed on. Not with a small unit of trusted allies, but with the whole army of Traytos to rescue a single girl. It was a noble act but a foolish one as the army was needed to protect the kingdom and its surrounding 'investments'.

A soldier of notable rank approached Fameborn to discuss the plans for some of the soldiers to return to protect their land. The soldier was well known in the ranks. She was an elf, but unlike many of her race, she was not of noble birth. She was an abominable half-breed. Her other half was not of human origins. But she had the esteem of Robyn clans and the Oakyn clans. Commander Peren had even accepted her as an elf and sister within his own Ambyr clan. She had the pride of the giants and the strength of the dragons. Many of the female soldiers saw her as a role model. They knew her as Rubee Scartlyt but those that had the chance to fight by her side knew her as Ru. Short and simple. She wore a soldier's garb and she too was injured. Dark blood dripped from her wounds as she approached Commander Fameborn. Her fiery hair drooped from the lack of care and her determined eyes burned with fury, like that of a dragon.

'Commander, Sir,' said Ru with heavy determination. As Rubee tried to get the attention of her commander, unfortunately, her words had fallen on deaf ears.

'Commander Fameborn, Sir,' said Ru with a much louder tone and even more urgency in her voice. But again, Fameborn ignored her. Many of the soldiers were there at her attention and understood her intention. So they looked towards their commander, willing him to notice such a well-known soldier among his men.

'Commander Fameborn, Sir!!! We have more pressing matters to take care of back in Traytos to continue the fight,' said Ru with as much gusto and formal grit she could muster at being ignored more than once. She had been given orders by commander Peren to return to Traytos. And she also knew many of the ranked soldiers had been given direct orders to return to Traytos to head back to their daily duties.

Coming out of his fantasies with charging forward defeating fiends, demons and dark creatures, swooping into the dungeons to rescue the princess from her assailants, Fameborn finally took notice of a rather rambunctious soldier of a much lower rank. She had no right to interrupt him in these grandiose plans of victory and honour. So not only did he use his 'temporary' rank to his advantage, but he also looked down on her. For being nothing like him, a pure bred human, the superior race. She was an elf and a half-breed at that. And she was only a measly sergeant. How dare she break the code of honour by addressing him at all? With a face only a smug rich child could ever muster, he addressed her concerns.

'Stand down. SOLDIER!' said Fameborn with a commanding tone. His face showed he did not care for her demands at all. He wore a nasty grin as he looked down at her. His face was darkened by the shadows of his height and his unprofessionalism.

'Commander Fameborn, Sir. I have other orders from…' said Rubee with determination and esteem that she was following the correct protocol when addressing was concerned. She was rudely interrupted by the commander in mid-sentence. Rubee could feel the negative emotions from her commander, knowing he was wrongfully using his rank and power to undermine her.

'I. SAID. STAND. DOWN. Do you not understand the situation?' said Fameborn as he put his foot down. Commanding soldiers was easy as a soldier only needed to follow his orders. After all, he was their leader.

Rubee tried to get another word in, but with the motions of the commander's fingers in a circular fashion, she had been surrounded and restrained. Rubee was being held by an older knight. She knew not to resist, as she had not done anything wrong. She wore a stern face and tried to keep her emotions hidden. The knight restraining her had her by the arms in a sleeper hold. Rubee was shorter than the old knight and knew she could easily get out of this situation, as her size did not show her strength.

Rubee was quickly disarmed by other knights of the commander's unit. Her weapon and shield were removed from her side. Her boots were also rudely removed from her feet. This was wrong, very wrong indeed. What was Fameborn doing? As strange as this situation was, she kept a stern but determined look on her face. The commander slowly approached while he waved his fingers left and right to clear a path. The commander was now face to face with Rubee and what he said next sent chills through the spines of all who saw this.

'Your name soldier?!!!' said Fameborn with a sinister tone.

'Sergeant Rubee Scartlyt,' said Rubee in reply.

'Well Sergeant, I hearby dismiss you of duty. For your insubordination to my orders,' said Fameborn with the tone of an executioner.

'Sir? I don't understand. What insubordination?' said Rubee in confusion.

Fameborn had turned around to address the rest of the soldiers to show what happens to those that disobey. He then pulled his sword out from his side with menacing dread. Fameborn then lifted the heavy weapon and casually rested it on his shoulders for a dramatic show of strength.

'My loyal soldiers, we are to march to the tower to rescue the gracious Princess of Traytos. But this wench has dark thoughts of undermining my orders and operations with false orders from less righteous commanders,' said Fameborn, addressing his men. He then lifted his blade and took a flourished step back to extend his blade, while using it to point at the restrained elf.

'She wishes to thwart the glory and victory we all deserve. She is a harlot, a half-breed and an enemy to the conquest to reach our true purpose. To save our Princess. Princess Dawn,' said Fameborn with dramatic phrasing.

'I, Wilbur L. Fameborn, declare those that disobey must be punished,' Fameborn continued with his commanding presence. At this point, Rubee had started to panic and stress. She did not know this man, but there were always rumours of the 'Fameborn clan'. Most of the rumours were of men in the family being righteous and courageous in battles. The acts of immeasurable kindness and charity were also implied. But there were dark rumours as well. They were less known and the only ones that could tell wouldn't be able to a second time. These dark rumours told a different story of how the Fameborns were actually a ruthless band of Twilight knights that would steal the 'fame' of others and make it their own.

Rubee was now struggling to escape as Fameborn made his speech, but for some reason the knight restraining her was stronger than her. It was impossible. She had the ancient strength of giants and dragons. How could an old man hold her with such strength? Was it magic? She could not tell. After Fameborn had finished his speech, he had turned back towards her, his sword raised high and ready to strike her down.

'Do you have any last words? Whore!!' said Fameborn with a dark and sinister tone. Fear and anguish now showed on Rubee's face. She showed regret and confusion. The stern determination lost and the strength she relied on gone. She gave her reply as loud as she could. 'Liar!'

Fameborn, with eyes dark, full of murderous intent, brought down his sword on the helpless elvish sergeant. She had broken command and disobeyed his orders. Her punishment was just. Her death would remind the rest of the masses that he was justice. She would not be a martyr for disobedience, she would not be remembered for her acts, but for the fear in her eyes as she tried to escape her fate. The sword came down swiftly but had not killed her as he had intended. Fameborn thought the half-breed would be cut in two, right down the middle, but her skin had been tougher than anticipated and Fameborn needed to exert more force. In doing so, he had also killed the old knight holding her in position. From the adrenalin of the kill, he had forgotten him as well. Turning in righteous triumph, he addressed his soldiers and ordered them to leave the weak and march to the tower.

The path ahead was filled with treacherous and deadly traps. Some were buried underground, some hidden in plain sight, while others were hanging invisible in the sky. The soldiers who had witnessed the atrocity of the commander's actions and argued against the cruelty of the deed, had been given the same fate as the honourable sergeant. While the others that had obeyed knew the fate that had befallen them. The rest of the soldiers that had not witnessed the scene followed their commander begrudgingly. At the end of the trapped fields, the army's march was halted by an explosion that killed seven fighters and injured thirty bowmen and gunmen.

The commander took notice of this immediately as he saw his limited mortality flash before his eyes. He ordered his men to stop. But ordered some of the weak and injured to sacrifice their lives to save the strong. They did not agree straight away, but when forced by the death of another, they marched forward.

The traps were there to stop large armies from approaching the tower. King Aroduct had designed it that way long ago and did not want his soldiers and his inventions to meet. It would have been a waste of good materials. But because Fameborn was such a fool, he had done just that. Explosions occurred often and lives were lost. More lives were lost to the insidious traps than the war with the mages. Only a small handful of soldiers remained by Fameborn's side by the time they had reached the camps near the base of the tower. The rest of the fallen soldiers were all either left behind or forgotten.

CHAPTER 53
TRAP OF DESIRE

The sounds of explosions and cries of soldiers for help echoed in the background as Fameborn emerged out of the trapped fields. He was accompanied by a small band of strong survivors. Many of who had no skills to besiege a tower controlled by mages. All the survivors were warriors and knights, all brawn and no brains. After a short breather, Fameborn ordered another charge at the lower camps. As they made their approach, some haggard as they were, pushed on with pure will and cause. Reaching the first tent, they struck like wild animals, causing havoc and destruction, then the next tent, killing and rending with their swords and axes. They split up to trample as much as they could before the tower. Blood spurted with each cut, bones snapped with each strike and adrenaline surged with each stride. As the warriors' weapons dripped with the blood of their enemy in its spherical form, reaching the hard dry stone of the ground, the warriors all roared in fury. The taste of victory just short of their lips, they slumped towards the ground. Their backs straightened and they looked to the skies at the top of the tower and saw the damsel in distress waiting for her rescuer. The soldiers marched to the gates and then found themselves back to the edge of the clearing again. Fameborn, not noticing the change, ordered another charge.

Perhaps twice or three times the soldiers had charged with the energy from the previous attempt, but after the fifth time they no longer have the same ferocity to attack. They had exhausted their energy and struggled to take even the smallest steps or lift their master weapons of choice off the ground. Fameborn's soldiers were tired. There was nothing else to it. Why had Fameborn been the only one unaffected? No one could answer such a question. Indeed, no one could even muster the thought of the question of why. Every assault and every attack of the camps below had been reset and exhausted even more energy from surviving soldiers.

Fameborn, with all the energy of rescuing the princess, had ordered the charge to attack the sleeping camp below the tower. His troop had followed him to the gate and they had defeated and vanquished every threat of the camp site. As he entered the gate, he ordered the charge to push on to defeat yet another incoming wave of enemies, but with each wave, his men reacted with less and less ferocity. What was on their minds that they could not push past such weak foes? He ordered the charge again and again and again. With each push, not a single one of them had gone down, but they lacked more and more conviction. They were losing, but Fameborn, not knowing what was actually going on, kept ordering a fatal charge. His men looked at him like they'd fought ten or perhaps fifteen battles non-stop, but that couldn't be true, it was just waves of enemies. As Fameborn looked back to his troop, he saw them change with every glance.

At first, they appeared with the muscles and strength of survivors emerging out from the dreaded field of traps. Then slowly they appeared to shrink, they seemed to deflate. At first, their muscles were bulging with masculine power, then shrivelled to fatty loose skin, then to dried out husks. Their demeanour had also been changed with each attack, from eagerness so ready to win, to tired determination so ready to rest, then to dead eyes exhausted from years of torment so ready to simply give up. His soldiers were suffering not from each order, but from the land at which they stood. The only difference between the commander and his soldiers was a level of stubbornness, but he too, had been affected by the mysterious energies of the tower. Soon he too would slump down, lacking the energy to push forward like the dry husks they were all turning into. What was going on?

CHAPTER 54
KITRETH OF THE FLAME

Sitting at a desk by the window of the highest floor on the tower of rivals, Kitreth waited for a signal of the approach for her kidnapped cousin. She had arrived at this 'abandoned' tower right after her first meeting with her uncle, the king of Traytos. Her own father had ordered her to wait for a clumsy mage to arrive with her cousin and she was tasked to make sure Dawn was healed but locked up safely. She had been waiting for two days and her patience was starting to wear thin, as she had experiences and rituals back home to attend to. But the annual culling ritual needed to be attended to. Kitreth was overjoyed when her father had invited her to join this year's culling ritual. She was overjoyed to meet her cousin and her uncle. She had been properly groomed on the history and politics of both Bataros and her neighbouring kingdom, Traytos.

The true history concerning Traytos and Bataros was a well-kept secret among the monarchy, as it would cause more than a stir among the common folk and the lesser races. To the common folk, the kingdom had been split due to war and opposing conflict. But to Kitreth, the true history of the split was due to a method of controlling the masses. The reason the kings of old had separated the kingdoms in two was the constant population growth due to refugees from other sectors. Some sectors were being affected by the aftereffects of the 'thrust' while others were being affected by wars and conflicts of the two factions of magic and technology all over the world. Due to the kind and generous nature of the leaders of this sector, which allowed refugees and outcasts to migrate, this sector had become too over-populated. There were great plans and inventive solutions to this problem, but none of them had worked. So, a decision had to be made and in the past the ruler of this sector had not even been a monarchy, instead it was governed as a republic with different representatives leading different parts of the sector. In fact, this tower used to be called the tower of rivals because it was the place where rivalries of different sectors would solve their differences. Some would be solved using words and long discussions, while others were solved with martial combat. There were rules for everything and the archives below the tower served as a storage chamber for it, an ancient library of how conflicts could be systematically resolved. Peacefully or otherwise.

Kitreth had these very thoughts in her mind as she waited for her cousin. She had been a curious and inquisitive child, meaning she broke the rules a lot. What rules? You might say. Why every rule that would limit her imagination or task. As a child who grew up in a castle of mages, she was spoiled but with a sadistic mother in tow, growing up was not one filled with good tidings and noble grooming but a dark upbringing no child should ever experience. Death, suffering and torture are notions not spoken of to children brought up in a wealthy upbringing. In short, death and dark topics are censored or sugar-coated to ease the explanation. Although many suffer the reality of death through wars, sickness and untimely ends, Kitreth was taught about death at a young age of three, by her mother no less. Her father, on the other hand, had taught her about life, which would confuse any child with what was right or wrong. Her mother wanted her daughter to know the world as she knew it. The reality of life. It was a cruel and terrifying place, filled with dark rituals, human sacrifices and wars. Instead of teaching Kitreth how to be a mage of high standing, she taught her the ways of the warlock. Daily lessons about ritual sacrifices, using the already condemned prisoner as test subjects. Daily lessons about the finer ways of how to torture a man or woman or child, to get information from them. As well as daily chores in cleaning the blood, guts and sinew of an execution ground, to understanding the innards of malnourished, sickly and over fed criminals of the world.

Her father, on the other had was kind-hearted and naïve in nature. So he would spoil Kitreth in all manner of things. He had not fought with his wife on how to raise their child, he was happy just having the family he now had. He would teach Kitreth how to cast spells of light and power. Spells that could destroy as well as create. They would practice spells in the courtyard of the castle grounds, they would share secrets by exploring the passages of their home. They were both filled with smiles and laughter, in all the accomplishments, no matter how big or small. Even the smallest achievement, remembering something she had forgotten, her father would praise and honour her. She was her father's daughter, after all. He was always full of smiles when she was around. He even hid his own cowardice when his wife had taught her the ways of death and torture. Praising her, even though he knew it was wrong. Kitreth was a cherished child, in all aspects of her parentage. She was praised by her father and disciplined by her mother.

Kitreth had been waiting for her cousin to arrive for three days, when it hit her she shouldn't be waiting for the underlings but instead preparing the next stage of this scheme. Her uncle wouldn't mind, she had thought, as waiting long hours doing nothing was a waste of time and energy. Energy that could be spent on an experiment or practicing spell casting or perfecting ways to interrogate prisoners. She decided waiting three hours was enough and headed downstairs to do something. This would break her promise to her uncle, but who cares? Cousin Dawn was going to be my prisoner. No warden ever waited for their prisoner: they simply came to them in due time.

Breaking the promise of the great Golem master was like breaking the rules. It was easy for Kitreth. She had broken practically every rule in her kingdom, which had a contradiction. Her mother had taught her to be merciless to the poor and the rich alike and her father had taught her that compassion was needed to understand all types of people. This simply meant she needed to be nice and ruthless to everyone who fell into that category. But to Kitreth's understanding, it could not be done. You could only be nice or ruthless. She had learnt this with every tutor that taught the history of her kingdom and subjects about the world, including laws, cultures and beliefs. Even the contracts and quests she had taken from local guilds had certain regulations required to complete a task. She had ignored them and completed what was necessary. No need for equations, just the answer. No need for understanding the significance of tribal rituals, just results. If someone wanted to fight, let them. Why stop it? That way, the stupid could die out and those needed were left to their own devices. So, following the exact plan of her uncle was too much of an inconvenience, instead she tasked a minion to do the deed.

As Dawn arrived in her shocked state, she was met with not her intended captor but one of Kitreth's lackeys, a blind goblin who had been instructed to 'scare' the poor girl. But this goblin had been used for a few too many cruel experiments that she had very little intelligence left. She had been used for target practice, torture examples, trap tester, lobotomies, transmutations, transmorphisms and the occasional stress reliever. Death was an occupational requirement for most goblins, as they were a species considered a pest more than a people. So dying to test a trap's deadliness was just another part of the job for goblins. The minion tasked to 'care' for Dawn was practically a zombie at this point, as Kitreth was taught never to waste life in any shape or form. But Kitreth was also lazy in a sense, in that learning names of creatures was a pain and a waste of time. When the goblin was ordered to scare and threaten Dawn, she had only understood a few words of the human language, so she only understood that killing Dawn was bad. And that anything else was fine. So of course, the goblin attacked Dawn at every opportunity, every chance, and every time she had had no jobs to do, but would never kill Dawn.

As you might think, there was a problem with this situation, as

Kitreth had been instructed to teach Dawn the lesson that the world was cruel and punishments happened to those who were foolish. Not a lesson that goblins were evil creatures. Because they weren't and everyone in their right mind had known this in every kingdom or empire or sector. Goblins were a resource to be used or exploited. Much like the prejudice of the less fortunate, by the rich and wealth, or the prejudice of giant races being savages, by the isolated and paranoid, every race and social standing had their myths and legends. The rich, believing the poor would rob them for their riches or their jobs, had been a threat to young nobles and lords to be wary. While creatures that kept to themselves could only read about other races from whatever source they could get. Most of the time, those texts were meant for entertainment – much like this book – or war propaganda. So back to the story, Dawn was attacked by a blind goblin to the point of death, but would be healed by another goblin to not anger mistress Kitreth.

Kitreth had ordered her minions to report everything done to Dawn, every word Dawn said, every plea she requested and every demand she made. But her goblins had only nodded to avoid being punished. So Kitreth never received a report concerning Dawn, the supply of the goblins' healing potions soon ran out. After thirteen days, Kitreth's goblins had run out of healing salves, healing potions and bandages. Too afraid to ask for more, the goblins decided to steal from the lab. They knew which potions to steal, since many of them had been the ones to test such decoctions. They weren't smart enough to read, but their primal instincts had been heightened, such as smell and touch. But since these goblins had been domesticated – in essence due to the cruel treatment they endured – they weren't very quiet or stealthy in stealing those potions. This caused more problems than just asking for more potions. For the goblins had ransacked the alchemist's laboratory for healing potions and they had also destroyed many of the delicate brews Kitreth and her sorcerers were preparing for the rite of cunning.

Two weeks had passed since Dawn had arrived. Kitreth had awoken earlier by two hours due to the noise from the incoming soldiers out in the dreaded fields. She was used to not getting much sleep since her early days when her mother was alive. She welcomed the new dawn with more appreciation than most. It was a new day and that meant the next day's progress. Patience was never her strongest virtue, as waiting was hard and boring. Her anticipation was always at its highest just after waking up. It filled her with excitement. She finished her morning ritual more quickly today as the noise from the distance was getting louder and louder with each passing day. Lord Idiotborn and his moron-zealots must be getting close.

I wonder how many lives he wasted in that war uncle set up. I needed to prepare the illusionary traps in front of the tower, so I could provide the report uncle asked of his soon to be idiot son-in-law. Illusions and mind spells are easy enough to cast, but trying to make them non-lethal was another thing entirely. I had my sorcerers prepare the ingredients in the alchemist's laboratory, so they should be ready by now.

As Kitreth headed to her main alchemy laboratory on the third floor, she was witness to the most horrifying sight of them all. All of her experiments ruined. All of the ingredients unorganised and some even destroyed. All her work, all that preparation, all her anticipation lost. But the energy within her was at a high. The joy and anxiety transformed to frenzied rage. Her face transformed slowly from the shock and awe to red wild anger. Her eyes closed and she took a deep calming breath to hide the killing energy bound to explode out from her finger tips.

Furious and upset, she spoke in a dark, heavy tone, much like an automaton or one of the golems her uncle had left on the floors below. With a swift motion, she raised her arm to point to the mess in the hallway as well as the laboratory. She spoke words of alarm and a warning. Only two words could be understood by those not too frightened by the aura of hate that emanated from her. Get out! Then a scream so horrifying most of the staff starting their daily duties were frightened and scared. Most wanted to flee, but the burst of arcane energy overwhelmed them. They were frozen by her emotions and energies combined. Only the goblins, the perpetrators of this whole disaster, were kept in motion for the writhing torture she would apply to the fools.

'Dis nut eye nid? Eye nid da no hurtie drinkie drink,' said the goblin as she grabbed and hoarded vials and flasks of liquid.

'You there!!! Minion number 43. What. Are. You. Doing?' screamed Kitreth with pure menace and malice. Goblins were known to be thick headed, especially ones treated as minions.

'Me! Mistress?' said the goblin in question. She had shock in her voice. The surprise from a servant that puts their actions to question. As though they had been doing the wrong task or accused of disobeying.

'Yes, you fool,' said Kitreth with a snarl. With a single finger raised and dark energies harnessing to that single point, one could see shit was about to go down. Kitreth was preparing a spell to immobilise her minion, but the dark energies would also torture the poor creature. More and more dark energy was concentrating on the tip of Kitreth's finger.

'Eye, loke fur no hurtie drink. Fur new pet of mistress,' said the goblin in confusion. Goblin number 43 did have a name, but Kitreth had no use for it. They were her toys. Things to be used, if they were still useful. But if they had broken, they would be discarded like old toys. The goblin revealed all the potions and elixirs, as well as the leaves of herbs she had found, to her mistress. Goblin number 43 had recklessly carried them in an old sack full of holes. The sack itself seemed to be an old practice dummy's head. The soft cotton or wool that filled the head was emptied out but all the knives and daggers used to strike it had left little holes and pieces of hard but sharp pieces of shrapnel. As goblin number 43 revealed the contents of her bag, she also revealed the nature and damage of those vials. Some were simply nicked and scratched, easy to fix. But many of the vials of irreplaceable elixirs were broken and had mixed with the rare and priceless ingredients.

With a single crack of lightning, Kitreth unleashed her spell. The goblin was frozen stiff, shrouded in a black film of tranquil energies. Only a few words could be heard by the other goblins waiting for number 43, as they witnessed the severe act of their mistress blast her with those terrifying powers. Those words were, 'Die you fool' and the awaiting goblins did not want to share number 43's fate, so they dashed up the stairs from which they came. The sudden rush caused quite a stir of feet stamping on the stone steps. Kitreth was startled but knew her minions were still around. Her rage and anger now filled her mind. She cast another spell to solidify her first prey. Then, with determined fury, she followed the goblins to the top of the tower. What had those fools done to Dawn? She better not be dead or they will all pay. They will pay with not just their lives. Death was too good for them. These thoughts filled Kitreth's mind as she headed towards Dawn's room in chase of her foolish underlings.

Upon arrival, the goblins had been caught at the door with many a potion in their hands. Some pleaded to be forgiven, some pleaded for their life, while others simply ran away, not wanting any of the consequences of number 43's actions. But the sight of Dawn made Kitreth even more furious. The last time she had seen her cousin was on her arrival. Dawn had been dirty from the journey to the tower, but unharmed. Here in the cell, Dawn was strung up in prisoner's chains, which had not been in the room before. Her clothes had been ravaged and soiled, she was covered in bruises and blood. On her left arm, a bone protruded from her skin, just shy of her shoulder. Though from a distance she appeared to be dead, she was very much alive. But only barely. Kitreth of the flame was her title, given to her by none other than her father. The goblins here now knew why she was called this. As Kitreth walked towards Dawn, flames started to envelop her surroundings. The temperature started to rise, beginning with the hallway just outside of Dawn's room and encroaching on the stairwell. The flames licked not only the ground, walls and ceiling but also Kitreth's targets. The goblins. The flames were quick to envelop, but slow to kill. Kitreth had intended to make them suffer for their foolish acts so they would remember if they lived this torture. The poor goblins writhed in pain as the flames slowly burnt them. It bit them like little rats. There was no way to put the flames out. Rolling on the ground, or patting the flames had no effect. They were suffering and there was no way out of this.

With screams and squeaks and screeches from the tortured minions, Kitreth cast a spell of silence, to save her ears from the cries and pleas of her disobeying servants. They were supposed to report to her. They were supposed to care for Dawn. Not torture her. She needed new servants after this debacle. With a mind filled with fury, looking at her poor cousin made her feel sorrow and pity for the girl. She was part of the culling ritual, but not like this. She could have helped with the plan if not for her evil father.

Healing was not one of the magical arts she was proficient in, but she could still cast some. The effectiveness was minor, but it was still better than what those idiots were doing. Looking around, Kitreth could tell her unreliable servants had been using goblin salve to heal her wounds. Those fools were lucky it didn't kill her. As goblin salves were for those wretched creatures only. It would have poisoned her to death. Dawn needed more powerful healing, but since her main laboratory had been ransacked and ruined, Kitreth needed to use someone else's. Anyone else's really. Her thoughts raced in her mind and the only way to help Dawn was to seek her professor's aid. He was in this tower as well, but why would he help? His mind had already abandoned the ways of the void, tranquillity and magic. But Kitreth was desperate. Minor healing was removing the goblin's salve, which was no more than first aid at this point. With all the first aid she could give to Dawn, Kitreth unchained her cousin and held her close. Slowly carrying Dawn in her arms, Kitreth walked out of that dreadful room. As she walked towards the stairwell, the goblins were still writhing in pain and horror as the flames devoured their skin, a slow and painful death.

The traps and obstacles surrounding the tower were planted many, many years ago, by none other than the Golem master himself. All Kitreth and her crew had added were some minor illusionary spells that would defeat the weak of wills. Though the thought had occurred to Kitreth, perhaps the spells maybe too powerful for thick-headed brutes that her uncle had entrusted to rescue their one and only princess. Dawn was carefully being watched by Kitreth herself, not wanting to repeat the same events that had befallen her with incompetence. She dutifully had taken on the task to heal and safeguard her cousin.

From the window, she watched as the soldiers of Traytos fell for every trap laid out on the field surrounding the tower. Who was the fool that ordered such a waste of good souls? Whoever it was, it did not matter much to Kitreth, as her original orders still stood. Fight the rescuers and make sure Fameborn lived. Whoever this Fameborn is, he better be worth the wait. It was quite strange her orders did not include the safety of Dawn. But she was her only distant relative and perhaps when it was her time to rule, they too would plan the purging together. With such thoughts, Kitreth gently placed the back of her hand to soft skin of Dawn's forehead. With kindness and worry and future conquests in Kitreth's mind, she gently stroked Dawn's cheek. With Kitreth's light caress, a sadness struck her as her fingers touched the scars left from the torture she had suffered. From the depths of her heart, a single tear welled up in her right eye and from that sadness, a fury like no one had ever witnessed, was churning inside, coalescing into magical energy.

CHAPTER 55
THE AFTERMATH

After the crash, Torbiro had been the one to come to consciousness first. He felt pain all over and he could not move. His first thoughts were to scream out for help, but as he took in a short breath, his throat and lungs were filled with dirt. So instead of his thought turning to action, he convulsed and squirmed in pain, coughing out the dirt and dust. Pain struck his entire body and as he lay on his back, the brightness of light blinded him with searing heat. One would normally react and raise their arms to block out the light, but Torbiro's body was shattered from the crash. Pain and suffering were the cost of survival. But with survival meant life, which in turn meant hope. There was hope. If he had survived, Memyra must have survived as well. His panicked thoughts were concentrated and focused towards the hope that Memyra was alive. This was a good distraction from the sharp pulses of pain surging throughout Torbiro's little body.

From above, Torbiro was about four metres away from the crash site. His body lay facing the sky, but his legs and his arms were bent and broken. To start off with, his arms had snapped from the elbow, bending and twisting in an unnatural manner. While his legs were as straight as a board but several sections of his thigh and shin had bones protruding out through his skin. His entire body was covered in mud, dirt and lots and lots of blood. His body screamed with every breath, but as Torbiro had something else on his mind, all other thoughts would be forgotten. At least for the time being.

The crash site was absolutely spectacular, shards of metal here and there. A black sun marked the soil with stumps of trees laid out burning from the explosion, like some angry fire giant's offspring had uprooted all the trees as though they were plagued with disease. The surrounding green grass and small shrubs were entirely turned to ash. But the further from the crash site you went, the greener the landscape became. Black to burning ashy remains, to a light sickly yellow green, then a lighter aqua, to finally a lush, vibrant natural green. Just a few metres away from Torbiro - in a northeasterly direction - lay an undamaged Memyra. The strange gnome too was there, but unlike Torbiro, he lay – more like he crashed and was imprinted into a tree – slumped inside a tree trunk, entering it from the side. The left side, to be more precise.

Memyra soon awoke after four short turns - hours – after Torbiro. She was careful even before putting on the rocket boots. The item that protected her was now a broken piece of leather, but before the explosion, it had been a belt of inertial absorption. In laymen's terms, a belt that could change your fate, so long as your fate had a lot of unchangeable energy. Like an explosion. She got up slowly, blinked from the brightness of the sun and then rubbed her eyes to readjust to the light. She stretched her back, then her arms and then jumped up and down a few times to limber up. After all of the stretching was complete, she checked herself to see if she had any injuries, scrapes or bruises. She silently complained about the nicks her trousers had on her knee. She also noticed her bag of tricks was not on her person, so she started to look around for it. Her thoughts were solely focused on her precious things back. Some of those items were not only precious but also dangerous. Immediately, she spotted her bag but did not notice the mangled body of her friend just a few metres away. Her bag was slightly singed but a bit of soap and dusting would fix that easy. In her bag she searched for a curative, to ease her mind of the events that had occurred recently. Finding one with ease, she popped the stopper and sipped the cherry flavour. Not her favourite, but it reminded her of Torbiro, he always likee the sweet flavour. Her thoughts of Torbiro were sadness. Solemn ones, as though he had died or worse. As she thought of her dearly departed friend, she had not noticed she was walking with a squishy, fleshy step. Did she finally notice her friend lying on the ground in a broken and contorted way?

With a yelp and stifled cry, Torbiro came out of his focusing – more like self-distraction than mental focus – meditation. Torbiro's eyes were squinting at the brightness of light, which made his face look like a shrivelled prune. Looking up, he could see an outline of a shadow stepping on him. His first thoughts were mixed from the idea of death to crying out and asking for help. He took a deep breath - as deep as he could anyway – and tried to call out for help, but the pain of his body only allowed him to whimper and sigh as he exhaled the pain from his lungs. With eyes squinting, he gazed up and saw only the silhouette of a person. The light was so blinding that Torbiro could only see a darkened outline from the knee onward. With a hand reaching out to him, Torbiro could only shield his eyes to protect himself from the dangerous figure trying to harm him. But unknown to Torbiro, it was just Memyra trying to provide him with assistance. With the sight of her stubborn and frightened friend on the ground, all she could do was giggle at the scene right in front of her. She tried her hardest not to laugh, but Torbiro was like a puppet with its strings cut off after it had fallen to the ground. It was not as funny as Memyra made it out to be, but her sense of humour was just that morbid.

With a familiar sound, Torbiro finally stopped squirming and finally accepted her aid. Not having much stability due to the lack of functioning joints and all his bones had been broken from the crash, did not help him. To his fortune, he had the aid of Memyra's bag of tricks. She managed to find a curative that healed his wounds but not the function of his bones. She had a different trick for that though and she wasn't going to reveal it until she got information from that runaway gnome. Memyra knew Torbiro, once healed, would run away to his all-important mission. So she told him the 'potion' was still working its magic, so he needed to wait a few hours till it took the full effect, with a nasty smirk no less.

'Hey, hey Myra, my body still hurts! Wasn't that drink supposed to heal me?' said Torbiro after he drank the questionable curative from Memyra's bag of tricks.

'It's gonna take some time, Torro. Just be patience. I thought you were a knight,' said Memyra, as she continued to look for the item in her magical bag that had the power to heal her friend more completely. As she dug and reached inside the small bag, she found the roll of bandages. These bandages were enchanted with magical healing properties, but would also take time. Time was what she needed the most, as Torbiro's track record had always been bad. She pulled out the roll of bandages to set Torbiro's legs and arms in the right position. She even had healing potions that would cure him instantly, but they would not help this situation.

'So why are you bandaging me up now?' asked Torbiro as Memyra started to bandage him.

'It's so… it's so you don't turn to jelly!' said Memyra, as she lied through her teeth.

'Jelly!!? What do you mean?' Torbiro was in a panic.

'Yes… yes. The curative has a jelly side effect that happens with patients with broken bones, but don't worry, I had these bandages to make sure that doesn't happen,' said Memyra with a smile. Sweat ran down her face as she said such an obvious lie, but to her luck, Torbiro was still very naïve.

Wrapping her friend in the bandages was short work and once she was done, Memyra surveyed the area and found it was still very bright. It must have been the effect of the explosion. She was very curious about the actual time, so she pulled out a timepiece. Just as she had thought, it was the middle of the night. How could it be this bright? It was definitely unnatural. She needed answers and she needed time.

Memyra searched and searched for the gnome from the crash, but she could not find him anywhere. Although she had only been searching the ground nearby and not the remaining trees, there was no chance, as the bright light had halted her view above. So, in her search around the area, she had missed her mark a good 15 times. She was thorough, but having not looked up, she passed the same tree with this gnome every single time. After searching for more than four hours, she headed back to Torbiro. Her thoughts were of disappointment, but what can you do, really?!

With Torbiro finally healed, Memyra told him what she had found and the two headed off, away from the bright light, towards the east where they had dropped off their friends. The journey would be long as the two were a fair distance away from the crash site. The two halflings had determined they were North West of the Dip Hills. The land in the north was very beautiful and bountiful, with wild fruits and vegetation growing all throughout the region. This land would have been enough for their people to live and thrive. So why had the king not mentioned this to his people. In all the years they had lived in Traytos, there had never been any notion of liveable lands within this sector. Torbiro made sure to burn this beautiful land in his mind to ask the king to move his people out here. Memyra on the other hand, had seen this untouched site before. It was when she had left to carry out a mission with her guild mates to steal and smuggle various magical artefacts. She had used this area to rest and hide from Bataros agents. The beautiful landscape was still surprising to her as well, just as it was for Torbiro, but she knew the reason why the king of Traytos had hidden this place from her people. It was his hate for her race and his prejudice for the small races. The two frolicked through the bountiful glade and even tasted the fruit from the nearby bushes. They were sweet and delicious enough that Torbiro wanted to take more to share with his old master, back at the tinkerer's shop.

After a week of travelling, they found themselves back at the foot of the Dip Hills. Torbiro had worried about his two companions, Robyn and Jimmy, and also about the princess. Torbiro was full of worry, but he had hope too. He knew Robyn wouldn't be alone as they had left them together with the other elves. But where was Jimmy? Was he back at the healing tents? Or was he still in the Dip Hills? It was a mystery in Torbiro's mind.

CHAPTER 56
JIMMY'S OBJECTIVE

Deep in the Dip Hills, through the caverns and even deeper still was where Jimmy had been all this time. He had needed to escape the prying eyes of both the soldiers of Traytos and magical merchants of Bataros, so he could plan and plot his scheme. His orders were simple, but his opponents were halflings. They had the gods' luck, so all loose ends needed to be cut and dealt with before executing any part of his plan. Jimmy's plan needed not to be perfect, but it needed to succeed. He was the best spy and instigator in all the land. His record of destroying lands or kingdoms had been forty-five and zero. With forty five threats under his belt, this was just another notch he could place there. But the issue was, his target this time was a halfling. He had dealt with their kind before and they just seemed to have a natural born gift that lets them escape traps, poisoning and even death. It was disturbing and annoying but that just meant he needed to make the proper contingencies. Jimmy needed to make sure Torbiro was at the scene of every event leading to the tower and once that idiot knight 'rescues' the princess, make sure Torbiro is the one caught as the kidnapper. But where in all the pulse was that halfling?

I know where the elf is and where the thief's agents are as well. But I can't pin point his location. He should not be able to hide from me. He wears that armour so proudly. The tracking spell I placed on it should be working. Just like I did with the others, with the exception of the thief. She is another matter I need to attend to.

Jimmy had kept a close eye on everyone he had met. With a simple handshake, he could cast a spell of tracking, a mark that was not so easy to find or notice. Making the mark look very natural on the skin or clothing of his target. If on the skin, it would be a small mole or a birth mark, but armour and clothing were much easier to disguise, as they could be anything from damage or a change of colour. On armour, the mark could be a dent or scratch and clothing, it could be a tear or a patch of ink or stain.

Jimmy started to use all manner of tools to search and find the troublesome halfling. He used magical seeing crystals, mirrors of power and powerful location spells that could find a mithral needle in a stack of steel needles. He used technology as well, seeing through the eyes of the automatons he placed in all the major locations, the Dip Hills south and east, the medical sector and even the front of the tower, where the king's daughter was being held. But no matter the tools he used, all he would see was a white light, like an orb of brightness. It was strange, the spells should be working, he thought, but why couldn't he find the halflings? It was a strange mystery and Jimmy despised mysteries. Perhaps searching for him was the wrong approach, but then he would have to reveal himself and would pose the risk of being discovered. He needed an excuse, but excuses were not in his repertoire and the lie would either become far too convoluted or it would be far too simple. With his plans and schemes put on hold to think of the excuse why he had been away for so long, it hit him rather quickly. Eureka, he thought. Amnesia. It was simple enough to work. He just needed to look like he had a severe head wound. Illusion magic would do. It's easier and less encumbering. Now, back to the plan.

CHAPTER 57
THE SEARCH FOR TORBIRO

Robyn had been with her newly found brothers and sisters for about a week since the terrible frenzy where the knight commander Fameborn and his men had tried to kill the innocent. She had not known how they all escaped from the battle but it was a blessing and a curse as they were left at the eastern most part of the Dip Hills. It was a blessing to escape the battles and dangers, but it was a curse as they were placed in a far more volatile area than the battle. They were in the middle of the fields surrounding the dreaded tower of sacrifice. To the kingdom of Traytos, its name was all but forgotten by the masses and to those in the service of Traytos, it was called the Tower of Rivals. But to the elves, they knew of its ancient name. The tower of sacrifice was a place where the evil controllers of the region had plotted to destroy the lives of others. They had left many lives in ruin for the sake of the rich. This tower was the central point of this sector to start a caste system where democracy fell and a monarchy rose.

We felt the dread of the place once we roused from the confusion of the transition of the rescue. Robyn may not have been the first to come to, but she was ready to protect and move the refugees to a safer location. The Dip Hills were no longer safe, as there were many soldiers in crucial parts of the valley. Torbiro, with all his good intentions, had made the lives of these elves far more dangerous. The Dip Hills were far too secure. So the only option was to head north to the ghost lands. Robyn had heard of the rumours regarding the ghost lands, but they were just rumours, right? She had hoped so, as the ghost lands rumours told of the area being tainted with the wild energies of the void and that creatures of the past would manifest and try to drag you into the eternal void. The thought frightened Robyn more than it did the children of the group. The merchants and elven families had known of the ghost lands by another name - Tranquillity plains. The plains were said to emit healing energies cast by those of the past and in turn you could regenerate and rejuvenate your magical capacity. It was more a holy and sacred zone for these travellers, as there were different rumours from different regions. But to those who had visited the ghost lands before, they knew the lands were once the homes of the elves, then the nomadic tribes of the giants, then the small lands of the halflings. But after each time the people were driven out, the land was simply abandoned and nature grew with the energies of the void. So the land glowed with the vigour and fervour of life. The glow attracted visitors but did not have the healing properties or the energies once known to the clans of elves that once lived there. It was simply the land abandoned by people without the choice or the strength to stay.

The journey north started out with many difficulties, as they needed to evade and avoid the traps placed by the terrible owner of the tower of sacrifice. The traps were magically and technologically made, so the dangers were different for every occasion. The traps were easy enough to spot for the race of elves. In fact, they were very obviously placed, like the land was made as a training field for fools. The traps ranged from simple pit falls to illusionary mind mazes. The traps were designed to cull the fools and obtain the learned. The elves, aside from Robyn, were learned scholars and merchants for scholars. They were more the guide to escape than Robyn was. Robyn was not like these elves, as she had not been trained in her natural abilities. Though elves were magical in nature, she had either forgotten her abilities or not practiced them to have the keen eyesight or natural flexibility; or perhaps under stressful situations, she was not able to muster them. She was clumsy and appeared to the children as a newborn fawn.

Each trap had its purpose. If the individual was anything but intelligent, they would fall for those hidden traps. Pit falls would capture the slow and heavy. Rope traps would catch the speedy and light. But the most dangerous traps were the magical kind. They were designed to test the individual's personality, such as their courage, determination, spirit and their will to overcome. While these individuals were trapped, they would experience the challenge until they had succeeded, but the magic would drain them of their life force and return their souls to the void, even if they belonged to the pulse. Touching the traps were enough to keep you there forever, but to Robyn's fortune was her allies could dispel some of these magical dangers.

Once out of the trapped fields, the march north was more of a pleasant one. The plains were flat and full of vegetation to forage, so food was no issue. But after only three days on foot, the elves spotted something very odd on the horizon. An orb of light. It was massive and the brightness was blinding, even at this distance.

'Young one, do you know what that is?' said a male elf.

'Ha ha ha ha, please stop, not there,' said Robyn as the children played and teased her.

'Young knight, I need your guidance. Please children, this is not the time,' said the male elf. With a groan of disappointment from the children, they stopped tickling and teasing Robyn.

'Yes, sorry, sorry. What is it, Korvin?' said Robyn as she caught her breath from the jovial activities with the children. With a deep breath and a long sigh, Korvin rubbed his forehead with his forefinger and pinky to massage and relieve the annoyance he felt at this non-magical elf.

'Young knight, do you know what that brightness is over yonder?' said Korvin, using his right hand to point, while shielding his eyes with his left.

'Korvin, you mean that bright light up ahead?' asked Robyn as she too shielded her eyes from the bright light in the distant.

'Yes, my child,' said Korvin with a quick reply.

'No, no, I don't know what that is. Maybe it's magic?' said Robyn. With eyes shielded, she could only make assumptions, as she could not actually see the source.

'It must be very powerful magic, if it is, my child,' said Korvin, with a calm tone as if trying to analyse the light from its intensity.

'Mr Korvin, it's bright over there! Is that the ancient spirits from the void?' said an elven child as he rubbed his eyes from the blinding light.

The elves, with the exception of Robyn, were stopped by the light as they approached the northern lands. As their keen sight had actually hindered their approach. Robyn marched on to see what the light was and how to stop it, so her new friends could find a new home. Robyn put on her rifle goggles to help protect her eyes from the light, but the intensity of the strange illumination seemed to get closer and closer, even though her approach was a slow pace. As Robyn got closer, the light seemed to bounce up and down as though it was moving towards her. The light couldn't be alive, right? With fear entering her mind, she started to move in a westerly direction to see if the lights would follow her. Unfortunately, the light stopped and started to approach her. The more Robyn moved away, the more intense the approach of the light was toward her. At some point, Robyn thought she was hearing things, as if she heard Torbiro's voice.

'Heeeeey, Torbiro, is that you?' Robyn called out to the blinding light.

'Ro…by…n…' came a distant voice.

'Heeeeey, Torbiro, are you out there?' Her voice had gone raspy and was filled with concern for her friend. The voice became clearer as the light got brighter and brighter.

'Robyn, this way. Stop running away.' Torbiro's voice came through the light. Torbiro could see Robyn running away from him rather than towards where they could regroup and exchange notes.

'Hey, Torbiro… why are you so bright? I can't see you, the light is blinding!' Said Robyn, shielding her eyes with her arm. At this point, the illumination was so intense that closing one's eyes was the only way to block it out. As bright as the path was, Robyn needed to walk in the darkness if she wanted to continue to see.

'Bright? What do you mean, bright? Do you mean me?' Torbiro questioned her meaning.

'Torro, who are ya talkin' to?' said Memyra in reply to Torbiro's confusion.

'Myra, it's Robyn, can't ya hear her?' said Torbiro.

'Robyn? I can't hear anything. Have you been smoking some snuff?' Memyra's sarcasm so obvious, you needed to be a deaf and blind fool not to notice.

'She's right there. I can even see her a bit!' said Torbiro in protest. Torbiro extended his finger in the direction of where he had seen Robyn.

'All I see is nothing!!! Wait, did you say bright beforehand?' said Memyra. Upon speaking those words, she realised there was something amiss with her earlier conversation. Where was Robyn and why could Torro hear her?

'Torbiro, I can hear Memyra. Is everything alright?' Robyn replied to Torbiro as though he were talking to her. At this point, with the extreme brightness searing her eyes, Robyn was starting to become delirious and confused.

'To… Torbiro. Me… Memyra. I… I'm scared. This light. It's…' pants Robyn with panic and fear in her voice. The concentration of the light was increasing and its intensity causing greater harm than just blindness.

'I can. Hear. Her. She is. Just. Over. There,' Torbiro was panting too. As Torbiro moved closer and closer to Robyn's location, he too was affected by some hidden force. His breathing was erratic and his voice was very distant, although from Memyra's point of view her friend was only about two to three metres away.

'Torro, Stop,' said Memyra, commanding Torbiro to not go any further. She didn't feel danger or some instinctual sixth sense telling her to stop her friend, but rather it was more of a sisterly love stopping a wandering brother going the wrong way before they were both separated.

'Torro! I said stop right now. That's an order.' Memyra, this time, had a more commanding tone. Like a commander in an army or a leader of a band of thieves. But her effort was not rewarded with an obedient ally but rather a stubborn child not listening to her as the big sister. Memyra was now panicking as her friend disappeared in front of her, through what appeared to be thin air. Then, without a moment's notice, she too started to approach the same area.

Through the conversation, Robyn had lost all the energy to move any further. As though her body was completely drained of power and she was moving with nothing short of her sheer will to find her friend and ally. With eyes completely shut and a loud throbbing beating in her ears, Robyn collapsed from the journey. Torbiro was near, but she could no longer hear him. What replaced her friend's voice was a loud heartbeat pounding in her ears. On her knees and no longer moving, the noise got louder and louder as though it approached.

What Robyn was experiencing was also being experienced by Torbiro, as he approached her silhouette. He could still see, but there was a strange force that pushed him down. Like the gravity of the planet had just focused on a single spot. It felt as though he was moving through a solid wall of steel, or the moment one swims up from the deepest part of the sea to break through to breathe life-giving air. Torbiro, with all the determination in his being, continued to approach. He was no more than twenty to thirty centimetres away when his body finally collapsed. His stubbornness was not enough for him to push any further.

Memyra, in her panicked state, tried to calm herself. She used a breathing technique and even a calming mantra, but with each attempt, she failed to break free from her fear. She searched her person for some kind of memento to remind her of peaceful times with Torbiro. But she was at a loss. Then she searched her bag for her trusty grappling hook so she could reel him back towards her. Although she was a halfling, her natural fearlessness was lost due to the disappearance of her friend. Her bravery was a façade in the presence of her friend's stubborn determination. It is said the race of halflings were never afraid of anything, but that was just a myth. A myth told by adventurers who had encountered their race in the most dangerous of all situations, like a dragon's lair. But the truth of the matter was, halflings were luckier than they were brave, as most of the time they were only in said dragon's lair due to another reason, like stubbornly retrieving a valued item. At this exact moment, Memyra was at the point of breaking down into an emotional wreck when she grasped the familiar handle of her grappling hook. She thrust it out and aimed for the last known location of her friend. Breathing slowly before taking the shot seemed to calm her down, even if only a little. The charge of the weapon was loud, louder than Memyra had anticipated and the shocked surprised her more than the recoil of the pop, as she pressed the trigger to release the hook. What happened next was something out of this world.

The hook went in the direction Memyra had intended, but what she expected was grabbing Torbiro from the other side and dragging him back to her. Instead, the flying grappling hook went through the mysterious veil just as Torbiro had done and a shattering effect reverberated throughout the space she stood. The mysterious veil started to spill out like a mist or a fog, then the scenery around Memyra warped and shifted. It cracked and broke like her surroundings were actually made of glass. The sound was oddly soft and quiet but then there was darkness and all of a sudden she felt her knee buckle and she hit the ground, hard. A sharp pain, then breathlessness, and back to darkness and emptiness.

CHAPTER 58
THE ELF TRADER

The smell of warm stew woke me up. I wondered how long I had been under. I could also hear Torbiro speaking to Robyn and a few other elves. For them to be chatting in such a fashion, I must have been out for quite a while. Torbiro would have been very suspicious about people with magic and magic in general.

Memyra thought all this to herself as she tried to rise from the soft bed she laid in. But it was either some unknown injury or magic that held her down, as she could not move what-so-ever. In fact, she could not move due to the draining energies of the zone she and Torbiro had been in, but why had she not noticed the transition? It was from her actions to breakthrough, rather than pass through, the erratic barrier made of both the negative energies of the pulse and the void. Memyra was at death's door when the elves had found her. While Robyn and Torbiro were in the same state, the shattering of realities had further drained Memyra of her life force. She was too weak to speak or to move. But halfling luck would always have their back – so long as you didn't use it too often, that is.

From her bed, she could hear Torbiro talking about his mission to uphold his knight's pride. To rescue the princess. The elves, as well as Robyn, seemed to think it was a deadly venture and suggested he find another way through the deadly traps surrounding the dreaded Tower of Sacrifice. The Tower of Sacrifice? What tower is that? Maybe they were talking about the Tower of Rivals. These thoughts were in Memyra's mind as she listened to the conversation, which was starting to heat up into an argument.

'Torbiro, you have to be reasonable,' said Robyn as she pleaded to her friend and ally the dangers of his proposed mission.

'What do you mean, reasonable? Robyn, this was an order from Commander Peren.' Torbiro stubbornly stood his ground on the matter at hand. His pride was more on the line than the actual mission, but he was a knight of Traytos, already forgetting his actual mission.

'Mr. Halfling, please understand the journey back south is a dire peril. It is simply too dangerous.' Korvin the elf, stood his ground knowing the elves had had enough dangers in one lifetime.

'Robyn, our mission is to rescue the princess, remember?' said Torbiro, being as obstinate as a dwarf.

'But Torbiro, I thought our mission was to capture your friend Memyra, since she was a wanted criminal of Traytos,' said Robyn, trying her best to remember the actual orders of their commander.

'Maybe you're right Robyn, but we should still rescue the princess since it's on the way back to the kingdom.' Torbiro tried to be matter-of-fact to divert the conversation.

'Look, young master. You have your mission and Robyn has hers,' said Korvin, pulling Torbiro back from his diversion. The elf could tell when the situation was about to go sour. It was not magic, it was just having dealt with other merchants like himself, sly and cunning fellows. Regardless of race, a good merchant had their charms and wiles.

'I'm talking to Robyn, ok?' said Torbiro, trying to take control of the conversation.

'Torbiro, that is very rude. You're starting to act less and less like a knight. Just...' said Robyn, trying to settle the situation. She was being helpful but neutral as Robyn did have orders from her commander and she had also promised to aid these elves. As they too, had saved her. The argument at hand was known to Robyn alone, as Torbiro was trying his best to deny it.

The issues were very simple to understand. Torbiro wanted to go and rescue the princess. Korvin wanted to go to a safe haven for his people and Robyn needed to help both. She was being indecisive about which side to choose. And so she was between a rock and a hard place. But her naïve nature made her torn between being loyal to both but also to neither, which made Torbiro more aggressive, which was very odd.

'Torbiro, I understand you want to go and save the princess but...' said Robyn as she was started to explain everything again but again was interrupted by Torbiro.

'Robyn, please I know this...' said Torbiro. Robyn had finally had enough of the same conversation over and over again. It had already been three turns – which was known to all others as three hours – and there was no further understanding from both sides. She needed to put an end to it.

'Torbiro, I tried to be polite and noble like a knight, but you are starting to act more like a child than a warrior. I can see there is only one option, though I still want to aid both of you and I owe both of you my life,' said Robyn, stating the facts. Torbiro was shocked that his friend had just dropped such an accusation towards him. Robyn could see the remorse on his face. She could also see, although Torbiro could be stubborn at times, he was very fragile and could be confused very easily. Torbiro really wore his emotions on his sleeve. Maybe that's why Memyra was such good friends with him, as she was more controlled and mysterious. Robyn had thought they were the same coin, but were each its own half. They really did complement each other.

My words had already cut him down and I was just starting to form my view of it all, Robyn thought.

'Torbiro, please understand that I want what is best for everyone. Not just for my pride or vanity,' said Robyn, making an apology.

'Miss Robyn, please inform your friend you are trying to rescue many, while he only rescues one,' said Korvin, stating the important facts to sway the situation his way in an elvish manner. Passive but manipulative. With calm in his eyes, Korvin looked at the defeated halfling and made a slight smirk, so very slight that even with Robyn's elven eyes, she didn't notice it.

'Yes, Korvin, that is right. The needs of the many outweigh the needs of the one. But you also need to consider that the one Torbiro wishes to rescue is the princess Dawn.' Robyn also stated some the facts.

'Yes, you are correct, Miss Robyn, but your kingdom would have no doubt sent knights and soldiers to save such a person of importance,' Korvin, continued to make his point that his plight was more pressing than the course Torbiro was proposing to achieve.

'Mr Korvin, you are right. We must find a home for your people, but I believe the best way to do that is to head back to Traytos and ask our kingdom for land that you can live on,' Robyn stated her opinion on the matter. She wanted to help her saviours, the elves who had aided her through the area of traps with their heightened insight and magical prowess and Torbiro, with his crafty relations with thieves and the like. Both had saved her and both wanted and needed her help.

'Perhaps you are right, Miss Robyn. Though I hope your king is more understanding of our magical nature than the commander that ordered the assault on our kind, simply to gain supplies. Not for free, but with trade,' said Korvin.

'Our king is understanding. My cousins and other magical folk do live in Traytos,' said Robyn. 'They were elves but a bit different, but all elves were magical in nature.' Robyn had started to explain the different jobs and professions her cousins and loved ones had to work with and for the kingdom. Korvin could see the reasoning in what Robyn proposed, but there were also dangers to her approach. In Korvin's thoughts and memory as well as the hearsay of the king of Traytos, he was known to all as a tyrant. Merciless and cruel. It would have been safer to go with the halfling in his quest to rescue his daughter first and ask for clemency.

With the look of compassion and kindness on Robyn's face, she managed to convince Korvin of her plan to head back to Traytos to find the elves a home to call their own. The two elves had made a decision, but they had forgotten about the still stunned Torbiro. He was crouching down, hugging his knees. His face still had the shocked look of a fawn caught in the headlights. He was only noticed when one of the children approached and started to pull at him. He would not move from the spot, but only then did Robyn and Korvin finally notice. Robyn felt embarrassed to have forgotten her other ally. Korvin had known Torbiro was indeed still in shock and the spell he had cast on Robyn had broken. That child will pay once this is all over. He had wanted to gain not only her trust but also her mental capabilities. This was good. It would serve well to gain control of all the elves in Traytos to start a revolt. But the halfling was still in the way.

With a false act of kindness, Korvin made an over exaggerated apology to show Torbiro he did matter and he was sorry they had forgotten about him in the discussion. In a crude elvish dialect, he called the child something and it had frightened the young boy. The word Robyn heard was 'Valtra' and in her misunderstanding, she smiled at the young boy, thinking she had heard 'Valpra' which meant small protector. She spoke to Torbiro and explained they had made a decision to head back to Traytos and report to the command that they had succeeded in the capture of the leader of the thieves' guild and to get an audience with the king of Traytos to help provide for the livelihood of the elves seeking refuge. Torbiro did not respond at first, but since they would be headed back to Traytos, he thought there may still be a chance to save the princess on the way back.

Torbiro stood up slowly, as though he too was affected by some magical spell. This was true indeed. Korvin had placed a minor charm spell to control and stop him from interfering. Although Torbiro had not interfered in the conversation, his idea to save the princess was still on the table. The plan Robyn had in mind was far too dangerous for the likes of Korvin and his supplies. The other elves really had no say at this point as Robyn had naively thought Korvin was their representative, but in fact he was their master. To be more precise, he was a thrall. A thrall was a sorcerer capable of enslaving others with mind controlling spells. He was dangerous and only Memyra would be enough to handle him, but she was absolutely incapacitated from her previous encounter.

With all parties involved updated, with the exception of Memyra, they had their plan. Korvin even apologised to Torbiro about his idea and had agreed to rescue the princess so long as the others had a safe place to stay. Torbiro, not knowing what Korvin had meant, agreed without hesitation. He was just eager to save the princess to prove to the king he was a knight to be proud of. In Torbiro's mind, the safety of the refugees would be solved if he just sent them to Traytos, as the kingdom was very safe with large walls that surrounded it. But since he would be heading for the Tower of Rivals first, he would simply take them and protect them as best he could. Quite foolish if you think about it, but Torbiro was quite a naïve person. Naïve and trusting. He still believed all people were filled with good intentions. In turn, he had hoped people would also believe in him as he trusted them, but that's not how this world works. Only two things protected him from the truth: his friend Memyra and his luck.

Torbiro was now overjoyed to start planning for the rescue of the princess from the dreaded Tower of Rivals, but he needed Memyra's advice as well as the others. The main reason for that was she ''told him she had been inside the tower before and gaining advice from someone with knowledge of its layout would make the operation more successful. The elven healer had been performing some sort of magical ritual to ease her pain, as well as cure whatever injury she had sustained. From the outside, there was no mark, or scar, or broken bone that showed what was affecting her. The elves had called this aura sickness, which was something many young magicians experienced in their first year of studying on how to cast spells. The elven healer was a good friend of Korvin, but due to an issue concerning identity safety, she did not give her name. Which was odd in Torbiro's mind. He introduced himself, just as a courtesy, as that's what you did when meeting new people, but he did not wish to disregard their customs or their culture. He would simply ask Robyn about it later to understand elves better, so he did not make any misunderstandings and mistakes. What both he and Robyn would never know is these particular elves were enslaved by Korvin and they were his merchandise he wished to keep safe.

After ten hours, Memyra had woken up from her sickness. The healing ritual had worked and she had the same vigour and sassy attitude she always had from the beginning. Torbiro was overly excited his friend had finally recovered from her mild injury and fatigue. Robyn had been worried sick because Korvin had said her illness was a very common type of fatigue that young apprentices get from the lack of arcanus or energies from the void. Korvin had explained that energies from the void not only provided magic to hurl spells but they were also the life blood of all tranquillity, which meant they could also heal and replace the energies lost, to rejuvenate and restore. He also added that the energies of the pulse were the cause of this sickness. To use magic with the power of the pulse was usually impossible. The pulse was a chaotic unnatural energy, the fuel of technological advancements, but Korvin's knowledge of both the pulse and the void were very minimal. His powers to convince were of the void, which in turn meant he just fabricated stories of void propaganda and pulse falsehoods. To try and control the foolish and weak minded. Memyra was not one he could control, not because of her halfling luck but because of her own knowledge on the matter. She did not know the theories of pulse matrices or the religions of the void, but Memyra knew that mixing magic and technology was dangerous. It would cause great catastrophe, as the gnomes of Traytos had found. Memyra herself had worked with many races that used either the void or the pulse, but never both.

As Memyra rose from the soft bed roll, she felt an unusual ripple from her body. Like the vibration of a factory engine or the rumble from a purring cat. There was no pain, just a sensation. When Memyra touched the origin of the ripple, time seemed to slow. She turned to her friend Torbiro, who had a gleeful smile on his face. What a fool, she thought. But she waited for him to jump and nuzzle her in the same manner a child would hug their older sibling after being scolded. Her usual patience did not award her with the gentle scent of her friend, as he was still moving very slowly toward her. Very odd indeed. Memyra could not believe it. Then she blinked and rubbed her eyes in disbelief. Once her eyes were cleared of whatever made things move so slowly, Torbiro reacted at a normal pace, jumping to hug and nuzzle her. Though it was very flattering, Memyra allowed it for no more than a few ticks, then shoved Torbiro roughly to the side. She then crossed her arms and threw a light insult to her friend. It was the usual banter between the two. Memyra did have feelings for Torbiro, but he was just the kind of man who barely noticed the obvious signs. So she kept her feelings hidden through her actions of aggression.

Robyn too, was quick to move toward Memyra but decided not to catch and lift her up, since she was still injured. Her delayed action was enough that she was able to see Memyra shove Torbiro to the ground, but not the look of pleasure on the young halfling's face as Torbiro nuzzled her. Korvin was the only one to witness the emotional display of the injured female. It made him think it was a good weakness to manipulate. A wily grin emerged from Korvin's face, but he too quickly returned to his passive look. The pair had exchanged some weird banter and started to discuss their plan. Torbiro explained to Memyra they would need to find some place safe for the elves to stay while they went to explore and rescue Princess Dawn from the Tower of Rivals. Memyra suggested they all should just go back to where they came from and be done with it. But that was not an option if Korvin was going to help them through the Field of Dangerous Traps. So Memyra simply refused to help the suspicious elf and would follow along until they parted ways. Memyra had a strange feeling about Korvin, like he was hiding something or much like herself. An outlaw trying to gain profit at the cost of others. Memyra couldn't trust him so blindly like the others, but once Torbiro was convinced there was only one way to stop him. Put him in a cage. But it wasn't right at that moment.

With the plan set, mostly agreed upon by the party with the exception of Memyra, the group of elves and two halflings started their journey back south. It had taken Robyn and the elves almost 10 cycles – 10 days by normal counting– but with the halflings in tow, it was going much faster. Memyra was leading the group, since she had the most insight of the terrain in these parts. Memyra had been here before and the land had not changed too much that she wouldn't find her way. Though Memyra was acting as a guide, Torbiro was the one pushing the party faster and further. This did not bode well for Korvin, as he needed to mentally push the other elves with his will. But with Torbiro not allowing him to rest, his grip on each of his captives had started to gain control of their mental and physical faculties. Robyn, none the wiser, did not see the difference and how the others were acting to this point. By the fifth day, the team had reached the northern part of the Dip Hills. This was where Torbiro needed to find a rare place to hide the elves. Upon their arrival at the foot of the first ring of hills, Torbiro stopped the team for a few turns –hours– to plan out his next move rather than rest. A few turns had past and Torbiro had made crude dirt drawings with a sturdy looking stick he found on the ground. He was making plans and had forgotten about the time.

'Hey… Hey, Torro!' said Memyra, trying to get the attention of the distracted Torbiro.

'Mi… Mister Torbiro!' said Robyn, also trying to get his attention. She was trying to tell him dinner was ready.

'Ah… Yeah, I got this,' said Torbiro in reply to both girls, without actually acknowledging what they were saying.

'Di… Dinn… Dinner is almost ready, Torbiro!' said Robyn. Even though she had travelled with Torbiro for more than a month, she was still shy around him. It was something Robyn had to overcome one day, but today was not that day. Her awkwardness was one formed from her upbringing. It was filled with both dark tranquillity and light pulse training. Which meant she was alone much of her young life.

'Rob'n, ya don't hav' ta be so shy around Torro,' said Memyra, trying to bolster her confidence. She could still see the lingering anxiety in her body language. By how she held a plate or how she presented them to the highly distracted friend of hers.

'TORRO!!!' shouted Memyra at the unresponsive Torbiro. Both Robyn and she had tried to call him over. She was already so sick of Torbiro just nodding along, ignoring both of them just to continue to draw in the dirt with his stick. Just what kind of plan was he coming up with that required that much concentration?

At the very loud, very intensive and very angry tone of Memyra's voice, Torbiro finally looked up and what he saw was the scariest image of her he had seen since they were kids. Though Memyra was only about two or three centimetres shorter than Torbiro, crouched on the ground, she looked like a monstrous giant with a great club in her hands. Before Torbiro could do anything or even react, Memyra was already looking down at him, in a menacing manner and flicking him with the grease covered spatula used to cook the elvish stew prepared by Robyn. Torbiro was struck three times before he raised his arms to defend himself at the angry Memyra. His head was covered in a mixture of brown sauce and a few vegetables flung with every strike and splutter.

'Mi…Myra, I'm sorry. Please…' said Torbiro as he blocked the frustrated attacks by his friend, while he tried to apologise. What Torbiro was trying to say was "Please stop hitting me" but Memyra had smacked his face to stop him from making an excuse.

'Torro, listen, I'm gonna stop but you hav' ta pay attention ta your surround…' said Memyra scolding her inattentive friend. But she too was interrupted by Korvin, who simply had had enough of this rowdy situation. He cast a paralysing spell and had directed at Memyra.

CHAPTER 59
KORVIN'S EXPLOITS

After two days straight of a warriors' march, I can finally rest my feet and relax my mind. I cannot believe it without seeing it myself. A halfling's agility is no longer a myth, or at least in my eyes. By the void, can they move? Their endurance is much like their greedy cousins the hill dwarves? They never seem to tire. I expected this Torbiro to be sturdy like his ally Robyn, as they are part of the Traytos knighthood, but the other halfling seems to easily keep up with the one called Torbiro. The exhaustion I have experienced from the first day was almost enough for me to lose control of my wares, if not for my memory of the pain from my employer, or I might have lost at least one of my slaves. As powerful as my kind are to charm spells, they have a low threshold for endurance, so powerful spells can be resisted but minor spells with enough effect and constant casting can weaken even the most powerful elven wizard or sorcerer. To my fortune or misfortune, in my opinion, I have an ancient bloodline meant to guide the elves to the void. But of course, due to a few unfortunate circumstances, I've been forced to use my ability in a perverse manner. But life is full of misfortune. Controlling and manipulating my kind for money has been my way of life for more than a decade and the only way for me to change is either death or banishment and either option means death, as banishment means to become an eternal servant of the master through spirit transformation. Which would destroy my body and have my soul service the master for all eternity as a ghost or something of the sort. It wasn't something I ever wanted, but the alternative was to sell out my kind.

My thoughts were muddled with ethics and moral for the first time in at least three decades. It must have been the halflings. They're the ones to blame.

With an angry grunt, Korvin spat out his anguish, in silence of course, but control of his emotions was teetering back and forth of his own threshold.

The halfling by the name of Memyra had stopped the group only to check if we were going the right direction. I thought it was odd we had stopped at all, but I needed to massage my poor feet; they were absolutely sore from the continuous marching. If I ever get the chance, I'm going to kill that halfling. Torbiro, you're on my kill list, too.

As Korvin was finally able to catch his breath, take off his boots and massage his feet, the group started to move again. It was the most irritating thing Korvin had ever experienced. He had been in long marches before, but most of the time, the one leading the pack would inform the group how long they would be stopping. But these halflings and Miss Robyn had no coordination what-so-ever.

If I was in the right mind, I could have led them in a more organised manner, but this was ridiculous. I grabbed my boots and started to run after them. There wasn't even any time to put my boots on. Another day had passed and during our march we had stopped only once to look for a landmark on the map. I was tired and I was reaching my limit, my physical limit. Which meant if I did not get any rest soon, I would be reaching my mental limit of endurance as well and I would not allow that. My merchandise was literally my life. If the master ever found out I lost even one, I could be killed. Before my mind broke from lack of energy, I wanted to demand a moment's repose. But as soon as I was about to complain, the group started to set up a campfire.

Three days of marching and finally Korvin could actually rest his body and mind. At last, he thought, I can finally take a breather.

With all my energy almost drained, I started to look forward to the nasty tasting stew young Robyn was going to make. I was so tired from the constant trek that my mind could only focus on keeping the slaves in check. I couldn't even plan my way into Traytos with magic, let alone think about the way to the dreaded tower.

With a big sigh of relief, Korvin sat by the warm fire to massage his sore feet and meditate to allow the void to replenish his magical and physical energies. Such meditation needed peace of mind and quiet. But this quiet only lasted for two straight hours. Korvin needed at least four hours of meditation to complete his rest, but he was interrupted by the squabbling of two squeaky halflings. Korvin could hear them during his state of meditation, which allowed him to perceive his nearby surroundings in case of danger. With a common mantra, he managed to block out the noise. The words of his mantra were peace, tranquillity and void, void tranquillity. Calm repetition of these words in elvish was like a lullaby. In his mind Korvin repeated, 'tero tero yareso, kon trah kon trah yareso.' With repetition, the loud, noisy voices slowly faded away. He was again at peace, able to meditate, to rest and restore his depleted energies, his stamina and arcanus. Korvin could see the white plains of the void when a loud screeching voice completely broke his lullaby-like mantra. This time it was young Robyn that had screamed. Was there no end to this chaos? I had the right mind to blast them with a controlling spell, but that would break the rest of the slaves and they might go rampant. Korvin again tried to block out the noise, but the halflings were simply too annoying. Their voices were like rapid squeaking, like the sound of a rusted door hinge opening and closing.

It was breaking my concentration. I could no longer handle the noise. The voices and the arguments. It was maddening. My void, the peaceful void in my mind, shattered by the creatures of chaos, like the infernal pulse had invaded my innermost being. I tried to control my anger. I tried to extinguish my emotions of rage and fury. I tried and tried and tried. But my mind was about to break. I couldn't take this anymore. I needed the pulse of chaos to stop. It was interfering with the energies of the void. To be able to concentrate, I cannot... this whirling of chaos must stop... I must stop it... but I must stay... in control... I must. I mus... I.

The pulse had entered Korvin's mind, but although it is the energy of technology, it does not conflict with the void. But due to the crazy and unpredictable nature of certain chaos creatures, such as gnomes or goblins, they tend to push the limits of the pulse and experience these dangers. People of the void have made a misconception that all creatures of the pulse are exactly like those on the extreme side of the spectrum. Alternatively, the creatures of the pulse have also been made to think all creatures of the void were passive in nature, like praying monks or religious fanatics. So too, did Korvin judge Torbiro and Memyra as goblins or gnomes. He could not break free from his own prejudice, which had caused his downfall. Overlaying grotesque versions of them, taunting him, breaking him and stressing him out. The pressure was so strong he simply did not have the willpower to overcome this adversity. What happened next was through Korvin's instinct to quiet the pulse, to absorb the energies and unleash it towards his intended target. Korvin no longer had control of his mind, as it filled with his own terrors and machinations of the pulse. He lost control. He forgot. He only felt rage, wrath and fury. He had forgotten his task to deliver the slaves and he had forgotten his fear, the threats and the consequences.

From his meditative pose, seated on the ground cross-legged, he floated in the air, using what little tranquillity he had culminated from his two hours of meditation and cast the most powerful spell he knew, to shut the maddening pulse, to return to the peaceful void and to defeat the evil goblins taunting and harassing him. Korvin raised his hand in front of him, with an open palm targeting the filthy evil goblins in his mind, but in actuality he was aiming for Memyra, who was not even the target in his mind. Korvin believed he was silencing his enemy. He tried to cast a spell of destruction but he did not know the incantation, instead he unleashed all the energy he could muster with a spell he had passively memorised. A minor charm spell. But a minor spell can become more powerful with more energy concentrated into the incantation. With all the energies within him, chaos or tranquillity, he blasted a paralysis spell. He had done it. The noise was now quiet. He had won. Korvin could now return to the peaceful void. But to his misfortune, even though he had stopped the bickering of the two halflings, his place of peace never returned. Instead, more chaos reigned. He had been lost in his rage and had not only unleashed his stored energies but also those that maintained his control over the other elves. The slaves were free. He tried to regain control, but it was too late. He lacked energy. He had neither arcanus nor any energy from the dreaded pulse, he was completely exhausted.

CHAPTER 60
TRAPS AND MORE TRAPS

With Korvin's action, his control over Memyra was secured but due to the irritated nature of his mind, he had inadvertently released his merchandise from his control. The elves in his care had suddenly awoken and their first action was to shout and flee. Their words cried out 'Murderer' and 'Traitor' and 'Monster', then they all fled in different directions. There were twenty elvish slaves Korvin had tried to control and then sell to whomever paid the most. Due to his own irritation towards the quarrelling halflings, Korvin had lost control over his pawns. The smaller elves that had acted much like young children were a sub-race of elves known as faerins. They were a combination of halfling and elf breeding. A very rare and unwanted race. Most of their kind were used as play things by the rich and wealthy races, such as the human nobles and eccentric gnome entrepreneurs. These faerins had a unique ability; they were able to phase and transport from realm to realm. It was a legend that faerins were created long ago by the 'Thrust' when both factions of the most prominent pulse technologists and the most faithful void zealots had competed to achieve the next phase of advancement. But it was simply a legend or perhaps a fabricated myth. These little elves did not act like the others and they decided to frolic around before disappearing into the brush.

Korvin, completely dumbstruck, spun a few times before completely collapsing to the ground. His body was stiff, but with a closer look, he was in a panicked state, trembling with either fear or anger. Robyn was the only one to see the state of Korvin, as the halflings continued to argue. The elves that had fled only spoke in elvish and from what Robyn could surmise, her halfling friends could not understand the language or they too would have reacted like herself. Shocked and worried. She approached the depleted elf and could see it was not anger he wore on his face but rather the utmost terror. What was he so afraid of that would frighten him more than a near death experience at sword-point? Robyn tried her best to get Korvin's attention, but he was too distraught to acknowledge her presence and remained in a catatonic state, clutching his knees in a foetal position. Not knowing what to do next, Robyn screamed as loudly as she could to grab the attention of her small friends, but her loud voice was still too quiet to be heard by the halflings. What could she do?

Memyra, in her moment of paralysis, thought she had been struck by some unknown force but she could clearly see Torbiro, and he wasn't holding a weapon to immobilise her. What had happened? As soon as the thought had passed, she was able to move again and her friend was still prostrating, like he was about to be hit. Memyra, not letting such an opportunity pass, hit him hard enough so the stubbornness would leave him and allow him to learn his lesson, but not hard enough to break his skin. With a thud and a satisfying slap, she scolded Torbiro but also helped him up, so he could join in to eat the stew Robyn had made for them. They had been arguing for no more than a few clicks, so the food should still be warm. But once the two had finally turned toward Robyn and Korvin, the scene in front of them was a bit odd. Memyra could remember Korvin was sitting on the ground, cross-legged and mumbling something in elvish. The other elves were just a few metres from the campfire, huddled and resting. Robyn too was by her cooking pot ready to serve the sweet-smelling stew, but now Korvin was in a foetal position clutching his knees, like some subdued babe and the other elves were gone. Huh? It was a little strange, but maybe they have just gone for a walk or to stretch their legs.

I looked at Torro and tilted my head in question. He looked back at me and glanced at Korvin and the pot of food and simply shrugged his shoulders like nothing was wrong or different.

'Wow Torro, you haven't even noticed the other elves have gone missing, but what do I care?' said Memyra, silently in her thoughts. It was time to eat.

After being scolded by Memyra, Torbiro noticed she stopped for a moment. 'I really thought she was gonna hit me but I guess I was wrong,' he thought.

But the instant I decide to stand up, she bonks me on the head hard and then gives me a slap. I was shocked at first, but then she helped me up. What was going on? I had thought it was time for dinner. Myra didn't have to hit me as she had already won and got her way. I was getting close to a solution to keep Korvin's friends safe when she started to shout at me. I know it was rude to ignore the girls, but I was so close. Our problems would have ended and we could have marched to the tower to rescue Princess Dawn from the clutches of evil. As I stood up, I could smell the delicious veggie stew Robyn had made and my stomach started to growl and grumble. As we started to move to the campfire to eat dinner, Myra gave me a confused look. I didn't know what that was all about, but her eyes were telling me something. So I looked at the campsite. It looked normal to me. Korvin looked a bit pale, but he always did after a short run. I looked back at Myra and shrugged my shoulders, telling her nothing was wrong. She immediately rolled her eyes like I missed something, but I couldn't figure it out. She could had just told me instead of using her silent treatment. Girls! I can never understand them. But that didn't matter now because it was time to eat.

After his big meal, Torbiro had planned to discuss his plans with Korvin about how to keep his part of the bargain. To keep his elven friends' safe, while they traversed the minefield of traps near the Tower of Rivals. But as Torbiro was about to start, Robyn stopped him with a look of panic in her eyes. Torbiro did not understand why she looked this way, but it must be important. Just before Torbiro was about to say something completely inconsiderate, Memyra smacked him. Even before he could respond in complaint, he could see his friend was pointing at Korvin and she had an upset look on her face as well.

I looked where Korvin had been sitting next to Robyn and that's when everything clicked. He wasn't moving. I thought he was just being quiet, like how Commander Peren is when he waits, but I guess it must be something else. I looked more closely at Korvin and he was as pale as a sheet of freshly cleaned cloth. I could only think to poke him, just to make sure he was alive. I approached slowly and very carefully, before doing anything, I looked at Memyra. I tilted my head to the left and gave her a thumbs up with a smile and pointed at Korvin. I didn't want to do anything that would anger Memyra as she hits really hard. I think she just likes to hit me. Man, I hope Korvin is alright, I still need him to guide us through the Fields of Dangerous Traps. I moved closer to Korvin to poke him and then check if he was ok. But what happened next was really unexpected.

The stew Robyn had prepared was really delicious, but I did wonder why she wasn't eating dinner with us. I understand Torro is a bit dense, but he was still good company. Just looking at Torbiro eat, reminds me of when we were little. He used to eat so fast so he could go back to planning to be a knight, to be a hero and to be admired. I remember like it… like it was yesterday but enough of nostalgia. I looked at Robyn and she had been speaking in elvish again to Korvin. I couldn't understand what she was saying, but it must have been serious. It seemed as though he hadn't moved since my argument with Torro. I wondered what his problem was as I ate the veggie stew. After my meal, I could see Torbiro not understanding the situation, so to interrupt him, I used my plate to tap him. My intention was to stop his oblivious nature and actually look at the situation, ya stupid genius. But he must not have seen me put the plate in front of him and he ran into it. I could see he was about to complain as well, but I gave him a stern look, as if to say, look before you leap. I pointed at the very pale elf and made sure Torro knew what I meant. From the way he responded, maybe not, it looked as though he was going to help Robyn, but then he turned back, gave me two thumbs up with both hands and smiled oddly. Now I knew he didn't understand. I stood up and started to approach Torbiro to tell him to help Robyn. But what he did next was unexpected. It looked like he was going to poke Korvin, like he was some kind of dead body. I slapped my hand on my forehead. By the pulse, why are you so dense, Torro? Read the situation. How can someone as smart as you be this stupid? I had just eaten, so running was not a good option. Just before I could signal to Robyn, Korvin did something completely unexpected for such an apathetic and pious figure. I never trusted anyone that looked suspiciously calm all the time, but his reaction to being poked by Torbiro was utterly surprising. It shocked me. So much so, I fell to the ground from such an action. My mouth agape with shock and awe.

Robyn was very worried about Korvin that she too, had forgotten to eat. She heard Torbiro and Memyra talk about what to do next and how much they really liked her cooking, but it was not enough to stop her from caring for one of her own kind. Korvin was still in a catatonic state and no manner of soothing words had affected him. Robyn had hoped her friends would help care for Korvin, but they must have been too hungry to notice. I looked at Torbiro, but he seemed not to notice, then I looked at Memyra and she was very quick to notice my distress, but she did not act immediately. Did she not care? No, that cannot be. It must be a halfling custom to finish one's food before aiding others. After Torbiro had finished his third helping of my vegetable stew, he stood up and started to approach me; I looked down at Korvin, who was lying on my lap. I smiled and spoke only hopeful things to Korvin, that things are okay, or that good things are coming his way. I spoke in elvish saying that mother used to say, that fortune smile upon you. I heard a clang and quickly looked up to see Torbiro on the ground, rubbing his head. I wondered what had happened; I looked frantically for an assailant, but there was no one and only the four of us were in this clearing. Torbiro looked back strangely and gave Memyra his thumbs up. I did not know the meaning of this gesture, perhaps it was a sign of good faith. I waited for Torbiro to come closer and help Korvin, but instead he slowly approached and lightly poked him. I slapped his hands away and told him off.

'What are you doing?' cried Robyn, ready to slap Torbiro again if he came near Korvin.

'I was checking if he was still alive! Why?' said Torbiro, with a confused look on his face.

'You can't just poke someone in this state. That's just rude and…' said Robyn. She was interrupted by the sudden action of Korvin, from lack of motivation to bursting full ferocity. Korvin looked at Torbiro with an accusing stare. As though all the anger and fury was festering within that single look. Clearly Korvin was putting all the blame on Torbiro, but Torbiro was just shocked at the sudden action of Korvin, as he leaped up and started to rant about whose fault all of this was. The situation was shocking, a very calm, emotionless and enigmatic elf turned to a raving lunatic spouting nonsense.

'You halflings, ca…caused all this!!' said Korvin, waving his finger at Torbiro while he shook erratically.

'What do you mean? I didn't do anything.' said Torbiro. Again, he wore confusion on his face.

'You're the… You're the one that pushed me. You pushed me so hard…' said Korvin. At which moment, Korvin started to panic from the weight of the stress he himself carried. He was now in full blown panic mode. He pointed his finger at Memyra as she approached and started to mouth an incantation to cast a spell.

'Noooooooooowwwwww… Diiiiieeee!!!' screamed Korvin in an attempt to blast Memyra. But nothing happened. Not even a puff of smoke was released from his hand. He was out of magical essence, but the adrenaline he felt was urging him to attack.

'Miss Memyra, look out!' said Robyn, trying her best to distract Korvin without harming him. Robyn had jumped in his path and started to wave her arms frantically, like some crazed fan or someone trying to fly using skinny arms. Memyra was more concerned about the spell Korvin had tried to kill her with and jumped behind a nearby shrub. Memyra had reacted right after Korvin started his incantation. So Robyn's warning was very late.

'Memyra, where did you go?' Torbiro still did not understand the immediate situation. He was asking where she was to check if the spell had hit, since Torbiro had no knowledge of spells what-so-ever. He assumed she was gone because of the strange words Korvin had spoken.

'I'm okay, Torro.' Memyra responded to the confused halfling. She was very understanding, but this situation was so obvious that even Robyn had figured it out. 'What is going on in your head, Torro?' Memyra asked herself as she smacked her head with her palm. Even Robyn had acted on her instinct to protect others first. Just what was Torro thinking? Just what kind of knight is he? And just as she was thinking this, her question was immediately answered. He was just a fool. Like he had always been.

'I am Torbiro, of the knights of Traytos. You sir, Korvin are under arrest!' said Torbiro with arm extended, chest puffed out and his hand pointing at the elf. He was proudly posing like he was some hero in the Traytos gazette. At his declaration, Memyra and Robyn reacted with uncontrollable laughter while Korvin had been so shocked that all he could do was be stunned. Both the girls were in stitches as Torbiro marched towards Korvin.

'I… Said… Die… Half…Ling…' Korvin did attempt at casting a deadly spell, as Robyn lay on the ground just a few centimetres away, laughing and coughing at the weird situation created by Torbiro. Robyn was incapacitated from laughter and lack of breath. But Korvin was determined to end the two little halflings in his path. The ones, in his mind, that had ruined his life and the operation of his master. The only course of his life was death, so why not take down a few enemies with him?

'Memyra, I've got this. You no longer need to worry.' said Torbiro, with more gusto and pride than he should have. It sounded like a joke, more of a joke than an actual command or an order of reassurance. Torbiro was filled with confidence as he continued to approach Korvin to arrest him. There was no plan in Torbiro's mind, just baseless scenes of grandeur. The picture in his mind was of himself, gliding towards the criminal with his red cape – which he did not wear – gallantly floating behind him, as his prey cowered in fear – which was not true either as Korvin was just dumbfounded by the ridiculous scene in front of him. Torbiro could see his honourable friends cheering him on – in fact, they had been on the ground, laughing out loud as both tried to catch their breaths– to capture the criminal. Torbiro could hear the fanfare, graces and adulations of a crowd that was not there.

As Torbiro reached Korvin with the biggest smile on his face, he turned to his public audience. The veil of his grandiose illusion Torbiro created, had fallen. His heart was crushed and he showed his embarrassment as his face quickly turned bright red. But to Torbiro's further misfortune, Korvin had not only broken free from his shock, he had gained enough energy to cast a spell. The elf could feel the energies coursing through his veins. He was finally ready to kill his prey. His target this time was Torbiro, who was just within reach and his allies were completely incapacitated from their own amusement. This was Korvin's chance. His target was vulnerable and distracted by his own illusions. There was no way Korvin could miss and this was it. But unfortunately, Korvin had not been thinking straight. His target was a small creature in a prone position, which made it very vulnerable and easy to strike, but Korvin, in his wild machinations of revenge and retribution, had forgotten Torbiro was a halfling. All Korvin could see was a dark silhouette with a sad looking smile and as he looked at his surroundings, he could only see the dark waves of energy seeping out of the trees and the ground. The dark waves were his own darkness, blinding Korvin from the true scene unfolding in front of him, just like Torbiro, but in a dark nuance rather than a bright confidence. The laughter was more like taunting voices telling him to attack. The voices so warped that his view of them had become grotesque, feral and unrecognisable. To Korvin, they looked like gelatinous oozes with freaky and misshapen eyes and mouths that mocked and teased the viewer no matter where they looked. He could not recognise the race of his target. With a sinister smile on Korvin's face, he blasted what he thought was the defenceless Torbiro. Phantasmal Death. What Korvin had thought was Torbiro, had actually been Robyn, who was only a few centimetres away as well. Since it was an illusion spell, that only had an effect on those that had lost all hope and were in the midst of despair. But Robyn was in a state of bliss, so nothing had happened. Again, the halfling had won. That failure had broken the dark illusions Korvin had succumbed to, but his revenge was over. His mind was shattered and he had returned to the void. He was again calm and the scene he saw in front of him was chaos. With a final word, he declared his revenge on them all, but then fled to plot his revenge.

After the group had come to, they all realised Korvin was missing. At first, Torbiro wanted to find him but reluctantly refrained from this act. He remembered what he had done and what he had declared, which made him feel embarrassed. Robyn was next to try and look for Korvin but had no way to track him, since the foot prints all around them were from the other elves that had also left. Robyn tried her best to find Korvin, but to no avail. After all the searching, the two looked at Memyra to help look for this lost elf that had promised to help them through the trapped lands near the Tower of Rivals. But she shrugged her shoulders and said , "I don't know how to find him." and started to walk towards the tower. Robyn protested until they had found Korvin as he was a vital person to traversing the trapped fields and Memyra threatened to leave her behind, since she didn't care for the elf. Either elves, for that matter, she just wanted to go home with Torbiro and make mischief on the city of Traytos like the thief she was. Robyn was nice, but was not worth her time. She was more of a burden than Torbiro and just Torbiro's ally, not even her friend. Why should I care? She thought. But the cautious elf decided that searching alone would not help their real mission which was to return to Traytos with Memyra and arrest her.

Robyn thought it strange Memyra did not want to search for Korvin, since it would have been quicker for them to complete the mission Torbiro wanted. But if their search had taken more time than needed, then going to the Tower of Rivals would have been a waste of time. Memyra must have thought things through and had seen a bigger picture than she had. Was Memyra's thoughts also honourable ones, where she too, wanted to rescue our beloved princess? Robyn had started to unravel within her own optimism and naïve nature. Her thoughts of Memyra at first were right on the mark. She had seen her as selfish and uncaring, but slowly she had placed her positive outlook on life towards her new friend. Robyn was always looking for a positive overview and could not see the dark aspects of the world. In a word, she was naïve. So naïve that her suspicions turned into trust and then into faith.

Two days of constant travel and the three had made it to the edge of the trapped fields. On arriving, the three of them noticed the massive devastation on the field. Soldiers and warriors, suffering and struggling with the traps. Some traps were simple like pit falls but others were more complex, like mechanical circular blades. Although only one of them had keen senses, they could all hear the terrifying screams and torturous moans of those stuck in the traps. It was gut wrenching and painful to listen to. Even Memyra, who had seen far worst could not resist the urge to cover her ears at the sound of those suffering. As the group moved through the field, their agile bodies were able to naturally evade the simple traps that were triggered with a certain weight before dropping the unfortunate victim. The trapped fields were very flat, as though the surrounding lands had been crafted for trap testing. There were a few trees and rocks, but the even landscape meant the traps were all either well-hidden or very obvious. With Robyn's keen eyes and the agility and reflexes of the three, they were able to traverse the land of traps with only one weakness in their mind. Compassion. The compassion to save others was always on their mind. For Robyn and Torbiro, it was the need to help their kinsman, other soldiers of Traytos. As the two knew, the more lives they saved, the more potential allies they would have. But Memyra reminded them not everyone could be saved. She, on the other hand, had only wanted to save Torbiro. Save him from all of this, the situation they were in, the mission he gave himself and being a knight. His dream of being a hero was a long shot, especially in a city that practically hated their kind. But when they passed the third victim of these traps, the man crying out had broken the two. They needed to save him and an argument between the three started.

From a short distance away, they heard the cry of yet another desperate soldier caught in one of these deadly traps. After passing two soldiers who could clearly help themselves, from the perspective of Memyra, the two kind-hearted souls could no longer ignore those that needed their help or those that could clearly be helped. At first, Memyra reminded them they could help themselves, but Robyn had to disagree with her.

'Help, someone please help me!' cried a female soldier. Bracing the sides of the pit trap with all her strength.

'Ignore her! Let's continue,' said Memyra, reminding the team that not everyone could be saved.

'Ok,' said Torbiro, but in the back of his mind he wanted to rescue yet another damsel in distress.

'No, not this Memyra, we must help her!' said Robyn in protest. Her caring nature could no longer endure the struggle of another.

'Robyn be realistic, we can't save them all, plus what if the princess is being tortured? She won't last long,' said Memyra, again trying to convince her the princess was the main mission and a soldier should complete the mission before it's too late.

'In fact, we should just head back to Traytos and complete your first mission of my capture,' said Memyra with such sarcasm that even the dense Torbiro understood the urgency of rescuing the princess.

'No! Memyra, you cannot expect me to let more people die. I will not walk over this body to save another. Please Torbiro, we must save her!' said Robyn, pleading for his kind heart to protect life. Her plea was noticed by both halflings but Memyra crossed her arms and made an expression of obstinacy, to announce she would not take part in helping this one or any other in this dangerous field.

'Myra, can I borrow some rope?' said Torbiro, as if he would only help this one and they would continue on. But Memyra knew once they helped one, they would need to help the others too. With an 'hmmf', she uncrossed her arms and pulled some rope out of her bag, gave it to Torbiro and whispered, 'be quick'.

'Help me please, help me. I can't hold on much longer. Please hurry,' cried the soldier again, feeling her weakness overtaking her from the lack of rest.

'Yes, we will help you, please try to hold on,' said Robyn, reassuring the soldier.

'Torbiro, please be careful not to fall,' said Robyn.

'Yes, yes. I will,' said Torbiro, but in the same moment he had gone straight for Robyn's position, instead of going around the pit trap and fell in. With Memyra watching, her reflexes managed to react before it was too late. She had dived to grab Torbiro but was only able to grab the rope.

'Torro, you idiot! Use the rope!' screamed Memyra at her clumsy friend. Her eyes could not see into the black abyss of the pit, but she hoped late advice was better than no advice at all. Holding on to the rope, Memyra fell to her knees as tears started to well up in her eyes. She had lost her dear friend and it was all his fault. She had felt regret and could do nothing for him now. Paralysed from her pain of loss, she held the rope tightly as tears started to fall down her face.

'Torbiirroo, nooo!' Robyn had cried out as she watched Torbiro fall into the pit, regretting her choice of rescuing another and endangering her friend. Even with her keen eyesight, she could not see her friend and comrade. What had she done? Regret was setting in her mind. But

Torbiro had actually planned to drop down to help the soldier. He had his plan and he had not told his companions about his process.

'Guys, don't worry, I'm fine.' Torbiro called out. He executed his plan quickly, dropping down and lightly landing on the soldier, while using the rope to secure a tight harness. Torbiro thought, if this soldier had been here for more than a day, holding on to a rope would be hard, so she might fall if she let go of her life saving hold on the walls of this trap.

'Guys, I have a plan and Myra, can you let go of the rope?' called Torbiro, trying to calm his friends.

'Torbiro, you're alive. That's wonderful.' Robyn wiped a tear from her eye. She took a deep breath to calm herself and looked up at Memyra, who was wiping tears off her face.

'Memyra, pass the rope, please,' said Robyn, once she saw Memyra was calmer. With all their strength and a few gadgets, the two girls managed to pull both Torbiro and the soldier out of the hole.

At first, Torbiro thought his actions had more merit for the deed he had committed to, but then he put up his guard as his instincts told him to beware the wrath of those around him. From a heroic pose to arms up shielding his face, to block thrown objects. But to his surprise, Robyn was the only one to scold him while Memyra rushed past the soldier they had just rescued and gave him a very tight hug. In his shock, all Torbiro could do was push her away and escape. He was not used to this kind of reaction from either female. Each had their own reasons for their actions, but he just could not figure it out. Once he was released from Memyra's grasp, then reality struck him. The look on Memyra's face was regret and pain for nearly losing a friend and Robyn had a look of anger. One he had never experienced until now. It had only dawned on him he had forgotten to explain his plan to his friends. So jumping into a hole was very dangerous indeed.

'Torbiro, why did you jump in the hole without telling us what your plan was?' Robyn scolded him for such an absentminded action. It was rude of him to think before he leaped and not told anybody.

'I'm sorry, Memyra. I mean Robyn,' said Torbiro, forgetting who the one was scolding him. Usually it was Memyra and she was always very violent about it.

'I had thought the soldier was in grave danger so time was of the essence, but sorry, I forgot to tell you the plan, Robyn. Will you forgive me?' asked Torbiro, apologising for his rash action. His arms instinctively lifted up in guarding himself from a physical attack, but nothing happened.

'We can talk about this later, Torbiro. First, we need to help her and find out how many there are here in the fields and just what their plan was,' said Robyn, in a stern and commander like tone. By the pulse, she sounded just like Commander Peren, thought Torbiro.

'Tor… Torbiro, I'm glad you didn't die.' Memyra sniffed back her tears. She was very relieved her friend had not died. To her misfortune, Memyra could not gain control over her emotions. She normally acted in a calm and scrupulous manner to avoid emotional attachment or even being caught at her most vulnerable.

'Who are you?' said Torbiro. Instead of thinking it, he had just let it burst out. In his mind, he was more confused about this situation than the one with Korvin. Memyra was always strong, but having her cry and sob like this was too strange. Torbiro had never seen her like this before, not when they were children and not when they were poor and abandoned. But the soldier came first, so he pushed her aside and helped the injured soldier they had just rescued. Memyra simply turned away to deal with the overwhelming emotions she was feeling.

'Soldier, what is your name and rank? And what was your mission?' said Torbiro, quite forcefully, not even allowing the woman to catch her breath.

'Torbiro, please. Can you not see she is in no shape to answer such questions? Do you need food or water, dear?' said Robyn, trying to console the soldier.

'Water, please. It is fine, madam elf and thank you for rescuing me. My name is Saara Redfellow, rank private,' said Private Redfellow, answering both their questions. She was proud but fatigued and had no choice but to answer them.

After providing Private Redfellow with some water and a bar of rations, the group started to talk about what had happened and what was in store for the gung-ho army of Traytos. Before Saara explained anything, the sobbing and highly emotional Memyra had finally gained control of her feelings, or at least that's what it looked like on the surface. In fact, Memyra had taken a potion to keep her face stoic, but the overwhelming and crippling emotions were still there. In her mind, this magical potion had managed to totally suppress the feelings. Private Redfellow explained about one revel ago – one week – the commander of the army had rallied the remaining troops and his personal knights, to charge for the Tower of Rivals. Without a careful plan, many of his troop had fallen to the surrounding traps. She had been the medic of a group when she was ordered to charge forward with the wild and mindless troops. At first, the traps were easily avoided but after a certain distance from the tower, many of the traps had propelled them back to where they had started from, near the edge of the field. With each charge they made, the fatigue and stress caused even the most patient soldiers to make very trivial mistakes, such as letting emotions take control. Which had blinded some and made others more and more violent, even towards their fellow comrades. She had also fallen victim to the latter. She had been helping another soldier when she was kicked into the trap she had pulled them out of. Her equipment had fallen down the same hole. After the explanation and just before Torbiro was about to welcome her to the group, the two girls grabbed him and started to talk in a distant huddle.

'So, what should we do?' said Robyn, feeling a bit of mistrust for the young private.

'What do we do, you say? That's easy. Ditch her and continue to the tower,' said Memyra. She was still feeling the overwhelming feelings towards Torbiro and only wanted to protect him from everything, as if she were a doting parent.

'No. we should rescue the rest of the soldiers!' said Torbiro in protest. His thinking was simple and very trusting. With every soldier rescued, the stronger they were to rescue the princess. The more the merrier, was one of the human sayings back at the tavern.

'Torbiro, ssshhh,' said both Robyn and Memyra in unison. They were worried about the situation,

'Look. Friends, the more soldiers we rescue, the more people we have for rescuing the princess. That would mean we could do the rescuing and the soldiers would hold back the kidnappers. Doesn't that sound like a good plan?' said Torbiro. The girls had loosened their grip on Torbiro just for a moment and he broke the huddle to welcome the newest member to the 'Princess Rescue Team'.

'Welcome, Private Redfellow. Would you like to join us to rescue the princess? But before that, we must rescue the rest of the soldiers too,' said Torbiro.

'Thank you for helping me, but I do not even know your names or rank. Why should I follow you?' said Saara.

'Well, I do apologise for the late introduction, but I am Torbiro. A knight of Traytos and my companions are Miss Memyra, a friend of mine and Miss Cyan Robyn, who is also a knight of Traytos,' said Torbiro, answering her question very nonchalantly.

'As you can see, the three of us are on a mission to rescue the princess of Traytos, just like you and your commander. With your help, we can continue that mission and bring back our beloved princess,' said Torbiro. Again stating the obvious, but in a knightly fashion, poised and cultured. As cultured as he could, at least. Although it seemed like an act, Private Redfellow needed to follow them just to be sure they weren't like Commander Fameborn. As he had given the order to charge, blindly at that and denied aid to the troubled and trapped, he was also the man who had pushed her into the hole after she pulled him out. She did not want to repeat such a mistake that would cost her, her own life.

'Thank you, Knight Torbiro. Let us rescue everyone else,' said Saara.

Only a few metres away, they had spotted another victim of a commander's foolish order and yet again, with rope in hand, Torbiro jumped into the hole to rescue the soldier. Only Robyn seemed to be shocked by his actions, but the other end of the rope was held by Private Redfellow. With only a tug on the rope, they managed to save yet another soldier. This time, it was a male ogre. Very odd, for such a creature to fall in, let alone to get completely wedged in the walls of the hole. He was stuck, but with the four of them, they managed to get most of him out of the hole. With a single push of the ogre's bulky arms, he was out.

'Little one. Thanky you,' said the ogre. He gestured a sign of peace, which was to hug and lick Torbiro very violently. It was a cause of alarm for Robyn, who had never seen or encountered an ogre, but Torbiro had known a few of them from visiting various factories Master Dorian had done maintenance for. They were creatures of habit, but they were a misunderstood race, just like the giants.

With ogre saliva dripping down Torbiro's face, he quickly wiped enough of the liquid and gave the ogre a sign of peace most common for the dwarven tradition, which was to slap the big man on the chin. The nameless ogre then gently let Torbiro down and took a knee.

'Big one, what is your name? What do they call you?' said Torbiro as he continued to wipe off the slobber still coating his face.

'Me namez… Borgar. But shiny man callz me, Stupid! What Stupid mean?' said Borgar, confused on whether or not he was being insulted or it was a common human phrase.

'Borgar, stupid means…' said Torbiro, but was stopped by Memyra. She had grabbed him and blocked his mouth with her hand. She may have just saved his life from his own stupid and naïve acts.

'It means friend in the human words!' said Memyra, trying not to anger the very large creature.

'Oh OK. Me stupid then. Ha ha ha,' said Borgar, just happy to know he was not being made fun of and to learn a new word. His race was not intellectually inclined but they could still learn and new pieces of information were a joyous thing for giant races.

The three girls looked at Torbiro and Memyra whispered to him, 'Don't say anything', to warn him the ogre was still capable of killing the four of them if it went on a rampage. Memyra had not known of ogres, but she had seen them go on a rampage before and it wasn't pretty. Fear started to set in the minds of the women, but Torbiro reassured them Borgar would never kill them. Borgar was in Torbiro's debt and giants were an honourable race, much like the orcs and half-orcs. But simpler. Just as Memyra loosened her grip on Torbiro, he walked up to Borgar and again started to explain what the meaning of 'stupid' was.

'Borgar, stupid doesn't mean friend. It means to not be smart. It means to be a blockhead,' said Torbiro. Robyn and Private Redfellow were preparing to run away from the large man. Memyra, on the other hand, was preparing to jump into the hole for safety.

'Oh, ok. Is 'stupid' bad word?' asked Borgar. Confused, but still wanting to know more.

'No, Borgar. It is just a word humans use. But you are very strong. Can you help me rescue the others from the traps?' said Torbiro, distracting him to ask for help in their rescue attempt. The girls, who had feared the worst out of this very large creature, sighed a breath of relief. Torbiro really was lucky. They all thought.

'You save Borgar. Borgar help little one,' said the ogre with a toothy smile in agreement.

With the aid of Borgar, the team were able to rescue many soldiers from simple traps such as pitfalls, net traps and caged traps. After about a turn – so one hour – the team had not only rescued soldiers but marked all the simple traps and how they were triggered. Most of the soldiers agreed to join their honourable quest, while others simply wanted to return home to their loved ones. Torbiro did the humble thing and let them go. He made sure to ask them to send for reinforcements if a cycle – a day or two – had passed. At which point they had 50 men and women who still wanted the glory of rescuing the princess. The problem now was the magical traps. How would they get past them and safely at that? As they marched carefully forward with all they had helped, Torbiro and Robyn heard a familiar voice. To them, it sounded like Jimmy, but that couldn't be. The two looked at each other and warned the others to wait, only taking Memyra and Borgar with them toward the noise.

'Peep, Pooh, Peep, Pooh.',said the floating gnome, in the middle of a swampy area. His body was moving like it was swimming or treading water, his face was positioned upwards and he was saying strange words like he was trying to breathe underwater.

'Jimmy, is that you?' Torbiro asked the odd-looking gnome. He looked familiar, sounded familiar, but was just a bit odd.

'Torbiro, peep, is that pooh, you? Peep,' said Jimmy, struggling to catch some air. Jimmy was trapped, but it was a self-inflicting spell he had cast on himself to reunite with his prey.

'It is Jimmy!' said Torbiro, very eager to help his lost and now trapped friend.

'How can we help you? Jimmy, we have an ogre. Borgar can pull you out!' said Torbiro, starting to give instructions to Borgar, to grab the little gnome.

'Nooo, pooh, if you, peep, have Robyn, peep, with you, pooh, that would, peep, be better. Pooh,' said Jimmy in reply. An ogre, how did Torbiro get an ogre? It didn't complicate the plan, but it would be another thing to consider. He could easily dispel this spell, but that would need an explanation. If the elf just touches the field, I can say she was the one who saved him.

'Yes, Jimmy. I am here,' said Robyn in reply. She was thrilled another one of her friends was found and she was willing to help. Memyra, who was sitting on top of Borgar's shoulder, was a bit more sceptical, as she watched from a distance.

Jimmy had always appeared clumsy, similar to Torbiro, but the first time I met him, he had a wily and scheming appearance, like he had some ulterior motive. But he also had a strange aura about him, like my magical items. He was odd and I didn't trust him.

'Robyn, peep, can you, pooh, come close, peep? I believe, pooh, you can, peep, help me. Pooh,' said Jimmy as he calmly instructed Robyn. Robyn happily followed his command, like it was a friend's request. As Robyn approached, all saw a bubble-like substance appear and glow for a moment. This was the first time this had occurred. But Jimmy explained every few turns or so, this strange containment had glowed. He had explained his gnomish curiosity had been the cause of his entrapment. After a few moments, Robyn was instructed to touch the bubble to pop it. And with a loud boom and a lot of sticky and gooey liquid, Jimmy and Robyn had been covered in the blast of the strange orb. Torbiro was in the right place at the right time, which allowed him to avoid any of the goo. There was enough of the liquid to even reach the feet of the ogre, but just a small patch around his toes. Borgar quickly wiped the sticky goo on to the ground and managed to smear enough of it off his toes. Robyn and Jimmy were completely covered in the substance and as close as Torbiro was to the explosion, he was absolutely clean. Must have been the innate luck that halflings had.

In Jimmy's mind, this was a test to see and view the extent of the luck Torbiro had. As Jimmy pretended to complain about the sticky liquid he was enveloped in, he viewed his surroundings. Jimmy had noticed that even though Memyra the bandit was on the ogre, she too had a bit of the liquid on her clothing. Sure, it was small, but she was still affected by the event. Unlike Torbiro, everyone who was affected by the glowing sludge had been enchanted by one of Jimmy's spell. This Torbiro had a level of luck beyond, even that of a normal halfling. This was troubling indeed. But I can just trick him while the others are not around. Jimmy thought this as he made a fool of himself, slipping and sliding on the ichor that still covered him.

After cleaning themselves with a dry cloth, the team of 50, plus Torbiro, Robyn, Memyra and Jimmy, had confirmed the plan of action. With all of them helping each other through the rest of the traps, they would reach the commander and march to the tower and rescue Princess Dawn from her evil captives. The plan was simple enough and only a few turns later, the band of soldiers had reached the outskirts of the tower of rivals. Their numbers had also increased with all the fatigued mercenaries and knights that followed the commander. Their number was now almost two hundred. Upon their arrival, they were met with one last trap. One that was hard to detect and even harder to break free from. The team experienced the trap which held Commander Fameborn at bay, drained and stunned by the contradiction of the trap's complexity. All but one were caught up in it. Only Torbiro had escaped the strange trap.

CHAPTER 61
THE TOWER OF RIVALS

The original design of the Tower of Rivals was a training ground for assassins from nearby kingdoms. The terrain was designated by rings of difficulty. There were five rings in total and tested a different part of the killer's instinct. The first and outermost ring was to train young children, orphans or the forgotten. This part of the training course was designed to test the simplest of instincts. And children who wanted to survive had the greatest of instincts, relying on their animalistic natures. The next ring was designed and intended for young adults, either recruited from nearby cities to become legal killers for hire, or they were the children that had survived the first ring. This method might seem cruel, but it was reality. An assassin who could not pass a simple trap was worthless and so the first traps were to weed out weaklings.

The second ring tested a natural born agility and flexibility. Anyone who was slow or clumsy would be stuck here. This part of the ring was also a test of loyalty. Who were they loyal to? This was always a question when hiring an assassin. Money? Or just the task? If it was for money or some kind of wealth, their loyalty lay with themselves and they would do anything to get it, even kill their allies. If their loyalty was for the task of killing, then they were the perfect assassin. As the job was enough to satisfy the creature of death.

The third ring was to test intelligence. Not many children made it this far and even young adults that had survived the second ring could be trapped here. This ring tested, not just intelligence but teamwork, since this was a survival ground, sometimes survival meant sacrifice. Not of life, but of pride. These grounds had traps only those that had allies would be able to overcome. Betrayal meant death, not just for the one being betrayed but also for the betrayer as the field was full of dangerous inescapable – if alone – traps.

The fourth ring was to hone the three skills combined. These traps were magical in nature but could be overcome by a team of three or four skilled in survival instincts, agility and flexibility, loyalty and intelligence. Those that had innate magical abilities had an advantage here, but many of them would not have lasted this long. As most magical creatures had a level of arrogance, that would have been the death of them via a betrayal. Which is why mages and other such souls were never assassins. The traps in this ring would ensnare and immobilise. But due to their magical nature, only those that were capable of being charismatic would be able to convince, connive and merge with an enemy group. A small group of thieves could make it this far, but a lone talent would need to seek the aid of another and hide their real intent.

The final and innermost ring was, of course, the most dangerous of them all. This too was of magical design, but the intent of the trap was to test out their grasp on reality. This trap tested the strength of will and the power of their mind. It was an illusionary trap designed to test the true desires of the creature. If again it was for wealth, the trap would provide them with their deepest desires of pleasure and wealth. Whatever made them happy was the trap. Ultimately, to escape was to release it, as this happiness was not real. It was not true and therefore they would be released. But after perhaps days or weeks within this training facility, an unprepared soul would greedily seek nourishment, rather than wealth or treasures. Children who made it this far would seek the joyous life with a family, to be cared for and pampered. This ring was to test each individual and no alliance would prepare them for this task. Some would make it through. Most of those that passed this test were just useful accomplices, to aid in a task but have no real desire besides the job at hand.

And so, those creatures would be the true warriors of death. But since the tower is now being controlled by a single kingdom, these training grounds have been modified, to have a secret method to pass the traps and enter the tower, such as an underground tunnel. Those with magical means use their powers, which allow the person to materialise themselves from one location to another in an instant. One such individual is Kitreth from the opposing kingdom of Bataros. She is now within the tower caring for her cousin, daughter of the kingdom of Traytos. With the aid of an expert in the healing arts, she is waiting patiently for any signs of her cousin's recovery. Not aware of the arrival of a new force to thwart the plans of her uncle. Kitreth had known about the history of this tower and the changes made to manipulate who would survive and who were controlled. Those changes had weakened the natural powers of the land and she had decided to enhance them back to their original power. But with such an enhancement, Kitreth was unaware those that broke out would never leave the trap. Only those with assistance would be able to escape the final trap. Or perhaps those with luck could break out of such a powerful mental trap.

The trap in the innermost area near the tower triggers without provocation. The trigger is the sweet desire of triumph. Those that see their goal just within their reach tend to create a fantasy of victory and the ease of attaining it. For Fameborn and his men, the trigger was just seeing their glory so close within their grasp. The defeat of their enemies, the rescue of their maiden and the rewards that would come with their efforts. The escape and the solution of the trap was to realise such a thing was all fake, to mentally overcome the fantasy with a realistic reality and to become humble in their attempt. But greed and the lust for power were their downfall. For Torbiro, it was much the same, but he did not lust for power. His desire was adulation. Of becoming a man that could be noble and appreciated, to be able to be relied upon, to reach above the prejudice of others and to be a knight. But his escape would be much easier, since he had all of this already, but he seemed not to acknowledge it himself. He was his own enemy, a contradictory solution. For Memyra, it was to keep Torbiro safe, but since her trap would consist of her desires, then her way out would be to have her friend come to harm. Memyra had vowed to never let that happen ever since they were younglings, but every act Torbiro had made would always put him in danger and she would be his saviour. She could have overcome this fear, but her emotions were still on a high, ever since Torbiro jumped into the pit just hours ago. If she had been calm like usual, this trap would not even affect her. For Robyn, her desires were to keep not one person safe but all the people they had brought. Her compassion was her downfall and the only way for her to break out of this trap was to understand life was not eternal and everyone had their moment. Although she was an elf, and mental traps were their speciality, which gave them an advantage to resist them, Robyn was not magically attuned. She had been trained but in the end she had chosen the path of chaos rather than the path of tranquillity. Making her susceptible to this mental trap much like the others.

Much like Fameborn's dream of success, Torbiro and his group had experienced the struggle and success of this horrible mental trap. After the first time, they repeated their rescue of Princess Dawn, much like the first time, though the second time had been harder to accomplish, they would burst through the tower doors, defeat the countless monsters, climb the tower, defeat more enemies and free and retrieve the princess, charge back down the tower and out the door. But once out, many of them would turn back and start this process again and again until they escaped their desires. The trap was relentless, but after the second cycle, Torbiro had broken out.

On Torbiro's second rescue attempt, he decided not to turn around and continued to march with the princess in his arms. With a few steps, he was out of the mental trap. Bumping into Memyra, who was always behind him, he crashed into her physically, which had broken him out of the trap. Oof! And he was on the ground. When he arrived, there was still plenty of light from the sun, but now it was night. How did this happen? Where was the princess he had rescued? And why was he still at the edge of the field, near the Tower of Rivals, which he had traversed and rescued the princess? Torbiro rubbed his eyes and noticed Memyra, Robyn and the others were standing asleep. It was strange. He looked around and could see the knight of Commander Fameborn as well as the commander himself start to look odd. Many of the knights were starting to shrivel up, but Torbiro had thought maybe they were just old humans. But what Torbiro did not know was three of these men were actually the same, or perhaps younger than the commander and he did not know there was a trap of mental desires here that would drain a person of their life force for being obstinate and stubborn. Humans without beards looked alike to Torbiro, so these people were just that. They were old. What Torbiro needed to do was save the princess from the evil people that had kidnapped her. He stopped inspecting the knights and headed for the door of the tower. He gave a signal to his friends and the soldiers that had followed him, but no one responded. Being quite dense, he charged forward without noticing he was alone. To his luck, there were no guards near the tower. There was the door and with every step closer, he started to notice the strange difference between the other times he had rescued the princess. The first thing was the steps of the tower to get to the front door. They were huge. They were similar to the steps of the castle in Traytos. Why were they so big? He wondered. But there wasn't enough time to ponder and investigate, so using his agility, he jumped, not straight up but from the side of the first step. To bounce off of it and jump again to the top of the first step. To his luck, this was easy, since he was not wearing the heavy encumbering knight's armour, or this would not have been possible. Not wasting time, he repeated this until the top of the stairs, at which time he turned around to check on his friends' progress and at that time he noticed he was alone. He looked around to where they all were and in the distance; he had found them. They were all still with the sleeping knights, standing asleep. What were they doing? They were wasting time, so Torbiro started to call out to them, but his voice was not quite loud enough to rouse them. Seeing how high he was from the ground, Torbiro slowly climbed back down to gather his friends. Why were they not coming? He thought. He was already very drained of energy from the trap and by the time he had climbed down from the stairs, he had started to feel the weight of his exhaustion. One step, two steps and he was down. Collapsing from lack of energy, Torbiro blacked out.

CHAPTER 62
SLEEPING FRIENDS

The next day, Torbiro was awoken by something entering his mouth. Normally, he slept very peacefully on his side, curled up in a ball. But due to the events of yesterday's trap, he had passed out on the ground, on his back, no less. His mouth was wide open as he slept and an unfortunate flyby had landed into his mouth. A crow had pooped directly in there, with the nasty projectile touching his tongue. He awoke with the utmost revulsion. He spat and emptied his still empty stomach as he hurled all of its contents out. What a way to wake up! After cursing the accursed bird that had violated his mouth, he stood up and brushed all the dirt off. He looked at the tower and remembered he needed to rescue the princess. He took a few steps to the tower and realised he needed to find out why his friends were nowhere to be found. Turning around, he investigated.

At Torbiro's return, he could see the same scene as the previous day, with the exception that some of the human knights were now on the ground as pale as ghosts. Without knowing what to do, Torbiro started to check on the other soldiers and his friends, especially Robyn and Memyra. Torbiro had tried to speak to them, softly and then gradually, very loud. But to no avail. With his finely thought-out speeches having no effect, Torbiro started to use Memyra as a guinea pig, by trying to annoy her. First, he would call her names, such as thief or wolf. But his friend did not budge. Secondly, he tried to tell her nice things, but these words too were lost in the mind of the unconscious. He even tried to use physical contact such as trying to move his friends, but this too had failed to do anything. He had tried to push and coax the large soldiers to budge, but they simply were too big and too strong for a small little halfling to affect. Getting frustrated, Torbiro went back to Memyra, as she was his size and would be easier to move. He tried to pull her arms, push her back, trip her, flip her and use choke holds to get her to budge, but nothing was stirring them. How could he get his friends and allies to rouse from whatever sleep they were in?

It had been a few hours since he started and he had gotten nowhere with his attempts. Torbiro had also become quite exhausted, so he sat down next to Memyra and tried to think about how he would get them to move and start the rescue mission of the princess. Sitting cross-legged near his halfling friend, Torbiro then noticed the magical aura around all the trapped individuals. He had no understanding of how magic worked, let alone how to disarm the trap these people were encased in. His halfling instinct started to manifest from the intense frustration he felt. So he took off the shoes Memyra had given him. They were very comfortable, but when Torbiro was beyond the point of stress, he would naturally want to relax and that meant being bare-foot. He kicked these shoes off. One landed just a few centimetres away from Memyra and the second shoe flew all the way to Commander Fameborn. Torbiro had not seen where the second shoe went, as right after he kicked it off, he immediately curled up in a ball to rub his toes. The feeling of massaging his toes was amazing and he managed to calm himself from his inadequacies and relax to allow him to find a solution to the problem. Although Torbiro was in a moment of thought, he had missed a crucial moment, when he accidentally freed Commander Fameborn.

CHAPTER 63
POPPING THE BUBBLE

I must climb the tower and save the princess. I must march forward and defeat my enemies. I need the glory and honour. I am the hero she is waiting for. I must… oof. In the dream-like trance, Commander Fameborn had been climbing the tower with sheer will power. His mind was weakening and his body was almost broken. But in a sudden instant, upon climbing the tower once again, he was struck with a boot of all things and had been brought out of the magical trap. At first he was confused, but from the energy draining properties of the trap, he could no longer muster any mental will to push himself and with blurring eyes, a shrivelled up body and a broken spirit, he was about to collapse from exhaustion, but his last image was a small boot striking him and a small soldier curled up in a ball, vigorously making pleasuring sounds. It must have been the void. Had Fameborn entered the void through the trials of death and devastation? This must have been the dishonour his liege had warned him about. What shame this must bring him and his clan. Fameborn could not keep from losing consciousness and so he blacked out with a thud of his body to the ground and the clank of his armour as he collapsed.

After a few clicks, Torbiro was startled by a very loud sound of heavy armour crashing to the ground. From his view, it appeared to be from where his commander had been standing straight and stuck in place. Torbiro released his feet and bounced to a standing position after a slight roll. He could see Commander Fameborn collapsed on the ground only two metres from where he was last standing. How could that be? He hadn't budged when Torbiro had tried to move him and yet there he was, on the ground face first in the dirt. What had happened? Torbiro wondered, but from what he could see, he could not make heads or tails at how the good commander had moved. At which point, Torbiro had not realised his technology-made shoes had been the solution to break the magical spell. It was a clockwork item which contained energy emanating from the pulse, which in turn could naturally disrupt the energies from the void. His shoes were the key, which was a strange turn of events. Memyra was also being affected by the clockwork shoes but not by much as those did not strike her like one did with the commander. Although Memyra had been wearing both magical items and technological items on her person, the effects of the mind trap had a full effect on her. It was as though the controller of the tower had anticipated this fact. Torbiro approached the now prone commander and tried to coax him. His words were effective, but the only response he could receive were moans and grumbles of fatigue and exhaustion. At least he was alive, was Torbiro's thought, but now he needed to awaken all the others.

At first, not knowing what had affected the commander, he picked up both his fancy shoes. Rather than putting them on, he continued to be barefoot and held the shoes in his hands. He went back to Memyra and tried to talk to her, but as with his last attempt, nothing had affected her. As a gesture of annoyance, he poked her with the shoes he had been holding. Not being able to see the aura affecting his friend, this act was weakening the mind trap and as Torbiro spoke, he had started to get a slight response from Memyra. Though it was just her face twitching and her brow wrinkling, but it was a start. Something he was doing was working. Was it the shoes? He thought, but that didn't make sense, as he had been wearing those shoes beforehand and had poked and kicked her from his other attempts. This situation still puzzled him, but something he was doing was working. In fact, it was not the clockwork shoes that had awoken Fameborn and were affecting Memyra, but actually an innate ability which all halflings have. Luck. Torbiro's luck was so immensely strong, it had the ability to change the chance of effect by tenfold. To put it in perspective, a human who was born under some mystical factor would have a one in five million chance to break the mind trap with technology. A normal halfling such as Memyra, has a one in fifty thousand chance to do the same, but Torbiro has both abilities. He was born under an unknown mystical factor like some god giving him absurd luck and he is a halfling. So Torbiro has a one in twenty-five chance to affect a magical spell that has been fortified by technology to cull the weak and unprepared with a technological item.

In Torbiro's mind, poking Memyra with the clockwork shoes was the solution, so he did so until she broke out of this insidious magic that affected her and the others. In a few short clicks Memyra blinked, squinted and stared blankly at her friend before collapsing from the magical drain. The last thing Memyra heard before blacking out was Torbiro's voice exclaiming excitement, with a very loud 'Yes!' Torbiro, on the other hand, had found his solution, or at least that's what he thought it was. So, not knowing the real solution, he continued to poke the others until they too dropped to the ground after breaking free from the mind trap. There were many soldiers and only one Torbiro, so he got to work. It took him two cycles – two days – working alone before someone finally awoke from their normal slumber. The first to wake was of course, Commander Fameborn as he was the first to break free of the mind spell, aside from Torbiro. He was not forthcoming about aiding the others but only wanted to selfishly gain honour and glory by rescuing the princess.

'You there! Little man,' said the commander, pointing at Torbiro with a sinister glare.

'Me? Sir?' said Torbiro, a little startled since he had been hard at work for the past two days rescuing everyone from the trap.

'Yes, yes, now tell me quickly, are you the one that put my men to the ground?' said the commander. His tone was very dark, as though it were a threat.

'Well, yes, but…' replied Torbiro. He was immediately interrupted by Fameborn as he leaped into action.

'You monster!' said Fameborn, as he charged toward Torbiro, who was still poking another victim of the mind trap with his clockwork shoes.

'No. Wait, sir, I'm helping every… ah!' screamed Torbiro. Although he was about to poke yet another soldier with his shoes for the tenth time, just to awaken them from their slumber, Torbiro was still able to duck, dodge and dive away from the attacking knight. As Torbiro screamed, it was not because he was being attacked but rather because one of the soldiers he was trying to help, was stabbed by the commander who was supposed to lead them.

'First, I will avenge my men. You have bewitched and then I will save the princess with the power and justice of all of Traytos. Now, die you evil imp!' Fameborn continued to slash away at Torbiro, with little regard to the fallen, though in his defence he had thought they were all corpses.

'Please, sir. Ah… No! Don't attack. Please!?' Torbiro tried his hardest to evade the attacks and get away from his assailant. After about four or five swings, Torbiro was far enough away that he could no longer help those soldiers from the mind trap. He had also dropped one of his shoes as he evaded and weaved among the still affected soldiers, but to help both himself and the soldiers, Torbiro could only think to leave the area.

After only saving about half of the trapped soldiers, Torbiro had run away from his commander, who had accused him of being the cause of the situation. He could not have known that he was a knight as well, since he did not wear the traditional armour of the knights. Instead, he wore leather armour for mobility, which Memyra had advised him to wear. If he had just been wearing his proudly polished armour, maybe the commander wouldn't have attacked him. All he could do now was wait and try to save as many soldiers as he could with the single shoe he had left. Finding the left shoe would be a waste of time and rescuing the princess was indeed his task, but there was no way for him to do so if Commander Fameborn was around. Torbiro took refuge near a single large stone, to catch his breath from the attacks by the confused but upset commander. As he sat down on top of the stone, something underneath him seemed to shift. To Torbiro's surprise, there was a path that had revealed itself behind him. There was a slight mechanical sound like clockwork, gears and sprockets scraping on rusted and ill-maintained parts. Though the sound was fairly quiet, once the hatch had opened, he could clearly hear the mechanism shift and move as though it was an echo throughout a vast chamber. Torbiro was curious about the path, but saving everyone was first priority. He looked back to where his commander was and he could see some of the soldiers and knights were being roused by the commander. From this faraway, he could not see whether Memyra or Robyn were among them, but he could clearly see his friend Borgar, who was being attacked for some reason. Torbiro wanted to help, but what could he do? His commander had attacked him and some of the soldiers were being attacked by the knights of Traytos. He couldn't break rank, he was just a probationary knight. No one would listen to him and to add more salt to the wound, Torbiro was small.

Thinking of all the possibilities, Torbiro decided that heading into the mystery underground path was better than confronting the Traytos knights. He felt a heavy feeling in his stomach as he turned away. It must have been guilt. The guilt that he was not as brave as the knights in the stories he had idealised. The guilt was there in the pit of stomach, but it was not going to deter him from moving forward. Maybe this path would help them in the long run, he thought. The main question swirling around in his mind was, why was it here? Why was there a hidden path so close to the tower when one could just enter it through the front door?

Looking back one last time, Torbiro viewed the rally of the troops he had saved from their deep sleep, as Fameborn forced them to prepare for the assault of the tower. This made Torbiro regret not being part of that glorious team and turned to scout out the path. The steps here were made for humans to traverse, so going down them was still a bit of a task. The path ahead was very well lit and it was a magnificent sight to behold. The stairs aside, since there were no handles to grip, they were a bit dangerous to walk on but the walls were lined with steam pipes whistling, as though there was an immense amount of pressure within them escaping from small holes. There were so many colours that the wall almost looked like a gallery for art. As Torbiro looked closely, he could almost see a mosaic from the different coloured valves, gas cocks, the galvanised pipes and brass fittings. But that must have just been his imagination or the constant lectures from Master Dorian about the intricate differences between an oil pipe and a water pipe. Torbiro still didn't know the difference, besides the colour of the valve or if the pipe had a gauge that said water or oil on it. He was no engineer after all, but he had some experience with working at Dorian's store front, selling parts. The walls and the corridor seemed to change as he moved along the path. But that could not be possible. What kind of crazy technologist could make a moving corridor? Torbiro pondered this until the floor turned to dirt and was no longer made of the metal, similar to the pipes. The path behind him was still there, but as he moved forward down the corridor, the stairs behind him started to merge with the walls.

Torbiro thought he was trapped but as he started to move toward the stairs, they emerged from the walls and formed the stairs again. 'Wow' was the word that came to mind. A corridor that could react to your thoughts. He tested the mechanism a few times to see if it wasn't just a coincidence. But to Torbiro's lack of technological knowledge, this chamber was not magical and could not sense his thoughts, but rather it was motion activated. The creator of this technological marvel was none other than the king of Traytos himself, Aroduct the Golem master. This corridor would form and reform depending on where you would step. The brass platforms were very sensitive to the touch so that even a small mouse could be detected.

This was the passage he had made to trick would-be assassins into a trapped corridor he had designed, but the Golem master was not all knowing when he had made this trap. He had designed it for medium-sized creatures like humans, who would be at least 130 centimetres tall and not halflings who were at most 130 centimetres tall. Torbiro was also very lucky to activate and evade much of the traps still in use. As he had been looking at the different colours of the pipes, deadly gas had bellowed out above him and as he walked step by step down the stairs, he had escaped sharp rivets that had ricocheted off other pipes. Without seeing any dangers, he walked through the corridor, designed to test the most tactful assassin. He had even broken one of the trapped hatches as he was testing the formation of the stair as he stepped back and forth, seeing if it would appear and disappear from his 'thoughts'. The tunnel was still deadly with traps but Torbiro had either stopped just in front of the trigger switch or touched a lever or a valve that disrupted the circuit of the mechanism and damaged the system through a cascading effect. At the end of the tunnel, there lay the bottom layer of the Tower of Rivals. How did Torbiro know this? Well he didn't, but there was a sign with a map on it. This discovery would lead the warriors and knights of Traytos to victory and Torbiro wanted to share it with the others. Again he shouted with glee, saying 'Yes' very excited and dashed back up the corridor with the moving pipes and intricate clockwork traps that had been damaged beyond repair from Torbiro's accidental touching and meddling.

CHAPTER 64
FAMEBORN'S CHARGE

With the evil imp gone, Commander Fameborn started to look for another target to vent his anger and frustration on, since his prey was just that much quicker than he was. He found his next target, a large ogre. He could see it was wearing the symbol of Traytos, a cog with a crown in its centre, but he couldn't care less for the creature. If it died, it was weak anyway and didn't deserve to continue living under his command. With rage and malicious intent, Fameborn started to hack and slash at the rather large ogre. It awoke and started to defend itself, not by striking back, as Borgar could see the young knight held a weapon of the commander, but instead by blocking and trying to snatch at the weapon to stop his assault.

'Beast, you shall die by my hands. Ahhhh!' Fameborn continued his assault at a prone ogre and a defenceless one at that. This was a disgrace, but there was no one around to witness this aside from Torbiro, who was too far away to be seen by others and the ogre soldier. Fameborn thought it was the perfect crime. No one would believe the words of a soldier over a knight, so he was safe in his mind.

'Ka pu ten, Not. Enemy.' said Borgar. He tried to say, 'captain, I am not an enemy' while trying to snatch at the sword that had stabbed him several times.

'Soldier, I have been possessed by an evil imp. I can't stop. Please help me!' Fameborn lied through his sinister eyes and gritting teeth.

He continued to attack Borgar with even more ferocity, with mention of the imp, as though he was trying to resist something.

'Sowee Ka pu ten. Me. Smash evil imp. Where?' said Borgar. He had almost grasped the sword when Fameborn had made his plea and Borgar was distracted for a moment. This moment would have been his last, but some of the soldiers and knights started to rouse from the commotion. This was not good for Fameborn. More witnesses meant more trouble, and so with a single thrust he aimed for the thigh of the creature and the single arcing cut sliced Borgar's leg. This act had forced Borgar to scream in pain and lose his balance, toppling face first to the ground. Fameborn approached Borgar's ear and said, 'This was the only way.'

'My friends. This ogre has been possessed by an evil sorcerer, and he has accosted me. This beast must die,' said Fameborn, declaring a different lie to cover up his previous one. But to his misfortune, many of the soldiers were not his knights and they had gone to defend and aid Borgar, as they knew he was a gentle ogre. He would not attack anyone and he was very loyal to Traytos. The symbol Borgar wore was not a simple badge that could be taken off, but rather one sealed to his very skin. That badge meant he had great fortitude and will to resist magical influences.

'Sire, Borgar is one of us,' said Private Redfellow. She blocked the commander's path in striking the lethal blow.

'Out of my way, soldier. Attacking a knight is a sentence for execution. Now move aside. Or I shall cut you down as well,' said Fameborn, with an air of superiority in his tone and command.

'Borgar not enemy,' said Borgar, with a soft whisper. The pain of losing his leg had given him strength, but he knew death would be the only outcome if he attacked the commander. Borgar wondered where Torbiro was. As even though he was little, he would have helped him. He was a kind knight.

'BORGAAAAR. NOT. ENEMY,' shouted Borgar, as he breathed through the dirt and grass. The ogre's roar was so startling, even

Fameborn was taken aback. His will wavered for a moment and fear had set in his mind.

Fameborn needed to back off, or there would be consequences. It would mean his death if he pushed further. So, in an awkward display, he tried his best to pretend he had fallen on his back and started to fidget and spasm like he was the one being possessed and then being released by an evil spirit. Private Redfellow did not believe any of this, but Fameborn still out ranked her and he was the commander that ordered a foolish charge, almost losing all the soldiers to those traps. Saara also wondered where Torbiro or Robyn were. They were knights that could have stopped this from ever happening. But with a quick glance, she spotted Memyra and Robyn. They were still unconscious, but starting to rouse from the roar of Borgar. But where was Torbiro?

After Fameborn's poor man's acting, he forced himself to vomit to show he was coming out of being possessed. Many of the soldiers and his loyal knights, that had survived the deadly trap, had started to assist him. He graciously refused and told them they had more important matters. And that was to save Princess Dawn. With his sword in hand, he gave a rallying speech, pointed his weapon upward and charged for the main doors of the Tower of Rivals. Many of the soldiers Torbiro had saved knew this was their mission, so they charged and followed the commander blindly. But those that had protected Borgar, as well as Memyra and Robyn, stayed behind.

Borgar had just lost his leg and he would not be able to move without proper support. Robyn was filled with so much grief and sadness that she could do nothing. She was shocked by the gruesome state of her friend. The world was dark indeed, she thought. Memyra, on the other hand, could not care less for the creature and was more worried about Torbiro. He had been there poking her with his clockwork shoes before she had collapsed from the strange level of fatigue. Memyra started to rummage through her magical bag and pulled out a potion and a crystal orb. She uncorked the potion and gave it to Robyn to drink, but Robyn had misunderstood and instead thought it was a potion to help the ogre. The potion did have healing properties, but Memyra did not know the extent. More concerned with Torbiro, she spoke a command word and the orb lit up. 'Find Torbiro.' The orb glowed and an arrow appeared in his direction. Memyra started to move when they heard the soldiers, under the command of Fameborn, had crashed at the main doors of the tower. Instinctively, they all turned to the sound and missed seeing Torbiro emerge out of the hole he had been in.

CHAPTER 65
UNSIGHTLY INJURY

After climbing out of the hidden passage he had found, Torbiro could see many of the soldiers were already at the front door of the tower and were slamming against it. He was so happy about the passage he had found he did not notice Borgar on the ground clutching where his leg had been completely severed. Torbiro was so distracted by the knights and the soldiers bashing at the tower for entry that he bumped into Memyra, who had just turned to look back, only to see her friend crash into her. With a resounding 'oof' from both halflings, the group looking after Borgar turned to see the little commotion behind them. Even Borgar seemed to forget his leg and was looking. Human, elf, gnome and ogre alike were all puzzled at the halflings. One was rubbing his head, which was obviously Torbiro, their missing companion, and the other just grabbing the male and shaking him furiously. Her actions were so out of the park that it made everyone laugh.

Robyn was stunned by Memyra's actions towards their friend, which had distracted her long enough to accidentally pour the potion on the severed leg rather than the ogre. The full contents of the potion soaked the ogre's severed limb and by the time anyone else realised what had happened, it was already too late. Robyn's shoulders, arm all the way down to her finger tips were slumped in a downward fashion. The potion in her hand was just an empty glass bottom and the last drop of curative wasted. From being distressed to distracted to dumbfounded, Robyn was as still as a statue. The words coming out of her mouth were a sigh. 'Ah' was all she could say. Jimmy was so distracted by the halflings that by the time he too turned to see the potion, which he knew was one of regeneration, the contents of the flask were healing the severed part of the ogre's lost leg. Though it was a waste of magical resources, Jimmy tried not to express his concern, but the potion was valuable. He too said 'Ah' in distress at the misuse of such an asset. The magic of the potion was strong and although Borgar was a stupid creature, the leg started to move as though it were still part of the lumbering ogre. Saara turned back from the squabbling halflings to see a frightening sight. The severed leg was moving on its own. She too screamed in terror with an 'Ahh'.

Everything was happening within a single moment and the chaos of the halflings was the cause yet again. But Torbiro and Memyra had no idea what was happening behind them. This was the scene that had distracted the others. After the two crashed into each other, Torbiro was the one to start the fight by complaining about how she needed to watch where she was walking. In Torbiro's mind, it had been Memyra's fault, even though he was the one that barraged into her at a full run. Torbiro had been focussed on the door of the Tower of Rivals. Memyra was at first just glad to see Torbiro was safe and sound, but when he started to accuse her of being the root of the collision, her irritation switch turned on. She could not back down in an argument that was clearly not her fault. She may have been looking down when she was following the orb's direction, but the item was glowing and it blocked her vision, although she was also not moving very fast, just walking, slowly at that. It was Torbiro's fault.

In fact, it wasn't either of their fault alone. It was both of their fault. One was moving at top excited running speed without looking where he was going and the other was also moving directly at the other with a glowing crystal in her face. They had both been distracted and had crashed. But that wasn't going to stop Memyra from scolding the high and mighty Torbiro. The banter between the two was much the same argument they had had throughout their friendship. First it was the finger pointing. It didn't matter who was right and it only mattered that the accuser was the one that was right. Second came the staring contest with added taunts and bickering. The two would slowly approach each other for the third round, which Torbiro was never good at. The halfling wrestling. Which was not a contest of strength, but a contest of endurance. Whoever could endure being spat at the longest was the winner. To some, this act was of a feral display, but to many, seeing halflings duke it out in this manner was more confusing and amusing than anything. Even the halfling language was an annoying screeching and squeaking sound like a very high-pitched recording sped up to just sound like chipmunks or squirrels chattering. In a few ticks of a clock, Torbiro had been defeated and Memyra was on top. Both their faces were completely soaked in saliva, phlegm and mucus. Then after their battle, it was the halflings' turn to turn around at their companions' predicament.

Torbiro was defeated. His face was sticky and slimy and needed a good wash. He politely asked Memyra for a cloth to wipe his face. Just to tease him, as always, Memyra handed Torbiro the cloth she had just used to wipe away the oral ichor from her face. He usually fell for this prank, but not today. He must have found something amazing that he was able to see past the prank and asked for a dry cloth. Once their faces were dry, the two headed for the commotion over by the ogre Borgar. They walked up to the group of frightened humans and a stunned elf. Jimmy was there too, with his mouth agape and shock in his eyes. Only Borgar was still sitting down with a confused look on his face, not understanding the situation at all.

'Hey guys? What's going on?' asked Torbiro, as he approached his friends.

'The leg… It's a… alive!' said Saara, with terror in her voice.

'The leg? What do you mean?' Memyra still did not understand Robyn had magicked the dead leg of Borgar with the potion she had given her for self-use.

'Look… over… there!' said Saara, wincing at the gruesome sight of a fleshy dismembered limb. Saara was usually calm when dealing with most injuries, but any form of necromancy was another matter. She had been told the scariest stories growing up about people coming back from the dead and eating flesh.

'Private Redfellow! Why are you on top of Borgar?' said Torbiro, asking a strange question, but then again she was clinging on for dear life on top of Borgar's head like a housewife freaking out about a cockroach she spotted in the kitchen. As Torbiro asked that question, he saw Private Redfellow was looking away and pointing her index finger in the opposite direction.

'Saara, just tell me what it is. Stop with the guessing games,' said Memyra, trying to force the issue out. This was no time for games, but she still expected an answer. Torbiro was now closer to whatever it was Saara was afraid of. So she asked him what it was.

'Memyra, it's a leg. But it's moving on its own. It also looks like Borgar's leg,' said Torbiro, giving a short reply to the question on both their minds. It was like one of the golems back in Traytos that the technologists and engineers would build, but this one was just fleshy and bleeding out.

'Hey Memyra, I think Robyn is stuck again. Hey Robyn are you ok?' said Torbiro, moving past the dismembered limb and heading towards Robyn and Jimmy, who were stunned in place. Both stunned for entirely different reasons.

'Oh! Is that all? I can fix that, easy,' said Memyra, nonchalantly. She knew this situation could be solved by an item she had in her special bag. This time around, she pulled out a pretty ordinary item. A needle and string.

'Can one of you big soldiers carry that leg to Borgar? I'm going to stitch it back on,' said Memyra, ordering some of the soldiers that stayed to help out with this operation. Two of them agreed, but in the end, Borgar was the only one able to carry his meaty leg. He put his leg on the same place it had been cut off and Memyra started to sew it back on the ogre. It was clumsy work, but the medic was of no use in the current situation. Saara had fallen off the ogre and fainted from her necrophobia. After the quick patch work, Memyra came over to the shocked elf and gnome Torbiro was now poking with a single clockwork shoe.

'What in the pulse are you doing?' said Memyra, very annoyed at Torbiro for doing something frivolous. What would poking someone with a shoe do, anyway?

'Can't you see? I'm going to revive them, of course! What else would I be trying to do?' said Torbiro, answering Memyra's question. This was what saved so many people before so, this too should have an effect, thought Torbiro.

'Stop that. How's that gonna revive them? Huh!?' Memyra slapped the shoe and Torbiro to the ground.

'I'll revive them, like this.' Right after she had slapped Torbiro, she leaped forward at Jimmy and with a clenched fist, clocked him in the face. On the return, she somersaulted quickly and leaped at Robyn and opened her hand for the heaviest slap to the face. She even left a small red hand print and everyone watching made a sound of pain. Like clenching your teeth and inhaling, while recoiling your head in surprise.

This action was effective although Robyn had hit the dirt hard, but she broke out of her trance. Robyn put a hand on her cheek and could feel the pain from the slap. Jimmy, on the other hand, was not affected by the punch, but to Memyra she had seen something odd about him then and there, like there was an illusion transposed or overlaying his true form. It happened too quickly to verify, but now more than ever, Memyra focused more of her attention towards Jimmy. He was up to something and Torbiro was involved, but what was it?

Their scuffle was only for a few clicks – a few minutes – and they could all still hear the soldiers at the Tower of Rivals attacking the front door. Torbiro, remembering something important, quickly said, 'Wait here, I'll be right back.' and dashed towards the Tower of Rivals.

Soon Jimmy was also on his trail. Memyra, not trusting him, chased after the both of them. Robyn, Saara and the other soldiers decided to wait and rest for the time being and gather their thoughts on what had just transpired.

CHAPTER 66
LITTLE HELP

The rally was a success and the men were as ready as ever to take back our damsel in distress. But those insubordinate troops will pay for their insolence, but I won't be able to kill them myself. I will just have to report them when I return to Traytos. I must get through this infernal door and save her. For the king, for the honour and for the glory.

With these dark thoughts in Fameborn's mind, he continued to urge his soldiers to carry on the assault of the tower doors. Each attack was one step closer to breaking down this obstacle and one step closer to the rescue of Princess Dawn. Fameborn could only think of himself and of the glory and power this rescue would bring him. He was trained to be good, not in heart, not in nature, but as a soldier, ruthless and merciless. He would be the perfect general, just like his father and grandfather alike. This was the kind of man Aroduct wanted, as these types of men had a simple weakness. Their pride. Pride could be easily manipulated, taunting their strength, pushing their prowess or even goading their ability. But there was one problem: compassion and kindness could confuse men like this. As easily as they were to be controlled, they could be just as easily swayed. But this was the Tower of Rivals and those that emerged would have no rivals left to contest with.

With each attack, the door was damaged, but with each pause, the door was repaired by some mystical power. Fameborn continued to use the force and ferocity of his soldiers to make a breach. But to no avail. In the meantime, Torbiro, followed by Jimmy, who in turn was being stalked by Memyra, had arrived behind the crowd of soldiers and knights trying their hardest to breach the front door and defeat the evil within. Torbiro, not wanting to waste any time, started to climb the stairs. Rather than informing the resting troops, he wanted to aid the commander who had attacked him earlier, but that could be dealt with after their mission was completed. The rescue of the princess. Torbiro was much quicker this time around as he was able to climb on the knights and soldiers as leverage, rather than trying to physically climb a set of steps made for the tall. Using his agility, Torbiro managed to first climb up soldiers' pants from the ground and hop from shoulder to shoulder, to reach the frontline where the commander was. His report would not only gain him some adulation but also a higher appreciation for his contributions. Torbiro could see it now, smiles and handshakes and pats on the back. Continuing to jump from soldier to soldier, he finally arrived at the frontline. Alone, this had taken Torbiro almost three turns – three hours – of a clock, but with the mass of people helping him move, with more agility, this had taken him only five clicks – five minutes – which was very quick for a hundred metre climb.

Although Jimmy was following Torbiro, he wanted to catch him out then and there, to be the traitor, to be used as the scapegoat for the king's plans. It was perfect and all he needed to do was plant an incriminating note on his person. But the only problem now was his halfling friend. But she could be dealt with easily enough. 'She thinks I can't see her. What a fool. I'll just have to kill her if she finds out any more of this plan, but for now I'll let her follow me and act out this pathetic role of a loyal 'friend'.' Memyra continued to follow both the suspicious Jimmy and her friend, who had started to climb the soldiers like some sewer rat scurrying up the drain pipe. It made Memyra feel a little proud to see Torbiro using his nature skills, but it did make him look a lot like a thief. She continued to watch Jimmy to see what he was up to. There must have been another reason for him to follow Torbiro and it made Memyra feel a little sick thinking about it. From what Memyra could see, Jimmy had stopped to talk to the lazy-looking soldier by the foot of the stone steps leading to the tower. He pulled out a note and handed it to the soldier. It was too obvious, but then he started to head back to the camp. Just what was he up to?

As I passed the female halfling, I used my subtle magic and cast a suggestion spell on her. I needed to frame Torbiro now, as it was the perfect moment, where he would be too distracted and there would be too many witnesses to verify any claims against him. If he pulls out the note in front of Fameborn of all people, he will be sacrificed and placed on display all throughout the city, but I needed to get rid of her first. Killing her is out of the question. There are just too many witnesses, such as that elf and if that ogre sees me it will be troubling. "No," thought Jimmy as he placed his hand on Memyra's shoulder and said, "I just wanted to wish them good luck." in a happy-go-lucky manner. So Jimmy would need to distract her instead and the best possible method of distracting a foe was to control them and a spell of suggestion was the perfect enchantment to do this. This spell required a basic one sentence command that would control its target, but it would only work on weak-minded fools. In Jimmy's arrogance, he believed Memyra was weak-minded in the first place. An error in judgement. He cast the spell on Memyra, using his mind to speak the command, which was to 'turn around and walk to Robyn'. This command was simple indeed, but it would be effective for the moment needed to distract her and frame Torbiro.

Upon executing my spell, I could feel it working its magic as Memyra started with a slow turn and motioned to walk as instructed. She would be distracted for at least a minute and I would be by the side of that troublesome scapegoat. I quickly cast another spell, using my mind to evoke the words silently as to not be detected and discovered.

With the blink of an eye, Jimmy had disappeared and reappeared in the crowd of soldiers below where Torbiro would be at this very moment. He pulled out a sheet of paper and cast another spell to write the letter. Even with the small amount of light created from the spell to inscribe the letter, there were so many people pushing on those stairs, it would have been impossible to see.

After Jimmy patted Memyra's shoulder, she had a sudden and involuntary thought to turn away and walk back to Robyn. She couldn't understand why this was happening, but it must have been Jimmy's doing. Memyra tried to resist, but it was no use. It must have been magic and this made her worried, as she could no longer see Jimmy.

He must have found me out, but how? I was being extra careful not to be spotted, so how? I continued to walk towards Robyn when it hit me. If I couldn't resist, then I would go with the flow and just walk there faster. I couldn't turn away, but if I got to Robyn faster, it might break this hold on me. I had heard of magic such as this and there was no way for someone like myself to break out of it, as I'm not trained for such a task. I tried to run, but I was beckoned to walk there, so I walked as fast as I could. It would still take a few clicks, but it would be faster and on arrival the unknown force stopped. Robyn was confused but very welcoming. However, I had to ignore her. I needed to help Torbiro, that fool.

Torbiro had finally reached a shoulder close to the commander to tell him there was another way. At first, Torbiro motioned to the knight he stood on to get the attention of the commander, but from the loud screams to attack, he could not be heard. Second attempt, he tried to yell out to get everyone's attention. This only annoyed the knight he stood on, which had compromised his footing as the warrior tried to fruitlessly bat him away. Thirdly, Torbiro made for the commander himself and tried to give his report directly but this would be risky as if he missed he jump, he would land on the ground where he could get stomped on by all of those soldiers laying siege to the door. He counted 1,2,3 as the crowd swayed forward to attack the door and 1,2,3 as they stepped back from the door to ready themselves to attack again. That would be the right time to jump, just before they attacked as they took that crucial step back. As Torbiro counted, Jimmy pushed one of the soldiers, which caused a cascade effect where all the soldiers fell like dominos. This situation had made Torbiro leap too soon and instead of landing on his shoulder, he got caught by the sword of none other than the commander on the downward swing.

Torbiro was now hanging from the tip of Commander Fameborn's sword and had the attention of all the soldiers who had fallen. All looked angrily at Torbiro, but this was his chance. He would tell them of the secret passage and they could all save the princess together. He could feel a great speech welling up inside himself, but just before he could speak a word, the commander interjected.

'How dare you befall my men. Little imp!' said Fameborn, as he lowered his blade to release the halfling.

'Thank you, sir. I mean commander. I mean commander sir. But I…' said Torbiro, trying to address the commander in the proper manner so he didn't offend. Although Torbiro had important information to tell the soldiers, the commander did not wish to hear it and kicked him aside, ordering his men to continue the assault.

'Men, ATTACK!' boomed Fameborn. He had to stand up to get back into position to continue attacking the door with brute strength alone.

'Sir, please listen. I have important…' yelled Torbiro. He wanted to say, "I have important information about a secret passage" but his small voice was drowned out by the roar and shouts of the soldiers following Fameborn's command. In this situation, Torbiro had lost. No one would listen to him and no one could see him under the shadows of the soldiers. Try as he might, no one was going to listen to him now. And he was just in the way. Torbiro had to be careful, otherwise he would have been pushed off the ledge of the stairs and it was a long fall.

Although Torbiro was being very careful, someone still managed to push him and he tripped, causing another pile up. For such an act, even though this was his first, all the knights nearby were very adamant about stomping and kicking the poor halfling. Bruised and battered, Torbiro stumbled out to the side of the steps and failed to see a misstep here would cause him to fall. To his fortune, there was Jimmy to the rescue to catch him. Both of them on the ground, Jimmy stealthily slipped the note in his cloak pocket and helped him up.

'So, Torbiro. I guess the commander is busy right now. What should we do?' said Jimmy, in a very gnomish fashion.

'I… Just… wanted to … help,' said Torbiro, dejected. At this moment, Memyra was only a few metres away. She had seen her childhood friend fall near the top of the stairs and she had used her clockwork boots to run as fast as she could to catch him.

'Torro, are you alright?' She looked worriedly at the slumped down Torbiro.

'I just wanted to be of help. Myra, what should I do?' Torbiro's tone was grim and depressed. It was like he had lost all hope.

'Torro, forget about them. Come on, we can just go back home.' Memyra was hopeful they could just put this silly adventure to rest and head back home.

'Yeah, maybe you're right, Myra. The commander has everything under control.' Torbiro had been persuaded by his friend and maybe the adventure just needed to end.

'No! We need to save the princess,' said Jimmy. It was such an outburst that it shocked the gloomy Torbiro out of his slump. Even Memyra hopped a little from it.

'What do you mean, we have to save the princess?' Memyra crossed her arms and looked Jimmy up and down, trying to investigate his angle. This was the first time Jimmy wanted to do anything. Usually, he would go missing.

'Um, well you see… I just thought we could be heroes,' said Jimmy. He also didn't know why he made that outburst. He had no interest in saving Dawn, since Fameborn had been tasked to do just that. Besides, he had already done his part of the plan. Jimmy tried to play it off, but Memyra didn't believe him at all. In fact, the only one that had believed him was Torbiro.

'You're right. Let's go guys!' said Torbiro, with all the gusto he could muster. With newfound confidence, Torbiro strode proudly back to his friends with an idea of becoming a hero.

CHAPTER 67
ENTER THE DUNGEON

Down in the tunnels that Torbiro had secretly found, he had brought with him a loyal group of friends. Or at least that's what Torbiro thought. He brought Memyra, who was very upset about not going back home and instead was following this crazy band of miscreants. Robyn was also with them, who was now quite rested and a bit more together than before. She was happy to accompany Torbiro since they were going to save someone again, which intrigued her compassion to aid others. Private Redfellow, Karl, Wilrokk and Borgar had also come along to continue the mission. Karl and Wilrokk were soldiers that had stayed behind to help Borgar when he was being assaulted by Commander Fameborn. And the one covering them from the rear was none other than Jimmy, who was just as begrudging as Memyra at the idea of going down a mysterious tunnel to get inside the Tower of Rivals.

Upon entering the passageway, everyone could feel the deadly dangers within. The only exception to that feeling was Torbiro, who had said this was much safer than the traps above. For the team's luck, Private Wilrokk was a learned engineer and gearsmith for the army of Traytos. Meaning he was someone who knew about technology and any technological items. He had found out in this tunnel there were about fifty different traps that could kill instantly. But Wilrokk had also disarmed enough of those traps to have somewhat of a safe journey through this passage. Wilrokk questioned how Torbiro had managed while all the traps were active, but they left that discussion for another time as it might take longer for Torbiro to explain, since he had no idea how he had survived either.

Jimmy was the most terrified of the passage, as he had experienced its deadliness when he had first come here to take the assassin's test. Clearly he had passed, but the trauma still haunted him to this day. Jimmy's movements were the most paranoid among the whole group. With every step came with it the dread of the past, but he needed to stay with Torbiro since he was clearly the scapegoat, so he could report all his actions. Fameborn was never going to listen to him now, not that that idiot ever did. Well, it all comes down to who is tending to the monsters in the dungeon. Please, for the love of the tranquillity, let it be anyone but Rat.

Past all the traps at the end of the passage way, the team was astonished by the size of the underground that was meant to support the tower above. They had arrived in the lowest part of the underground from the map Torbiro found attached to the wall. This place was the dungeon. It sounded so cool to Torbiro and Borgar, but the rest of the team were more frightened than anything. Jimmy was just as surprised when entering the dungeon as it was his first time entering it from the most dangerous of levels. The lowest level. This level was supposed to house the breeding factory, which was an alchemist's dream but a prisoner's nightmare. As this was the floor, that would test the deadliness of the monsters they would use to thwart off intruders. Like themselves, right at this moment. The lower dungeon housed dragons and their terrifying spawn. The middle dungeon housed more humanoid creatures, like minotaurs and centaurs. And the upper dungeon housed simple monsters like goblins. But from the look of this tower, it was about thirty floors from ground level. The map Torbiro had found showed the layout of the dungeons and who was in charge of the floors and what creatures were out for testing. Torbiro had never seen a live dragon before and he was curious about what they looked like, how ferocious they were and if they could really shoot fire from their mouths like a lot of the legends from tavern stories said. Borgar was on board with Torbiro to explore this place, but the rest of the more sane party members had put the two of them on a leash. Borgar was their only real muscle. Robyn and Memyra were the quickest and quietest, so they gave themselves the role of scout. While the rest were on leash duty. Torbiro had a knack for doing random things and causing trouble, so to stop this Memyra devise her plan that Torbiro must be watched at all times. 'Do not let him out of your sight no matter what.' was what she had told everyone but Borgar and Torbiro.

The scouting team went ahead of the group to see if the coast was clear and although both Memyra and Robyn were in that team, they would alternate scouting times so Torbiro wouldn't get too suspicious and complain. All was going well until the team took a short break near the stairs of the lowest floor going up to the middle floor. Torbiro had gone missing.

It was Memyra's turn to scout ahead. The group had been keeping a close watch on Torbiro for a few turns, as the path ahead was still filled with dangers. Like those ferocious dragons. Memyra had experienced a dragon attack and they had melted everything they let their flames touch. It was not cool or amazing, as the storytellers in taverns told stories about them. They were terrible creatures that destroyed and burned. Memyra did not want that experience to happen to Torbiro. It would break him forever. She thought only of his safety, so they might return home safely with no more crazy adventures. She found a safe path that led to a stairwell to the next level. But upon her return, she could see most of the team were resting. She smiled at how cosy everyone looked and would have joined them, but when she looked again, Torbiro was nowhere to be found.

'Guys, wake up!!!' said Memyra, as she looked frantically around for any traces of Torbiro. She kicked Karl and Wilrokk as they were supposed to be watching him.

'What do you mean, Memyra? Torbiro is right here?' said Wilrokk, pointing to a small sack with an imprint of a halfling's head. Looking down at the lack of a halfling on the sack they had used as pillows, Wilrokk blinked and rubbed his eyes with a clear realisation Torbiro was missing. He let out a scream of panic.

'Ahhh! What do we do?' shouted Wilrokk in panic. His voice had also echoed throughout the caverns of the dungeon. This was the worst-case scenario. They would be found out. They were all in danger and worst of all, Torbiro was somewhere else.

In unison, Karl and Saara punched the idiot to shut him up. They were already in danger considering their situation and shouting in panic wasn't helping, so the two soldiers knocked some sense into him. Wilrokk's cry had echoed throughout the dungeon and they could hear the growls and snarls as though the creatures above and below were answering the call.

'Wilrokk, are you nuts? Don't ever shout in a place full of monsters. At least while I'm here,' said Memyra, very annoyed and frustrated.

'We look for Torbiro, of course. No time for resting. Now move,' continued Memyra, as she shouted her orders to the lot of them. They had one job and they still made a mess of things. Where in the pulse is Torro?

While this was happening, Torbiro had fallen down a secret passage while he slept next to Wilrokk. He was where he was meant to be, but when Wilrokk rolled over, Torbiro had accidentally found a hidden panel and was pushed in. He still slept while Memyra and the others were arguing about where he had gone. With the shouts and snarls echoing all around, Torbiro was awoken by a strange gnome. Unlike Jimmy, this gnome was much older, his beard was completely white and it looked very frizzy. As though it was not looked after at all. He looked familiar, but Torbiro just could not put his finger on where he might have seen him before.

'Hello,' said Torbiro, to the strangely familiar gnome, very politely.

'Will you get 'tup ol'redy?' said the gnome, pointing out to Torbiro he was actually sleeping on his laboratory bench.

'Um, you said I was on your bench, but wasn't I sleeping on the floor? Where am I exactly?' Torbiro looked around. There were many flasks and beakers and other glass containers. There were piles of powders on papers all over the bench and a black cauldron on the far side of the table.

'Mister Torbiro, you are on the third floor of the Tower of Rivals, why do you ask?' said the gnome, a little matter-of-factly, while he poured ingredients into a glass beaker and started to slowly stir it.

'How do you know my name?' asked Torbiro. Torbiro hopped off the bench and started to explore the room.

'Please, Mister Torbiro, do not leave the room or touch anything. All of these are very precious experiments I must complete for my mistress,' said the gnome.

'So, mister gnome, what's your name? And who is this mistress of yours? Is she nice?' Torbiro asked questions left, right and centre. Torbiro was curious considering this gnome knew so much about him and yet Torbiro didn't even know his name.

'Mister Torbiro, 'course you know my name. I gave it to you just moments ago. Is this that halfling joke you have been trying to tell me 'efore hand?' said the gnome. He was chatting to Torbiro like they were old friends, but Torbiro had never met this gnome before, or had he?

'Well alright, I'll tell ya ma name again, its Raaket Apollo Tenan or Rat for short,' said Rat, a little annoyed but intrigued as well.

'Well, that's a strange name, but I won't ever forget it. Nice to meet you,' said Torbiro, as he extended his hand for a friendly handshake. Rat took his hand and before shaking, Rat inspects Torbiro's hand, then when he is satisfied, said, 'I see' and gave Torbiro a most joyous hand shake.

'Hey Rat, you said we were on the third floor of the tower, but how can that be? I was at the very bottom floor of the dungeon. See here on this map,' said Torbiro, showing his new friend his map.

Rat inspected the map in Torbiro's possession, hummed a little, then said, 'It's magic.' He warned Torbiro that the dungeon was very dangerous and shouldn't be taken lightly. He also warned not to touch anything and don't use the gem Rat had given him. Torbiro looked puzzled at Rat, for he did not know this gem he spoke of. He shrugged and left to explore. Rat was about to say something else, but as soon as Torbiro left the door's arch, he found himself in front of a set of stone stairs, finely carved and heading upward. He could hear a loud banging sound at the door behind him. It was odd. If Rat wanted to go out, he could just open the door, very strange indeed. Torbiro was starting to get annoyed at the banging sound and approached the large wooden door. He had seen this door before. It looked like the front door to the Tower of Rivals, but how could that be? He was on the third floor. Well, Rat was a bit weird, so maybe he was mistaken.

Torbiro had viewed the window from the third floor and they were quite high up. Now when Torbiro looked out the window on this '3rd' floor, he could see the warriors and soldiers attacking the door on the other side. It was very odd, what a strange tower. In fact, what Torbiro could not understand was the Tower of Rivals was enchanted, which meant its floors could only be accessed through the control of one's will. In essence, you needed to understand magic to go to the places that you wanted. Since Torbiro was not magically trained he was going to be wandering around until luck brought him to his desired destination.

The door in front of Torbiro was simple and all he would need to do was turn the doorknob and let them in. He waltzed up to the door and started to turn its handle, but it wouldn't open. It must have been locked. Of course it was locked, otherwise Commander Fameborn would have made it inside by now. How silly of me to think it was going to be easy, thought Torbiro. He started to look for a key, and just as Torbiro started to think about the key, there it was. Right in front of him. Though he was in a completely different room from before. That didn't matter. He grabbed the keys and thought about opening the front door to let all those hard-working soldiers in so they could help. Again Torbiro, upon that simple thought of helping, he was back and unlocking the door just like that. As the door swung open, Torbiro thought of the words that would come from those that would thank and appreciate him. The tower's front door was very large considering how small Torbiro was and it had taken him a few minutes to fully open one door. By the time he was done, he came around the front of the door to receive his reward. But no soldier or warrior or even the commander was anywhere to be seen. Where had they all gone?

CHAPTER 68
FEARSOME FOES

Torbiro had only been missing for fifteen minutes and in that time he managed to meet a new friend by the name of Rat, found himself at the entrance of the Tower of Rival and get the keys and unlock the front entrance. In that time, Memyra and the others were frantically searching for him in the dark underbelly of a dangerous dungeon. Due to Wilrokk's panic shouting, the search had been much slower as they had to hide from the guards of the caverns. They could have fought them, but they were absolutely out-numbered. Memyra wanted to split up the party as that would mean covering more ground, but Robyn and the other soldiers of Traytos advised against it.

Looking for the missing Torbiro was far more dangerous than they had all anticipated. At first, they encountered drake hatchlings, who had already been hunting for prey. Drakes were a wing-clipped dragonnoids breed for ground assault. They had the senses of their dragon cousins, but were more aggressive and far more effective for tracking their prey. Since drakes could not fly, their bodies had adapted for agile runs, flexible footwork and a light and slender body for manoeuvring. Normal drakes had the colour of their dragon counterpart, green, black, red, white, blue, gold, silver, bronze and platinum. But the drakes in this tower did not have any of these colours. Rather, they had all the colours making them an abomination to nature, but this meant these drakes were even more deadly. It gave them all the unique traits of the others into one creature. Green drakes could blend in with the environment like stealth camouflage. Black drakes could melt into the shadows of its prey. Red drakes could burst into flame which gave them more range when pouncing on their prey. White drakes could freeze their prey to make it that much easier to catch. Blue drakes could move as fast as lightning itself. Gold drakes were known to have great healing properties, which provided them with increased endurance. Silver drakes could produce illusions of itself to fool its prey. Bronze drakes were known to be the most common and their ability was a quicker breeding cycle. Platinum drakes were known to have the strongest defence among the rest, as their scales could withstand an assault from a powerful siege cannon.

'Guys, those are drakes. We should run for it,' said Karl, with fear and a tremble in his voice. Karl was more of a long-ranged specialist like Robyn but being an orc he could handle being in close quarters as well.

'Karl, don't freak out. What colour are they?' asked Saara. She had a lot of knowledge about creatures since she had come from a hunter's family. She knew drakes were much like dragons, but depending on their colour, one would know their weakness.

'Um, I think it's red?' said Karl in a panicked reply.

'What do you mean? You think it's red?' said Saara in annoyance. It was dark but orcs, much like elves, had darkness vision, which allowed them to see in the dark. Saara was only a human, so she couldn't see in the dark at all. Well, without tools, that is. Memyra had provided her with night vision goggles to look for Torbiro.

'Um, I… um. Good lizard. Ahhhh!' screamed Karl as he defended himself from the creature. With an orcish cry, Saara and Robyn turned to see Karl was fighting a fiery shadow drake.

'Robyn, can you see that?' asked Saara. She could only see a strange aura of silver and red with her goggles. It couldn't be. Saara had thought.

'Saara, do you mean the drake? Yes, I can see it. I think it's red and black, but how can that be? Drakes are only supposed to be one colour,' said Robyn. She was taking out and preparing her triphil just in case.

'Karl, are you ok?' said Wilrokk. He had seen Robyn get ready for battle, so he too equipped his trusty battle-axe. This battle-axe was a standard issue from Traytos, but being a technologist himself, Wilrokk had modified it slightly, by having the axe head rotate like a buzz saw. To do this, he would need to pull out or extend the shaft and start cranking it in a circular motion.

'Guys, run! I'm… Ahhh!' Fighting in the dark was nothing new for orcs like Karl, but this was nothing like a brawl at the tavern or a blindfolded match in the arena. This was for survival. His last words were a warning. He had been ambushed by not one but six of these rainbow drakes.

With the final cries of the orc soldier Karl ringing in their ears, his gurgling corpse was shredded by six agile drakes. Robyn could only make out three of these drakes and so she shot her weapon at them. Her actions were not made by a calm person but rather someone who was now fighting for survival. Memyra and Jimmy were also close by but just at the other end of the corridor, so they had been the furthest away from where the drakes had attacked. But they were shocked to hear Robyn, of all people start shooting at the creatures in this dungeon. What could have happened to make her attack? This was Memyra's only thought besides her worry about finding Torbiro. Memyra motioned Jimmy to see what was going on, but then the two were immediately picked up by Borgar, who had swept them into his arms. Memyra could see Saara and Wilrokk running behind Borgar with Robyn still firing her weapon further behind them. Memyra refused to be carried by Borgar, so she crawled out of his grip and climbed to his shoulder and there she could see the desperate attempt at stalling the six creatures with amazingly precise shots. Where was this beforehand when they were in the Dip Hills? Either way, this was crazy. Robyn was a friend. She was too nice to die this way. This was the very first time Memyra felt pity, or maybe it was compassion towards another person aside from Torbiro. Memyra had bonded with the overly compassionate elf and she needed to be saved, unlike these cowards who ran for their lives.

With Karl dying in front of Robyn, Wilrokk and Saara, the three of them poised to attack and get their revenge on the death of their friend and comrade. All of them had heard his last cry to run away, but with blood rushing through their veins and adrenaline starting to fortify their fighting spirit, they were ready to fight but not flee. Robyn was first, her triphil already in her hands. She took aim and fired at the nearest drake. One, two, then three, all shots were fired and in three successive bursts, they hit their mark. The drake recoiled, revealing its strange scales under the cloak of its own shadow. The scales shone a bright, prismatic rainbow of colours. It was beautiful to look at. But Robyn knew this was a battle they would all die in if no one ran. At least Torbiro was safe. He could save the princess and tell everyone their story. Again, in a split second, before the adrenaline took over her emotions to fight, she needed to act like a knight. She needed to protect the others and be a proud elven knight, just like her cousin, Commander Peren. That image of Peren managed to quell some of the emotions and calmed her enough to give an order of retreat. Before speaking a word, Robyn reloaded her precious gun. Getting the cartridges into the weapon used to take a few clicks, but with Wilrokk's help, this was reduced to a few ticks.

I was ready and I could sense my friends coming to help, but they needed to save the princess with the help of Torbiro. They must survive.

Using her elvish powers of telepathy for the very first time had saved precious time, but shocked the two soldiers. Her telepathy had activated and in her stress, she ordered her friends to run. This was an ability that even the youngest of elves in her clan could perform, but she was thought to have a disability, since she could not use it. Her telepathy was not powerful enough to reach Memyra or Jimmy, but it was able to reach those she wanted to retreat. Karl was right. Running now would be a victory in the long run. Robyn could hear their voices of refusal, but she would hold firm and hold the line here.

'Karl! Noooo… I'll make you pay for this,' yelled Wilrokk, as he started to charge. The last words of Karl were lost in his ears.

'Robyn, wait for us. We can back you up. Move to the rear!' cried Saara, as she started to charge forward, brandishing her sword in both hands. The rage and anger in her eyes fuelled by the dying last breath of their comrade.

'No! You must stop,' said Robyn, as she unlocked her telepathic powers. At first she had spoken those words, but it did not get through to them.

'Robyn, we must avenge Karl. We must…' said Wilrokk, his orcish blood giving him an extra thickness and toughness to his resolve.

'I said. NO.' Robyn was determined and blasted her influence to change their minds and save them.

'I will remain. I will hold the line. I will not let any of them pass. Now run.' Robyn's back was to her friends. Poised to aim and strike true.

'Now go. First, get everyone to safety, find Torbiro and save the princess.' Her determination and purpose to serve and protect, shining through.

'Robyn, are you sure?' said Saara. Her tone was one of fear and regret. She asked a question she had already known the answer to. But she needed to make sure.

'Yes,' said Robyn, as the image of a tear falling down on her face was projected in their minds. Saara and Wilrokk could feel the sadness in their hearts quelling the rage and anger they had felt when Karl had died. Now only sorrow and hope remained. Was Robyn always this powerful? Saara thought, but why only now had she used this ability? At that moment, the two had turned and run back to escape, just as Robyn had ordered, relaying the message to Borgar. The two could see Borgar had been affected by Robyn's telepathic message as he was crying, but did not understand why. With words not spoken, the three understood with a simple nod. Saara was the only one to turn back with regret, but ultimately she would remember her sacrifice. And so they ran.

On top of Borgar, Memyra called out to Robyn to run, but she either could not hear or was refusing to listen. Memyra needed to act quickly. Robyn was all alone and none of those Traytos soldiers would help. Cowards, all of them. She knew very little about drakes, but if they could fly, she could at least slow them down. If only Torro was here, she thought. He would be able to figure out a good plan to handle them. If I find that idiot, I'm gonna kill him. Memyra pulled out a small gun from her magical storage bag and adjusted its projectile to a sticky net instead of a cannon ball. The weapon she pulled out was something she had fixed from an old gnoblin workshop. It was a multi-purpose grappling hook, but gnoblins were notoriously bad inventors, since they were the abomination of a breed between a gnome, a creature of chaos and a goblin, a creature of tranquillity. Which meant everything they made blew up. The weapon was loaded and ready. Memyra just needed Robyn to run and then they could all escape together and find that idiot that caused all this.

'Robyn!!! Run away. I can help you,' yelled Memyra as she aimed her weapon. She was getting further and further away since Borgar wouldn't stop. She could see the rainbow drakes were starting to learn Robyn's tactics, as they started to move as a pack. Robyn must have heard because she turned to face Memyra but only smiled with her enemy charging behind her, as though she had resigned her life.

'Thank you Memyra and take care of Torbiro when you find him,' said Robyn in a silent prayer. She knew running would only put her friends in danger. So she turned around to say goodbye to her friend, but then she heard something. It sounded like Torbiro, but how?

'Cyan, run now. I can distract them.' Came the familiar voice.

'Torbiro? Is that you?' Robyn looked around in confusion.

'Cyan, I need you to run. I can distract them. Just go.'

Robyn had never been called by her first name, with the exception of those from her close family. Not even her cousin Peren had called her that, but this voice sounded like Torbiro, but different. It was deeper and yet not. Who was calling her out so casually in the midst of things? Robyn tried to turn around to see where the voice was coming from one last time, but all she could see was a short human child of a shadow waving their arms around, as though he could cast spells. But Torbiro couldn't cast spells. Again, the voice came and warned her to run. This time, she felt like she had no choice but to run. It felt like someone or something was controlling her to move. Robyn started to move from a slow walk to a light jog and then to a full run. It was as though someone had cast a spell on her, but what spell was cast and who cast it?

In fact, that mysterious person had cast a mild suggestion spell on Robyn and the command to get her to move was, 'Run away as fast as you can.' In Robyn's mind, the spell had control over her and all she could think of was to do as it said. With Robyn moving away from the drakes, it was time to launch the sticky net. Memyra had to wait just long enough to make sure Robyn was out of its range. Once Robyn was safe, Memyra fired. The shot was very loud, Vaphoomf. It was also very bright but ultimately it should work at stalling the vicious drakes and they could reach the second level and search for Torbiro there. The net landed on a few of the drakes and all of them could hear the snarls and pained shrills of the beasts as they struggled to move from the sticky net's grasp. The net was used to entrap much larger prey such as flying vehicles, which were the size of a noble's wagon, to keep them on the ground. The gun could only use this feature once, as the sticky ichor needed to be cleaned out of the weapon before one could use it again.

Their escape was successful, but they couldn't stop since more of the monsters from the floors above had seen them and were now after them. No time for rest, they just needed to keep running. Drakes were dangerous, but the minotaurs were larger and the centaurs were faster. The team were never trapped, but they had no choice but to forgo the search for Torbiro and evade the creatures in this dungeon to survive. The minotaurs patrolling in threes and fours wielded giant axes which had a wide reach. So wide, in fact, Borgar got clipped a few times while they ran for cover. With every step away from the hulking minotaurs, the group needed to dodge the spears and arrows launched at them by the centaurs from a distance. To Memyra and Jimmy, running was not a problem, as the two had been riding atop their hardworking ogre friend. But since Borgar didn't bother with dodging the projectiles, he would often get struck. They were little more than an annoyance to the ogre, but to the small creatures on him, these projectiles were deadly. So both Memyra and Jimmy needed to work as a team to deflect as many of the missiles or else it meant death and that was not an option. The team had been running for three hours straight without getting any rest and after they turned a corner on the first floor, that's when they saw Torbiro go into a room. With the exception of Borgar, who just wanted to leave, the team had all thought menacing thoughts of confronting Torbiro and beating him to a bloody pulp. They turned and followed him into the room and there he stood, arms crossed, with an annoyed grin on his face.

CHAPTER 69
THE WAY IS OPEN

'Come on men, push,' said Fameborn as they continued to siege the front door of the tower of rivals.

'I said push,' continued Fameborn, but the door just wouldn't budge. They had been at this for hours and nothing had changed. Little did he know the next push would let them all into the depths of the tower. At that exact moment, Torbiro had just opened the front door and with all the strength of the soldiers, they breached the tower. The normal layout of any building was entering it from the ground floor, which then would have stairs going up and down, or a hatch or ladder going down. But this was not a normal tower. It was the Tower of Rivals and it was currently managed by the mages of Bataros, so it was a jumbled mess of floors. Which meant any door inside the tower could lead to any other part of the tower. Only the person's thought could take them to the place they desired. Fameborn had been tasked to rescue the princess and if he was true to his mission, he would have arrived there upon entering the tower, just like in his dream, when he was trapped in the mental trap. But he and his men plus the soldiers with him had been influenced by his bloodlust and rage to kill the evil in this tower. So where did they all end up, you ask? To the dungeon.

'Men, we must defeat those evil monsters and save the princess. So who's with me?' rallied Fameborn as he and his troops arrived on the first floor of the dungeon. The soldiers and knights all brandished their weapons and with a resounding battle cry, roared in response. The first floor of the tower was mainly home to the servant class monsters, such as goblins, animated skeletons and lesser demons. They weren't a threat to soldiers and knights, but monsters were monsters to these men. They chased, killed and ransacked these unarmed and unprepared creatures. It was a slaughter. But Fameborn wanted more. He gave in to his bloodlust and death-lust. As a paladin-classed knight, it was true that all evil creatures needed to be vanquished but some of them had already surrendered but were slaughtered, anyway.

Fameborn wanted more of a challenge, so his thoughts remained in a battle lust frenzy, which transferred to his knights and some of the soldiers that followed him. So each staircase they entered would lead them to a lower level of the dungeon. The second level had more formidable foes, minotaurs and centaurs. These creatures had tactics and had slain unprepared soldiers too confident with their skills. And so the battle for the tower went on, for Fameborn and his brood.

CHAPTER 70
SEARCH FOR DRAGONS

Being alone in the Tower of Rivals was pretty boring, so thought Torbiro as he wandered the empty halls. He wished to see dragons, since he had never seen one before. He was also warned not to take the dungeons carelessly, but his curiosity just peeked more of his interest. He held the map for the tower in his hands, but he could never get to the place he wanted to go. Torbiro had also wondered whatever happened to his friends. Were they lost? He needed to find them too, but dragons? He was torn, but standing still was never his suit. Rather than thinking of the "what ifs" he decided he would eventually meet them if he just kept on moving. Every time Torbiro thought about what a dragon looked like, he could only ever think of the descriptions the tavern storyteller would say. A lizard with wings, claws so giant they could crush a house with a single attack. And they could breathe fire. Sometimes it was acid and other times it was lasers. Must be hard for it to try and talk. With every room he entered looking for a dragon, he would end up in a laboratory with giant claws or a room with a water tank full of lizards or into a library with laser lights. So in the library, he searched for a book on dragons, just to get a picture of it, since his imagination wasn't very good and he had been walking for two hours, but still no dragon or his missing friends.

Torbiro found many of the books in this library were indecipherable.

Some were written in elvish, others in dwarven script and others had glowing words, but he still could not make heads or tails what they said. Torbiro could read a little bit of dwarvish script but not much and he only knew of elvish script because Commander Peren had some fancy looking notes on his wall in his office back in Traytos. After grabbing plenty of books and making a mess in the library, Torbiro ultimately gave up trying to read any of those strange books. He was about to put them away when a goblin girl started to do just that. So, thinking it was her job, he left in search of the mystical dragon. As Torbiro left the library, an idea popped into his head. Rat. He knew about this place. Maybe he knew where the dragons were and would be able to help him find some. Not knowing how to go to Rat's room, he just thought of wanting to see him and there he was.

'Mr Rat, sir, can you help me? Find a dragon?' said Torbiro as he entered the room.

'Ahh, where did you come from?' said Rat in a panic, turning and clutching his chest. He was breathing very rapidly from the sudden shock of Torbiro's question.

'I'm sorry, Mr Rat. Are you alright?' asked Torbiro, concerned he may have scared his new friend to death. He just wanted to know where the dragons were and what they looked like. Not kill a friend, which would be rude.

'No, no, I'm quite alright. I thought you just left?' said Rat a little bit confused. He tilted his head like he was looking for something behind Torbiro.

'Left? I just got here. But do you know about dragons?' said Torbiro, in a very inquisitive manner. His desire to see a dragon was the only thing distracting him from rescuing the princess.

'What do you mean, dragon? I know plenty, but I swear I've already had this conversation with you today?' said Rat, with even more confusion. Had he already spoken to Torbiro about dragons today? Must be déjà vu, or was he going senile?

'Huh? What do you mean? This is the second time I've talked to you today?' said Torbiro. He looked confused and reacted to the same look as Rat. As Rat looked past Torbiro, Torbiro turned to see what he was looking at, but nothing was there.

'Ok fine, it would seem you might have forgotten what I just told you, so this time let me show you what a dragon is and what they look like. Explaining it to you is a really long process and I just don't have that kind of time today,' said Rat, explaining the lack of free time he had due to an abusive mistress.

'Thank you Mr Rat. If you ever want to work for someone who is nicer, you can always join me if you'd like.' Torbiro understood what it felt like to not be appreciated.

'Thank you Master Torbiro. I may take up your offer, but be careful not to underestimate those dragons. They are quite deadly,' said Rat, thinking he had another case of déjà vu. He had done this before. As Rat had taken a moment to pause and think about the early visit from Torbiro, Torbiro had already left to seek out his fabled dragon. Rat turned to give him another piece of crucial advice, but Torbiro had already left. Drat.

With the image of a dragon in Torbiro's mind, he dashed out the door and low and behold, he finally arrived in front of a massive dragon. Torbiro was so delighted that all he could do was marvel at its size and colour. The storytellers were wrong, dragons were not one colour. They were a rainbow of colours. It was the size of a castle; it was just so majestic and wondrous that Torbiro had even forgotten about the warnings Rat had told him. To Torbiro's fortune, the creature was asleep. But that did not stop him from getting close to touch it. Being a halfling had its perks when it came to being naturally stealthy, which had kept Torbiro alive in his encounter with the enormous creature as he climbed all over it. From on top of its snout, to its wings and all the way to its tail. But on the way back, the creature started to stir as though it was about to wake up. Torbiro was surprised it would wake up, but then Torbiro had noticed something odd about one of its scales. It was jutting into its skin, as some humans referred to an ingrown nail that was usually in the toe area. It looked painful, so like a nice fool, decided to help the dragon by pulling it out. But to Torbiro, the scale in question was about the same size as himself. It was the size of a shield, which was about 30 by 30 centimetres, but only about one to two centimetres thick. So prying this scale out would take some time. But as luck would have it, it came off very easily. Torbiro was happy to have helped, but now what would he do with the scale? Maybe he should keep it as a souvenir.

With a job well done, Torbiro put the scale away and went back in search of his missing friends. He had been wandering around the top of the tower and now he was back at the bottom. How would he get back to the top? He wondered, but started walking nonetheless. He had found an archway when he saw his friends running away from a band of big cow-people. They were minotaurs, but Torbiro didn't know that. Torbiro tried to catch them by going to a different corridor, but he was unable to find them again. He had chased them for a few clicks when he found an interesting room full of levers, buttons, valves and switches. It was a room much like the one in Master Dorian's breakroom, where he would watch his hometown game of dwarven-bowl. Such a rough game. This room too, had a glass-like view screen, but unlike the one back in Traytos, the screen here was not flat but round, like a crystal ball in those fortune teller's tents during carnivals. Torbiro didn't know how it worked and didn't want to damage it, so instead he left the machine alone. But what he found odd was a lever with the words "reset tower" on it. What did that mean? He wondered about it at first, then pulled it. But nothing seemed to happen. He put the lever back to the position he found it and left.

What Torbiro had done when he pulled the lever was remove the magical circles in the tower so that movement was no longer dependent on the thought of the individual, but rather their physical movement alone. This was bad for the exhausted and overworked patrons of the tower, but it was good for the heroes trying to rescue the princess. All they would need to do was go up. Indeed, nothing had happened for Torbiro as he could not feel the magic, but it was a disaster for everyone else in the tower. Especially for Kitreth.

275

CHAPTER 71
TROUBLING SMOKE

Kitreth had been hard at work healing and caring for her injured cousin all this time. It had been her priority to keep her safe since if she died, the plan would not only go south, but she would be killed by her uncle. She could have just fled, but that would dishonour her family and most of all, her pride as the next ruler of Bataros. She did not want another event like this to happen, so she instructed her mages to place a maze in the tower so t only those with the mental capacity would be able to enter a certain room at any given moment. Which meant magical glyphs that could read the mind of any person and then transport them to the room they needed to enter. The servants were then manipulated to not have the word princess in their memory, so no matter the order they were given, they would not be able to enter the room the princess was in.

This also meant anyone could enter the secret room of the princess if they were there to rescue her, like an idiot knight, who would get lost in this labyrinth of a tower. This plan would drain the rest of the mages, but it would make the confrontation with Stupidborn, aka stupid Fameborn, just that much swifter. He would be at death's door anyway and uncle needed him to be alive. So I just had to wait a few more days until I released him from that trap I enhanced. So I could blame everything on Stupidborn for being the worst hero in the history of heroes. He had been trapped for four days now and in just two more, he would be so weak that the only thing on his mind would be recue then heading home. It was a perfect plan.

The tower had been quiet ever since the maze was put inside it. This was good, but it had also drained the mage's energy to work on breeding the monsters and brewing elixirs for the market. Progress was slowed, but it was better than having every goblin killed then having to breed more of the filthy things. Master Raazet had been making great progress with healing Dawn, but this too was slow, as though he was distracted by something else. He would never betray me. He was my loyal master after my mother passed away. So it might just be my imagination, besides I too needed to prepare for the battle with Stupidborn so I don't accidentally kill him.

Kitreth headed for her training chamber when she heard an unusual commotion from the level below her. It sounded like arguing from the mages. She decided to leave them be while she prepared her spells, her equipment and her appearance. She needed to look devilish to appear as the propaganda uncle made out the Bataros soldiers looked like. Kitreth could just cast an illusion spell, but that could be risky, so she prepared her dress and mask. She started with the mask and in just a few short, painstaking hours, she was done. Lost in her own focus, Kitreth had not heard the happenings of the tower but upon completion, she headed back to her quarters and in the corridor near her room she spotted a halfling of all things. He had an old scrappy looking map in his hands and seemed to walk blindly into the next room.

Kitreth had no time for such creatures, but why was there even such a creature in this tower? Halflings only resided in Traytos in a special sector and her uncle had hated their kind for some reason. So why was there one here? Perhaps it's a missing specimen from one of the labs. I should ask around if it is, as I do not want random creatures wandering around this tower. So Kitreth headed for the stairs rather than using the archway's glyph. Walking was much easier anyway and as she took the first step down, she heard an explosion. It was near enough that it actually shook this part of the tower. She needed to know what had happened and ran down the stairs.

Down a single flight of stairs, even before she could see the smoke, she could smell something burning. The smell was of burning flesh, putrid and rotting. The smoke's colour, once Kitreth had seen it, was also not black, but a reddish purple. This was bad. Had the mages summoned a demon again? If that was the case, this tower and everyone in it would be condemned. But to her luck, this was not the case. The mages inside the room were arguing about having screwed up and mixed two different recipes together. One was the recipe for a regeneration curative and the other was a recipe to ward off demons. Hence the explosion.

'Look, it was clearly your fault,' said a mage, dressed in a red robe.

'No, it was your fault. You're the one who poured demon's blood into a cauldron for a healing potion. What are ya, an apprentice?' said a mage, dressed in a black robe.

'You're the one in the wrong laboratory. So there!' said the red-robed mage as he spat on the floor.

'It doesn't matter whose fault it is, just clean this mess up. Now!' said Kitreth, annoyed these mages were bickering instead of just fixing it. In unison, the mages said "yes" and begrudgingly went back to work. How could an argument like this even happen? The glyphs I prepared earlier should have prevented this altogether.

'You, tell me why you aren't at your station?' said Kitreth, pointing at one of the mages, trying to investigate what was going on. The accused mage revealed that it seemed something either had gone very wrong with the glyphs or an outsider had entered the tower. Kitreth also asked if any of them were missing a halfling specimen. They looked at each other, shook their heads, nodded, then looked back at Kitreth and shrugged their shoulders, confused. They did not have such specimens, but maybe the other magi had lost a halfling.

With a mental spell, Kitreth sent a message to all the mages in the tower to check if anyone was missing any specimens in their labs.

She did not mention that the specimen was a living halfling, just so no one started to make fake claims just to get the creature. She waited for a response and only master Raazet was the one to answer. He had been missing one for the past hour. It must have slipped out of it's cage. With a private message sent to its last location, Kitreth went to investigate the issues with the glyphs. She found immediately they had been turned off. She tried to cast a teleportation spell to go directly to the control room, but this had failed. For some reason her spell had fizzled out. What was going on?

As Torbiro had been exploring, he upturned various objects in the tower. Some of these items had been placed in a certain location and position to enhance the effectiveness of the tranquil energies gathered from the void, but if these items were disturbed, the arcanus returns to its natural flow. Torbiro had thought upside-down pots were strange, so he put them right side up. He had also changed the positions of elvish writing displayed on picture frames, which were crooked, so he made them straighter. He thought the rooms to be in need of tidying and wanted to help as he searched for his friends.

Why was Kitreth able to cast some spells but not others? Perhaps it was because of the type of spell? Or maybe it was the amount of arcanus needed to cast the spell. As Kitreth had these thoughts, she headed down to the dungeon via one of the secret passages. It would not let her get there directly, but it would certainly cut the travel time by half. She decided to take the two mages with her for punishment and upon their arrival in the dungeon, the three spellslingers saw their worst fears had indeed happened. There were intruders inside the dungeon and they had been wreaking havoc on the poor little monsters. Kitreth grabbed one of the mages by her side and squeezed hard. She had grabbed his left shoulder. The gnome mage winced and struggled from the pain. He begged for mercy, but it was a mistake. Kitreth gave him just that, but not in a manner he had thought. She used her necromancy to drain the life out of the mage. She didn't stop when she had enough energy, but rather continued to drain until the poor unfortunate gnome was nothing but dust. Kitreth the Flame was her title, but not many knew of her real title, Bloodletter. The other mage had sensed danger, but there was no place for her to escape. She should have stayed in her lab, but now a rival mage was consumed even past death. Just to be used as arcanus. It was truly terrifying. The aura mistress Kitreth had was always terrifying, but now it could be seen. Its appearance was more like an ooze that coated her entire body with the faces and visages of those creatures from the void, the undead. She ordered her remaining mage to handle the control room while she dealt with the unruly intruders. Kitreth cast a teleportation spell and an egg-shaped portal cracked the very air. Within the portal was the control room. It looked untouched, but that didn't mean no one had been in there. The mage jumped a little too high into the portal and scraped the edge of this demonically created door with her arm, which shrivelled up. All of the fluid was drained. It was painful and the mage screamed after moving through. The problem was, the mage had disregarded the after-effects of the mummification of her arm. After entering the control room, rather than severing her arm, she started to work on what was wrong with the tower's glyphs, but in a few seconds, the draining effects on her arm had spread to her entire body. Killing her slowing and painfully. Just like the male mage, she was no more than a pile of dust after eight seconds.

CHAPTER 72
ANOTHER TORBIRO.

Memyra and the others had finally found Torbiro and it was time for some payback. He had indirectly put them through hell and there he stood nonchalantly tapping his foot with arms crossed like he was mocking them. How arrogant, indeed. Memyra was the first to approach him. She was covered in blood, most of it was Borgar's, but some had been hers as well. With fists clenched, cracking her knuckles, then her shoulders, she was ready. Not even Robyn would be able to stop them from ambushing him, as she too, wanted something from him.

'Torro, I gotcha!' said Memyra, as she jumped head long and grabbed the unprepared prey.

'Me… Memy… Memyra, is that you?' said Torbiro, with a puzzled and shocked look on his face. Tears started emerging from his eyes as though he hadn't seen her in a long time.

'That's right. Torro, it's your worst nightmare,' said Memyra, as she held him in a headlock. She was so angry with Torbiro, she had not seen the different reactions and nuances. She had expected him to recoil and put up more of a guard to her attacks.

'Nightmare? What do you mean? Woah, is that you, Borgar? Looking slim.' Torbiro tried to change the subject. Torbiro had to get out of this situation. Being here with Memyra and the gang was nostalgic, but he needed to find his clue. This Torbiro was not the

Torbiro Memyra and the team had known. This Torbiro was from a different timeline and he had a different task to achieve. Being here might change the current timeline and therefore, screw up his present.

'Hey, Torbiro. It's time to pay!' said Wilrokk and Saara. Both of them were covered in blood and had open wounds. These too, had lost a friend through this entire venture and it was time for Torbiro to feel their pain. Maybe not emotionally, but for all the running they had done, he was going to suffer for it physically. From the shadows created by their faces and the blood running down them, it made an exhausted-looking smile look so sinister. Both soldiers had such sinister smiles on their faces that it made them look like witches.

'Sergeant Redfellow and Officer Wilrokk, why are you looking at me like that? Myra, can you please let me go? This is all a misunderstanding?' said Torbiro, pleading to be released. Torbiro had said something he shouldn't have, but that didn't quite get caught. Memyra, Wilrokk and Saara were too tired to care for Torbiro's excuses. Robyn, on the other hand, had caught the slip of the tongue. She did have keen senses, after all.

Torbiro looked left at Saara, looked to his right at Wilrokk and tried to break out of the headlock from Memyra. With the three of them wanting payback, they held their positions and asked Torbiro for any last words. All he could muster was, "Not the face" and after a combination of punches from Wilrokk, a few slaps from Saara and a lot of spit from Memyra, with a few gut punches tossed in there for good measure, the crew was satisfied with their revenge. Even though this was not their Torbiro, they beat him to a pulp. Only Memyra had not listened to his request of not hitting the face. Torbiro was slumped on the floor of the room with bruises and lumps from the beatings. Robyn was the only one with the least bit of concern for the poor little halfling.

Robyn slowly approached Torbiro and helped him sit up. It was a strange sight to see for Robyn. As soon as Torbiro was sitting up, he smiled and said very softly, "Missed you guys." Robyn kept this to herself, since she didn't know its meaning. The team didn't have any healer's kits or even a first aid kit to help bandage Torbiro up, but instead the injured halfling just popped a blue-coloured potion in his mouth and the swelling and his injuries started to vanish. Robyn wanted to ask Torbiro something, but he stood up and patted off the dirt on his clothes and addressed everyone.

After being beaten up by his close friends, Torbiro could only think of the good times they had all had together. He was reminiscing about his past and started to wonder where he was at this time. He knew that at this tower there were two of himself here. One from this time and the other was him, the one that got mistaken for the Torbiro of this timeline. Searching his memory for where he was in this time was a mystery. He could only remember vague things that happened: discovering a dragon, getting a dragon scale, losing the dragon scale and finding the princess and then rescuing her. Where the hell did I go? With that thought in mind, just outside the door's archway, Torbiro could see himself walking by with a large map covering his view. There he is. Now it's time to jet.

'Guys, I don't know why you needed to attack me but it is time for me to go,' said Torbiro, as he started to chase his other self, walking by in the corridor.

'Torbiro, where do you think you're going? We have to save the princess, remember?' yelled Memyra, warning him if he left again he would get another helping.

'Myra, I know but see ya,' said Torbiro, as he dashed past Borgar and Jimmy at the door.

'Ah, Master Torbiro, where are you headed off to?' asked Rat, seeing Torbiro run past, in a panicked and frantic manner.

'Not now Rat. I got to lose them,' said Torbiro as he turned a corner.

'Guys, don't let him escape. Go after him,' said Memyra, very cross for not tying up his legs.

The only one not chasing Torbiro was Borgar, as he was far more tired from the running. It wasn't the running at all. In fact, it was the large amount of blood loss he had suffered from all the missiles that struck him. It is very surprising he was not dead. But the team had a moment's respite so, sure they could not keep up, but they could continue the chase. The team had been slowed down by a gnome mage in the corridor, but Memyra was able to get past him. She told the rest to grab him as she sped forward. Torbiro had turned a corner, but was it left or right? Memyra knew he had a tendency to always go right, so she turned that way, but the corridor was empty. No Torbiro in sight. Had she lost him? But in that short moment of thought, she heard Torbiro from behind her.

CHAPTER 73
RAAZET APOLLON TENAN

'Hey, Myra. I finally found you.' Torbiro happily waved the old map in his hands. Torbiro had been searching for hours in this tower for his friends and now he was very glad to have found them.

'Found you? What do you mean by that?' Memyra noticed Torbiro was not frantically running away, but he was his oblivious self again.

'Huh? Well, you guys must have gotten lost in the dungeon, right?' said Torbiro. He was confused since he was the one looking for them and not the other way around. After all, he had the map, there was no way he could have gotten lost with the map.

'Lost? Grrr, the dungeon? You have no right! Errr!' said Memyra in frustration. She was no fool and Torbiro was the one who had gone missing. With such high tension coming from Memyra, one could clearly see the thickness of the pulsing vein on her forehead. The stress had already been released when she had beaten him up, but a second beating was in order. Memyra clenched her fists, cracked her knuckles and salivated for a second round of punishment.

Torbiro completely ignored her and went to see the others. He greeted them well and mourned at the loss of Karl. He hadn't known Karl for long, but now he was with the dragons. Torbiro could also see they had met Rat. Wow, when did they become friends? He patted Rat on the back, as though to say, "welcome to the crew" and started to say a speech about it being time to rescue Princess Dawn. Just as

Torbiro was about to speak, Memyra turned the corner and headed back to the crew to get some information from the gnome that tried to stop them.

'My good friends, now that we are all together again, it is time to rescue our damsel in distress,' said Torbiro, with the poise of a leader. His confidence was glistening brightly as he spoke.

'But what should we do with this gnome?' said Saara, confused to see Torbiro was already treating this stranger as his friend. When did that happen?

'Huh? What do you mean? This is Rat. He's our friend, right?' Torbiro was also confused. With a perplexed look on Torbiro's face, he misunderstood the situation with his usual assumptions.

'Out of the way, Torro! We need to find out if this Rat is a friend or foe?' said Memyra, as she pushes Torbiro aside. With her right index finger, she thrust it into Rat's face, just short of his little nose. Rat could tell she was more of the leader in this band of ruffians.

Raazet or Rat, knew he was in a dire situation. He was surrounded by large and unscrupulous characters; an ogre was dangerous enough but an orc too. What kind of adventurers were they to have two halflings, an elf, a human, an orc and an ogre with them? Three of whom had symbols of Traytos' crest as though they were soldiers. If he could only cast a spell, he would be able to push them away so he could easily escape. But none of the ingredients in his pockets were responding to his arcanus.

I could pretend to join them and then flee as soon as possible, but the female elf might be a problem. Torbiro did say we were all friends. Perhaps that would be my only escape.

'You! Mage. Are you working for the master of this tower?' Memyra interrogated Rat in a threatening manner.

'I, well, I do indeed but I am a friend to Torbiro there,' said Rat, as he pointed his finger at the halfling. Rat had about ten possible answers prepared at the question of "Are you friend or foe?" but the question was not asked. This halfling was going to be a problem, too.

'Okay, Borgar, you can eat him now. We can't trust him,' said Memyra, as she read the facial expressions on the gnome.

'Ogay, I eat it nawu!' said Borgar, as he started to lift the gnome from Saara's grip and licked his lips, preparing to eat the poor gnome.

'No, please. Don't eat me. I will talk. I can help you. I know where the princess is. Just please don't…ahhh,' screamed Rat as he flailed around, slapping and kicking the ogre about to eat him.

'Borgar, put him down. He is our friend, not food!' said Torbiro. To stop Borgar from eating Rat, instead of simply telling Memyra to stop this, Torbiro started to slap the ogre, as if he were a disobedient animal.

'Borgar, not bad. So Borgar not eat little gnome,' said Borgar as he only managed to lick the gnome and drop him next to Torbiro.

'Thank you, friend. I can help you but please don't let me be eaten,' said Rat as he hid behind Torbiro, from the ogre.

'So, what is your name, gnome?' said Memyra, using the most threatening tone to intimidate the gnome in question.

'His name is Rat,' said Torbiro, trying to protect his distraught friend.

'Yes, yes my name is Rat,' said Rat, as he wiped off some of the saliva on his leg. He was agreeing with Torbiro and nodding frantically. Rat was still surrounded and some of the ingredients in his cloak had gotten wet, so he was still unable to cast any spells. This was really, really bad.

'Torro, shut up. And you tell me your real name or else,' said Memyra. She was now putting on an act to get this gnome to; one, tell them the truth and two, tell them everything else about this tower. She pointed her finger at Borgar again to emphasise that a single lie would get him back in the mouth of the creature.

'Myra, I…' said Torbiro, as he tried to again defend his new friend but was interrupted by Borgar, of all people. Borgar had grabbed him and covered his mouth.

'Now, answer my question, gnome!' said Memyra, again in a sinister tone, still keeping up appearances. Though Memyra was no shorter than Rat by a few centimetres, she had a menacing presence, which frightened the defenceless but powerful gnome mage.

'Ma… My name is Raazet Apollo Tenan, but you can call me Rat for short,' said Raazet as he answered her question. In his fear, he also revealed vital happenings in the Tower of Rivals, such as what his mistress looked like, her name, and where she was. Raazet had also explained where they could find the princess in the tower and what his occupation was and all the details he could muster from the fear of being eaten alive by an ogre. Raazet was going to ask for mercy, but Torbiro was their friend and ally and he was being treated far less gentle than Raazet had expected. So instead, out of a survival reflex, he spilled the beans.

Rat was still their hostage and so long as Borgar was with them, he would obey all of Memyra's commands. Rat was the only one who knew where the exact location of the princess was and once she was found, this silly little rescue mission could be completed and they could all finally go home. Just in case he tried anything funny, Memyra tied his hands to Torbiro. That way, both of them couldn't disappear. Torro was the only one to complain, but this was for his own good.

With Rat somewhat recruited, the team headed for the top of the tower. They needed to head there on foot since the glyphs weren't working and it would take a long time. The tower may have seemed small on the outside, but was a very tall structure. By Rat's explanation, the tower loomed to a massive height of forty metres tall with twelve floors. He had also explained the dungeons underneath housed many of their business opportunities back in Bataros. Considering they had started on the third floor; it would take them just over an hour to reach the princess.

CHAPTER 74
THE CORRIDOR IS CLEAR?

The climb up the tower was stress free and relaxing compared to their earlier run through the dungeon, but something on the eighth floor had stopped them. The path was clear. No one was around to block it, but they could not go any further. Rat was not the one responsible for this and did not know what was going on. He was tied to Torbiro and any time he tried to explain something, he would add some hand gestures. Torbiro's left hand would also flail about.

On the eighth floor, the rooms here all contained laboratories that made potions and elixirs. Potions made here would be sold to the people in Bataros and other surrounding kingdoms that ordered magical goods or accepted magical wares. Elixirs, on the other hand, were the private supply for the royalty of Bataros. These elixirs needed to be carefully stored in an aura of arcanus or they would not only lose their intended effect, but could summon the creatures used as an ingredient. Since the field of arcanus was disrupted by Torbiro during his earlier exploits, the aura used to contain these items had lost all of their power and had summoned a very annoying but dangerous creature. An invisible mimic. Mimics were not creatures per se, but rather ordinary objects enchanted to become a creature. As an example, a table mimic was an ordinary table turned into a creature. Now why would anyone make such a dangerous thing? For convenience, of course and skilled mages would create mimics out of everything. But the wizards of Bataros had found that certain variations of this creature could provide beneficial properties when consumed properly.

This particular mimic was made from glass, as it was a glass-window mimic. It was practically invisible and had the ability to blind and disorient its victims. Once the victim was immobilised from panic, that's when it would go for the kill and consume their life force. The reason this mimic was so annoying was the wizard who had created it, had also imbued the creature with his sense of humour. So it would only devour creatures that did not respond to their harassment. These creatures could morph into different shapes and move wherever and however they wanted.

'Rat, what's going on in this corridor? Are you behind this?' asked Memyra, as she jabbed her finger into the back of the gnome. She started with poking where his kidneys would be.

'Ow... Ouch, that hurts, you know. For an old gnome like me, it could be fatal. Now stop that.' Rat winced in pain.

'Myra, can you stop poking Rat? It's hard enough to move tied to him. Stop making it harder to move when you poke him,' said Torbiro. He had only used Memyra's nickname when he was annoyed and after being used as a shield for Rat so he could evade being poked.

'This is not...ow... my doing. Please stop,' said Rat as he tried to defend himself.

'Then what in the name of the pulse is pushing us back?' said Memyra, now questioning the group.

'Allow me to check but you must untie me so I can cast a spell,' said Rat, trying to genuinely help. Sure, it was to persuade them that he was on their side and then make a run for it as soon as they turned their back, but what would any desperate mage do?

'Robyn, hold the gnome while I untie him,' said Memyra. She signalled to Robyn she wanted to talk to her in private, before they untied the suspicious sorcerer.

'Memyra, do you trust him? Are you really going to untie the gnome?' asked Robyn. She did not trust the gnome, since he had helped the other Torbiro get away. Robyn still had a few questions for the halfling, but now it was impossible. She followed Memyra's lead and ducked behind Borgar to talk more privately.

'Hey Robyn, I want you to hold him down while I tie the two of them by the waist instead of their hands.' Memyra didn't trust either of them to act on their own. Especially Torbiro, since he had the gall to lie about his "other" mission. The gnome was a mage and considering the mages they had already encountered in the last toggle – last month – were less than friendly, how could this one be any different? Korvin was very suspicious and he turned out to be some crazed nut job.

'No, Robyn. I don't. I trust you more and that's saying a lot. Now make sure he doesn't notice and hold him still,' said Memyra, as she whispered to Robyn.

'Um, Memyra, I was wondering what happened to Jimmy. Did you see him leave?' said Robyn. She had been keeping close watch on Raazet and had asked Wilrokk to keep an eye on Jimmy.

'Ugh... Just another gnome to worry about. If he ever comes back, we can just tie all three trouble-makers together,' said Memyra, with stress inducing annoyance starting to build up. With all the gnomes she had met, Memyra could now say they were the worst, most annoying and most unreliable race of creatures ever. She had blacklisted gnomes at that very moment.

As Robyn held Raazet, so he could not flee, Memyra pulled out a lodestone magnet and some rope lined with a magnetised iron to reinforce it. In this case, it would be used as an invisible anchor and the anchor would be Torbiro. Memyra had quickly disguised the rope to look like a fancy belt to award her troublesome friend. And the lodestone would be attached to the gnome. What Memyra didn't know was the lodestone would also disrupt spellcasting and protect him from spells cast at him.

'Ok, you're untied, for now. If you make a run for it or do something else to stall us, he will eat you!' said Memyra as she pointed to Borgar, threatening the already frightened old gnome.

With a nod, and a quick scan of the area, Raazet started to cast a spell. Investicato was a spell to scan and identify objects and creatures that could not be seen by the natural eye. With a masterful technique, he cast the spell, but nothing happened. If Robyn was better trained in the mystical arts, she would have seen the lodestone collect the energy and disperse it upon the casting of the spell. But no one could see that aura and the spell seemed to just fizzle.

Since nothing seemed to happen, Raazet cast the spell again, but again nothing happened. Why was his spell not working? Raazet then tried to cast a much simpler spell, like a cantrip he had learnt and memorised as an apprentice, but this too had failed. He was useless. If he couldn't even cast a beginner level spell, then there would be no hope for him to escape. He spent a few minutes casting and invoking some spells, but nothing was happening. Raazet slumped in complete defeat; he could not cast spells. This had never happened to him before.

Not being able to move from this location, Memyra and the others discussed how they could move forward. They needed a plan, but they also needed to know what could be on the later floors. This was a magical tower full of magical creatures and obstacles and of course, the mages themselves. And all they had to work with were soldiers from Traytos, one of which was an elf with keen eyesight but far too clumsy with her weapon to be trustworthy, an orc with knowledge of technology and machines, all of which was useless here but he could put up a good fight, an ogre, enough said there, all strength and no brains, a gnome mage who could not cast any spells, so just a gnome with information about where the princess was located and two halflings, one of which was good at making unsafe plans but would work out in the end and Memyra, who couldn't care less for the mission or the princess. Her plan was to go home, but Torbiro insisted there had to be a way for them to climb the tower. And with a single word, he got another crazy look in his eye and they started to plan.

CHAPTER 75
YET ANOTHER TORBIRO

Meanwhile, elsewhere on the lower levels of the Tower of Rivals, Jimmy had followed who he thought to be Torbiro. This happened when the others were pummelling the other halfling they had assumed to be the real Torbiro. But Jimmy had magic inside him and was trained in its ways, in truth he could see the aura of people. In their first meeting, Jimmy had seen the very bright tinge of yellow that engulfed the halfling. This aura was something all creatures had starting from birth. Every aura was different and every person had a unique aura about them. Many magi needed to train to gain the ability to feel the presence of the aura to understand and control the powers of arcanus, which was the essence of the void. Being able to see this aura was the next step in arcanus control training. Not everyone could complete this highly advanced form of arcanus perception training as it had a great consequence for the ability. Jimmy had to sacrifice his natural sight to be able to see the aura. In his training, he had lost his physical eyes, but for a mage of his calibre, it was barely a loss. He had known the risks involved, but he had a contingency plan. It was simple, just cast a spell to regrow those eyes. But having a physical eye did not provide him with the ability to see the aura and discarding his natural sight was his decision in the end for the pursuit of power.

The Torbiro they had encountered in the room did not have a yellow tinge, as it was more like a deep green colour for his aura. Clearly, he must have been an imposter, but Jimmy would find the real one, subdue and capture him. Jimmy left the group silently as he followed his real prey. This one moved less erratically than the Torbiro he had met and studied, but that did not matter.

I will corner him and this will be the end of my mission. All I need to do is cast a spell to immobilise him and he will be mine.

Jimmy had chased this short creature with the same colour aura as Torbiro to the end of a corridor on the fourth floor and it seemed as though the halfling still didn't know he was being followed, as he continued on the same path until it was too late. Torbiro was cornered. Jimmy came out of hiding and before he could cast his immobilise spell, his prey turned around. And said something very shocking.

'It's been awhile, Zyro!' said the halfling with a yellow aura.

'How do you know that name?' said Jimmy, confused but intrigued at the same time.

'I'm the one that gave it to you, of course,' said the halfling. His voice was different but Jimmy couldn't quite understand why.

'It does not matter how or where you got that name from. It's time for my mission to be completed. Now submit!' said Jimmy. He was full of confidence and had underestimated his prey.

'It is unfortunate, as you have the wrong Torbiro. The one you seek is downstairs searching for his friends,' said Torbiro. He was yet another Torbiro of a different time and this one seemed to understand who his opponent was and how to deal with him. Immediately, Torbiro pulled out his weapons and launched a flurry of quick slashes.

Jimmy was surprised by this development. His spell was still in the incantation step and wouldn't have been cast for another few seconds. How did Torbiro cross seven metres in an instant? Getting cut a few times wouldn't stop or disrupt Jimmy's concentration, so at point black range he cast the spell of immobilise. A sinister grin appeared on his face as the energy was unleashed. He had his prey and his mission was completed. But the spell had no effect. Torbiro continued the assault with another barrage of quick slashes and jabs. Jimmy was overwhelmed and all he could do was leap backwards to avoid any more attacks. As Jimmy leaped back, Torbiro followed him. This is definitely not his prey. This was not only bad, but a miscalculation on his part. Simple spells weren't enough, but more complex spells needed time to cast and the constant assault Torbiro made was so skilled that even a misstep would have killed Jimmy. He needed to get away. Perhaps if he turned invisible, Torbiro would not be able to continue his assault and it would give Jimmy the chance to prepare and capture his prey. He knew of one spell that could provide him with cover, but it would absorb and neutralise all the arcanus within five hundred metres. Jimmy was desperate, so with a single word, he cast the spell, Conseeltos. And he vanished, but the halfling didn't falter and continued to attack. Jimmy was in trouble. His trump card had failed. His only choice was to surrender and die.

CHAPTER 76
WHAT HAVE THEY DONE?

Down in the chaos of the dungeon, Kitreth went on her rampage to remove those pesky intruders. Her power was simply too much for the would-be soldiers and knights of Traytos. They weren't supposed to be here in the first place. Why were there so many of them? But a few blasts of fire had weeded out the weak and a few spears of lightning would simply take care of the remaining ramble. This was the first floor of the dungeon and Kitreth had still not seen where that hero Fameborn was. Where in all the void was he? Kitreth had taken care of thirty or so soldiers when she realised the knight in question must have gone down further into the dungeon. Why would he do that? He had his orders and I remember uncle telling me to keep Dawn at the top of the tower for this reason. Well, it was time to knock some sense into him.

Fameborn had faced goblins and weak undead on the first floor of the dungeon and then proceeded to the next floor to face the more formidable minotaurs and centaurs, but this was not enough to satisfy his bloodlust. He needed to face something more; he needed to defeat the foulest creature in this place, the creature that had the gall to attack Traytos and kidnap the lovely Princess Dawn. He needed to kill more evil and cleanse this place, for the glory of Traytos. He had Dawn in his mind, to rescue her, but it had become a secondary priority. He needed to find the mastermind of this tower and defeat them. At the death cries and shouts of his faithful knights, Fameborn looked up and there he saw the most terrifying creature of them all. He had seen the sorcerer with a shade of purple manifesting about her body, like some kind of terrifying armour. Fameborn had seen Kitreth. Though he didn't know who she was, it didn't matter to him. All that mattered was to defeat the witch and climb the tower and rescue the delicate flower that was Dawn. Fameborn held his blooded blade in one hand and rushed back to the first floor. This must be the mastermind, he thought. It was time to finish this and complete his mission and return to Traytos in triumph.

CHAPTER 77
THREE PLANS

On the eighth floor, the gang had come up with three possible plans. Two of those plans were from Torbiro's crazy ideas and the contingency plan or Plan C was made by Robyn. The first plan was to climb back down to a lower floor and find a window to use one of Memyra's grappling hooks and climb to the higher floors. The second plan was to have Borgar use his strength to barge through whatever was blocking them and then push forward. And their third plan was to find some wizards who had not lost the ability to cast spells and get them to help.

Since the team was already on the eighth floor, they went with the second plan first. The order of the plans was when Torbiro had come up with them, so of course the team voted for which plan would be executed first, with the first plan going last as it was the most dangerous to try. Memyra wanted to make sure the ogre could bust through the strange wall that had blocked them, so provided – on loan – a pair of ramming gloves used by ogres and giants for use during a siege of heavily fortified walls or gates. Why Memyra had them on hand was for another time and she would answer any questions about them once they had finally left this accursed tower. These gloves were adorned with a heavy, cylindrical battering ram. Its size was about fifteen centimetres by fifteen centimetres and its length was about fifty centimetres. The gloves also had a small lodestone magnet to provide some extra power to the wielder. With a single glove, an ogre should have the power to break down the front gates of Traytos on his own, but with a pair, it would be overkill.

The instructions Memyra gave to Borgar were pretty simple. They were to thrust his arms out with the gloves. Torbiro had also wanted Borgar to charge at the corridor to make sure he had enough force behind him. What the gang didn't know was the things that were stopping them were very mischievous creatures with a bad sense of humour. From about ten metres away was the starting line for Borgar. Equipped with the gloves, Borgar got ready to run. On the signal, Memyra powered the gloves up with electricity and hid with the others behind the ogre. Borgar started to run and after about ten metres in unison everyone else shout "Now!", "Attack!" and "Pumpkin!" from Raazet. And that was when the plan failed, as Borgar met with no resistance as he thrust his arms forward. Instead, he tripped over some invisible force and continued to roll with the momentum of his dash. Borgar tried to get up, but something had pushed him and he continued to roll further down the corridor and by the time he was able to stand Borgar had made it to the next floor up, on his own unfortunately. The others had seen Borgar's success in passing the unusual barrier and dashed after him, with Wilrokk first, then Saara and then the rest of them.

With grinning enthusiasm, Wilrokk was the first to eat that confidence as he slammed hard on to an invisible wall, with so much impact that it broke one of his orcish tusks and three of his front teeth. Saara was next, but with her quick reactions, seeing Wilrokk crash into the wall head first, she managed to slow herself enough not to repeat his mistake, but she still hit the wall hard enough to break an arm and dislocate her right shoulder. With the exception of Torbiro, everyone else managed to avoid injury. Torbiro was not paying attention and smashed his hand into the hard invisible wall as he tried to leap through. Wilrokk, Saara and Torbiro writhed in pain from their recklessness. Plan A ended in failure.

After a few potions, the minor injuries of Wilrokk, Saara and Torbiro were healed, but as for their broken bones and missing teeth, they needed some stronger curative to fix those. If Plan A had failed, they would need to go on without Borgar and proceed with Plan B. Plan B was Robyn's idea and it was to head on to a lower level and get assistance from the other wizards with the help of Raazet. This was the non-violent method as well, but someone with a lot of charm needed to help Raazet out.

The problem with Plan B was it relied on Borgar still being with the team. His presence would have had a massive impact on 'convincing' the wizards to aid them. But with him not there, they could only rely on Wilrokk ,since he was the next scariest of them all. But he was too injured to even try, plus he wasn't scary in comparison. So the team headed down to try the plan, anyway. First, Wilrokk would be the 'assistant' to gather the poor sap. This failed immediately, as the mages they met were already in a panic from not being able to use their magic. None of them could help. So it seemed Torbiro's first plan was next. If this failed, they would have to come up with some new plans.

CHAPTER 78
STALEMATE

On the fourth floor, Jimmy continued to battle with a very formidable Torbiro. Jimmy had used his trump card and failed. His next act was to submit defeat and die, honourable or not. Death was the end. With the next attack, Jimmy would stop evading and take the fatal blow and with a single thrust of the halfling's weapon, Jimmy was cut. The strike was very accurate. In a single blow, he was going to die. Jimmy's invisibility spell cancelled on his death and his final view was of the aura leaving, but Jimmy still managed to hear the fiend's last words, "Until next time".

In the lower levels of the dungeon, Kitreth had fought more of the soldiers in league with Fameborn. She was furious it had not gone according to her uncle's plan. She now had to vanquish many of the soldiers herself. She cast all manner of spells to cull the herd, but then for whatever the reason they stopped. She could no longer accumulate arcanus, even though she had used the blood of her enemies as material. But since she had worked on the numbers first, she was now only outnumbered five to one. She was versed in melee combat, but it was not her forte and she was still outnumbered. If only master Raazet were by her side, she would be able to summon the prismatic drakes to hunt these fools. With that in mind, she headed for the high ground and called for re-enforcements from the first level of the tower. There were still the mercenaries her father had hired just in case things went bad.

Blast after blast, the witch continued her attack. Fameborn ordered his brave men to recklessly charge the one sorcerer as he continued forward. This act cost almost all of their lives, but their deaths were fuel for his vengeance. He had five good soldiers left and he ordered a charge with him in front, not to protect his men, but so he would greedily take the kill for himself. In their sloppy formation, his left flank started to fall behind, but to their astonishment, the mage had stopped with those infernal spells that had vanquished their friends and allies. And then the witch had fled. Fameborn was thrilled to see his enemy flee in fear, but he also grinned as now there would be a chance to hunt the bitch. He cried out, 'Charge' as he raised his sword in the air to rally his men. It was time for victory.

On the first floor, Kitreth called out to those hired goons to deal with the remaining soldiers so she could lead Fameborn to his task. She was exhausted from the climb up, since she needed to physically run. Being without magic truly sucked. It was mundane and too much work. Huffing and puffing to catch her breath, she reached the room where those lazy and overpaid mercenaries stayed. Kitreth was going to order them to hold the line and kill the men with Fameborn. But as soon as she got to the door, all the hired goons were scattered on the ground. Some were dead and others were heavily wounded. The only one left was a halfling, who was looting the dead. Kitreth had seen him before, but where? No matter, if he was in this room, he must have been one of the mercenaries and he would do. She ordered the last of the mercenaries to attack the intruders, but his response was unexpected, as he dropped his pants and slapped his bare arse, which infuriated Kitreth. This one halfling was no match for her if only she could cast her spells and punish this disobedience. She would not have this. She was the mistress of the tower and her position was the highest and should not be contested by non-magic folk.

'You there, I demand you dirty mercs to get to work,' said Kitreth, ordering her living mercenaries to get to work.

'Ye... Yes, mis... mistress,' said the other heavily wounded mercenaries as they struggled to get up. Their weapons were scattered on the ground, but as soon as one approached the halfling, they were instantly cut down.

'I don't work for you, little Kit,' said the halfling in a cocky manner. With a flourishing bow to show he was the one that had dealt this heavy blow to her, he started to walk out.

'How dare you, you little speck of existence. Now die!' said Kitreth. she had momentarily forgotten she could not use spells and instinctively extended her arm towards the halfling, as though she were to cast a deadly spell. But of course nothing worked. In her frustration, she kicked one of the corpses and ordered the remaining mercenaries to deal with the soldiers in the dungeon.

'Well, it's been nice catching up with you li'l Kit, but I gotta run, cya,' said the halfling, as he hopped over the dead and skipped out the door. Since there was only one way out, he needed to pass Kitreth, but he was counting on it.

With a quick flourish, Kitreth unsheathed the weapon on her hip. Her weapon of choice was a very elegant rapier, with a light blade and glowing gems on the pommel of the blade. Though the gems on her blade weren't there just for show, they were, in fact, gems of power. Even though Kitreth could not cast spells, she could still handle one little halfling, or so she thought. Underestimating an opponent was the first thing she was taught not to do when fighting an enemy. In this situation, her stress and arrogance were to be the cause of her downfall. Instead of using the full force of her weapon, Kitreth struck the halfling with it in its dormant state. If she was trying to kill her foe, she had missed it. The weapon struck, but not a vital spot and then got caught on the hinge of the door. It was truly unlucky.

With a flourish of his own, Torbiro bid farewell to Kitreth, stating the great halfling, Torro would never get caught by the likes of her. He made a fancy exit and managed to steal a few of those power gems from the rapier without anyone knowing. And by the time Kitreth got herself unhinged, the halfling by the name of Torro was gone. Now her only problem remaining – that she knew of – was Fameborn and his knights. She gathered what mercenaries and mages she could find and headed off to the entrance of the dungeon.

In a single clash, both sides were in a stalemate. Both sides were riddled with injuries, both sides fighting for their masters and both sides wanting their master's victory. On the side of Fameborn, there were soldiers and a few knights trying their best to push forward. These men and women had been fighting almost nonstop since the battle in the Dip Hills. On the side of Kitreth, there were half dead mercenaries still looking for payment and mages just wanting to go back to the safety of their workshop to continue their work. Some were suited for hand-to-hand combat, while others were using their numbers to trick and trip their opponents. With only their leader to rally or threaten them, no one was giving up a centimetre.

The knights knew if the leader was defeated, that would be the end of this struggle. In a valiant attempt, they hatched a simple diversion with the mages who could barely hold their own. And as soon as there was enough room for one knight to push on through, they signalled their young commander to pursue the evil witch and put a stop to this madness. In what seemed like a few seconds, the knights made a feint tactic and the mages fell for it. This allowed Fameborn's troop to break Kitreth's brittle line and with that single act Fameborn burst through, declaring he would finish her off and those that survived would reap the benefits, glory and riches included.

Kitreth saw the pathetic attempt at a feint as well as the next seasoned warrior. She had ordered her critically wounded men to let it happen. She had wanted a one-on-one fight with Stupidborn to finish this mission and go home. She had hoped next year's culling was going to be more fun than this, but she needed to survive first before counting next year's chickens. With her own lines broken, Stupidborn burst out and declared something incoherent about bony-fats and Gloria and leeches. What on Axelia was he talking about? His men cheer him on, as they must have understood. Kitreth prepared herself by using one of the gems on her weapon to conjure up an elemental cold about her weapon. And again another clash and yet again another stalemate.

305

CHAPTER 79
NEW LOVE

Meanwhile, back on the fifth floor, Torbiro, Memyra and the others were searching for a good vantage point to enact Torbiro's first plan, since Plan B and C had failed, unfortunately. The crew were looking for a good room with enough leverage to another window up above. They had found such a room, but they needed to destroy much of the lab equipment to fashion a makeshift anchor, just in case the grappling hook or the rope broke. Memyra informed them the only way this rope would break is if magic breaks it. The rope she had provided was made of mythril, a dwarvish metal that was light and damn near unbreakable by physical strength alone. She had confidently and with a lot of pride stated, if this rope breaks she would stop hating gnomes and with an arrogant gusto, she crossed her arms and said, "that will never happen."

The crew had decided Robyn should be the one to climb first, even though Torbiro insisted he should go first. But having the calm and responsible elf go first was what everyone agreed on, instead of a troublesome halfling with a wild imagination to create chaos as he arrived. So while Memyra setup and instructed the soldiers of Traytos to hold the line, she also instructed Raazet to fire the grapple hook gun. Why a gun? You ask. Well, there was simply no way for any of them to accurately toss a grappling hook up to the next window. Well, it could be done but time was of the essence and they needed to get that girl as soon as possible. Raazet was very much afraid to use an item of technology since he was a wizard of great power, but Memyra pushed the tool in his hands and slapped him, to stop being such a human.

With only Saara taking offence at that comment, everyone else understood. She was the only full breed of human in their group, but humans were normally such a pain to deal with. Some humans were fun to be with, while most would just be so judgemental on everything that was done. Doing good things is good and doing bad things is also good. Their race might have been worse than gnomes, but at least some of them were fun. Raazet did not understand Memyra's insult towards humans since he was able to teach and nurture a human child, so he understood their problems, but he also understood their potential. Humans had a curious mind and an ability to adapt no matter the situation. Raazet smiled at the comment, but with the weapon in his very hands, he remained as timid as a human.

With the lines secured and both gunners ready, they fired the grappling hooks. Memyra first, then Raazet. When Raazet fired his gun, he felt a sudden exhilaration as if the tension inside him was also released when the hook was launched towards its destination. He felt like a curious human, learning something new for the very first time. He imagined himself with the same eyes as young Kitreth when he had started her tutelage, those many years ago. But he was not as 'cute' as a young child of any race. He was a squinting old gnome with the fires of curiosity in his eyes. The blast, the recoil and even the smell of the fumes from the gun had excited Raazet more than anything in magic he had ever experienced. From a highly experienced arch mage to a technologist, it was a dangerous path, but his sudden extreme interest had internally persuaded him. At some point, Raazet was hugging and drooling on the grappling hook gun of Memyra.

The climb up was very easy for someone like Robyn, who had such agility. But once she was up, she was tasked to lower a rope to help the others climb the tower. She lowered the rope and was able to help Saara and Wilrokk up, but after a few short clicks –minutes – she had vanished. Raazet needed to be tied to the grappling hook gun as he would not detach himself from the now sticky with his own saliva, grappling gun. But once everyone had arrived, Raazet explained they should be on the tenth floor, considering the number of windows they had passed when they were either, climbing up to this room, or as they were held up by those up top. This room was much like all the other labs below but had active runic symbols all around the walls, doors and even the ceiling and the floor. What exactly was this room?

Raazet was the only expert in magic and with time, he was able to determine what these runes actually were and what their purpose was. The rune were used to catch and trap unwanted pests. In essence, they were a magical rat trap. One touch and you would be transported to a different location in this tower where all the pests would be taken. Usually that would have been the dungeon, but with the mistreatment of Princess Dawn, Kitreth had made sure all pests be brought to her to be punished. Robyn had accidentally touched one of these runes and been teleported to Kitreth's private chambers and without the magic glyphs, not even Raazet knew where that was exactly. The search for Robyn and the search for the princess had commenced.

CHAPTER 80
THE TOWER OF SACRIFICE

The team needed to split up into groups so they could survey the floors more effectively and efficiently. But Memyra needed to keep an eye on Torbiro, just in case he did something completely outrageous, which might bring down the entire tower. He was lucky like that. Raazet could not be trusted to go with the soldiers of Traytos, so the group split into two groups. One had Torbiro, Raazet and Memyra and the other group had Wilrokk and Saara. Team TRM would search for the princess and Team WS would search for Robyn, as well as Borgar as a side note. So the team split up, with soldiers to search for soldiers and the short people to search for the princess. What could go wrong?

Wilrokk and Saara used their military training to search systematically room by room. They searched every nook and cranky but found nothing. From what Raazet had described, this Kitreth was a mean-spirited mistress which meant she could have kept her pests in boxes or cages and that is where the soldiers had gone wrong. The two did not have too much experience with mages, but they would upturn everything in every room until they knew there was absolutely no trace of Robyn where they searched. They had started on the tenth floor and went up to the thirteenth floor with no results. Where in the pulse was Robyn?

Memyra made an error of choice to team up with Torbiro and Raazet. One was Torbiro, enough said, and the other, Raazet, was a gnome and she hated gnomes. Memyra hoped the other two were making more progress than her chaos riddled team. Though Memyra had doubts about her teammates, Torbiro was one lucky halfling and Raazet was someone who knew the little nuances of magical displacement and could spot where an illusion might be or if a wall was fake or not. Within three clicks – three minutes – of splitting up the party, Torbiro had already found a clue to where Robyn might be, but Memyra simply ignored his insight and findings. Torbiro had found a clue that led him to believe that there were false walls in this tower. It was possible Robyn might be inside one of the walls in the first room they entered. It sounded far too outrageous to Memyra, since that would mean the tower was a mechanical maze with mages practicing magic inside of it. It was like a dream or a nightmare. If it was a dream, then this building was designed with the intention to have both magic and technology work within it, which would mean it is knowledge from before the 'Thrust effect', meaning it was fantasy or lost knowledge. Either way, it was maddening. If it was a nightmare, it would have exploded as soon as someone cast a spell in this tower, since magic and technology could never exist together as an intertwined system.

Torbiro felt disheartened at not being trusted, just because Memyra had gotten lost with the others down in the dungeon. But he felt more determined to follow his own insight, since he had heard Robyn's voice in one of the walls. Memyra kept a watchful eye on the two, but with Raazet's help, he might be able to prove to Memyra he was right. Torbiro could see Raazet was very fond of the gun-blasting tool they had used to climb the tower from the outside. Torbiro approached Raazet and told him Memyra had more of those gadgets in her magical bag of storing. If he could help him with a little distraction, Torbiro could show him more gadgets back in Traytos when they returned with the princess. Raazet was not immediately convinced, as he was still loyal to his mistress and he wished not to leave her side until the very end. But Torbiro added, he could always visit Traytos on vacation to explore the unknown and wondrous. Normally that would not have pushed Raazet but looking at his drool-covered gun and looking back at the very angry Memyra and then looking at Torbiro, he said, 'I guess I'd have to return this to her' with a sad expression on his face. Raazet had found a new love and it was technology. He knew it was forbidden to mix the two, but studying them separately would be fine, right? Staring lovingly at the gun, Raazet peered slowly at Memyra and under his breath, agreed to distract her if he could get more devices like this gun. And with that, the two acquaintances become accomplices.

Raazet gave the signal and started to distract Memyra by trying to give the sticky and slimy gun back to her. Memyra reeled in disgusted at the thought of gnome germs, but she had waded through much worse, so she punched him for being annoying. Raazet didn't think she had it in her to attack an old man, so he felt a lot of regret and pain for helping Torbiro escape. As Memyra continued to look for any hint of the princess, she noticed Torbiro was missing again. She immediately looked for Raazet. Old man or not, he must know where Torbiro went. He was still on the ground where she had punched him; he wasn't that frail that the punch had taken him down, but at least it was easy to find him. The old gnome was still trembling from before and Memyra almost felt sorry for him, but she had to find Torbiro, so she picked him up and shook him. After only a few clicks of shaking an old and near broken gnome, he told her where Torbiro had gone. Into the wall.

While Raazet was distracting Memyra, Torbiro was hugging a particular wall. He had been hearing whistling from it and the feint sound of someone calling out for help. To Torbiro, it sounded like Robyn, so it must be her trapped inside the wall. But how would he get inside? Torbiro had heard from master Dorian that his homeland had built secret passageways in stone caverns, to hide from nearby raiders that would try and attack his people. He had said touching the stones or bricks on the wall in a certain combination would open it. Torbiro was very lucky indeed and his first try to open the wall worked, but he had been touching the stones randomly so he did not know the code for entering.

The wall swung open only slightly and Torbiro slipped past. Inside, the wall was unusually bright. Torbiro had not brought any torch or even a lamp, but the illumination of the passageway had orbs which contained light. These light orbs were much the same as the ones back in Traytos. They appeared to be similar to Torbiro, but were slightly different. The ones he remembered in Traytos were lamp lights powered by electric generators. They were also attached to large lamp poles over-arching a main street to provide light, albeit dim light from such a large orb. These light orbs were much smaller and they floated on the very air the walls produced. The whistling sounds Torbiro had heard were steam pipes releasing air to push the orbs off the wall. The entrance remained open until Torbiro moved further into the tunnel. It shut without a sound. Not that Torbiro was very observant in the first place. The hallway was a cornucopia of different colours, gears and valves, much like the entrance to the dungeon, but the difference here was the unusual feeling of familiarity. The pipes were cold to the touch, but the air inside the tunnel was warm. The tunnel was narrow but also spacious. The pipes here were not a marvel to look at like before. They were placed neatly and accordingly; the floor too was very soft to walk on like a thick cotton blanket but not hard to move through. Odd was the word that came to Torbiro's mind, but he pushed on.

At the end of the tunnel, there were three doors to choose from left, right and down. Down was the easiest to enter, but the left one was slightly ajar and it was where Robyn's voice was coming from. So naturally Torbiro followed her voice but made a note of the other doors to explore later. Inside this room he could see not only Robyn but also all of his friends through simple looking mirrors. But Robyn's voice was coming from a brass pipe with a loose hatch protruding from the wall. There were many pipes like this on the wall. They curved out from the ceiling in fact, like the talking tubes in factories. Torbiro went over to the tube and said 'Hello' in an awkward manner, as though he was unsure if anyone would answer. But to his luck, Robyn was able to hear him.

'Torbiro, is that you?' came Robyn's fearful voice.

'Yes, it's me, Robyn. I came to rescue you. Where are you?' asked Torbiro, very excited that he had been right all along. It was time to rescue Robyn and then the princess. Torbiro had been distracted at this point, but now he was in full focus.

'Torbiro, I'm in a room with only a window. There are no doors or a way out. Where are you?' Robyn's voice was starting to calm but there was still a bit of trembling. She was still afraid.

'Don't worry Robyn. I'll come find you. I'm in the wall right now,' said Torbiro as if being in the wall was nothing new. But once he had said it, it definitely sounded cooler in his head.

'In the wall? What do you mean, Torbiro?' said Robyn. She was in a panic now. The fear had started to rise again. Her anxiety and situation were no help either, nor was Torbiro being helpful with his vague and ambiguous explanations.

In the few seconds and then minutes that Torbiro didn't return her answer, Robyn tried to calm herself, knowing that at least one of her friends was out looking for her. Robyn had never been this scared before. She was alone and stuck in a prison. Her prison was small but was big enough to allow her to stand and stretch her arms and legs, but that was it. There were no doors, a single but small window and no light. It wasn't dark for Robyn, as she was an elf with vision in darkness, but this type of room would make anyone worry. No sounds could reach her with the exception of where Torbiro had found himself, so for the past couple of hours Robyn had been alone in silence.

Torbiro, thinking he had given his friend a sliver of hope, had dashed off to find his friends to rescue Robyn where ever she was located. On his way out, he saw the three doors yet again and paid them no mind as Robyn came first, then the princess, while exploring came last. But what Torbiro didn't notice was, he had gone in the wrong direction and was going further into the secret passage rather than back the way he had come. After a few minutes of running, Torbiro came to a dead end. 'Where was the door?' he thought, but he knew pushing some stones would let him through. He did just that and instead of coming out in front of Memyra and Raazet, Torbiro had found himself in front of Saara and Wilrokk. Had he gotten lost or what?

CHAPTER 81
SECRETS OF THE TOWER

Wilrokk and Saara had been searching the eleventh-floor rooms for Robyn when something odd happened. The stone wall to the north started to shift and turn. Wilrokk was so surprised he leaped backward, colliding with Saara, who had a handful of books as she too, was rummaging through bookshelves and desks for anything noteworthy. Wilrokk started to reach for his weapon when Torbiro emerged from the wall.

'Wilrokk, Private Redfellow? Where are Myra and Raazet?' said Torbiro with confusion and curiosity.

'Um, Torbiro. They're downstairs, but that was a few turns ago. They could be anywhere. Where did you come from?' said Wilrokk, relieved it wasn't anyone dangerous.

'Huh? I came from the wall, can't you see? But good news! I found Robyn. Well, sort of. I came to find Myra because she might have a tool to help,' said Torbiro in a rush. The information he had was said all jumbled up and both soldiers just looked at him with even more confusion.

'How did you get to the eleventh floor anyway?' said Saara, trying to divert the confusing conversation.

Without saying another word, Torbiro just pointed at the wall that was still ajar. The passage was dark from the outside, but Torbiro had explained it was nice and cosy inside. With a new lead, Wilrokk and

Saara followed Torbiro into the secret wall passage and there they found themselves at a crossroads with three doors. One on the floor, one straight ahead and the other on the right. These were the same doors Torbiro had found before, albeit their positions had changed a little, but they must have been the same ones. Wilrokk noticed something on the floor of this crossroads. There were cogs and gears. These intricately carved gears were turning only slightly, like a clock or a delicate machine. Wilrokk had only seen them because Torbiro had tripped on something as he walked by. The little halfling didn't fall down, but he did perform a clumsy hop like he was covering up his excitement.

Hidden within the gears were circular handles. It seemed as if they were levers or something else. Wilrokk examined them more thoroughly, while Saara and Torbiro went inside the opened door. Wilrokk was not quiet either as he examined the floor gear, as he did not want to be separated from the two. So he would call out every two clicks on what he had found. Meanwhile, Torbiro and Saara had entered a completely different room from the one Torbiro had described on their way here. This room had mirrors, much like the room beforehand, but there was also a table with a model of the Tower of Rivals. This was very strange. What was the purpose of this model and why was it here in an unknown location? Torbiro had explained that the brass tubes were supposed to be on the eastern wall with a weird-looking barrel in the centre of the room. Torbiro couldn't find anything familiar in this room, so he started to call out to Robyn, but there was no response. Saara was curious about the model tower, so she started to investigate it.

The model was very detailed, showing different floors and rooms with very precise furniture placed in various rooms. Though Raazet had told them there were thirteen floors of this tower, the model revealed the tower actually had over twenty floors. That was strange. How could there be more floors? It must also include the dungeon floors as well. But that was not the case. This model of the Tower of

Rivals was the exact replica of the tower, just a 1:25 scale. Although it did not show the occupants in the tower, you could still affect them by moving the floor or the furniture in the model. Saara had picked up a small sized table to have a look at its intricate design. It was unusually precise. It had even captured the details of the table's small stains, but after looking at the marvellous piece, she put it back.

Saara had even seen the mess of some of the rooms they had searched in. This model was fun and very interesting, but this was no time for fun, so she continued to look for something useful. Torbiro, on the other hand, found something on this odd table that held the model. A switch. Being curious, he pressed it without even telling Saara what he had found and the table lit up, revealing different coloured lights and a wooden board with writing on it. The script used was in human letters common in most of this land. But neither Torbiro nor Saara could read it.

The tower was lit up with lots of small, coloured orbs floating in each of the rooms. Wilrokk was still shouting out what he had discovered back in the passageway and he had figured out what the gears were for. This part of the passage was actually an advanced elevator, which allowed a person to travel directly up and down from this spot. Torbiro must have come from downstairs and accidentally kicked it on his way out. But how was it he hadn't noticed the change? Was it so seamless that he had not noticed, or was Torbiro really so absent-minded that he didn't notice? Wilrokk called out one last time to tell them his report on his finds. In a few minutes, the three of them had more questions than answers about this place. But at least they could now travel the floors with ease. Torbiro and Saara had also showed Wilrokk the model tower. Wilrokk could appreciate the model for what it was, an intricate display of art and engineering. But what he saw within the model shocked him.

CHAPTER 82
THE GUIDING TOY

Memyra and Raazet were still arguing when something inside their room made a sound. It had startled them both enough to stop their argument about Torbiro going missing. The table had moved. But how? Was it magic, or was someone else inside with them? Memyra grabbed a pair of goggles from her bag and put them on. She then made a quick scan of the room, but found no-one.

'What was that?' said Raazet and Memyra in unison, as they heard a table shift loudly on the floorboards.

'Is someone there?' Raazet asked the empty room with more of a curious inquiry than fear.

'No one invisible is in here,' said Memyra, putting her see-through eyes away. Memyra was more on edge now than ever before. Torbiro was missing. Robyn was missing and worst of all, she was with a gnome.

'What was that?' Again, in unison. This time, Raazet was pointing at a floating table, his mouth agape. Raazet could see the spectral hand that held the table and this act had frightened him. He looked at Memyra and she too, seemed to be screaming silently.

'Do you see that?' Raazet pointed to the spectral hand.

'What? The floating table or the ghostly hand holding it?' Memyra hissed.

'Well, both. But what is that?' Raazet had spotted a very large eye peering down at them. Raazet was a reputable mage in the kingdom of Bataros, but he had never seen anything like this before. Magical or conjured hands always had a caster nearby as the spell required constant incantation and there was a certain range to the spell as well, so the caster needed to be inside the room or just outside in the corridor but considering both had a view of the corridor outside and no one was out there, this didn't make sense. Memyra had said no one invisible was in the room now. 'How she could tell that with a pair of goggles is beyond me. But technology is still fascinating, to be able to see the unseen without the aid of the mystic arts is truly amazing,' thought Raazet.

'What is looking at us? Is that a monster? Use your magic to get rid of it.' Memyra whispered an order to Raazet, like the master of some pet.

'No I can't. Why don't you get rid of it? Use a device from your magic bag, huh!?' said Raazet. He wasn't her pet and he wouldn't risk his life for her when she was being so mean. After that, the two continued to argue about who should take care of the monster eye in front of them. By the time Raazet caved in, due to a well timed bonk on the head by Memyra, the spectral hand and the mysterious eye were gone.

Wilrokk had seen the chamber the three of them were in, or at least the small, scaled version. He could also see three different coloured dots, one green, one purple and the last one yellow. The yellow one was moving around sporadically, while the other two stayed near a table at the centre of the room. Wilrokk looked up and could see Saara was looking around the room, keeping an eye out for Torbiro, just in case he left or did something dangerous. Torbiro was about moving somewhat sporadically around the room as well.

'Torbiro, stop.' Wilrokk wanted to see if his theory was right.

'Um, ok,' said Torbiro, a little bored as he really wanted to save someone soon and be a hero instead of waiting around playing with little toys.

'What is it, Wilrokk?' Saara was curious to see what he had

discovered. Before Wilrokk answered, he looked back down at the model of the tower and the yellow orb was not moving. Could it be the yellow orb represented Torbiro? But there was another yellow orb in a different room with a red orb.

'I think these orbs are us.' Wilrokk concluded.

'Torbiro, I want you to zig-zag around the room. I think I found something important.' Wilrokk kept his eyes on the yellow orb to see if his theory was true.

'Um, ok,' said Torbiro. He was a bit confused, but he had nothing else to do. So he started to move in a zigzag pattern all around the room and with that, the yellow orb also started to move in the same manner.

'Eureka! Excelsior! Exciting! But what did the colours mean?' said Wilrokk in astonishment at his discovery. Though it did give them a clue to where they were, they still needed more information. They needed some with magical skills like Raazet had to help them.

After a bit of explaining, Torbiro understood what the little orbs were. They represented people and he had devised, the colours meant their race. Yellow was for halflings, green was for orc and purple was for human. Red must mean gnome because it was near a yellow orb, which must be Myra and Raazet. It was all just speculation, but it was good enough for now. There were a lot of red orbs at the bottom of the tower and two purple orbs chasing or dancing with each other at the top of the tower. But what colour would an elf be? If they only knew this, they could find Robyn. The princess was purple, but there were a lot of purple orbs not moving. Which one was she? Team TWS could see that Team MR was just four floors below them. Wait, why was it four floors? They were on the tenth floor and we were on the eleventh floor. Shouldn't it have just been one floor? These were the many thoughts in Torbiro's mind as the three of them headed for the elevator shaft just outside in the corridor.

After reaching the right floor with the elevator, team TWS headed for team MR. In a short time, the whole team was back and after a short punishment session from Memyra, Torbiro was just like Raazet, in pain and regretting his life choices. Memyra did not provide any healing potions to either Torbiro or Raazet, not because she didn't want to, but because she had run out. She had in fact, one more potion, but that was for emergencies as a last resort, not for minor injuries. So Torbiro, Wilrokk and Raazet remained injured, just minor swelling, bruises and little cuts. It had made them ugly to look at. But appearances aside, they conveyed their findings from within the secret wall.

Raazet was amazed at the corridor alone and was shocked at the technology within the tower hidden away all this time. If the mistress had this knowledge, she would have used it by now. 'It must be unknown to her as well, even though we had made the preparation of scanning the contents of the tower upon our arrival three years ago.' he thought. Before making more of a thorough investigation on hows, whys and the whats, Memyra reached out and grabbed Raazet. Telling him without a word to stop what he was doing and find who they were looking for - Robyn and the Princess.

According to Robyn, her location was somewhere within the upper floors of the room, where the team was able to speak to her. That was three maze-like floors, as indicated by the model of the tower. They had also found a possible location where the princess could be, but they needed to split up again. To make sure the team could meet at an exact time, Memyra produced time pieces; a hand crafted watch and a clock small enough, it could be carried or attached like an emblem or badge. Everyone was given a simple watch to keep, with the exception of Torbiro, of course. He was given a gnoblin watch which had a shocking alarm. The simple time pieces were scuffed, worn out and had scratches from wear and tear. Torbiro's watch was pristine but near deadly. Memyra had explained she was the only one to know how to stop the alarm and if it rings more than three times, the electrical charge would explode. A possible killer. The little watch couldn't actually kill a person, but it could stun them to the point of near death. This warning was enough to scare not only Torbiro, but Raazet and the others as well.

The plan was simple. They would split up into single person search teams. Though they would be alone, they could recruit whoever they rescued or met along the way. Raazet ,going by himself was trouble, but he couldn't use magic so he would just be slowing whoever he went with. Since Robyn was alone, Memyra and Wilrokk would search for her. Meanwhile, Torbiro and Saara would go in search of all the purple orbs of the tower on the upper levels. Raazet would stay behind at the model tower to help direct them. Memyra had given out message stones to each of them so they could communicate with each other and as a precaution, Memyra had given Raazet a belt of location, similar to the one she had given to Robyn. That way, she could find them with the Mask of Location. With everyone going their separate ways, Memyra told them to meet back at the model tower room in three turns to report what they had found and start the search again. Three turns was fairly short for searching a large tower, but it was a way to keep Torbiro from going missing again and from Raazet to escape.

CHAPTER 83
RESCUE TIME

Robyn was found almost instantly with the help of Raazet directing them. But it was all thanks to the Mask of Location. Why hadn't Memyra used it earlier? It was due to her current emotional state. She had yet overcome her feelings of loss when Torbiro had jumped into that pit trap. This emotional state was still making her act unrashly, which put a dampener on their quick progress. Had Memyra been in the right state of mind, they would have all been back in Traytos by now, with the princess in tow, but emotions always cloud judgement and decisions.

With Robyn's help, they could cut the searching of the princess by half. But another problem had occurred that only Raazet and Torbiro knew about. Commander Fameborn was with mistress Kitreth in a deadly cat-and-mouse chase up the tower. Torbiro had thought those two purple orbs were fun dancers, but they might make a mess of their search. He found dancers to be more annoying than any goblin or gnome he had ever met. He had only met a few dancers at the Traytos tavern. In the dancers' defence, it was his fault for eating his meal at the dance floor, so really it was a self-inflicted irritation.

Using the three hours they had been given, they searched frantically, using the process of elimination. There were five of them and there were thirty-three purple orbs in the tower above. With that in mind, within the time allocated, each person could reach about six orbs so long as there were no delays. Memyra and Robyn knew that was not possible for Torbiro, as he would get lost and then distracted. He could follow a plan, but he was absentminded when he was alone. So they could possibly find the location of the princess after five turns – five hours - with the four of them searching. Little did they know that with Torbiro, he would find her almost immediately because of his stupid luck.

At the point of separating, Torbiro headed for the closest orb on the tower's model. He knew it was part of the mission to explore, but searching was technically exploring, so he could bend the rules just this once. He wanted to know what that strange pink orb was and everyone in the party had agreed Torbiro was right about the colour coordination of the orbs, so they would all look for purple orbs only. Out of all the colours he had seen, the pink one in the model was speaking to him, as though it was beckoning him, calling out for help but the others had said no. So Torbiro silently agreed, but also making his own plans as the others organised to rescue Robyn or search for the purple orbs.

Torbiro had arrived where the pink orb was located, near the corridor of the thirteenth floor, which was no more than an attic from the looks of it. There were no doors or windows, but there were a lot of singe marks and ash lying on the ground. It also smelled unusually pleasant. Like the princess' bed chambers back in Traytos. He could remember the smell, since he had been one of the trusted guards appointed to protect her in his short time at the castle. Torbiro had always been meticulous when it came to work, so he had learnt a few things about the princess, to not offend her when it was time to work with her. The attic was a dead end, but it did smell like sweet lavender and freshly baked bread. It was nostalgic and made him hungry. But there was no princess in sight, so maybe he was in the wrong place after all.

Just before Torbiro started to head to the next location, as Raazet had been yelling at him from the message stone to stop wasting time for fear of Memyra's wrath, he took a moment to bask in the smell and moment of his memory. He approached the strongest scent in the room and leant on the wall to rest for a bit. Just as he touched the wall, he had accidentally come in contact with the combination of the stones that opened it. Torbiro never got the chance to lean but instead fell on his back and rolled to the foot of the bed of the princess. He had done it. He had found Princess Dawn. She was asleep on the bed and had grave injuries. What had the kidnappers done to her? It was time to bring her to the team, but how?

CHAPTER 84
RESCUING THE PRINCESS

'Um, madam Memyra.' This was Raazet, 'Torbiro is not listening to my instructions. What should I do?' He was reporting only three minutes after starting the search for Robyn.

'Forget him for now. Robyn first and then talk to me. It's only been three clicks. What the hell Torro? Errr.' Memyra replied, irritated. In just a short twenty clicks, Robyn was found and rescued. After all the hugs and tears, Robyn was caught up to date with what they had known about the tower. In the short wait, Robyn knew rescuing the princess would allow all of them to finally go home to Traytos.

'Raazet, this is Wilrokk. Some of the rooms containing the purple orbs have strange human like golems inside but still no princess. What should I do?' Wilrokk reported his findings after discovering three out of three of the purple orbs weren't the princess.

'Master Wilrokk, please go to the next one. What kind of golems? Machine like or flesh golems?' Raazet replied back with curious gusto.

'Machine like. What are flesh golems? Never mind, don't answer my question for now.' Said a confused Wilrokk.

'Raazet, this is Private Redfellow. All of the rooms I've just searched have human like golems inside. What should I do? I have yet to find the princess.' Saara reported back similar findings.

'Miss Redfellow? Who is this? Are you Saara?' Raazet had not known her by that name since Memyra had been calling her Saara.

'Yes, I am Private Saara Redfellow,' she replied.

'Oh, ok. Well, if you're done with your rooms head back to the model room. I can direct you,' said Raazet.

'Raazet, have you heard from the others?' Saara asked, as she started to head back.

'Yes, Lady… um, Madam Memyra has located and saved Robyn and she will be aiding us in the search for Princess Dawn. Master Wilrokk has found similar things as yourself but he continues his search. And… Torbiro is..' Raazet was a little reluctant to badmouth a friend of the terrifying Memyra and was hesitating to say more.

'It is good that Robyn was rescued but what is it with Torbiro? Did he disobey his orders again? Well, so long as he didn't go to the pink orb like we told him sternly not to, it is fine,' Saara said, in reply to the quick report of everyone's successes.

'Yes,' said Raazet, embarrassed she had guessed exactly what he so fearfully did not want to disclose.

'Hey Raazet. Can you reach Torro?' said Memyra, trying to hurry back to the model room with Robyn so they could help the others searching for the princess.

'Hi, Madam Memyra. Um, I… Um can't? He will not respond, but he is at the pink orb, so at least we know where he is. Please don't hurt me!' He recoiled at the fact he might be hit, but only after falling on the ground did he realise he was safe and alone in the model room.

'Wilrokk, this is Myra. I want you to forget the rest of your rooms and get back to the model room. I'll contact Saara to do the same. We need to talk,' said Memyra as she ran with Robyn to the model room. It had only been two turns since they separated and getting back would be pretty quick since they had the aid of the secret tunnels that were woven throughout the tower.

'Roger that,' said Wilrokk. He was about to enter the final room he was designated when he was ordered to return. He left without opening the door, but something had happened to all the rooms they had already searched. The golems were about to awaken. Opening their door was the initialisation process to awaken them. But Wilrokk and Saara had not known this, so even if they were to blame for the incoming danger, there was no way of stopping it.

With everyone arriving almost at the same time, with the exception of Torbiro, who was still with the princess, the remaining team had to discuss what they had found and what to do next. Wilrokk came out with a theory about what the golems were that he and Saara had found. He believed they could only be the guardians of the place from when it was built. Saara explained they were very human-like but just mechanical, like a mini golem. Even automatons made by dwarves weren't this sophisticated and intricately designed. If they were indeed guards, the team would be in trouble, as the original creators were long past dead and none of them would know how to stop them.

At the point of realising the dreadful situation they were all in, that was when Torbiro arrived with a smile on his face, though it was still swollen from his earlier beating. He had arrived with 'I did it. I found Dawn.' No one quite heard him at first as the atmosphere in the room was so glum and distraught. Not being able to read the room, Torbiro shouted, this time with glee and excitement that he had been right all this time and found the princess. His words were so fast and cheerful that it almost sounded like the halfling language, but in fact was just the human dialect spoken really fast. To everyone but Memyra, it sounded like the cheerful chirping of morning birds and squeaking of small rodents. Memyra finally looked up and what Torbiro saw was a truly terrifying sight. It was the face of a sinister rogue smiling deviously, coupled with the face of a crying maiden as tears fell from her eyes and down her face.

The team knew where the princess was and they could get there very easily, too. This mission was almost complete. The only thing left to do was grab her and bring her back to Traytos. Although Raazet was not part of this mission and his part to play had also been completed, he was simply too frightened of Memyra to leave their side. He had inadvertently joined them. He hadn't forgotten about his mistress and the tower itself, but due to the eminent danger of being smacked, he would obey. They had all agreed that getting the princess – which Memyra insisted on calling 'the little brat' – out of the tower and back to Traytos as soon as possible was their current plan. But what they hadn't anticipated was the involvement of their next obstacle. Fameborn.

CHAPTER 85
FAMEBORN'S BATTLE

The battle with the witch raged on. Sometimes there were opportunities to strike her down, but at those moments Fameborn's movements slowed or he wasn't able to make his tired body respond. The two had been in conflict for several turns and the witch was not tiring. It must have been sorcery, an evil power only those of Bataros would ever wield. But Fameborn had the fervour of battle and the morale of a man seeking vengeance. Fameborn was not going to stop until he had vanquished the bitch.

Kitreth had been chased so clumsily and without coordination by Fameborn, that it had taken a toll on her body not to laugh out loud every time he came in for an attack. She was agile and lithe in her movements. At times, when she was having a little too much fun being chased by an idiot with his pointy stick, she had to slow herself for him not to get lost. Kitreth needed him to rescue Dawn and this whole culling plan of her uncle's would be completed. But was the chase really what she was enjoying, or perhaps it was the 'being chased' by a man that had excited her? She did not know, but what she did know was she was not in love with this fool chasing her. Her mind was filled with the exhilaration of being prey, of being wanted and of being the only one to be able to give that satisfaction. But whenever Kitreth looked at her pursuer, it made her feel sick to her stomach at the stupidity of this whole act.

The two had been climbing the tower very slowly as Fameborn would take a breather every flight of stairs. But Kitreth needed to vanish when they were near the chambers of Cousin Dawn. Kitreth had felt the arcanus return to her by the time they had reached the eighth floor, where she had found an ogre stuck half-way through a wall. How in blazes did an ogre get this far up? It did not matter, since the creature couldn't move, but Kitreth needed the idiot knight to focus on her as they climbed to Dawn's chamber. She cast an illusion spell to disguise the ogre as scattered barrels of dirty laundry and continued to climb.

The humanoid automatons glow with a dark energy. Only when their chamber has been opened will these killers activate. Their mission has always been simple: to cleanse the tower. All creatures within are their targets. They do not discriminate; they do not choose, they simply cleanse. They were originally created for simple cleaning. They were a custodian class of automatons, but after the catastrophic event known as 'The Thrust', these machines started to malfunction and cleaning turned to cleansing and cleansing was redefined as killing. So the creators of the tower had sealed them away and hidden the floors on this tower and made sure only a creature of their kind could access them. And only through magic would these dangerous machines awaken.

Upon casting her illusion spell, Kitreth felt a sudden chill down her spine, as though to warn her of imminent danger. She had never had this happen before, but Fameborn was hot on her trail as she spotted him staggering up the hallway with an exasperated expression. 'Tell her to stop running.' This put a mischievous smile on her face and she continued to goad him.

CHAPTER 86
SWARM OF CLEANERS

As Torbiro and his friends travelled through the secret tunnels, they started to hear a strange humming sound. It wasn't an eerie sound either, with the exception of Raazet, everyone found it to be a familiar humming, like the start of an engine or the bubbling of a water boiler. It was familiar, but they all felt a sense of dread. Even halflings can feel fear and this was one of those times. They didn't stop to think about or discuss this feeling, but with a single look back, they knew they needed to hustle. Get the princess and get out.

They passed several corridors before arriving at the entrance to the room in which the princess was being kept. The team could hear a loud commotion on the other side of the corridor. In unison, the three who had recognised the voice, said 'Fameborn' with a sigh. Torbiro had left the door open by jamming a chair in the entrance way so it wouldn't close again. Torbiro pointed out that he could not lift her safely as he had tried and the evident bump on the girl's head was proof of that. With comments from all the women, Torbiro smiled, trying to look innocent, though he had no real excuse. Wilrokk was then ordered by Memyra to pick up the girl and go. Raazet instinctively wanted to help cast a spell and purple, glittering, spectral hands appeared to remove the medical tubes from the poor girl's body. He was the one who had applied them, so he knew full well the danger if they were just yanked out, as Wilrokk was about to do. Raazet's magical expertise made quick work of the removal and then they had the princess.

Dashing as fast as the team could with an unconscious princess on the shoulders of Wilrokk, they headed down a secret passage, as they had discovered it was a shortcut through the tower. Reaching the elevator gear was only a few metres away when something unexpected blocked their path. The humanoid automatons were activated. With rust, cobwebs and loose chains, the machines slowly approached them. This stopped them in their tracks. Even Torbiro didn't try to befriend them. The team turned to head back the way they came. To their luck, it was not blacked out yet.

Out of the wall and into the battle between Fameborn and Kitreth. A stray arcane missile would have made for a nasty accident as it headed straight for Wilrokk, who was the mule carrying the precious cargo, but with the return of arcanus in Raazet, he was able to quickly deflect the missile with a magical barrier. Memyra had a new appreciation for the gnome and her hatred towards Raazet was lowering. He wasn't a useless burden anymore. Torbiro and Robyn tried to call out to their commander they had the princess, but he must not have heard them through the bloodlust. Memyra could see their allegiance to Traytos was still strong, but urged them to forget the fool and just leave. But their loyalty to their commander seemed to cloud their judgement.

The battle raged on and on. Kitreth could see Fameborn was nearing collapse. This was her chance. Her performance needed to be believable, so she cast a spell to aid her. Another illusion spell where she grew horns, dark wings and a flaming orb that surrounded her. She looked terrifying to those not versed in magic. Kitreth then delivered her threat and she heard a scream from behind her. She had not been aware of Torbiro's team, but what distracted her more than the scream was the rapid shifting of the walls.

They shuttered, rumbled and moved like a mechanical machine. Then large numbers of humanoid automatons marched forward, like a mass of mechanical zombies. What terrified her the most was seeing an aura of arcanus shrouding those machines. She instinctively took a step back, which would have killed her if not for the illusion that portrayed her physical form. With that step, Fameborn took his chance and tried to cut her down. He had penetrated the illusion and the spell was broken. What emerged was the form of the witch he had been chasing all this time. He had won and she was no more.

Kitreth saw she was surrounded by a real threat and the buffoon Fameborn was still making threats, like she cared. He was a minnow compared to the swarm of sharks slowly approaching. The threats that Fameborn made were lost on deaf ears. But the fool continued his victory speech. Kitreth, not wanting death to befall her, crawled away and cast a levitation spell. Though it worked, it was not at full power, as though some of the arcanus she generated for the spell was being absorbed. It was, in fact. The automatons ran on both arcanus and chaotica, not melded together but as separate energy sources and with every spell cast, the automatons got stronger. Dread slapped Kitreth in the face, as more and more of her arcanus was absorbed. She needed to flee, so Kitreth searched for a window or an exit to leave this tower. The thought of saving Dawn did pop into her mind, but saving herself was top priority. A tear welled in her eye as she turned to flee. With quiet words of 'sorry' towards Dawn, Kitreth left the tower.

CHAPTER 87
BATTLE FOR OUR LIVES

In the adjacent corner, just a few metres away from the battle between Fameborn and Kitreth, the team were cheering for each side. With Raazet cheering for his mistress, everyone else was cheering for their commander, with Memyra, the only one not cheering for either side, trying to coax her allies to move on. But no one could hear her and she had to smack Torbiro to get his attention. As Raazet had spells to protect him now, Memyra did not want to incur his wrath. A single look told Torbiro it was time to move. Memyra looked pissed and getting any more bruises was not ideal since they had the princess with them and Torbiro wanted to impress her with his bravery and good looks.

As the battle was nearing its end, Torbiro and Memyra finally could be heard from the spell-slinging and curse slurring. 'It is time to go,' was all they said and with a nod, they started to pick up their things and move. Saara had turned around, since she dropped her weapon behind her and there she saw the most horrible creatures her mind could conjure - zombies. Saara screamed, but what she was looking at were actually the automatons with a visible aura of arcanus and this made them look like the living dead. The automatons looked like human cadavers, with skin showing muscle and bones, with strange tendrils spewing a yellow fluid seeping into the ground and everywhere else they touched. That was the appearance that had manifested in

Saara's mind, but what they looked like to the others were mechanical puppets with wires and coolant leaking from loose joints.

The scream from Saara alerted and alarmed Torbiro and the others. Raazet could see that Kitreth too, was distracted by the scream and cast a slow spell on the attacking Fameborn to protect her. As Raazet finally turned around, he could see a hoard of those machines and he could feel his magic slipping from his control. The creatures must run on arcanus. Casting spells would just hinder them from escaping the marching hoard. Wilrokk now had both the princess who still remained unconscious – man, the girl could sleep – and the petrified Saara on his shoulders. 'This overtime better pay off,' thought Wilrokk. Memyra and Robyn both armed themselves with a sonic piston and a triphil, respectively. They needed to slow the hoard down while the rest got away far enough. Torbiro wanted to fight but didn't have any ranged weapons on hand, so instead called out for help from his commander, but he seemed too busy taunting the already defeated spellcaster.

Another scream from Saara at the opposite side of the corridor. Torbiro turned and could see the wizard by the name of Kitreth had cast some more spells and more of the automatons had come around and blocked their last way out. What could Torbiro do? He looked at his unused mythril daggers and started to frantically think of a plan. He had two options: one, he could strike his commander to snap him out of his victory, or two, he could try and fight off the blockage. The safest was to get Fameborn's help, but attacking a commander was treason no matter the situation, but his other option was a deadly battle. He had a slim chance of true victory.

Saara screamed for the third time. She was having another traumatic experience and Wilrokk was totally defenceless. Robyn and Memyra were doing their best, but with each shot, the more stable the automatons became. What was powering them? Torbiro was desperate, so he stabbed Fameborn in the back. The man was two, maybe three times the size of Torbiro and the strike had gotten his attention. Fameborn turned for Wilrokk and charged to save them. But Fameborn wasn't in the right mindset to save anyone but Dawn at that moment.

Fameborn charged, seeing his precious prize being carried by a green demon and a hoard of zombie minions about to consume the princess. With a battle cry, he leapt into action, his weapon drawn high, about to slash another killing blow to another enemy of this cursed tower. Raazet could see this and warned Robyn to shoot him or Wilrokk and Saara would die. Raazet, thinking all elves had immaculate accuracy, had asked Robyn instead of Memyra to help their friends. But just as Robyn took aim, Memyra had shot two sonic blasts in that direction and then kicked the gnome for his prejudice and assumption. Memyra's shots had cleared the path but affected all parties present. Wilrokk was down, stunned by the sonic weapon. Fameborn was also down, subdued by the loss of blood from all of his injuries, and Saara was catatonic. Only Torbiro was still conscious but suffering from ringing in his ears and vertigo from the sonic blast. Ironically, this loud sound was the only thing that had stirred the princess. She was awake.

Raazet needed to step in. They were in deep shit. Disregarding the consequences of fuelling the enemy, he cast a massive spell, summoning a giant. The majesty of the spell coated the entire hallway and adjacent rooms with blue and white light. Runic words spilled out from the gnome and magic circles, squares and triangles surrounded Raazet. It was soothing and mystical. This brought Torbiro out of his funk and distracted the princess from their dire situation. With a few gnomish words, a giant manifested, but everyone was not expecting Borgar to be summoned. Borgar appeared out of thin air upon the spell being cast. Borgar appeared to be confused about how he got there, but then saw Torbiro and the others were in trouble. Before he could act, the halflings shouted, 'Pick them up, let's go!' Torbiro was shouting and pointing at Wilrokk and the others while Memyra and Robyn ran toward Borgar for a hasty escape. Raazet was quickly scooped up by Robyn as she leapt on top of Borgar's large shoulders.

CHAPTER 88
I SUMMON YOU

Borgar was indeed bigger than everyone else, but he could not possibly carry all of them at once. That is, until Raazet, with his last bit of arcane power, enlarged the ogre with yet another spell. Torbiro was amazed that he was so powerful. Why hadn't he cast spells when Robyn was lost or when they got stuck on the eighth floor? 'Maybe he was tired,' thought Torbiro. The enlarge spell didn't just help them, but it also powered the automatons. But as luck would have it, at least it only powered them instead of enlarging the frightening troop. With more size to Borgar's body, he was able to carry everyone, but he no longer fit inside the corridor. So, with his giant's strength, he ploughed through the tower's walls, creating a path of destruction throughout the halls.

One and then two floors later, Torbiro suggested it would be much faster going out the window instead of destroying the tower. Memyra liked this idea and started to rummage through her pack for something to soften the landing, but Robyn and Raazet insisted on taking the stairs, since they were on an ogre and they had injured and unconscious people with them. It was too risky to jump out of a twenty-storey building, which was stupidcide (a stupid suicide). It came down to Borgar to decide, since the princess was too concerned with Fameborn and his injuries. How kind, thought Robyn and Torbiro, and how rude, thought Memyra and Raazet. With not even a thank you to her rescuers, each team member awaited Borgar's decision. The ogre chose to jump.

Crashing and smashing into walls and breaking things was a favourite pastime of every ogre, but Borgar had a secret fantasy and it was to fly like a bird. Memyra had convinced Borgar he would be able to fly all the way back to Traytos if he listened to Torro, his saviour. The ogre liked the girl halfling and instead of waiting for Robyn or Raazet to argue against them, Borgar had run straight out a window. And they were falling. Memyra was laughing, Raazet and Robyn were screaming in terror while Torbiro was cheering and pointing at Traytos. The princess had been shocked by the fact she was going to die, falling from that height.

Memyra made quick work with the rocket pack and put it on Borgar as they continued to steadily fall toward the ground. She shot a net around the rest of the unconscious and shouted, 'Hang on!' and then kick-started the rockets. Boooom, they were off.

CHAPTER 89
THE RETURN HOME

In the distance, the Tower of Rivals slowly disappeared as the rockets propelled the heroes' team back home. Before their arrival and back in the tower, a different Torbiro saw the collapsed Zyro bleeding out just outside Raazet's laboratory. This Torbiro checked him and nodded. Checking for potions on his belt, he pops one open and forces the dying man to consume it. With another nod, Torbiro puts a note into Zyro's pocket. With that, he returns to the laboratory and vanishes with a blast of prismatic light.

Approaching Traytos after three turns, Torbiro started to worry, just like Raazet and Robyn. Borgar continued to cheer as one of his secret dreams had been fulfilled and without a care in the world. Memyra, on the other hand, just watched the scenery go by. First the Fields of Traps, then the Dip Hills and the line of soldiers heading back home after the war. The walls of Traytos never looked so homely until now. This made Memyra warm to the idea she was almost home.

'Myra, how are you going to stop this thing?' asked Torbiro, worried they might crash into the ground. The team was only two hundred metres away from the high walls of Traytos and if the rockets didn't stop, they were going to crash and maybe die. The mission would be a failure if that happened.

'What do you mean, stop? This baby doesn't stop, but I can turn it off.' said Memyra. She was already preparing to leave the soldiers, as she didn't want to be executed by the king's stupid orders. Memyra had a pair of floatation devices on her back. They looked like rockets but were different. These devices would create a cushion-like bubble to shield her from the impact. One device would protect two medium sized creatures or a single large creature like Borgar, but it could protect four small creatures with only one device.

'What?' cried Robyn, Raazet and Torbiro. They were shocked this free and fast ride would kill them, anyway. 'What about the princess? How were they going to protect her?' Wilrokk was still unconscious and Borgar was having way too much fun. The three of them started to panic but then Raazet thought to cast a spell.

'Noooooo,' shouted Robyn and Torbiro at Raazet. They warned him that magic was forbidden in Traytos, but he cast the spell, anyway.

With the amount of arcanus being generated from the panicking mage, the alarms and sirens of Traytos activated. Dwarven and goblin searchlights surrounded the group and large cannons blasted projectiles at them. Death by crashing may have been better, they all thought as cannon balls, large whirling blades and steam powered harpoons headed their way. Memyra was the only one not screaming as she had done this before, entered town illegally and evading the poorly aimed projectiles was easy enough. She guided Borgar towards the castle while teaching him how to spin. The spinning would make the large but stupid ogre do a barrel roll to evade the projectiles. Raazet had almost fallen off Borgar, since he was trying to cast a slowfall spell, but Robyn was quick enough to catch and hold him while she hung on to the ropes that held everyone else.

They approached the castle in just a few clicks. Crash! Borgar had been spinning as they all crashed into the front of the castle and flew through the courtyard, landing in front of the king himself. Borgar had broken everyone's fall, so injuries were, at most, minor broken bones.

CHAPTER 90
UNEXPECTED ARRIVAL

Prior to the crash, the king of Traytos, Aroduct, had been awaiting Zephyr Spike's report while tending to his normal duties of upholding his kingdom. It had been three revols – three weeks – and his last report had been on the battlefield about finding the most suitable scapegoat. Aroduct had hoped it was anything but a halfling, as halflings had the devil's luck. The king had been receiving reports of more refugees and soldiers coming back from the war. What? How could that be possible? Fameborn was a fool and had no experience leading soldiers. He should have had the lot of them killed. What could have happened?

Every year Aroduct would plot for the sector's annual culling and every year previously had been a success. Less people meant more jobs and more jobs meant more servants. Slaves were one thing and he had kept these creatures under wraps, but each culling had a purpose in the long run. Continuing stability. But now, with so many people returning, what would he need to do? Send them away? No. Aroduct would just have to raise tax levies to exile those people, but what of the 'small' businesses? Would they be revealed? No, they would just have to be closed down for a time. With a grunt of irritation, Aroduct mulled over what changes had to be done and then he heard the sirens.

Magic was being cast in his fair kingdom. They better be shot down or those goblins are getting turned to glue. On his raised throne, King Aroduct was warned a flying ogre was headed for the castle and he should be evacuated to some place safe. Lost in his thoughts about the failed culling and the events to come, Aroduct could not hear those warnings from his knights and then there was a crash.

CHAPTER 91
SHOCK OF THE KING

The east wall of the castle had burst inwards. Stone, bricks, mortar and gems came raining down on the guards below. Some were vigilant and managed to shield themselves from the debris, but the others were less fortunate and suffered grave injuries. The massive gear, the symbol that hung at the front of the castle for all to see, had been dislodged and fallen on top of soldiers guarding the entrance of the great hall and killed them instantly. That single event had brought about the death of seventeen soldiers and knights loyal to the king. Aroduct was in shock as he saw a single ogre with a pair of dwarven blast packs crash through and destroy the main entrance of his beloved castle.

The creature wasn't in control of the device on his back. The king needed to move or he might die as well. The king was not known for being agile, but to his fortune, Peren was just a few metres away, about to give yet another report on the incoming soldiers. Peren was quick to act. Using his innate magic of teleportation, he popped in, grabbed the king and popped out. Once the king was safe, Peren put on a belt filled with clocks to hide his magic. Peren had always kept weapons by his side in case of emergencies and equipping them, he prepared for battle.

After the crash, Torbiro was first to emerge from the ogre. He moved in a topsy and dizzy manner and after a few steps, he looked up at Peren and said, 'Commander Per..' in confusion, as though not believing his very eyes and then hunching over and vomiting on the ground. Robyn was next to emerge with a gnome drenched with liquids of fear, clinging to her breast with a death's grip. Robyn was bleeding from her head, but the adrenalin must have kept her from passing out. She addressed her cousin Peren very politely and bowed to her king. The throne room was a mess. The king had never shown this kind of shock before. King Aroduct was always calm and collected, but today Peren had seen him catatonic from shock. Mouth agape, eyes bulging and heaving a sigh.

Memyra never appeared, as her landing was much safer than the others. She activated her bubble, which had protected her from the crash and just before they landed in the king's great throne room she drained a potion of invisibility. She wasn't completely invisible, but it was enough to conceal her from typical knights. The elf standing next to the king would be trouble, so she waited until she could flee. And as she held her breath, Torbiro came out of the crash site, wobbled over to the king and threw up. That was her chance and she legged it.

CHAPTER 92
REPORT OF PEREN

'Lord Fameborn! Lord Fameborn!' said commander Peren, as he tried to wake the knight. The king had tasked Peren with finding out what the pulse was going on. The king had retreated to his chamber for some needed rest with that order.

'Fo… Foul fiend. Have at thee,' said Fameborn, as he sat up with a start and nearly head-butted Peren in the process.

'Lord Fameborn, thank the chaos. You are alive. Congratulations are in order,' said Peren, avoiding the attack with a roll.

'Ahh, Commander Ambyr. What are you doing in the Tower of Rivals? I dare say, wait congratulations, for what?' asked Fameborn in confusion and puzzlement. Fameborn was still thinking he was battling the endless hordes of zombie demons.

'You have successfully rescued Princess Dawn. You have returned to us in Traytos. You are our hero,' said Peren, trying to get more from the stupid knight. Every knight worth his salt knew just how much of a fool Fameborn and his family were. They weren't real knights, just rich merchants who could buy the title. The last comment about being a hero left a nasty taste in Peren's mouth.

'Why, yes, I am the great Hero of Traytos. Of course, I rescued the fair lady Dawn. I await the feast to celebrate. Where is his majesty, Commander Ambyr?' said Fameborn, taking the credit for what he did not achieve.

'Our lord is resting right now, mayhaps the festivities will be on the 'morrow. Can you tell me about your friends?' said Peren, pointing to Torbiro and the others. Peren had placed and separated them so the medics and doctors could tend to them more efficiently. Peren could see Fameborn had no idea who these people were, not even the ogre. Just typical. Torbiro was among them, so maybe he knew what was going on.

CHAPTER 93
THE REWARD

As the king stumbled to his chamber, he could hear Commander Peren address the halfling. His name was Torbiro. Now, where did he know that name from? As he reached his bed and sat down, Aroduct was bombarded with the memory of who and where he had heard that name before. It was the probationary knight. The halfling that was supposed to catch the thief. He had better have completed that task or else. Aroduct had grabbed one of his larger pillows and started to wring it, as though he was choking the halfling who had ruined his castle and the hidden contents of the walls.

Aroduct plotted to give him his just rewards. A good hanging.

CHAPTER 94
CELEBRATION

After a short rest, the king came out of his chambers to address the hero who had saved his dearly beloved only daughter. Aroduct assumed the kidnapping side of the plan had at least worked, but there was no one to address back in the throne room. Not Fameborn and not even that filthy elf, Peren. Where were they? With a single order, Aroduct was informed most of the soldiers were heavily injured so they all had to be taken to the infirmary. The soldier also promptly asked if there was to be a celebration since the princess had been returned, as it was a request from Lord Fameborn himself. The king simply nodded in acknowledgement, but did not have an answer for a lowly soldier.

Aroduct ordered three of his men to inform him when any of the party were able to talk and for the time being, he would start making preparations for a town festival and a town hanging. His men promptly made preparations for everything the king had asked. Aroduct returned to his quarters to make one speech to address his people and another to warn his enemies.

Inside the infirmary, doctors had frantically been working to save the lives of the party involved in the crash back at the castle. The little halfling was the luckiest of them all, as he only suffered vertigo and a few scratches. The female elf had received a slight concussion and several broken bones. The healing pod would do the trick. The female human was suffering from PTSD and had several broken ribs and a fractured spine. This one needed surgery or else be paralysed from the neck down. The gnome was bleeding internally from a broken rib. He too, needed surgery. The half orc had two mangled legs that needed to be reset. For him, the healing pod after leg resetting. And the ogre was worst of all. By all accounts, the creature should be dead, deep lacerations, skull caved in from the impact and all his bones were shattered to the point of being fragments. This creature must be part troll to still be alive from all this. The doctors could not do anything for Borgar, so they had to send for giant experts to determine his prognosis. Lord Fameborn was already up and about. He was saved first, since they all thought he was the hero to save the princess. But Commander Peren insisted on getting the halfling awake as soon as possible.

Peren needed to get to the bottom of this and Torbiro was the one who should know. After a few turns, the doctors informed Commander Peren Torbiro had finally awoken. The boy was barely injured, so he ordered him to his office for a private report.

Torbiro entered Commander Peren's office for the last time. He was thrilled to see his commander since venturing out of Traytos and to tell him of all the adventures he had experienced. But to his great surprise, Peren was not amused in the slightest. He just wanted the facts. Torbiro reported in the most formal speech he had ever given about his mission. He told him how he had helped with the war and saved as many lives as possible in the Dip Hills and how he had surveyed and conquered the entire surroundings of the Dip Hills for later use. He told Peren how he rescued more soldiers and knights that had fallen in the Trapped Fields near the Tower of Rivals and how he found some dragons underneath the tower and last, but not least, how he uncovered a secret chamber in the Tower of Rivals, saved the princess and heroically returned to Traytos with the help of his companions, naming everyone, even Memyra.

Peren grimaced from behind his desk as Torbiro recounted each and every event the king had been complaining about since the soldiers started to return. At the mention of Memyra, the thief he was meant to capture, Peren asked if she was with him at all those events Torbiro had recounted. To all those questions regarding the presence and help from Memyra, Torbiro had answered 'yes' with pride and honesty, like the knight he wished to be. 'Where was Memyra now?' That was the next question the commander asked and Torbiro assumed she was with the others since he did not see anyone in his room when he had awoken? At this point, Torbiro was all smiles, but Commander Peren was the opposite. The commander did not want to do this, but it was necessary to protect such a loyal knight of Traytos. He dismissed him from duty. The smile on Torbiro's face started to fade and worry and sadness replaced it. Torbiro was in denial, but it couldn't be. He was the hero. This must be a mistake. So instead of returning the badge of the knights of Traytos, he demanded to speak to the king and walked off. Peren tried to stop him, but the little knight did not understand the fate of those who follow Aroduct and many of them weren't even knights. Most were corrupt merchants in the king's favour.

As Peren noted down all that had been recounted, Torbiro had left to see the king. By the time Peren had noticed Torbiro was gone, he knew it was too late for the halfling now.

CHAPTER 95
A SOLDIER'S REWARD

After being healed and bandaged up, the soldiers in Commander Peren's report would receive a reward and commendations for advancements. With the exception of Torbiro, but since Peren did what any good soldier of the realm would do, he told the truth about what he had found out from a young knight upholding their duty. He did not leave out any detail and passed it to the king. Peren knew what would come next and hoped Torbiro's loyal friends would help him, since he could not.

All recovered soldier and knights who had survived were in the presence of the king and the preparations of the festival. The king had ordered his men to gather all names of those to be rewarded. Cyan Robyn, Borgar, Wilrokk Spinner, Saara Redfellow, Torbiro and Wilbur L. Fameborn. These brave souls would receive their well-earned reward. To rise in rank and gain honour and glory as well as reverence for the rescue of their Dawn. With the exception of Borgar, everyone attended, even Memyra, disguised as a gnome servant.

The king gave a speech, thanked the heroes and awarded each and every one a new rank. Torbiro was no longer probationary, becoming a fully-fledged knight. Saara and Wilrokk became sergeants and Robyn became a first-class knight sniper. Torbiro was proud and happy for his new position, but he had been blinded by his reward to not see the truth. Memyra and Raazet were watching the ceremony and had seen a sinister look on the king's face as he looked at Torbiro.

CHAPTER 96
TORBIRO IN THE KING'S WEB

When Memyra had left the castle grounds, she ran towards the old shop Torbiro used to work at. She looked for the dwarf Dorian, who had taught him about tinkering and inventing, to ask for his help. As she entered the small shop, she spotted the dwarf immediately; he was behind the counter, asleep. Memyra could use his help so she tried to wake him, but after a few clicks, she gave up. This dwarf was, as they say, stubborn and thick. So instead of just leaving, she left a note and hoped he would get the message.

She ran back to one of her hidden caches to resupply and headed back to the castle. Torbiro was blinded by his own pride and was in deep trouble. There was no way Aroduct the cruel would ever reward a halfling, no matter who he or she was. Memyra knew halflings weren't allowed in the castle but gnomes were fine, so putting on some makeup, she disguised herself as a gnome servant to get past the guards.

As Memyra climbed back to the castle, she could see the preparations for the festival. All the gossipers were saying, Fameborn this and Fameborn that. There was not even a mention of the rest of the team, let alone the real hero. But what Memyra found truly terrifying was the upper west town. This was the main road to the entrance of the castle and she could clearly see soldiers setting up a public hanging. This was bad. She needed to hurry.

Raazet could see through the obvious farce of this king. Clearly Torbiro was in trouble, but magic was easily detected here so he could not cast anything unless he wanted to share Torbiro's fate. Compared to King Kerem, this man was pure evil. How could he lie to his loyal subjects like this? It disgusted Raazet to the core of his being, but the only way he could help was with tools. Where did Memyra go?

CHAPTER 97
A CLOUDY DREAM

'This was it,' thought Torbiro. His dreams had finally come true. He had become a real knight. A just, a true and an honourable knight. He had failed in capturing Memyra, but he could just go after her another day. He would be revered instead of threatened. He would be praised instead of taunted. He was now a symbol of justice, a part of the wheel and cog of society and this would help his kind become better citizens of Traytos. Torbiro wore the medal he received proudly and then turned to Commander Peren. Torbiro was hoping for a proud look or even a stern smile to congratulate him, but as Torbiro looked to his commander, he had turned away.

Commander Peren was right. He had heard reports from soldiers and knights that the king had planned to hang Torbiro for his transgressions.

CHAPTER 98
KARMA

Before the appointed meeting to award those who had helped rescue Dawn, the king hosted a secret meeting of his own, with his brother, the king of Bataros. They needed to discuss what had happened in the tower and why the culling plan this year failed. Kerem told Aroduct everything his daughter had reported. Kitreth had said halflings were involved. A man by the name of Torro had wreaked havoc on the happenings in and outside the tower. The tower was now in complete ruins since the ancient cleaners had been awoken. Anger and fury, frustration and hatred were all the feelings Aroduct had brewing within him, the more he heard. This was the reason he hated those foul creatures. But by the end of the report, there was no mention of Zephyr, so he must still be alive somewhere. Aroduct was going to punish the fool when he returned and he would return.

CHAPTER 99
ADDRESSING THE PEOPLE

As Aroduct presented and proceeded with his speech to the knights of how these soldiers were the ones responsible for achieving the deed of rescuing his daughter, all he could think about was torturing that smug halfling. Drowning him like a rat or squeezing the life out of him and then making him breathe nothing but deadly gas. Though he did not show his obvious hatred, there were small signs and hints that he was plotting.

Once the speech was over and the cheers and adulations had quieted, the king addressed Torbiro for a private meeting, as he was about to receive his next assignment as a real knight. Only Torbiro was approached and Aroduct had done this when all the others were surrounded by crowds of adoring fans, wanting to hear their side of the story. The epic tales and the heroic escapes and the like.

CHAPTER 100
TORBIRO'S VALPRA

While the ceremony was proceeding, Peren had ordered knights loyal to him to watch out for those people being rewarded as he knew they were in danger. Peren would watch over his cousin Cyan since she was much like Torbiro. She was naïve. These grandiose ceremonies were always a farce and not a single one of them would receive a real reward. Most likely, they will be sent to a dangerous impossible mission to get rid of them for good. And it wouldn't even look like murder, since the mission was impossible to begin with.

Peren had been a knight in this kingdom long enough to have lost friends and clansmen by the order of King Aro. But by the order of his clan, he needed to stay and find out what sector 133 was hiding. There must be some secret to this mysteriously friendly sector. But climbing the ranks was not just hard, but also deadly. Not just to the one climbing, but also for their loved ones.

He hoped Torbiro had enough luck to come out of this alive.

CHAPTER 101
HALFLING REWARD

After the ceremony, Torbiro was asked by the king himself about a new mission. Sure he would do it; it would be an honour. That's what Torbiro was thinking. He proudly walked to the meeting place. He was a knight, after all. Torbiro the knight, Torbiro the knight, Torbiro. The knight. It had a nice ring to it. Torbiro repeated his new position until he was satisfied, but what he didn't notice was Memyra stealthily following him.

The meeting room was dark at first and once the curtains were opened, Torbiro could see the king was already inside. There were ten knights and soldiers inside the room, too. This must be a really serious mission for so many knights to be involved. The king then ordered his men to close the great doors once Torbiro was fully inside. Memyra had been tailing him and she needed to keep that door open otherwise she wouldn't be able to listen or see what it was Aro wanted of Torbiro. But Memyra was too late. The doors were shut.

'Torbiro the knight, please stand on the podium,' ordered the king. Torbiro, not understanding the meaning of the podium, climbed to the top. A smile on his face and eager to please.

'Torbiro the knight, this is your trial.' The king announced the halfling's punishment.

'Trial? What do you mean, sire?' Torbiro was puzzled. He still had faith this was another test, so he stood on the podium at attention, ready for anything.

'Silence, you traitor. You will only speak when you are addressed,' said the king, commanding his knights to strip the halfling of his medal and knighthood.

'Did you capture the known criminal Memyra of the Gearspark Guild?' said the king, prompting Torbiro to tell the truth.

'No, but I...,' answered Torbiro truthfully. But once he had said no, he was interrupted with another question.

'Did you kill the enemies of Traytos, the Bataros barbarians?' asked the king, prompting Torbiro to yet again answer with a 'no'. The king had already received reports on this halfling, how he healed the sick and injured and saved those that were meant to die. The war and those traps were designed to kill, eliminate and extinguish life. That was the whole purpose of the culling.

'No, but just let me...,' Torbiro was again interrupted by the king. He was about to say 'just let me explain' but he was not even given that chance. Another set of questions and accusations where the only truthful answer Torbiro could give was a 'no'. His spirit was being broken with each inquiry. His faith that this was still an important mission had waned and faded. And by the end of it all, he was treated just like he was back in the slums, back when he was a child. Blamed and taunted, persecuted and wrongly judged. They found him guilty. But was he?

Torbiro had been taunted, spat on, punched and pounded. He was stripped and chained and then they put him in a sack and beat him. The soldiers and the knights all laughed and laughed. When they heard the groaning had stopped, they dropped him out of the sack, where they beat him some more. Torbiro needed to be strong and he didn't desire this. When his body finally broke, the king's men made sure to heal his wounds enough for more torture. They repeated this until they had run out of healing elixir. And this was the last time Torbiro would see the light of day as he was finally bagged.

CHAPTER 102
A KNIGHT'S MERIT, BAGGING, HONOUR AND ANSWER

The trial was not just. It was just a way for the king to humiliate me. What had I done to desire this treatment? I am a knight of the realm. I must stay strong. No matter the questions they ask me, I will stay true to the ideals of a knight. Sure, I had failed in capturing Memyra, but she was my friend and what had she done that was so bad? She was a good person; she leads good-natured people and helps the poor. She is more of a knight than I am and yet she is the one who is being hunted. Why, why are we hunted here in Traytos? Have the halflings ever done anything wrong? Sure, some need to take food, but we still pay the shopkeeper when we have the money. We are not thieves and we are not rodents. We are people, too.

I worked with outcasts and refugees growing up and they had much better treatment than the halflings. What had we ever done so wrong that we desire this treatment? I am a knight and I will uphold the honour and pride bestowed upon me. I will not break, I will... not...break.

Why did they strip me? Hey, give me back my clothes. I will not break. Spit, eww, gross. I will not break. Chains really? I will not break. Hey! What's with the sack? I will not break. Ow, ouch, stop it. I don't desire this. I... will... not... break.

Why are they torturing me? Is this the real truth? I still believe I still have faith. The king will stop this. I am his hero. I will not break. Just let me go. I don't desire this. Please spare me some honour. Where is my honour? Knights get an honourable death, is this it? No, I will not break.

Torbiro woke in a damp cell with a flicker of light seeping in from the grates above. He was no longer naked, but he wore the clothes of a prisoner, tattered rags. His arms and legs were sore, but most of all, his chest burned. He could not see the mark, but he knew what had happened. He had been branded a traitor of Traytos. As a child, he had seen others being branded in the same way. It was a cruel punishment. The screams of so many people, many of them did not desire such treatment, such as selling a mouldy loaf of bread in the garbage or helping a slave up when their master pushes them in the mud or dung of an animal. This must be what Myra had talked about. He felt such a fool.

'My dreams implanted in me were just false hopes,' he thought.

Torbiro could not move, nor could he speak. He was truly broken. He was tired, so very tired.

'I should have listened to Myra. She was right, she was right all along. Myra, I'm sorry. For doubting you.'

CHAPTER 103
PRESENT DAY

'And that's the whole story. You believe me, don't you? Hey, are you still there? Hello!' Torbiro had finished telling his tale and the events that had put him in this situation. After shouting with all his breath, no one else answered. Torbiro was alone again, but even though he had lost hope a few cycles ago, he gained a new appreciation of life and where there was life, there was always hope.

'Sorry mate, cou'd ya repeat that part where you met the dragon? I had ta go wet the lizard, if ya know wh't aye meen? Ha ha ha,' laughed the bard.

'What? The dragon part. I just finished telling you that over a turn ago.' Torbiro was irritated that the one actually listening to him wasn't listening at all. Wait, did he say wet the lizard?

'Look, aye was busy with a sexy little lady, ok? So sue me!' said the bard. And with that, Torbiro could hear the bard kick the grate and walk off. How ungrateful.

Torbiro had been in these cells for a few cycles since the brand on his right breast was still sore. He thought they would just keep him in jail, but he had heard the guards talking about some ex-knight that was going to be hanged. This was bad and Torbiro had no way of escape. But then he had heard the door to his cell open as the lower part of it made a scraping sound on the ground. Someone was about to visit him. 'I wonder who it is,' he thought.

CHAPTER 104
UNEXPECTED VISITOR

Coming out from the shadows, holding an oil lamp, was his old commander. Commander Peren had come to visit him and give him his last rites. But Peren also had a message for the young halfling. The commander was not alone. He had brought Robyn with him and she acted as his guard by the order of the king. Peren was glad Robyn was the one the king had chosen to be his 'watchful guard' since they could speak secretly in elvish.

Robyn unchained Torbiro and gave the little halfling a big hug. Torbiro did not have much energy and his wounds from being beaten in a sack were still fresh. Robyn was so worried when Torbiro had disappeared from the party and when the king returned with a strange announcement. An announcement about catching a traitor by the name of Torbiro. Tears were running down Robyn's face when Peren spoke to her in elvish and then Robyn stopped.

'Torbiro the knight, I give you a choice and a mission,' said Peren, as quietly as possible, so as to not alert the guards.

'Yes, what is it?' Torbiro was curious and intrigued by the proposition of a secret mission.

'Let cousin finish, silly,' said Cyan as she pinched the pasty cheek of Torbiro.

'I would like you to bring Cyan home to the elvish groves of sector 045. There you can become a real knight if that is still your dream.

I have a mission from the homeland where I am not able to follow. I must stay here until we meet again, brave Torbiro,' said Peren, with a gentle smile that made him look more like Robyn. Until now, Torbiro had always seen Commander Peren with a scowl on his face, but that smile made him look so gentle. Torbiro actually blushed at his handsome face.

'Will you take her?' asked Peren. He had a worried look as he asked the question. With a gentle caress of Cyan's cheek, Peren's face returned to the stern scowl of a commander once again. But before Torbiro could answer, there was a scream from the guards outside.

CHAPTER 105
DISTRACTION

The alarms and sirens of the magic detection systems had gone off again. This was the second time this week and this time the very citizens of Traytos were in danger. As a huge stone giant busted from the large protective gates of Traytos. On top of the giant were Raazet and Memyra. The two had been searching for Torbiro ever since he disappeared from the party celebrations back at the castle. They were teaming up again for the sake of their friend. Raazet was still waiting on Torbiro's promise of more technological devices and Memyra was out for blood.

The two had rampaged throughout the lower city, where the factories and returning soldiers were denied entry. To help them with their problem, they made a sizeable hole in the wall. There was panic as the magic detectors went off. The soldiers guarding the gate were outnumbered by the returning soldiers, so there was a stampede of people going all over the place. Raazet and Memyra had known about Torbiro's location for some time now, but they needed a distraction to get him out. Hence the ridiculously-sized giant.

CHAPTER 106
TIME FOR AN ADVENTURE

Screams from the adjacent room made Robyn and Peren turn at the ready for a fight. Was this a jail break? What was with the commotion outside? Dust and debris were coming in from the guards' room. The wooden door slammed to the ground with a shatter bang and then there was another explosion. But there was something odd about all this, thought Torbiro. Peren was already here to save him. Who else could be out there?

Guiding Torbiro out of his cell, the three of them could see the guards were gone, with the exception of their pointy helmets. Their weapons were on the ground, but where had the guards gone? Peren, using his trained keen senses, could make out a short stocky person in all the dust and debris. The little fellow carried a shovel and wore a strange looking mask. As though the creature had found what he was looking for, he headed towards Peren and the others.

'Bah, th're ya 're lad,' said the stocky little dwarf. Torbiro thought he looked familiar, but it couldn't be? Could it?

'State your name, dwarf.' Peren had his weapons in hand, ready to defend his young knight and cousin. The dwarf removed his breathing mask and who would have guessed? Torbiro was right. It was Master Dorian.

Dorian of the clan Axefell. 'Wat de ye wan'? ya pointy eared pansy!' said Dorian, looking at Peren like he was a lost sheep.

'Lad, wat 're ya waitin' for? Come on, then!' said Dorian as he reached out to guide Torbiro. Torbiro smile and looked at Peren and Robyn. It was time to go.

EPILOGUE
A HALFLING'S LIFE

Traytos had been all Torbiro had known, but now he had the whole world to explore. He still had a mission and he would see it through. With all the ups and downs in his life, Torbiro had one thing he could always rely on. Was it his luck? Perhaps not yet. It was still very unpredictable. Was it his friends? Close, but not close enough yet. It must be his perseverance and his ideals to do the right thing. His life was filled with trial where he needed to endure, but now his life would start a new chapter and this time he had more people to encourage, push and inspire him. But Memyra would always be there to keep an eye on him. She had already declared her dibs.

The end.

Shawline Publishing Group Pty Ltd
www.shawlinepublishing.com.au